Origins: Reformation

By Mark Henrikson

Key Move Publications, LLC
Copyright Mark Henrikson, 2013
St. Louis Missouri

DON'T MISS THESE OTHER EXCITING TITLES IN THE ORIGINS SERIES

Book 1: Origins

Book 2: Centurion's Rise

Book 3: Reformation

Book 4: The Reich (fall 2014)

Book 5: The Greater Good (fall 2015)

.

Acknowledgements:

Friends and Family:

A big thank you once again to the usual supporting cast: my wife Tracy, my brother Jeff, my mother Donna, and Kim Callan down in Texas. It takes an army to put these books together, so thanks once again for joining me in the trenches.

The Reader:

Writing a novel is a lot of time and effort to expend if no one is going to enjoy reading it. Books 3, 4, and 5 in the Origins series might have remained in outline form had the wonderful fans of Hastelloy and his crew not spread the word. It has been nothing short of amazing to watch this Origins story grow in popularity over the last year.

Knowing so many of you were eagerly awaiting the arrival of book 3 was flattering, motivating, and to be honest a little intimidating since there is now the added pressure of expectations. Pressure makes diamonds though and hopefully you find that was the case here.

As always, I would love to hear your opinions on this novel or the entire series. Find me on Goodreads.com (a website every self-respecting bibliophile should join and use immediately), let me hear it on Amazon, or shoot me an email at originsauthor@yahoo.com. Good things are always nice to hear, and so is constructive criticism; just remember the constructive part.

ENJOY!!!

Prologue: Separation Anxiety

PRECIOUS FEW MOMENTS in life compare to the exhilaration of combat; mortal combat. The thrill of never being so alive one moment with the prospect of not existing the next was intoxicating. Kuanti embraced it, he craved it and he considered anyone who thought otherwise not a true Alpha. The only limiting factor to his high was knowing his adversary did not share the same mortal jeopardy.

The Novi and their infernal Nexus device that was capable of regenerating lives lost in battle was infuriating. On countless occasions Novi fleets were decimated by brave Alpha warriors and yet the Novi collector ship simply slipped away to safety through a space fold. Then the lives lost were regenerated, ships re-crewed, and the Alpha reengaged in battle like nothing happened. That was all in the past now though.

Space fold travel had one critical weakness. If the ship sensors detected a solid object between the craft and its destination, an event horizon could not be formed. This fatal flaw would be the Novi's undoing. The Alpha finally perfected the ability to generate a mass density field large enough to obstruct their escape.

Today, for the first time, a perimeter of Alpha constrainer vessels had surrounded a Novi fleet leaving no easy escape. Finally his adversary had to face the same specter of death hanging over their shoulder as Kuanti, and that fact sent the primal rush of adrenalin coursing through his body with renewed vigor.

"We've got them," Kuanti exclaimed while looking over Cora's shoulder as she strained to replace the last blown power relay feeding the wave blaster systems. "Their fleet is destroyed, and that collector ship of theirs is damaged and on the run. It's only a matter of time until we locate them and complete our victory."

"Yes, but the cost was disastrously high," Cora responded coolly without looking back from her repair duties. "Our fleet Commodore was an inbred pup. He had the advantage of surprise and four to one odds while the Novi faced the immobilizing fear of dying for the first time in combat. Even a half witted runt could have carried the day with a fraction of our losses."

4

Kuanti let loose a frustrated sigh. "You have to give the Novi credit. Rather than be rendered impotent with fear, they stood tall and held their own today. They battled through the odds in what has to be the single bravest act I have ever witnessed; the Novi collector ship flew directly though a constrainer ship causing its destruction to create a tiny gap in the constraint field to escape through."

Cora allowed an angry growl to resonate deep in her throat at Kuanti's praise for the enemy. "Lucky for us Captain Goron is in command now. He is the only reason we are even alive now to pursue that Novi collector ship. All the other captains went after those Onager vessels like they were females in heat to try and claim all the glory for themselves. Goron was the only one to use his head. He sensed the trap and pulled us away before those Novi ships self destructed. Otherwise we would be among the billions of atoms floating in space rather than making final repairs to win the day and possibly the war."

"Yes, Captain Goron is a worthy leader, strong and smart," Kuanti admired, but quickly changed the topic away from his better. "Stellar cartography limited the number of systems they could have escaped toward down to three, and we have already thoroughly searched two of them. I tell you, Cora, this is it. These next few minutes will be a turning point in our history, and it is a privilege to be a part of it."

Cora gave one last grunt and had her effort rewarded with a click of the power lead snapping into place and the soft hum of power flowing freely to the ship's weapon system once more. "Now we have them," she said with finality in her words as she stood up to face Kuanti, but only found empty air behind her when she completed the turn. Her mate was off to give the good news and claim the credit.

"Wave blasters are back on line and fully powered," Kuanti reported to his 'superior' with a familiar rush of adrenaline adding a hard edge to his words. Combat was upon him once more, even if it was just the pursuit of a limping and unarmed Novi collector class ship.

"Excellent," the chief engineer barked and then moved his relatively petite frame to a communications console mounted on the nearest wall. Elohim was a very capable engineer, but reporting to such an unimposing individual pulled at Kuanti's ambitious instinct. If only he had the courage to challenge his leader he could be the one giving orders in engineering.

"Captain," Elohim said into the intercom. "Weapons systems are now online."

"All of them?" came a curt reply.

An exacerbated sneer crossed Elohim's snout as he gently shook his head. "No. The fusion torpedo launchers are still offline and need more time to..."

"You've had almost an hour and only accomplished half of your orders. This is too important for your incompetent excuses," Captain Goron interrupted. "You are to oversee the repairs personally to get them back on line."

The captain did not wait for an acknowledgement; he simply cut off the conversation. Elohim looked at Kuanti with resignation in his eyes. "Even working miracles is not good enough for that man."

"That's why he's in charge," Kuanti offered.

"That and he stands a head taller than the rest of us," Elohim said on his way toward the main corridor. "You are in charge while I am in the torpedo room working another miracle for our dear leader. Can you handle that?"

"Of course," Kuanti responded with a bravado he knew deep down was only for show.

As he watched Elohim round the corner and vanish from view he felt a set of warm paws caress his shoulders from behind. He glanced to the side and found Cora hovering over his left shoulder. "Your first taste of leadership, he should not have done that."

"You're right, he should not have," Kuanti said while forcing a confident smirk to cross his lips for her benefit. The woman's ambition knew no bounds. If she were a male, he had no doubt she could rule the entire galaxy. Kuanti shrugged off her grasp and was about to address his subordinates looking on when the world around them erupted.

A powerful blast made the floor buck beneath them and sent everyone to the deck. A sudden surge of air rushing in from the exit corridor drew Kuanti's attention. He looked up in time to see an explosive fireball billowing toward the engineering chamber. An instant before the flesh of every occupant in the room was consumed by the inferno, a solid metal bulkhead slammed shut over the doorway.

A moment later Kuanti heard a deafening groan of metal shearing away from metal and then a sense of weightlessness overtook him. He floated several inches above the deck plating before emergency systems kicked in to reestablish gravity and environmental support. He landed painfully on his knees and paws but shrugged it off to stand and take command of the situation.

"What the blazes just happened?" Kuanti demanded of no one in particular.

A junior officer, whose name Kuanti was too flustered to remember at the moment, ran a damage assessment protocol on his console. A set of silent heartbeats passed and then Kuanti watched the young man's perky ears go limp. "A fusion torpedo from the Novi vessel struck midship and tore us in half."

"How is that even possible?" Kuanti asked in open mouthed awe, but realized the answer was unimportant. The question was not how it happened, but rather what should they do now that it did?

"Where is the rest of the ship?" Kuanti managed to ask. "Was it destroyed?"

"No, it's floating toward the third planet along with the Novi ship which was incapacitated by our weapons fire before the torpedo hit."

"What about us, where are we headed?" Kuanti insisted.

"Nowhere," the young man answered with the ominous resignation of a death row inmate to his fate. "We eventually might collide with a hunk of rock when we drift into the asteroid belt between the fourth and fifth planets a few hundred years from now."

Kuanti stood motionless in the middle of the engineering room with thirty crewmen looking to him for guidance. He was at a complete loss for words. The situation appeared hopeless.

After what felt like a silent eternity, Cora finally paced over to him and wrapped her reassuring paws around his shoulders once more. "You are in charge, Leader. How should we proceed?"

He swallowed hard and considered running from the situation yelping like a newborn pup, but then a familiar and welcome sensation lifted his spirits. He was scared to death and yet he had never felt so alive in his entire existence.

A true Alpha embraced fear. Fear of death, and now the fear of responsibility. Kuanti slowly looked around the room and finally said with remarkable confidence, "Here is what we are going to do..."

Chapter 1: Pleasant Voyage

KUANTI FELT A slight nudge to the shoulder that sent his body gently swaying in the hammock. Moments later a more insistent shove brought him fully awake. His upper body instinctively tried to sit up straight, but his snout smashed into the sagging occupied hammock hanging just above him. A frustrated growl escaped his throat as he laid back, rolled to the side and slowly rose to his full height and squared off against his disturber with teeth showing from underneath his snarl.

"Apologies, Leader," his subordinate responded with contrition. "It is time for a shift change."

Kuanti exhaled his frustration while he slowly put his back against the wall and sucked in his stomach so the crewman could climb into the hammock. "I will be glad when we land so this hot bunking protocol will no longer be necessary," he said softly to himself.

All along the narrow corridor hammocks were triple stacked and hung between structural support girders. Males and females alike were waking and taking their counterpart's place in bed to execute the shift change. Kuanti was anxious to reach the command deck and see if all was ready for their landing approach, but he had to wait. The backlog of bodies in front of him took a few minutes to file out of the narrow corridor. When he reached the exit portal, Kuanti had to bring in his shoulders and duck through a roughly cut hole in the bulkhead that served as a doorway.

The six foot gap between the outer and inner hull of the ship was never intended to house crewmen. With the exception of a few bare bulb light fixtures hastily added, the space was pitch dark and had extremely poor air circulation. As a result, the small, narrow space was hot and muggy like a swamp on a hundred degree day. The walls actually dripped with condensation.

Still, the crew needed somewhere to sleep. The engineering section had thirty crewmembers on duty when the Novi torpedo separated them from the rest of the ship. There were no sleeping quarters in this section so a solution had to be improvised. It was not ideal, but they were making it work.

Kuanti paused to bask in the relatively cool environment he stepped into. No longer feeling like a vegetable in a steam cooker, he zigzagged his way through a maze of occupied temporary workstations set up in the hallway leading to the command deck. Quarters were so cramped one could not help but brush against workers on their way past. Under normal circumstances such a violation of personal space would be a grave insult and draw a physical confrontation, but the rules of society had changed for the soon to be shipwrecked survivors.

As he approached the command deck Kuanti heard shouting that no doubt accompanied some sort of angry brawl. Not everyone on board was as accepting of the new social order as others. Kuanti finally stepped onto the slightly roomier command deck that was actually the main engineering work space commandeered for the purpose of piloting the ship. He saw a very pregnant Cora protecting another female in the corner. Kuanti swallowed hard upon recognizing the male attempting to assault the female. It was Priapus, and this would not be pleasant.

"You grubby little whore," Priapus hollered while trying to reach around Cora to get at his target. "I'll kill you for this."

Kuanti grabbed hold of the hound's shoulders from behind and threw him back against the nearest wall. "What is the meaning of this?"

"She's pregnant!" Priapus spat while pointing at the female cowering in the corner.

"Good. My orders were for every female on board to become pregnant as fast as possible," Kuanti stated firmly. "It will take several generations for us to leave the planet we will touch down on today. We need all the offspring we can create to make a colony that will survive long enough to harvest materials, construct manufacturing facilities, and reinvent technologies so we can eventually send a message home."

"Everyone knows I'm sterile and unable to father children," Priapus admitted. "She mated with another male. She dishonored herself and me. I demand satisfaction."

Kuanti released his grip on the enraged crewman, stepped back and braced himself for what he knew was coming. "I'm aware of her condition because she carries my seed."

Priapus spent several seconds processing the words. Finally the anger behind his eyes hardened to a murderous rage and he lunged for Kuanti's midsection. He easily sidestepped the attack and gave Priapus a hard shove on his way past sending the attacker headfirst into a workstation screen. Sparks and shards of broken glass shot past Kuanti as he pulled Priapus back to his feet, grabbed hold of his throat and squeezed.

Kuanti absorbed the moment with all his senses: the smell of his opponent's last breath, the soft gurgle escaping his throat, and the delicate feel of a limp noodle collapsing beneath his mighty paws. Most of all Kuanti took in the sight as pure panic overtook his adversary the instant he realized the fight was lost. Kuanti held tight until the body finally lay lifeless on the deck at his feet. Every instinct demanded a roar of victory, but for appearances he could not publically enjoy the moment.

He managed to contain his inner beast well enough to silently return to his full height and look about the muted command deck. When his eyes met those of his mate, Cora proudly stepped forward to stand by his side.

"In the years to come we all will have children with multiple partners," Cora declared. "It is out of genetic necessity for our survival, and it brings no dishonor to anyone. Kuanti is my mate and will continue to be even when I carry the seed of another. This is our duty."

"Understood?" Kuanti added. Silence and subtle nodding of heads lent the crew's tacit approval to their lot in life. "Good. Now get this impotent whelp out of my sight."

Kuanti stepped over the body and paid no mind as two crewmen dragged it away. With that little rebellion settled, he turned his attention to the real task at hand. After three months spent eking out an existence aboard the crippled engineering section, he was eager to land and get some space to himself for a change.

"Retract the solar sail," he ordered while looking back at the three occupied workstations now pressed into service as a makeshift navigation system for the crippled vessel. "We may still need the aluminized mylar material when we reach the surface."

It was by no means the best propulsion system since it took over three months to traverse the measly twenty million miles to reach the red planet after being separated from their better half, but it worked. Rather than spinning out of control in the vacuum of space until supplies ran out, the crew was able to fashion the solar sail to catch the high speed gasses ejected from the system's star. Unfortunately the current carried them away from the third planet where Captain Goron managed to safely land his half of the ship along with the Novi collector craft.

To be honest, Kuanti did not expect either craft to survive their perilous landings. Both ships approached the planet at a suicidal speed of 200 miles per second and needed to execute an impossibly precise landing maneuver without the benefit of propulsion systems. To his surprise, through the manual telescopes his crew fashioned out of spare parts, they were able to tell that no explosions or radiation spikes accompanied either landing. Therefore, Kuanti had to assume both ships survived their descent.

"Bring the landing program online," Kuanti calmly ordered. "Let's run through the scenario one last time before trusting our lives with it."

His subordinate complied by pulling up a three dimensional rendering of the red planet and the ship's approach path. As the sequence played out on screen, Kuanti watched the ship orientate with its engines leading the way and enter high orbit around the planet.

"The shielding around the engines is designed to withstand the rigors of a fusion reaction. Absorbing the relatively low heat from friction with the atmosphere upon reentry should not tax the design limits too much," the crewman narrated. "Once in the atmosphere, where the gravity coils have something to push against, we should be able to control our descent and have no difficulty landing among the mountains you have selected in the north eastern quadrant."

Kuanti watched the screen as his virtual ship blazed a trail through the atmosphere and then finally floated down among the tall mountain peaks to touch down near what they all hoped was a vast network of caves.

"If we decide the chosen landing spot is not ideal, will we be able to relocate the ship?" Kuanti asked.

"Only if we pick it up and carry it," the crewman answered. "We are missing half our gravity coils from the rest of the ship that landed on that other planet with Captain Goron. We can't form a complete field. All we can do is control our descent. We cannot lift off again."

"I certainly hope our geologist knows his trade," Kuanti exhaled, drew a deep breath and held it as he pondered his next order. Everything was riding on it. "We've done all we can. Turn the countdown over to the main computer."

Content that everything was well in hand for a safe landing, Kuanti turned his head to look upon Cora. She stood beside him beaming with pride. She leaned in to his ear and whispered in a sensual tone, "Well done, Leader. I can't wait for some privacy when we reach the red planet's surface."

Kuanti felt his pulse quicken at the sexual undertone of her words. "I thought being seen with the Leader by others was the whole point for you; power by association," he whispered back and concluded by shooting her a knowing stare.

Chapter 2: Bed Head

DR. JEFFREY HOLMES found himself alone inside Henderson Home Psychiatric facility during the dark hours of early morning. The prior evening his brother Mark called to inform him that his new patient, Hastelloy, presented a serious threat to his safety.

Jeffrey trusted his brother's judgment implicitly. What's more, he knew Mark worked for the government in some sort of security capacity that required a high level clearance. Still, Jeffrey couldn't shake the feeling that something was off. He had spent two whole days with the patient over the last week and was quite certain he had an accurate measure of the man. The only thing dangerous about Hastelloy, that he could tell, was the man's intellect and rapier wit.

Hastelloy's delusion of being an immortal alien trapped on this planet while fighting to prevent the evil species Alpha from conquering the planet was only harmful to himself, not those around him.

Against his better judgment, Jeffrey followed his brother's instructions. He phoned his wife to take the kids to a hotel for a few days and then spent the night on his couch in the office. Mark assured him adequate protection was already here. Henderson Home was the safest place for him to stay.

The stabbing pain in Jeffrey's back from laying on the overly plush couch all night let him know that the added safety did come at a price. Unable to fall back asleep because of his stiff back, Dr. Holmes sat up and rose to his feet.

He still wore his navy-blue dress shirt and khaki slacks from the day before, but his tie lay unknotted on the coffee table in front of him. He bent at the waist and arched his spine upward and drew a rapid fire popping of his joints moving back into proper alignment.

Jeffrey felt his mouth run dry so he stepped out into the hallway in search of a water fountain; closing the office door behind him. The long, dark corridor with doors on either side every fifteen feet had a haunting silence about it. The deep red lighting cast upon the white industrial tiled hallway by the illuminated exit signs on either side did nothing to alleviate his anxiety. It took very little imagination to picture himself just outside the gates of hell waiting for the devil to arrive and pass judgment over him.

Dr. Holmes forced his childish fear of the dark aside and headed toward the cafeteria water fountain at the far end of the hall. Midway down the corridor he saw a shape step out of the shadows. As the figure stepped under the dimly lit exit sign overhead, a devilish hue brought Hastelloy's features to light and Jeffrey felt a gush of ice water flood his veins.

Hastelloy said nothing. The man simply paced toward Dr. Holmes as if on a casual evening stroll. Jeffrey found himself instinctively stepping backwards from the patient approaching with an air of indifference.

Just when Jeffrey was about to call for Terry, or whatever orderly was on duty this time of night, a door slammed open from behind Dr. Holmes. He about wet himself as he whirled around to see the culprit and found it was his brother Mark. This wasn't the lighthearted brother he knew and loved. There was a primal anger in him that Jeffrey had not seen in his brother since the last time he tried to ride Mark's bicycle without permission when they were toddlers.

Mark pulled a gun out from behind his back, aimed a two-handed grip at Hastelloy, and silently stalked his way toward Dr. Holmes; never letting his aim waiver. Hastelloy's only response was to quietly raise his palms up to shoulder height in surrender.

When Mark reached Jeffrey's side, he motioned with his head back toward the office door. Slow and in step like ballroom dancers, the two floated ever closer to the closed door. At the same time Hastelloy paced forward, still with hands raised, to maintain the same threatening proximity to Jeffrey and his brother.

Jeffrey nervously fumbled around with the door handle until finally it turned allowing the door to open and reveal the familiar confines of his private chambers. Mark stepped through the doorway first and Jeffrey moved to follow, but was held back. He glanced behind to find Hastelloy holding his shoulders with an iron grip. Jeffrey faced forward once more to enlist the help of his brother, but jumped backwards at the sight of a snarling rabid dog lunging for his throat.

Dr. Holmes sat up on his couch with a start. He looked around the room to find himself alone in his office breathing heavy from the intensity of his dream. Jeffrey had tossed and turned all night with anxiety about spending the night away from his wife and kids. He must have finally relaxed enough to fall asleep.

Faint rays of orange and red light were peeking through the tall narrow window in the middle of the far wall to let him know dawn was approaching. Jeffrey finished rubbing the last remnants of sleep out of his eyes on the way to his desk. He opened a drawer and pulled out a fresh tie and affixed it around his neck. At least one part of his wardrobe would be fresh for the day; perhaps no one would even notice the wrinkly mess that was the rest of his ensemble.

A knock at the door was soon followed by the welcome sight of his secretary, Tara, entering with a piping hot cup of coffee in her hands.

"Morning boss, nice tie," Tara said with a set of raised eyebrows.

Dang it.

Tara was not one to let such things slide by without comment. "I saw your car in the lot when I pulled in and thought I would bring you a cup of coffee to celebrate you finally beating me into the office for once. Now that I see you cheated and stayed here overnight, I'm not sure you deserve it."

Jeffrey took the cup and loosened his back by flexing from side to side. "After spending a night on that thing I deserve this and a medal."

Dr. Holmes was not about to divulge the true reason he slept on the couch. Tara seemed particularly fond and trusting of Hastelloy's seemingly gentle nature; she might accuse Jeffrey of being the crazy one. Yet he didn't feel like making up an excuse, so he just dove right into his day before Tara had a chance to inquire further. "I'd like to have another session with Hastelloy this morning. Can you please have Terry escort him to my office as soon as possible?"

Jeffrey knew his brother instructed him, in no uncertain terms, to keep his distance from Hastelloy until Mark arrived. Still, he felt an undeniable compulsion, a necessity to understand what was going on. Maybe it was just curiosity, or perhaps an instinct to help or protect his patient. If the man truly was ill, then he needed an advocate. If he was indeed dangerous, then Mark would arrive in due time to handle things.

"You sure you don't want to freshen up a bit before receiving visitors this morning?" Tara asked while glancing up at Jeffrey's mangled bed-head hair.

Dang it.

Chapter 3: Indefinitely

PROFESSOR BRIAN RUSSELL'S head was awash with confusion, anxiety and chaos. One moment he nostalgically reminisced about his simple life as an archeologist. How excited he was a week ago to see his life's work culminate in the discovery of new chambers within the Great Pyramid and Sphinx in Egypt.

An instant later his mind was busy lamenting the weeklong captivity he spent with his research assistants, Alex and Frank. They were captured and held inside a chamber concealed within the body of the Sphinx in order to keep the discoveries a secret.

Then his emotions shifted to betrayal when he considered one of the captors was his trusted friend Dr. Andrea from the Egyptian Organization of Antiquities. Compounding the sense of double-cross was knowing Frank turned out to be an undercover agent working for the US National Security Agency.

If all that wasn't enough to make his head spin, then remembering what he witnessed while in captivity was simply mind blowing. His captors claimed to be aliens and to back this up they demonstrated the technological ability to manipulate the moon's orbit and the potential threat of bringing the celestial body crashing into the Earth to put an end to mankind. Impressive as that feat was, it paled in comparison when his captors executed an NSA agent sent to rescue them; then they appeared to bring the man back to life using a device called the Nexus.

Professor Russell was certainly not inclined to believe any of the loony alien on earth conspiracy theories floating around since Hollywood began making science fiction movies, but he had to admit that his captors put on a *really* convincing show.

The fear of knowing those supposed aliens could end all life on earth if they brought the moon out of orbit made the blood in Brian's veins almost stop flowing. He did take some comfort that the Nexus device apparently housed some 20 million life forces that the aliens were intent on preserving. This made the situation between these aliens and the NSA appear to be a Mexican standoff with both sides perfectly capable of destroying the other.

Following a heroic escape effort on the part of Frank's fellow NSA agent, Professor Russell now found himself walking through a metal lined tunnel leading away from the hidden chamber inside the Sphinx. Frank and his companion were up ahead presumably discussing the situation. It was impossible to tell for sure, given how quiet they kept the conversation, which Brian didn't consider to be a particularly good sign of things to come for him and Alex.

Meanwhile, Brian and Alex traversed the distance side by side with a team of six heavily armed Navy SEALs behind them.

"Ya know it's funny," Alex said. "The first time I walked through this tunnel it made me feel claustrophobic. After being cooped up for a week in that tiny cage, all I can think of now is a quote from Dr. Martin Luther King Jr., 'Free at last, free at last. Thank God almighty, we are free at last.'"

Professor Russell let out a quiet snort and leaned into Alex's ear for a private word, "More like we've fallen out of the frying pan and into the fire."

"What do you mean?"

"It's not like we just attended an Amway recruitment session in there," Professor Russell whispered. "National secrets were just revealed right before our eyes. Do you think they'll just let us go about our lives like nothing happened once we get to the surface?"

"We are American citizens who have broken no laws, what can they do to us?" Alex naively asked, but her wavering tone revealed less confidence. Professor Russell put his arm around his research assistant and felt her trembling through his touch.

"I don't intend to wait and find out the answer to that question," Brian said softly. "I'll think of something."

"Better make it quick," Alex observed as they reached the end of the tunnel and faced the three hundred foot ladder climb up to the surface, and potential freedom if they were able to think quickly enough.

As he forced his aging frame to reach for yet another ladder rung, Brian ran through a litany of escape options available to him and Alex. The tunnel entrance was nestled among a busy office park; they could make a run for it. Considering they were being escorted by Special Forces team members, each

18

of whom could probably run a five minute mile in full gear without breaking a sweat, that option seemed unlikely to succeed.

Wresting control of a gun away from the soldiers seemed equally absurd. This left Professor Russell with the most likely, yet painfully obvious option – his cell phone. Inside the Sphinx chamber and down in the tunnel he had no reception, but on the surface he would have a signal again.

Who to call though? It's not as though there was a *help the NSA is holding us against our will* hotline. Like a criminal held by the police, Brian figured he only had one phone call before being discovered; he needed to make it count. In the end, he decided his best bet was to phone his university department head when a moment of distraction or privacy presented itself.

Professor Russell reached the top of the ladder and found Frank's hand extended to help him out of the hole. Up above was a quaint little room full of dusty old shelves stuffed with files that no one gave a damn about, making it an ideal cover for the tunnel entrance.

Brian accepted the helping hand by grasping Frank's forearm. A moment later he was heaved up to the surface, bringing the professor face to face with the man who both betrayed his trust and helped save his life during the last week.

He tried to release the handhold, but Frank locked down his steely grip. He then reached with his free hand into Brian's pants pocket to retrieve the now fully functional cell phone. "Sorry, Prof, but we can't have ya phoning home just yet."

"Or ever," Professor Russell subtly added, but all he could do was purse his lips and watch the only real hope of contacting the outside world slip out of his reach. A moment later Brian looked on as Frank executed the same procedure to relieve Alex of her phone, though her response was not so understated.

An ear piercing slap bounced off the walls of the small room when Frank reached for the back pocket of Alex's jeans. "Touch me there again and I'll throw you down that hole. You got me?"

Frank immediately released his grip on her arm and responded, "I'm not lookin' for a date here darlin'. I just need that phone in your back pocket. Now we can do this the easy way or the hard way, your choice. Hand it over please."

Alex shifted her weight back onto her heels and crossed her arms. "Or what?" she demanded.

The instant those defiant words left her mouth, Alex had her feet swept out from under her from behind by the other NSA agent. The lightning quick move landed her face down on the floor. Next, a probing hand retrieved the phone from her now easily accessible back pocket and tossed it over to Frank. "Take the easy way next time," came an instructional reply from the attacker.

"Damn it, Mark, these aren't prisoners or suspects," Frank admonished while putting the retrieved phone in his pants pocket. "They were just in the wrong place at the wrong time."

"Now it's time to put them in the right place," the other NSA agent responded while pulling out a cell phone of his own to place a call. Brian only got to hear part of the conversation before the agent walked through the building's front door and out of earshot. "Tell the caretaker two high priority targets will be arriving ... indefinitely ..."

Professor Russell bent down to help Alex back to her feet. While she brushed off the front of her shirt Brian looked back at Frank with genuine concern. "Targets? Indefinitely?"

Frank gave an understanding nod, "NSA terminology, it's not what you think. We're not the bad guys, but you did see and hear some things you shouldn't have and now we need to manage that. Come on now; let's go for a little ride. It'll be like staying in a hotel for a little while."

"Indefinitely," Professor Russell repeated again.

Frank ignored the remark and simply gestured for the six SEAL team members to usher the captives out of the building.

Brian leveled a flaming stare of anger as he approached Frank with the muzzle of a submachine gun pointed at his back. "Indefinitely," he repeated one more time and then shouldered his way past.

Alex came to a full stop in front of Frank on her way out. "Just so you know. You would have been the one I called for help if you weren't also the one holding us against our will right now."

Out in the open among the low rise buildings of the warehouse district Professor Russell actually experienced a flicker of hope. He saw an Egyptian man in military uniform forcefully arguing with the other NSA agent.

His hopes were quickly dashed when he watched Mark dismissively order a set of SEALs to show the Egyptian officer to the back seat of an awaiting Humvee. Professor Russell and Alex were then crammed into another one and were soon followed by Frank and three Navy SEALs.

"Go," Frank ordered to the driver. The soldier obediently stepped hard on the gas and they left the other two Humvees to stand sentry over the warehouse hiding the tunnel entrance.

Chapter 4: Informing

OVER THE YEARS Mark had grown accustomed to receiving untimely phone calls from Terrance, his NSA executive committee watcher, demanding updates or issuing blistering reprimands. This was the first time in recent memory that Mark would be the one calling and issuing demands. When the other end of the call picked up, he steeled himself for the abrasive personality. "Terrance, it's Mark. I don't care what you're in the middle of right now, this is more important."

"It better be," came a flat reply, "because this is not how things work. I call you because I am the one who makes things happen, not the other way around."

Bureaucrats, Mark thought with a role of his eyes. "Oh have it your way then, Terrance. If you would be so gracious as to call me back, I will impart knowledge upon you that will literally make you soil yourself." CLICK.

Mark despised playing these little head games with Terrance, but found they were the only way to effectively get the man's attention and reinforce the fact that Terrance was nothing without Mark. Another moment passed and his phone finally rang. He waited for the third tone before answering just to make his point all the more obvious. "Yes, Terrance, how may I be of service?"

"Cut the games. If you have information you think I need; let's have it," Terrance demanded.

Mark took the next ten minutes informing his boss about recent events: the discovered Pyramid and Sphinx chambers, the tunnel, the gravity weapon, the aliens, their Nexus device, and the fact that two archeologists knew about all of it.

"Do you need a moment to change your shorts?" Mark politely asked.

"I'm starting to think I should wear adult diapers when talking with you," Terrance finally managed to spit out. "Basically you're telling me your absolute worst fears about an alien presence on Earth are now realized. You have thoroughly failed to manage or contain the threat and now our entire existence as a civilization stands on the brink thanks to this gravity weapon of theirs."

"You are such a pessimist; I'm actually rather encouraged," Mark jabbed back. "I finally know what I'm dealing with, and at least for now, I have an effective counter measure."

"How do you figure that? Are you still on friendly terms with the Greek god Atlas? Do you think he can add holding the moon up as well as carrying Earth on his back?" Terrance sardonically asked.

Mark failed to contain a laugh, but quickly regained his composure. "I've found the gods to be a little finicky lately. I prefer relying on the alien's attachment to the twenty million lives held inside that Nexus device of theirs. If they do pull the trigger on that doomsday device, they also destroy themselves and the Nexus. It has to be a measure of last resort for them."

"Well that certainly makes me feel safe," Terrance said with obvious sarcasm. "Why are you calling me again?"

"You called me," Mark quickly corrected picturing Terrance turning bright red and drawing his pistol to shoot an already bullet riddled picture of Mark mounted on his office wall. A silent couple of seconds let Mark know the time for playing head games had passed. "We know who and where they are now, at least three of them anyway. We need to lock down the Giza plateau and lay siege to the tunnel entrance so they can't get out once their Nexus device regenerates them. Then we just need to get permission from the Egyptian government to blow their national treasures off the face of the planet so the alien gravity machine no longer functions."

"Oh is that all?" Terrance responded with disbelief draped all over the four little words.

"Like you said earlier, Terrance, you are the one who makes things happen. Now is your time to shine," Mark continued. "Right now all we have are a dozen Navy SEALs and two Humvees guarding the exit point. We're going to need more. You have to call up every NSA asset within a ten hour travel radius and get them here immediately. That way Frank can lock this place down with as low a profile as possible."

"Frank? Why aren't you going to command the situation?" Terrance asked. "Is there something more important for you to do at this moment?"

Mark knew he had to sell his intentions just right. In the NSA your mission came first over everything else, even family. "When Frank gets done making his deposit at the safe house, he will take control of the situation here. I need to return stateside and pay my brother a visit in that psychiatric ward where he works."

Terrance immediately pounced on the opportunity to land a barb. "If you need time off just say so, you don't need to have yourself committed."

"Jeff is apparently being held captive by the leader of this alien presence here on Earth," Mark answered in a matter of fact tone. "It seems a man posing as a patient named Hastelloy is using my brother to get my attention. He wants to have a little chat with me, so I'm going to oblige him."

"Sounds to me like you're abandoning your post to rescue your brother from a potential mad man," Terrance countered. "We have assets in place there who can handle things if they turn ugly."

"They went to the trouble of bringing me back from the dead with that Nexus device for the express purpose of talking with this Hastelloy character," Mark insisted. "Whatever happens here, Frank can handle it. I need to go have that conversation, or at least kill the man. That way we'll have three of them trapped inside the Sphinx chamber instead of just two."

A few contemplative moments passed without a sound. "Fine. Wait for the site to be secured and then you may pay this alien leader a visit. In the meantime let me get things happening, but no promises on permission from the Egyptians to blow up the Pyramid."

"It may come down to us not having a choice," Mark cautioned before the other end of the line hung up.

****

On board the USS Ronald Regan a command bulletin came into the hands of the carrier group admiral by his first officer.

"Looks like we're being ordered to the Mediterranean off the coast of Egypt," the subordinate said while waiting for the admiral to finish reviewing the orders. "Another exercise?"

"I don't think so," the admiral eventually responded. "They don't usually pull the only carrier group in the Persian Gulf away for exercises; they bring in another. Plus four B2 bombers have already left Whitman. At two billion dollars a pop they don't send those things halfway around the world without a reason. While we relocate, we need to send up a second AWAC and constantly have one sitting on standby to coordinate all the aircraft that will be buzzing around this region a few hours from now."

Chapter 5: Long Range Planning

KUANTI DID NOT need to see the central gathering chamber to know it was fully occupied with young Alpha pups eager to learn their daily history lessons from him. He could sense their presence. He felt their individual moods and could hear their words, but that was all. As a relic he could not smell their individual scents, or feel the touch of an embrace from his great, great grandchildren. He dearly missed the sensations of his physical form, but alas, the physical body was a temporary tool granted by Mother Nature and taken away again at her leisure.

The vibrant energy of youth that filled the large room along with the soft chatter of individual conversations brought Kuanti's attention back to the moment. He had a job to do.

"Silence," Kuanti ordered in an expectant tone. The din of chaotic noise immediately diminished and was replaced by an attentive silence from four hundred youth ranging from five to fifteen years of age. "Take your seats."

"Yes, Founder," came a crisp chorus of voices followed by the Alpha youth obediently sitting on the cave room floor. The chamber was well lit with electric lights scattered along the twenty foot high ceiling. Kuanti occupied the place of honor at the head of the room floating atop a stone altar.

When the rustle of movement quieted once more Kuanti asked, "What is our mission?"

In unison four hundred voices replied, "We are the Alpha race. My enemy is the Novi. Their greed and aggression knows no end. For the sake of our people, the Novi must be destroyed. All that I am I dedicate to the annihilation of this enemy. I am willing and ready to give up my life for this cause."

"Covax, how did we first meet the Novi?" Kuanti asked one of his newest pupils.

"The aggressors landed on our planet claiming their ship had nowhere else to go. They took advantage of our hospitality to steal our resources and spy on our superior technology."

"How long did it take us to expel those spies from our planet?" Kuanti asked.

"Fifty years," every student, even the young ones, responded.

"Noren, what lesson did our forefathers learn from that time of occupation?"

"The Alpha race could no longer remain on our own planet," his brightest student recited. "The Novi aggressors were conquering new territories every day and the galaxy's sentient races needed the protection of the Alpha race."

"How long did we prepare for the conflict before initiating hostilities with the Novi?" Kuanti asked of Noren.

"Ten generations," came a proud response.

Kuanti lit up the chamber with his pride. "Very good. Ten generations of our Alpha ancestors labored and toiled and paid their efforts forward for the greater good of our race. The noble efforts of the Greatest Generations allowed the Alpha to beat back the Novi aggressors. Now, all of you find yourselves in the same situation."

"We are stuck on this barren planet," Kuanti went on. "Look around you. This chamber, the surrounding network of caves and constructed tunnels in the mountainside that provides a contained and habitable environment for you to live, were built by your ancestors. We paid it forward so that some day we will be able to communicate with the Alpha home world, or construct a craft to take us home."

"You are the inheritors and stewards of the efforts of every generation that has preceded your existence." For dramatic effect Kuanti let his last statement reverberate throughout the chamber for several seconds. Eventually an inquisitive thought from the student body caught his attention. "Yes, young Covax, you have a question."

"Founder, what are you?" came the young pup's shy voice.

"I am the life force of Kuanti, the Founding Leader of this colony," he boomed. The inner glow of his flowing life force hovering inches above the stone altar tripled in intensity at the pride he took in his revered title. "I labored all my life for this colony. Mother Nature reclaimed my body three hundred years ago. Now I serve your current leader as a guiding light to achieve the ultimate goal of returning every Alpha warrior and relic of warriors past on this planet to the home world."

"But how will we ever be able to do that?" young Covax innocently asked.

The negative tone of the question did not sit well with Kuanti and a frustrated shudder rippled up his flowing relic. "By paying attention in school, learning your lessons well and applying them to strengthen our industrial complex so we can advance and finally construct a communicator capable of reaching home."

"But why is it taking so long," Covax pressed further. "We had the technology once, why not now?"

"You are a curious one aren't you?" Kuanti commended. "The reasoning is threefold. First, the main computer memory core was on the other half of the ship which crash landed on the third planet in this solar system with Captain Goron. The only knowledge we had was in the heads of the original crew and our ability to teach the next generation."

"Second, we had to build a self-sustaining colony with a habitable environment, renewable power supply, and stable food source before focusing on technological redevelopment."

"Finally, the tools and ability to extract and process advanced building materials, power cells and complex metallurgy takes generations to develop. No one even knows how to build a flashtrans communicator anymore, but we know the steps we need to take to get there, so we progress. Generation after generation we move toward that technological goal we know is out there, but is for the moment beyond our ability to achieve."

"Let me ask you a question then, young Covax. What can you do for the greater good of the colony?"

"Learn my lessons, advance our progress and then pass that knowledge on to the next generation when I, too, become a relic," the youth obediently answered.

"Well said," Kuanti commended, "now get to it."

With his dismissing words, the chamber emptied quickly as the children headed to their respective grade level classrooms for specific instruction from other relics who served as instructors. He did sense a presence remaining in the chamber, however.

"How nice of you to take time away from your duties as administrator of my colony to consult with your Founding Leader," Kuanti admonished softly. "How do things progress, Quin?"

The old and frail figure of Quin hobbled his way to stand in front of the altar while leaning on a cane for extra support. In the old days this frail Leader would have been put down by a leadership challenge decades ago, but times were different now. Knowledge and planning abilities were revered far more than a set of strong muscles and the ability to use them in a physical confrontation.

"We had a breakthrough this morning," Quin reported. "We were able to hook the power leads from the broadcast tower to the central fusion reactor without melting them. It still can't handle the amount of power transfer we need to transmit a Flashtrans signal, but it is a considerable leap forward."

"Excellent," Kuanti exclaimed. "The third and fourth planets will move within forty million miles of each other in just a few more weeks. I was hoping we would have good news to report to Captain Goron. Otherwise it would be another two months of him insulting our intellect and efforts before we move out of contact range with his relic."

"What a whimsical ability an Alpha life force has," Quin admired in between a coughing fit that spoke volumes of the man's ailing health. "You are able to communicate and collaborate freely with any relic within millions of miles."

"Yes, and I fear you may be joining us in that fellowship before too long," Kuanti cautioned. "Don't be too eager to shed your physical form. While existing in the collective is a unique experience, it pales in comparison to the sensations of a physical body."

Chapter 6: Darkness Comes to Us All

A KNOCK AT Dr. Holmes' office door gave way to Hastelloy entering the room closely escorted by a brawny orderly named Terry. Jeffrey fought past the dangers his brother mentioned, and the disturbing imagery of his dream the night before, to greet his patient with a stiff handshake. "Good morning."

Hastelloy's eyes were busy giving the room a once over as he responded, "And to you. Two sessions in two days? Can't say I'm not getting my money's worth," he concluded as his eyes came back to meet Jeffrey's. "Nice tie."

Dang it.

Questions Tara may have had about him spending the night in his office Jeffrey could avoid, Hastelloy's he could not. The patient was far too intelligent and self-aware to let it go. As a principle, Jeffrey believed in being open and honest with his patients, but not this time. He was just trying to fill time while waiting for Mark to arrive and clear this matter up.

"A little domestic dispute at home I'm afraid," Jeffrey sighed and then ushered Hastelloy to his chair while dismissing Terry with a nod. He then took a seat for himself in the other chair nestled around a coffee table opposite the sofa. "Bad for me, but good for you since it gives us another opportunity to chat."

Hastelloy looked genuinely concerned. "You and I have certainly been spending a lot of time together this last week. I hope the situation within your family has nothing to do with me."

Dr. Holmes didn't feel like discussing the profound disturbance caused by Hastelloy. Instead he got out his pen and paper and sat ready to take notes once more. "Yesterday you finished with your subordinate, Valnor, ascending to the throne of the Roman Empire as Caesar Augustus; no small feat. Can you continue from there? What happened next to you and your stranded crew?"

Hastelloy's eyes snapped wide open in surprise at the question. "What happened? Prosperity. The Roman Empire served as a guiding light for the world to follow for nearly a thousand years. All my crew and I needed to do was stand aside and make sure nothing interfered."

"A thousand years is a long time," Jeffrey marveled. "You must have done a stellar job."

"Considering the Alpha threat on this planet was reduced to a formless relic holding Goron's life force, the task was not terribly difficult. Yet, either from my own incompetence or Goron's brilliance, he still found a way to completely unravel the marvelous work we achieved."

"Oh this should be good," Jeffrey prompted, thankful to be pondering events of the past rather than worrying about the danger Hastelloy supposedly posed in the present.

****

"Why, oh why, do I listen to your council," Alaric hollered at the wooden chest holding the sacred remains of his Gothic lineage. "We were prospering as a people up north, why did we need to come south and provoke the Romans?"

"Correction, you managed to get by up north, but even that meager existence was being threatened by the Huns coming West from greater Asia," a haunting voice that seemed to emanate from every corner of the small tent replied.

Alaric recalled the first time he heard the voices of his ancestors speak to him. He fell to his knees and buried his face in the dirt in reverence. With this latest defeat, the mystique of their presence had tarnished to the point that Alaric now had the nerve to challenge their divine guidance.

"We could have withstood a disorganized barbarian horde invading our fortified territory," Alaric countered. "Instead you insisted I lead our people against an established empire that has not lost a battle, let alone a war, for nearly a thousand years."

"The campaign is but in its infancy," the whimsical voice responded.

Alaric turned away from the chest and shook his head defiantly, "The campaign is lying on its death bed. No sooner had we crossed the Danube River did we encounter a Roman army to stop us. A professional army unbeaten for generations arrayed against my collection of farmers and their families, and I decide to attack? What lunacy!"

"Our people gave a good account of themselves on the battlefield," the spirit commended. "You managed to hold the Romans almost to a draw and escaped with most of your forces intact."

"We were beaten," Alaric shouted back. "Whether it was just barely or thoroughly matters not. My people know I am incapable of beating the Romans."

"There is more to warfare than winning battles. You must know and understand the ways of your enemy. The Roman emperor, Honorius, is a raving madman. Your attack will cause him to question the loyalty of every Gothic soldier and mercenary serving in the Roman legions. He is insane enough to order their collective executions."

Alaric collapsed into a rigid wooden chair and held his face in his hands. "What have I done? I have set into motion the extermination of my people."

"Do you really think our proud people will sit idly by while their throats get cut? No, they will resist and you will soon have legions of professional Gothic soldiers from the enemy defecting to your banner."

Alaric said no more. He simply shook his head in silence and reached for a flask of wine vowing not to see the bottom of an empty flask until the Romans arrived to finish him off. Weeks flew by amid a drunken binge until fate arrived at his army's encampment.

The sudden opening of the tent flap by his captain allowed sunlight to drench the inner sanctum with a golden glow that roused Alaric from his sleep. He fought back the urge to vomit as a result of the prior evening's binge drinking weighing heavy on his stomach and mind. Alaric finally found the willpower to look up at his officer with disinterest. "What?"

"A Roman army approaches," the officer reported.

"From which direction," Alaric asked. Not that it mattered at all. He intended to give himself up for execution in order to spare his people Rome's wrath.

"I'm afraid they have us surrounded, but they approach in marching formations rather than in line for battle. They have sent emissaries ahead requesting an audience with you."

Alaric raised an eyebrow and forcibly moved the haze clouding his mind to the side. "I'll be along shortly."

When the officer closed the tent flap once more Alaric heard an amused voice whisper from the corner. "Now the dismantling of Rome can begin."

Alaric donned the golden breastplate of his dress armor and paused on his way out of the tent to splash a handful of water on his face from a filled bowl. He dried himself and stepped into the midday sun with a relatively clear head and sense of purpose.

When he reached the central gathering hall, four Roman soldiers stood in the middle. Three held their crimson tasseled helmets in their hands to show respect and deference toward Alaric. The fourth held a long metal box that stood roughly three feet long and one foot tall and deep. "Welcome, gentlemen. To what do I owe this fine company?"

"The honor is ours, General. We come to join and aid your uprising in any way we can," the one holding the box declared.

Alaric struggled mightily to hold his poker face. "Why that is a *very* generous offer. Tell me though, why have you cast aside your Roman banners to join this upstart army of mine?"

"Emperor Honorius has gone completely mad," the soldier replied. "He questioned our loyalties following your uprising and ordered all soldiers of Gothic descent killed; he didn't stop there. His armies are rampaging across all Roman territories murdering our wives and children. We are being exterminated and cannot stand for it."

"How do I know your soldiers are not just a plant to infiltrate my ranks and destroy my army from within?" Alaric asked.

The man placed the metal box he carried on the ground, backed away and gestured for Alaric to inspect the contents. The man's distance from the box put Alaric on the defensive. Rather than risk setting off an explosive trap himself, he gestured for one of his soldiers to open the chest.

The man obediently stepped forward, knelt down and unfastened the lock without question or pause. He flipped the lid open and scampered back in surprise and horror. Not seeing an explosion gave Alaric leave to step forward and peer into the container. Inside, amid a torrent of buzzing flies, he saw four severed heads still wearing their Roman dress helmets signifying the rank of general.

"When we got word of the orders we killed our commanders and wiped out their armies before they could visit the same upon us," the soldier proudly reported. "Four Roman armies lay dead, and we present to you nearly thirty thousand soldiers ready to serve you, so long as you lead them toward Rome to save their families from the extermination order."

Alaric's face lit up with excitement at the proposition. It was better than he could have possibly imagined. He took a moment to clasp each of the four soldier's forearms to seal the arrangement. "Do not even bother having your men fall out of marching formation. We will all be on the move as soon as my men can assemble. The conquest of Rome is at hand."

Chapter 7: Breaking News

HASTELLOY STUDIED THE chieftain's eyes as they assessed the chess board. The game was only seven moves in and Hastelloy already had his opponent pinned. If he took the bait and captured the queen, Hastelloy could deliver check mate with his bishop. If the chieftain protected his king he stood to lose his rook, bishop and knight so the game was over either way.

Realizing the chess match no longer required any concentration on his part, Hastelloy looked around the meager Egyptian village that served as cover for the tunnel exit point leading to the Nexus chamber. The day was hot and sunny, but the tall tree outside his modest home built of clay bricks provided adequate shade to make things comfortable.

He came out of the Nexus regeneration chamber three years earlier. Per his own orders he remained as master of the village to watch over the Nexus until another crew member came out to relieve him of the tedious protective duty. Sometimes it was mere weeks, others it was decades spent living in the simple village before a replacement arrived. It was just the luck of the draw.

Though it lacked excitement, having a crew member perpetually stationed in the village was critical. Hastelloy still insisted no advanced machinery, like communication radios, could leave the village except in the most dire circumstances. If advanced tools were found by the humans, the potential for Neo Scale cultural contamination was just too great. This, unfortunately, left the crewmen scattered around the continents hunting for the last remaining Alpha relic with the difficult task of communicating with one another; which is where the village came in.

The one constant on this planet for the Novi was the hiding place of the Nexus. Whenever crewmen left the village they documented their identity, whereabouts and task to accomplish in a central log. If discoveries were made or anyone ran into trouble, they sent word back to the village where the caretaker could send couriers to the rest of the scattered crew. From start to finish the process sometimes took weeks, but it did the job.

"I know you are up to something, Master," his opponent said bringing Hastelloy's mind back to the game. "You never throw away a piece for no reason, but I cannot for the life of me figure it out. That leaves me with doing the obvious and possibly learning something for next time."

He captured the queen with his knight, and Hastelloy immediately moved his bishop into position. "Checkmate," he said halfheartedly. The village chieftain was a capable player, but this was just too easy to be even remotely enjoyable.

The Chieftain just shook his head and smiled. "I could live a thousand years and never win a match against you. You have played countless games against me and the others in your village and never lost, how can you be so consistent? How do you not slip up even once against a weaker foe?"

"A steady regimen of discipline, and unwavering attention to detail," Hastelloy instructed as the chieftain reset the board for another game. He omitted the fact that even if the man did live to be a thousand, that would still leave Hastelloy about ten times his senior.

The rematch was interrupted by the arrival of a young man running up from the grain silos. "We are about finished loading the wagons."

Hastelloy looked up from the game board to see twenty workers in the final stages of tying down tarps over the beds of a dozen wagons. "You made great time. I think we can hold off leaving for market until the morning."

The teenager was about to run off and enjoy his afternoon that was suddenly free of chores or responsibility. At the last moment the youth turned and handed Hastelloy a piece of paper. "I almost forgot. A messenger just arrived with a letter from your family abroad."

Hastelloy took the folded piece of paper sealed with the wax imprint of Gallono. "Thank you."

He was about to dismiss the boy and play another game of chess, but Gallono's brief letter put a stop to that plan.

Rome has fallen to barbarians from the north.
-Gallono

Hastelloy sprang to his feet, "Assemble the couriers. We leave for the port in Alexandria immediately."

Chapter 8: Reunion

AS HASTELLOY RODE his mount down the flawlessly paved streets of Florence he calmly took in the scene around him. Considering the recently sacked city of Rome lay only two hundred miles south, he expected the city to be in a frenzied panic. Instead of seeing bolstered defenses and the conscription of every able-bodied male into the army, it was business as usual.

The gladiator arena was standing room only, and deep cries of delight rang out across the city periodically as one combatant bested the other for the crowd's enjoyment.

When Hastelloy led his horse past the half-moon shaped amphitheater he observed the schedule of performances was uninterrupted by the calamity to the south. The masses seemed completely oblivious; as if their lives wouldn't be affected in the least by the city of Rome's downfall.

From a narrow point of view the people were right of course. From an individual perspective it made little difference. Whether they paid taxes to a far off Roman Emperor or a local Mayor did not matter to them. On a grand scale however, the fall of Rome made all the difference in the world.

The loss of a central, unifying government meant it was every tiny territory and city state for itself. Specialization of labor would be lost, replaced by a society focused on survival rather than advancing the arts and science that drove cultural and technological advancement.

Once again the crowd roared with excitement from the gladiator arena. Hastelloy envied them the luxury of living in the moment rather than always peering toward the future. None of them were constantly tested by an adversary who never slept or ate. Goron's entire existence was dedicated to thwarting Hastelloy's plans.

Hastelloy had proven time and again that he was the better man. He had the unparalleled advantage of existing for over ten thousand years and could draw upon that experience. As the centuries and millennia passed though, that advantage was fading. Goron was no simpleton. With every failed scheme he learned; growing in ability and cunning.

Goron's growing lethality aside, the law of statistics all but demanded the Alpha captain succeed at some point over the thousands of years. The situation was not unlike the prospect of Hastelloy losing a chess match to the village chieftain. The man was an inferior player, but if they played enough times, eventually Hastelloy's attention to detail would waiver or the opponent would get lucky. Either way, the result was defeat.

Eventually Hastelloy came to a freestanding building two stories tall just across the river from the city's center. The first floor displayed signage advertising a currency exchange while the second story served as living quarters for the proprietor.

Hastelloy tied his mount next to three other horses on a hitching post and stepped to the door. Since it was after business hours he rapped his knuckles on the door three times. Moments later heavy footsteps drew closer on the other side of the door until it swung open to reveal a silhouetted figure against the golden glow of a table lamp.

He gave his eyes a moment to adjust and then looked at the figure once more to see the clean shaven face of Gallono staring back at him. It had been decades since the two last crossed paths back home in the Egyptian village. The moment did not require words or tears. The bond forged between the two soldiers over thousands of years transcended all. The two men simply embraced and let the moment speak for itself.

Eventually, Hastelloy clapped Gallono on the back twice to bring the moment to an end. As Gallono ushered his captain into the room, Valnor, Tonwen and Tomal rose to their feet and acknowledged the entry of their commanding officer.

Hastelloy waved off the military protocol, "Sit, sit. You look ridiculous; now sit."

With that, everyone took a seat around a long rectangular table with benches along each side. Hastelloy looked past the table and saw the only other amenity in the chamber was a desk at the rear next to a steep set of stairs leading to the second floor. Completing the sparse decor was a stone fireplace with a roaring flame providing warmth to the chamber.

Hastelloy let his eyes wander to each individual seated around the table. It had been over two hundred years since all five of the Lazarus crew members were even on the same continent, let alone seated around the same table for a meeting. "It's great to have the whole family together again."

The comment drew all smiles while Gallono pulled out a letter and set it in the middle of the table. He pointed to the last line with raised eyebrows.

"I got your reply to my letter; we all did. I don't know about everyone else, but mine said to drop everything and get to Florence *immediately*. Yet here we all sit waiting for the author of these letters to arrive."

Hastelloy chuckled softly while he crumpled the letter and tossed it into the fire. "You had the benefit of traveling by land. Try finding a ship's captain willing to sail anywhere near the city of Rome while it's under attack and see how quickly you make the trip all the way from Egypt."

"Likely story," Gallono quipped, but then allowed his demeanor to harden and address the situation with the intensity it deserved. "You went to a lot of expense and effort to arrange this reunion, Captain. I take it you suspect the Alpha have a hand in the fall of Rome."

An affirmative nod prompted a frustrated huff from Tomal. "We rid that rabid dog of his hands a long time ago. How does he still manage to cause trouble?"

"He finds new hands belonging to those he manipulates," Valnor countered. "You ought to know," he concluded under his breath but still audible around the table.

The arrogant and rebellious Tomal of old would have continued speaking as though the cutting words had no effect. This new man took the shame of falling victim to Goron's control five hundred years earlier to heart. He was functional again, but the mere mention of his epic failure back then made the man revert to a child content with not speaking until spoken to.

Sensing the insult induced silence lingering for too long, Hastelloy spoke again, "Our searching for the Alpha relic has consistently pointed toward him hiding in the northern barbarian territories. Plus, a group of people don't just up and leave their homeland to invade a well established empire on a whim. They need a reason, a divine reason most likely, and we all know how fond Goron is of presenting himself as a deity to further his designs."

"I really don't see what the big deal is here," Valnor chimed in. "The Visigoths sacked the city of Rome, so what? They'll have their fun with the inhabitants no doubt, but in the end they can't hold the conquest. Eventually Roman legions will boot them out and order will be restored with relatively little lasting harm done."

Hastelloy shook his head with disappointment at his helmsman's thoroughly incorrect assessment of the situation. Valnor had come a long way in his abilities. He was even a key architect in shaping Rome into the long standing cultural and political icon that it was. Therein lay the problem, however. He had an unshakeable faith in the resiliency of his creation, and it shrouded his otherwise sound judgment.

"The preeminence of Rome has been shattered," Hastelloy instructed. "The few Romans ruled the many peoples of the world because everyone believed Rome could not be beaten. Now they know differently, and every ambitious governor and foreign power will line up to have a try at casting off the yoke of their oppressor."

Valnor looked insulted enough to draw a blade and challenge Hastelloy to a duel. "Oppressor? Rome is a noble institution that brought law and order throughout the Mediterranean to keep the peace."

"It is a hard peace," Tonwen interjected, "Enforced at the point of a sword against the will of the many."

"A hard peace is preferable to anarchy," Valnor countered. "We should reinsert ourselves into Roman affairs to root out the incompetence and corruption to set this ship sailing on a proper course again."

"The sudden empowerment of Rome's enemies aside. The Visigoths scorched half the empire on their way through Greece and northern Italy to reach Rome. There is no longer an empire to piece back together."

Valnor threw his arms out wide in exacerbation. "I guess we just sit here then and let Goron's barbaric anarchy wash over the civilized world we worked so hard to build for these people? Let all the technological and social advancements regress back to square one? I'm sure that will get us home sooner!"

Hastelloy felt all eyes on him. Valnor had a valid point and the entire crew awaited a retort. A sly grin crossed his lips before laying out his new plans. "Of course not, but Rome is not the answer. There is another unifying force among these people. One unencumbered by borders or nationality."

Hastelloy paused to look at his science officer. "Tonwen, former apostle to Jesus, would you care to venture a guess as to which entity I am referring?"

"The Catholic Church," Tonwen answered with glowing pride. "It universally guides the moral compass of society. It has the potential to carry unparalleled influence over both the working and ruling classes. Most important of all, the Catholic Church, if managed properly, will have enough wealth to encourage the arts. It can establish libraries to shelter and share the collective knowledge of mankind."

Valnor eagerly jumped in with his objection. "As you said earlier, Goron has a knack for hijacking religions to serve his purpose. Are you sure we want to promote a theocratic society that is even more vulnerable to his way of doing things?"

Hastelloy nodded his head slightly to commend Valnor's argument. Now the young man was thinking straight again. "It's certainly a risk, but considering the heavy hand we had in the widespread adoption of that faith, I think we can manage that risk."

Valnor's doubtful glare caused Hastelloy to raise his voice and steel his tone. "I know you gravitate toward a secular solution, but for crying out loud, Gallono and Tonwen were there at the start. Tonwen was declared a saint and posthumously named the first Pope of the Catholic Church. We have this religion under control."

"No," Tonwen interrupted. "We are only caretakers of his church on earth. It flourishes only by God's divine design and consent."

Hastelloy could clearly see the centuries since the death of his friend Jesus had not dampened the flames of Tonwen's faith. The former atheist and diehard scientist did not just speak the words; he was now a believer through and through.

"Christianity enjoys some prominence in the regions along the Mediterranean Sea, but not many other locations," Hastelloy went on. "Various pagan beliefs dominate everywhere else, and we need to change that. I am putting each of you in charge of a particular region. Your key objective is to proselytize as many as possible. Keep an eye out for Goron and his influences, but hunting him now is only a secondary objective."

Hastelloy pointed toward Gallono. "I need you to manage the northern regions, particularly the Germanic tribes. Keep in mind, Commander, that's also where all our evidence points to Goron holding the most influence."

Gallono silently nodded in agreement allowing Hastelloy to move on to the next crewman. "Valnor and Tomal, I need the two of you to convert the British Isles. Tonwen, you will own the regions of Northern Italy, Gaul and Spain."

"And what about you?" Valnor asked in the way a sibling might complain about chores being handed out unevenly by a parent. "What will you be doing while the four of us toil to spread superstition about the land?"

Hastelloy watched Tonwen's hands resting on top of the table turn into fists. Before the deeply religious man could explode in an extremely rare display of anger, Hastelloy spoke first. "The same as I have been for the last few years. I will be in Egypt coordinating communication."

Looking around the table Hastelloy could plainly see everyone except Tonwen was very uncomfortable with their assignments. They did not even know where to begin in order to accomplish their missions, and that made Hastelloy very happy. After hundreds of years spent fruitlessly searching for Goron, having the men step out of their comfort zones to confront a new challenge would be a welcome change of pace. Still, they looked completely lost on where to begin.

"I will not micromanage your efforts," Hastelloy went on. "You are all completely free to employ any tactics or methods you deem most effective to spread the Christian faith and enhance the influence that the Catholic Church carries over this continent."

"What about Alaric and his army?" Tomal asked. "If he's under Goron's influence he's likely traveling with the relic."

Hastelloy looked at his engineer with a stern face. He understood the man's need to prove himself once more to the crew. He had a certain determination to fight Goron at every turn, but he went about it in reckless ways. "No, that would be too obvious to fit Goron's mode of operation. He avoids our detection by doing the unexpected, not hiding in the most obvious location like with Alaric's army."

"At the very least, we cannot let one of his avatars rule the Roman Empire. Crumbling empire or not, that is entirely too much power to leave in Goron's hands."

Hastelloy let out a heavy sigh and lay his hands flat on the table and addressed Tomal with a very quiet and relaxed voice to convey how certain he was about his assessment of the situation. "Believe me. Alaric will not be able to hold onto Rome. Goron knows this, and he is already working his next scheme and hoping we spend all our time and effort trying to defeat this Alaric character."

Watching Tomal bite his lip as his analytical mind went to work behind those dark eyes of his let Hastelloy know the man was not convinced. "You are under no specific orders from me, Tomal. Proselytize the British Isles is all I ask. If you feel those orders take you to Rome to take a swing at Alaric, be my guest. Just make sure and steer clear of the brothel districts while in Rome. The four of us will be far too busy to come save you from another outrageous bill."

The joke drew some polite grins around the table, but everyone knew there was also a lot of truth to the words. With the orders given, all five men rose from the table, unhitched their horses and went their separate ways once more.

Chapter 9: The Mighty Have Fallen

EVEN BEFORE THE northern walls of Rome came into view, Tomal saw dark clouds of smoke billowing skyward. It had been nearly a month since the Visigoths savaged the city and still the fires burned. Word was the barbarian horde moved on to the south, but Tomal still had needs that required attention inside the city.

It was rumored that the Visigoths as a whole were devout followers of Christianity. This gave hope that the damage and slaughter might not be so severe. As Tomal passed under the northern gates into the city, that hope withered away with each and every stride he took.

He saw firsthand that the Visigoths went about their business without charity. In the hour of savage license, with passion inflamed and every restraint removed, the precepts of the Gospel held no influence over the behavior of the Gothic Christians.

The streets were littered with trash and debris jostled about by the foul wind that carried with it the rotting stench of decay. Herds of cats meandered from one trash pile to the next taking what booty they found, not unlike the Visigoths a few weeks before.

A closer examination of the trash lined streets revealed the cause of the foul odor in the air. Bodies young and old, male and female lay strewn about in every position imaginable. Most victims were citizens wearing togas or other garments of high fashion, but not all. The barbarian fury was clearly focused on the Romans, but even the innocent slaves and plebian classes endured the promiscuous massacre to some extent.

Tomal spotted a pack of vandals, at least thirty strong, moving from house to house in search of valuables the Visigoths may have left behind. Tomal crossed the street opposite the group and drew his blade as a deterrent in case they decided to take advantage of his lonely stature. They eyed Tomal for a moment, but concluded an empty house presented an easier target than an armed stranger; they let him pass unmolested.

He walked deeper into the city and passed the Mausoleum of Augustus. Glancing through the doorway as he walked by, Tomal saw dozens of urns holding the ashes of prior Roman Emperors shattered on the floor with the fine black powdered remains sloshed about the white marble floor in rhythm with the wind. Tomal caught the scent of that wind and instantly knew the Visigoths did not simply spread the remains of those great Romans to the four winds, they urinated and defecated on them as well.

The most shocking scene of all came when Tomal saw the forum. The once proud focal point of the entire Roman Empire with grand buildings, columns, steps and streets built of pure white marble now lay disfigured and charred. Statues shattered, columns toppled, entire buildings collapsed. In that moment he truly understood why Hastelloy abandoned any notion of piecing the Roman Empire back together again. The economically ruined city and empire was beyond any rational hope of repair. It could never be raised again to even a shadow of its former glory.

Tomal finally moved on to reach his destination, the one section of Rome still open for business. Tomal knew he could count on the brothel district to weather the ordeal. In a way, the sacking of Rome merely extended the debauchery of the whore houses to the rest of the city for a few days. The fact that men still frequented the establishments amid the chaos did not surprise him in the least.

What did startle even Tomal's admittedly shaky morals was the sight of a man bartering to sell his wife and three daughters into sexual bondage for no other reason than they 'allowed' themselves to be raped by the rampaging barbarians. All four women were of a decent age and attractive enough to serve Tomal's purpose. His reservations aside, Tomal overheard the prices being discussed for their purchase and could not say no.

Before a particularly unscrupulous proprietor could deliver a counter offer Tomal jumped in to end the negotiation. "I will buy all four of them for the asked price - one hundred sesterces."

"Hand over the coin and I'll hand over the girls," the man skeptically replied.

Without another word Tomal let his rucksack slide off his shoulder to the ground. He dug around for a moment and produced ten small bags of coin. One by one he dropped them into the man's eager palm and in exchange received the end of a rope binding the four females together.

"Lots of luck getting your money's worth out of that mangy bunch," the outbid proprietor hissed while glowering a murderous start at Tomal. They both knew the arrangement was an absolute steal. His instinct was to stay and gloat, but he had a more urgent calling.

Tomal led his purchased gaggle of prostitutes toward Rome's south gate. The girls were so beaten and demoralized that they put up no resistance whatsoever. They simply followed and did as they were told; resigned to their dismal fates.

Tomal planned on purchasing a cart and horses on the way out of the city, but there was no need. Horses roamed freely among the streets as no one had means to care for them any longer, and wagons by the dozen sat unused alongside the roads just begging to be taken. In no time at all Tomal and the four women were out the southern gate and on their way to catch up with Alaric's barbarian army.

The trail was not difficult to follow. A fifty mile wide path of destruction was carved across the landscape heading for the southern tip of Italy where Alaric apparently intended to cross over to Africa and secure a steady supply of grain for his most recent conquest. Rounding up enough ships to transport an army a hundred thousand strong took time. Tomal was confident he could catch them in time.

On the ride south Tomal invited the mother to join him on the driving bench of the cart to which she dutifully complied. "Fortune has done you and your daughters no favors these last few weeks."

The woman said nothing. She just looked straight ahead with a vacant, thousand yard stare.

"Believe it or not, I am the one ray of light shining through the darkness consuming your existence right now." A sideways glance from the woman let Tomal know he had a skeptic sitting next to him. "I'm not going to lie to you. You will have to perform lewd acts on men you would sooner drive a knife into, but only for a short while. It will be just long enough to gain access to the right man. Then you will exact revenge. For you, your girls, for me, and for every Roman, you will exact revenge from those barbarians."

Chapter 10: Payback

JUST AS THE informant said, Tomal and his wagonload of whores found Alaric's army camped just outside the southern port city of Cosenza. The bright sun was about to set over the horizon which meant it was prime time for Tomal's girls to ply their trade.

The week spent tracking the army down gave Tomal more than enough time to instruct the girls properly. Numerous lifetimes spent procuring the services of prostitutes rendered Tomal an unparalleled expert in the carnal ways to satisfy a man. All four of them, even the thirteen year old, proved to be quick studies; no doubt owing to the new found sense of purpose in their lives. It would not take long for their services to get noticed and recommended to the right set of ears.

Tomal brought his cart to a full stop at the camp checkpoint and waited for inspection. One soldier examined the undercarriage while another looked over the girls. "Well, what do we have here? Looks like some new flavors."

With that statement, the first soldier redirected his attention to the cargo. "Just in time too, but I am afraid we cannot let you pass without sampling the quality first."

Tomal just shrugged his shoulders. "Take your pick for a poke, but if you get rough I will cut it off. Do we understand each other?"

"Perfectly."

They each took their turn behind a tree and then allowed Tomal entry into the military camp with his whores aboard. Tomal looked back at the guards and saw bright satisfied smiles plastered across their faces, which gave him confidence his plan would work.

Three days later, after the girls were in almost constant use by the regular soldiers, Tomal received the invite for his whores to attend the king's banquet. Word of their talents had grown to almost legendary status among the camp. Naturally, King Alaric was compelled to indulge as well.

Just after midday Tomal ordered all patrons to be turned away from his tents. Most peacefully turned to other purveyors of the flesh once informed their King owned the four famous prostitutes for the evening. A particularly drunk soldier whose primal calling spoke louder than sound judgment found a blade drawn across his male appendage by one of Tomal's hired escorts, rending the man a eunuch. Following that bloody encounter there were no more questions or complaints about the brothel being closed for the evening; they simply moved on.

Now alone with his workers, Tomal invited them into his tent for a meal. One by one the girls paced into the tent wearing simple dresses made of a single piece of fabric tied at the waist that extended no farther down than the middle of their thighs. Their rustled hair and filthy garments gave evidence to their popularity with the men. The only aspect of the four women, particularly the mother, that did not look completely broken in was their eyes. They all knew they served a higher calling and were honored to perform that duty as true Romans.

Tomal kept his words short and to the point in case King Alaric had any spies nearby checking for plots against him. "Fortune casts a favorable eye upon us. Tonight you will be in the company of royalty rather than barbaric thugs. You have the rest of the day to bathe, groom and clothe yourselves adequately for the noble company you will keep tonight."

The four women bowed appreciatively to their owner and left the tent to do as they were told. That evening, an hour after sunset, the four returned for inspection. They stood in a line at arm's-length from each other as Tomal wove his way in between like a serpent sneaking through tall grass.

Each of the women stood utterly irresistible to Tomal. The spiced floral scent of their perfume was intoxicating. The exquisite dresses they donned were comprised of two rectangular pieces of cloth partially sewn together on both sides. The sleeveless dresses gathered over their naked shoulders by two circular pins were stunning. The coup de grace came at the waist. A delicate rope gathered the garment just above the hips and accentuated each of their hour glass figures to the fullest. King Alaric would be well pleased.

"Nearly fit for a king," Tomal commended. He paced over to a wooden chest he kept at the base of his overstuffed pillow bed. From the trunk he removed four gold necklaces which prominently displayed a pure black gemstone that contrasted beautifully with the pure white wardrobe the women donned. One by one he clasped a necklace around each of their necks. "Now you are ready. Go, perform your Roman duty."

In the early hour of the following morning, Tomal awoke to the sound of escorts showing the girls back into their master's tent. He rose from his bed wearing only a tunic and prowled toward his property. He stopped in front of the youngest, removed her necklace and moved on to the next without a word. When Tomal reached the mother he moved to recover his necklace, but found the black gemstone missing. "I knew you wouldn't let me down."

Tomal turned his back on the line of women and paced over to the chest at the base of his bed and returned the pieces of jewelry to their original container. He closed the lid and spun around to face his girls once more. His eye drifted away from their angelic presence to the two armed men accompanying them. "Show them back to their sleeping tent and do not disturb them for business until after lunchtime. They have earned a break."

The next day King Alaric became gravely ill. Two days later he succumbed to his illness which sent his generals and soldiers into a frenzy of activity. As a tribute to their fallen king the army officers chose to bury Alaric's body where it would never be disturbed. They labored for weeks to divert the Dusento River using a system of dykes and dams. Then, where the river once flowed they toiled to construct a tomb for their king and liberator from Roman tyranny. Once finished they would break the dykes to allow the waters to flow once more on their natural path and over the top of the tomb. The conqueror of Rome would forever be interred in the soil of the great empire he defeated.

Tomal used the distraction that the elaborate project created to full advantage. He managed to sneak his way into the King's private chambers. In the corner he found a stone altar standing waist high with an iron box sitting locked on the ground next to the altar.

He easily picked the lock with a set of fine wires and opened the lid. He had his doubts, but Tomal held out hope that Hastelloy would be wrong. He prayed that Goron's relic would still be in there. He wanted, no, he needed to be the one to extinguish the manipulative bastard's life force. It was the only way he could make things right. Alas, the container was empty except for a piece of parchment with a single statement written upon it.

Mission accomplished. Now it is time to tend a different flock. Remember, you have been and always will be a step behind me. Get used to it.

With both the Visigoth King and Goron gone, Tomal saw no reason to stay. He collected his girls, loaded the small fortune of coin he had amassed during their stay, and headed north with his horses and wagon load of valuables.

A few miles outside the city of Calabria, the only major Roman city in the south not to fall under the barbarian onslaught, Tomal stopped the cart and hopped out. He reached over the wagon side and loaded his rucksack with two handfuls of coin.

He momentarily paused to look up at the mother. The woman's eyes exploded to the size of saucers in surprise when Tomal announced, "All the rest is yours; payment from one devoted Roman to another for a job well done."

Then without saying another word he slung the rucksack over his shoulder and walked away. He didn't look back for fear he might let on that he had indeed surprised himself by walking away from the women and coin.

Chapter 11: Corruption

GORON RECEIVED WORD that Alaric had died in southern Italy just a few short weeks after conquering the city of Rome. The news was unfortunate, but of little lasting consequence. He fully expected the Novi captain to have Alaric assassinated, but the efficient speed with which it was carried out was admirable. Goron had hoped Alaric and his band of Visigoths would cause trouble up and down the Italian peninsula for at least a year or two in order to cement the state of chaos throughout the once proud empire.

In the end, Goron paid the news no mind. He had moved on to another scheme that showed significantly more promise.

By his estimation, Captain Hastelloy and his men had been quite active in the rapid spread of Christianity throughout the continent in recent years. Goron's initial instinct was to work against those efforts, but in the end saw no need. Why fight them if he could join them, or at least corrupt and take over what they labored so hard to create.

To that end, Goron's relic was hidden away among the white stones and stained glass windows of the Cathedral of Saint John the Baptist in Turin, Italy. There, front and center above the half-moon shaped altar alcove his life force rested, encased in red glass and revered as the perpetual flame of the cathedral. The position of prominence gave him an unobstructed view of the entire sanctuary and any worshipers who came to visit.

Initially only the local parish members entered his sanctuary, but now the flood of visitors for him to influence was nearly endless. Humans traveled long and far to see the charred piece of fabric housed in a protective case and proudly displayed near the altar. They referred to it as the Shroud of Turin. They prayed to it because the tapestry sized piece of linen displayed the charred image of a man who suffered wounds consistent with the crucifixion of Jesus Christ.

In reality, it was a piece of fabric laid over a woodcarving that was burned from the inside out to produce the lightly charred image. The work was exquisitely done by one of Goron's followers and served his purpose well as a draw for additional worshipers.

Goron was amazed how well the artifact worked. There was not even a need to convince people the shroud was legitimate. They wanted to believe. They were so desperate to feel the physical presence of their god that they would readily believe and do almost anything. They willingly gave away their wealth, left their families, and even waged wars and committed murder to be closer to the presence of their god.

Even in the late evening hour during the middle of the week, Goron felt the presence of several hundred worshipers filling the sanctuary pews, asking for divine guidance. If Goron still had lips, they would have smiled broad and bright. These people were in the right place.

"Do you come to worship my burial shroud or to worship me?" Goron asked in a soft, caring voice that seemed to emanate from the very stones making up the cathedral walls.

The barely audible murmur of individuals praying abruptly ended in dead silence as the visitors looked around the cavernous sanctuary. Eventually they turned to each other to try and confirm they were not hearing things.

"Are you prepared to carry out my wishes?" Goron asked a little louder this time.

Most remained reverently silent. Some allowed gasps filled with both fear and delight to escape their lungs, while a cowardly few ran from the place of worship in utter terror.

Goron addressed those who remained with a booming voice. "You are my chosen few. Will you accept my guidance without question?"

"Yes, anything you ask of me, Lord," came a bold reply from one man with all the others quickly joining the pledge.

"Then salvation in heaven and an eternity spent at my side shall be yours," Goron boomed. If he had eyes he would have rolled them at this point. These simpleminded creatures made it so easy.

Chapter 12: Batteries Included

TEPIN WALKED UP to a large clay vase that stood nearly as high as his seven foot tall frame. From the top he pulled out a long slender dipstick and observed the fluid level was running low. He immediately opened a two inch circular access hatch beside the dipstick, and attached a funnel. He then bent down and picked up, with the utmost care, an iron pitcher holding about five gallons of Carborane. He made sure not to spill even a single drop of the extremely potent acid as he poured it down the funnel.

With the fluid level topped off, he checked to make sure that the iron and copper electrodes were properly secure. He also made sure the power leads attached to the stone altar were connected and free of kinks. Tepin repeated the procedure on the backup battery located on the opposite side of the life force altar. He then stepped back and admired the device he dedicated his life to maintaining.

Mother Nature was such a wondrous and perfectly conceived deity. Not only did she provide sustenance in life, she yielded a perfectly natural process to maintain life even after death. The naturally occurring chemical reaction that produced electricity between the acid and electrodes was sufficient to power an iron-boron electromagnet that could pull a life force escaping its physical form to a focal point to preserve it for all eternity if desired.

Unlike the Novi who used a blasphemous machine to prolong their lives, the Alpha accomplished it through a completely natural method that consumed absolutely none of Mother Nature's precious resources.

"It's happening," one of Tepin's fellow monks said from the corner. Tepin turned his head to see the man sitting next to a bed where the oldest member of the red planet colony lay.

The elder had contracted the parvovirus a week earlier and his immune system was no longer able to cope with the particularly aggressive virus. He was in the final stages of respiratory failure and did not have long in this world.

Tepin slowly turned his attention back to the flat stone altar flanked by two seven foot clay vases. He closed his eyes for a minute to say a silent prayer; when he opened them again he saw the radiant glow of a divine spirit floating an inch above the altar's stone surface. The robust red and gold flame flowed like liquid metal from side to side with a divine fire burning from within.

He watched the life force intently for a few minutes because he had high hopes for this one. The man had lived a long, productive life and had much to offer the collective. All his life force needed to do was hold it together long enough for the others to accept him.

Tepin saw the vibrant glow flicker a bit, and then watched in sorrow as the glow slowly drained from the flame until the light was extinguished from existence. What a pity. Tepin only hoped that when his day came his life force would somehow measure up and be deemed worthy.

****

Kuanti felt the new presence the instant it arrived in the collective consciousness of the Alpha relics. There was a strange and unexpected harmony in the collective considering there were over a half million life forces present. These disciplined minds were able to shelter their inner thoughts from the others to the extent only relevant information was shared. The instant that harmony was disrupted by a newcomer it was open season.

In life the Alpha determined leadership and worth by one's ability to physically dominate others. Existing as a formless stream of consciousness did away with that tool. Alternatively, they made sport of mental domination instead.

Kuanti remembered how thoroughly violated he felt the moment his thoughts entered the collective, which only included a few dozen others at the time. His deepest fears, his most profound insecurities that he kept secured away in the back of his mind were dragged out into the open for everyone to feed upon. The humiliation was almost too much to bear; he contemplated letting his life force expire. The others sensed the impulse of course and egged him on to go through with the decision.

In the end, Kuanti found just enough hope and strength of will to hold on until his mind was able to keep his thoughts private from the collective. Since that day, existing among the others who were strong enough of will not to end their existence either had been a true pleasure.

Kuanti knew immediately this newcomer did not have what it took to survive; very few did anymore given the numbers they faced. Cora was the first to grab onto the man's humiliation of cheating on exams in school.

Another sensed his paralyzing fear of reptiles and projected into his thoughts an image of the newcomer being devoured by an enormous serpent. Cheating on his mate, fear of the dark, inadequacies in athletics all crashed in on the new arrival at once; it was too much.

The life force left the collective almost as soon as it arrived. The mental discipline it took to exist as a formless stream of consciousness took time. Time the weak-minded did not have.

Most newcomers chose to immediately extinguish their lives for all eternity to spare themselves the unrelenting scrutiny of stronger wills. This effectively served as a winnowing fork to separate valuables from the worthless chaff. Only the strong survived, even in the afterlife.

Kuanti had no difficulty dealing with the other relics now. He was the revered Founding Leader. His greatness was undisputed, and his mind had no trouble maintaining its mental walls to keep others away from his inner thoughts. The only time Kuanti felt any anxiety whatsoever was the couple of months every other year that the orbits of the third and fourth planets came close enough for Goron's life force to join the collective.

It amazed Kuanti how Goron was able to dominate the thoughts of everybody else without the benefit of constant contact with the collective. Life forces introduced for the first time spent years adapting to the rigors experienced inside the shared mental environment, if they survived at all. Their thoughts were transparent as a piece of glass, yet Goron's mind was about as easy to read as a book in a pitch black room. The captain was an absolute master of his thoughts and emotions, and had the uncanny ability to drill into those of others.

Kuanti resented the periodic interruption in his leadership from Goron's presence, but deep down he knew the captain was his better.

"Report?" came a question aimed directly at Kuanti's consciousness from the collective. He focused his thoughts and reached out to feel the new presence. It was not hard to find; Goron's life force shined through the din like a supernova. Kuanti had bad news to break to his captain. To hopefully ease the backlash he began the discussion by reminding Goron of his own failure.

"I still miss Elohim and his rather primitive psyche," Kuanti mused. They lost Elohim's life force several hundred years earlier, but Kuanti still liked to bring up the subject from time to time since it was the one and only example of Goron failing in his duties as Leader. "Don't you?"

"Yes, yes, Kuanti. The Novi succeeded in extinguishing his life force under my watch here on this planet," Goron replied in a very bored tone. "I am now operating alone on this world against the five Novi crash survivors. There, did I say my lines right? Did I adequately perform my part in your pathetic little play to dredge up that topic one more time?"

"I find it odd that the death of my engineer and the reduction in my influence on this planet seems to please you," Goron went on. "Explain yourself."

The captain was good, Kuanti admitted to himself, or at least he hoped was only himself. "We have endured a setback of our own. I simply brought up the topic in order to have a more understanding mind on which to convey the details."

Kuanti felt a flash of anger escape Goron's mental blockade. "Well, let's see. I am alone as a formless relic on a planet dominated by a very much living Novi threat that keeps coming back no matter how many times I manage to kill them."

"You are the only occupants of a planet with over ten thousand loyal Alpha warriors eager to do your bidding. Your only mission is to construct a Flashtrans communicator to reach our home world to get us the hell home. Yes, they are such similar circumstances, Kuanti. Your continued failure is completely excusable now that I give it some thought."

"The Flashtrans communications array is operational. It has power and is transmitting," Kuanti reported.

"How uncharacteristically competent of you," Goron commended. "Why is an Alpha fleet not already in orbit to finish off the Novi and take us home, or does your little setback ruin that happy ending for me?"

If Kuanti still had hands he would have punched something. He had done the impossible and yet Goron made him feel an inch tall. "The fault does not lie with us, Captain. The signal is being jammed by a device on your planet. The Novi are putting out a scrambling signal that will not allow any transmission to leave this system."

From across the forty million miles of barren space between the two planets Kuanti was impacted by a devastating wave of anger from Goron's mind. Yet through the anger he got a glimpse of another emotion –

admiration. Deep down the Captain admired his Novi counterpart and his resourcefulness. As soon as he detected the errant emotion it was sealed away once more behind Goron's formidable mental barriers.

"Too clever by half," Goron managed. "Damn that Novan!"

Goron brought his attention back to Kuanti. "Let me guess. Since discovering this interference you have just sat in a corner brooding."

Kuanti's mood perked up at the accusation of inaction. He was afraid the initiative he took would not be well received by Goron, but he now saw inaction would have been a far greater failure. "Not exactly. I felt the best course of action was to construct a craft that could transport an assault team to your planet to terminate the interference so that the signal can be sent."

"Excellent," Goron said in a rare display of commendation. "What sort of timeframe are you facing?"

"At least ten generations," Kuanti divulged and counted his blessings Goron did not have the physical ability to harm him, but his mental assaults could still be devastating.

Kuanti decided to explain himself before Goron had the chance to rip him apart in front of the collective. "We need to develop new materials to construct a spacecraft. We must invent and build a new fusion reactor to power that ship. We need to . . ."

Goron erupted with rage. "Have. You. Lost. Your. Mind? Why spend hundreds of years reinventing the wheel when you have a perfectly functional fusion reactor right now? Why can't you use the original reactor housed inside the engineering section of my ship that you crash landed aboard over two thousand years ago?" Goron insisted.

"If you had not allowed an unarmed collector class ship to get the drop on you in the first place perhaps we wouldn't be in this situation at all," Kuanti challenged. He knew it was imprudent, but it needed to be said.

"Your captain is waiting for an answer to his question, Ensign," Goron demanded.

Kuanti could feel the half million life forces mentally circling the two in the hopes of seeing a leadership challenge to entertain them. Goron was still the better man, even from forty million miles away, so Kuanti acquiesced to the order.

"That reactor powers the colony and our entire industrial complex. Most important of all, it powers the environmental barriers that allow us to maintain a habitable environment within these caves. We cannot survive without it, therefore another must be reengineered and built. Unfortunately that process will take a considerable amount of time."

On the fly, Kuanti thought of a way to save face. "A quicker solution would be for you to locate the signal and use the locals on your planet to attack and destroy it."

"Yes, it would," Goron conceded, "I am working tirelessly to do exactly that as well as disrupting the Novi's progress and influence on this planet in any way possible. In the unlikely event that I am unsuccessful, your efforts will be the backup plan. Now, with that settled, let's put our collective minds together and document everything we can recall about refining materials for a ship's hull and building a fusion reactor from the ground up."

Chapter 13: Beware the 99 Percent

"CLAY POTS WITH copper and iron electrodes dipped in an electrolyte solution," Dr. Holmes read back from his notes. "You're describing a Baghdad Battery right? Like the ones discovered a few years ago in Iraq dating back to the first century AD? Are you telling me these devices were used by humans to harness their life force after death just like the Alpha?"

"They certainly attempted to replicate the design. Fortunately, the Mesopotamians were only able to use very weak acid solutions like grape or lemon juice. Their version of the system could only produce one or two volts to charge the electromagnet, which is not nearly enough power," Hastelloy instructed.

"Well thank goodness," Dr. Holmes exclaimed. "I can only imagine the cultural devastation that could have been done if mankind developed a device to preserve a person's life force for all eternity."

"It would have been a catastrophe in line with the errors made during Novi first contact with the Alpha all those years ago which led to this war," Hastelloy confirmed. "It turns out the Alpha design employs a Carborane solution, basically a super acid that is several million times stronger than even sulfuric acid, let alone grape juice. The charge it puts out could light up a modern day city."

"What about now?" Jeffery asked. "We certainly have the technology to conduct enough electricity to make the device work. Why aren't mortuaries selling this as a service alongside their overpriced caskets and urns?"

The question seemed to throw Hastelloy off. The patient looked lost for words, but then recovered to finally explain, "Not many people could write back then. It really is something of a minor miracle that the designs were preserved from the original device the Alpha built in Ancient Egypt. It had to survive two thousand years of generations reciting the story until the Mesopotamians decided to give it a try and recreate the technology. When they saw it didn't work, they tossed it aside as folklore."

Dr. Holmes could only nod his head in agreement. "That does make sense I suppose. Now getting back to the fall of Rome, I do seem to recall the city of Rome falling to an army of Visigoths marching down from the north at some point. How could that one uprising, one of many hundreds over the course of Rome's rule, bring down such a well organized and prosperous empire?"

"The situation where a small, yet extremely rich and well organized, group rules over the impoverished masses is a precarious one," Hastelloy explained. "More than anything else, the continued dominance by the few relies upon their subjects believing they are inferior. Once the lower ninety-nine percent begin thinking otherwise, it results in an avalanche of change and rebellion that can only have one conclusion."

"Alaric and his army rampaged through the Greek peninsula sacking Athens and Sparta. Then they waltzed down the Italian peninsula and razed everything in sight along the Adriatic Sea until finally they reached Rome and laid siege to her walls."

"Didn't the vaunted Roman armies resist?" Jeffrey asked.

"Of course they did. Dozens of battles took place and after each, regardless of how many died, Alaric's forces swelled in number. The impoverished masses were drawn to him like ants to sugar. Rome, after a millennia of harsh rule, was on the ropes and everybody and their mother laced up a set of boxing gloves to try and deliver a knockout blow on their oppressors."

Jeffrey understood the logic, but still had a hard time believing the story. "What about the city walls of Rome? Why didn't they keep the barbarian horde out? I mean the defenses were constructed and improved upon for thousands of years."

"True, Alaric's army was incapable of breaching the defensive walls, but the weight of the rebellious movement made it so he didn't have to. Upon approach, slaves from inside the city opened the Salaria Gate and the Visigoths pillaged the city and revealed to the world that, yes, Rome could indeed be beaten."

"What about the Roman Emperor?" Jeffrey asked. "He couldn't have just sat idly by while his empire was devastated."

Hastelloy allowed a flat scowl of regret to conquer his lips. "Actually, Emperor Honorius did almost exactly that. The man was so out of touch with reality that when informed of the destruction of Rome he mistook it for the death of his favorite chicken named Roma. His exact words upon hearing the news were, 'How could it be? She just ate out of my hand this morning.' When his advisors corrected his mistake, the hapless emperor was greatly relieved."

All Jeffrey could do was laugh. "How could someone so incompetent rise to be Emperor?"

"He didn't, he had it handed to him as an inherited title. Skill and leadership had nothing to do with it. Furthermore, the penchant of Roman high society to eat off of lead dinnerware didn't help matters any since lead poisoning certainly does strange things to the human mind. Yet another reason why revitalizing the old Roman Empire was not a good solution."

"So what happened to the Visigoths once their King was slain?" Jeffrey asked. "Did they continue terrorizing the Italian peninsula or did Tomal's assassination save the day?"

"No, not really," Hastelloy answered. "Tomal's unilateral action didn't amount to much. Even if Alaric had survived, the swell of his rebellion all but vanished once the city of Rome was taken. With vengeance satisfied, people that joined along the way almost immediately began deserting his army to return to their normal lives. Eventually the Visigoth tribe ventured north to conquer Gaul and then turned south to finally settle in Spain."

"The Gothic people moved all the way from eastern Europe to settle in Spain?" Jeffrey asked for confirmation.

"I can tell you're beginning to see what Goron was up to," Hastelloy responded. "Under his influence, the Visigoths cut a ribbon of disruption and destruction all across southern Europe. In their wake they left a splintered series of tiny kingdoms ruled by petty warlords rather than one unitary empire."

"Why, to what end?"

"To disrupt my plans of progressing human civilization along at an accelerated rate so my crew and the Nexus could finally get home," Hastelloy answered sharply. "A unified empire allowed an unparalleled growth of science, technology and culture. Clearly Goron could not allow that, so he worked as an agent of chaos to regress mankind all the way back to feudal kingdoms. His actions threatened to bring all our progress to a grinding halt."

"As a solution, you sent everyone in your crew forth to make disciples of all nations," Dr. Holmes quoted from the Bible and then paged back through his notes. "Gallono was assigned Germany, Valnor and Tomal split the British Isles, and Tonwen basically had southern Europe. How did that all work out?"

"Considering Christianity spread like wildfire in those years following the downfall of Rome, and that each of my crewmen were named saints by the church not long after their bodies died, I'd say it worked out famously," Hastelloy stated with pride.

Jeffrey couldn't resist trying to guess who they were in Hastelloy's version of the past. "Let me see now. Tomal is an engineer and had a penchant for parties and drink. I am going to go out on a limb and guess he was St. Patrick."

Hastelloy graced Jeffrey with a smiling nod. "Predictable wasn't it. The patron saint of engineering who hailed from Ireland was indeed Tomal. Valnor stayed on the main island of Britain and convinced the King of Kent to ally with Catholic forces from the mainland to spread the faith. He later was named St. George and is considered the patron saint of Britain."

Jeffrey wanted another turn and jumped in with his next guess. "Gallono was in Germany so that probably makes him St. Boniface."

"Bravo," the patient commended. "For an atheist you are remarkably well versed in Catholic saints."

"My mother's side of the family comes from Germany. Having familiarity of the German apostle was practically a requirement, which is likely the reason I gravitate the other direction now."

"That leaves Tonwen who did far more than any of the others to not only promote Christianity, but set up a monastic system to record and preserve the knowledge of mankind. He documented the Rule of Saint Benedict which even today serves to lay out the duties, expectations, and behaviors of monks and nuns living communally."

"They certainly must have done something right since the Catholic Church still flourishes to this day, and is even the wealthiest land owner the world over," Jeffrey commended.

With the praising words spoken, Dr. Holmes watched his patient's demeanor melt away to a penitent man turning his head away with what could only be described as a look of shame. "Tonwen would likely counter your statement by asking: did the Church thrive because of, or in spite of my efforts?"

Chapter 14: Safe House

BRIAN RUSSELL TRIED his best to tune out everything from the outside world, but found the task nearly impossible. The roar of the mighty diesel engine powering the Humvee down the relatively empty streets of Cairo would have made even an eighteen wheel truck driver reach for a set of ear plugs.

He was still desperately trying to devise a plan for him and Alex to escape from the situation. He trusted that they were not in any sort of physical danger, but the prospect of being tucked away in some anonymous NSA safe house in a foreign country *indefinitely* for knowing too much was in some ways even worse.

Alex and Professor Russell were squished in the middle of the back seat with a well armed Navy SEAL on either side protecting the exit doors. That fact still didn't stop Brian from fantasizing about opening the side door and making a run for it every time the Humvee rolled to a stop. That plan was a no go though because every time the vehicle slowed, those soldiers visibly braced for action just in case the fifty year old professor and his undersized female research assistant decided to get feisty.

If hateful stares and ill meaning fantasies could actually harm a person, then Frank, sitting in the front seat alongside the driver, would have been a bloody mess. As the Humvee rolled away from the stoplight and picked up speed down the four lane road, Professor Russell glared at the back of Frank's head wishing it to explode for all the anger he bore the man.

His concentration was interrupted by Frank pointing out a slow moving truck ahead. "Don't slow down, just go around it."

The driver checked his side mirror and began the lane change but suddenly jerked the wheel back over and hit the brakes to avoid ramming the truck now only ten feet ahead and moving even slower. "Sorry sir, there was another truck alongside in the other lane."

The semi truck hauling a long cargo container continued to roll past as the truck ahead came to a full stop. Before Frank could unleash more than a couple of obscenities at the other driver, a powerful crash from behind smashed the Humvee into the back of the truck in front, pinning the vehicle.

An instant later the Humvee's hood erupted with a barrage of bullets targeting the engine block. Geysers of steam and black oil let them all know the Humvee would not be going anywhere anytime soon.

"Oh Jesus, those are fifty caliber rounds," the driver declared with his last words. A high powered round blasted through the side window striking the soldier in the head. The five inch long, half inch diameter bullet penetrated the armored glass and the man's helmet like they were made of paper to spread his blood and gore across the entire interior of the front seat. Frank also appeared to be hit; the NSA agent was drenched in blood and slumped forward, unmoving over the dashboard.

The two soldiers on either side of Brian and Alex decided to take their chances out in the open rather than let a skilled sniper play turkey shoot with them in the cramped confines of the vehicle. The two side doors flung open and the well armed soldiers jumped out to find any cover available. Brian and Alex, for their part, crawled off the seat onto the floorboards, went fetal, and started praying to survive the ordeal.

Outside the Humvee the world came alive with a terrifying gun battle that was nothing like the movies or video games. The SEALs unloaded their submachine guns into the truck that rammed them from behind. Shots from all directions came in at the soldiers as they moved around the rear of the Humvee. Between the two soldiers returning fire, Brian could hear them calling out targets to each other.

"Two on the right at three o'clock," pop, pop, pop. "Four on the left at ten and seven," pop, pop, pop. "Reloading!"

Then came a thunderous boom from the far right announcing another fifty caliber round had left the barrel of the sniper rifle. A heart wrenching squeal near the rear of the vehicle let Brian know the round connected with deadly effect.

Another minute passed filled with frantic breathing and the crackle of gravel just outside the opened door as the lone Navy SEAL scrambled for cover. Then a maelstrom of light machine gunfire culminated in a wet thump which reminded Brian of a watermelon being smashed by a sledge hammer. It evoked a muffled scream from the soldier still seeking cover just outside the open door.

Labored breathing was accompanied by the SEAL emptying yet another clip from his weapon, but two more wet thumps rendered everything outside completely silent. Neither Brian nor Alex dared look or even try to move. They simply huddled on the floor and waited for the inevitable to hit them and end the terrifying ordeal.

A silent minute passed before the cautious crunch of footsteps approached from all around the vehicle; dozens of them. Brian heard the front doors open so the bodies of the driver and Frank could be inspected. Then a set of hands belonging to a man in urban combat fatigues and wearing a black ski mask over his head grabbed hold of Alex and dragged her from the vehicle kicking and screaming.

"No, no!" she hollered before an injection needle penetrated the side of her neck bringing the struggle to an anticlimactic end.

A moment later a set of powerful hands pulled Brian from the Humvee. On his way out he looked to the front seat and found Frank still motionless and slumped over the dashboard.

Professor Russell did not bother trying to struggle. He felt the bite of a needle in his neck followed by the sensation of liquid fire injected into his veins. That fire quickly consumed all his extremities with a numb sensation that sent his mind into a tailspin which ended in complete darkness.
****

Frank slowly felt consciousness return to him. He did not dare attempt to test his motor skills just yet as the movement might still draw the deadly accurate sniper fire. He kept his eyes closed and allowed his sense of hearing to take over.

A motor was running in a vehicle parked alongside the Humvee which meant the sniper's view from that direction was temporarily obscured. This gave Frank an opportunity to open his eyes ever so slightly and steal a glance to the side. He saw a black paneled van with the back doors open. He silently watched the unconscious bodies of Alex and Professor Russell get loaded into the van and ten armed men of small stature climb in after them and shut the doors.

With all that going on outside, Frank felt confident a minor movement from his right hand would not be noticed. He reached toward his back pocket to retrieve his cell phone, but was disheartened to find his hand touching nothing but ass.

His phone had been taken, probably for intelligence gathering purposes. It was of little consequence since it could easily be disabled and wiped remotely. For the moment, Frank was just counting his blessings that he was still alive. The blood all over him was convincing, but the tablet he swallowed to temporarily stop his heart and breathing to mimic death must have sold the ruse considering the abductors did not finish him off with a round to the head.

Frank moved his probing hand away from the back pocket and toward his belt buckle. He was relieved to find his oversized 'Don't mess with Texas' buckle was still on him. He gently unfastened the buckle, pressed his thumb against the loop hook and snapped it off.

Frank then relaxed his hand once more and pictured in his mind the signal reaching an NSA hub and prompting satellite links to be pulled up and recorded.

Meanwhile, the van idling alongside sped off and Frank shut his eyes once more to play dead for the benefit of the sniper who might still be looking at him through a scope. Frank continued his impersonation of a corpse until the local authorities arrived along with the NSA recovery team posing as paramedics to bring Frank out of the situation unharmed.

Chapter 15: Time to Get Medieval

"WHY DO I see regret in your eyes when talking about the successful spread of Christianity across Europe?" Dr. Holmes asked of his patient. Hastelloy was always confident and composed, so this moment of vulnerability was completely out of character. Jeffrey knew this was likely his only chance to reach the heart of Hastelloy's issues before his brother arrived to hopelessly complicate matters, so he chose to press on the sore spot.

Silence lingered between the office walls for several seconds before Hastelloy reluctantly admitted, "Tomal was right to protest my plans. He was more in tune with the basic impulses of mankind than the rest of us, and I should have listened to him."

Hastelloy leaned forward to bring his elbows to rest upon his thighs with his clasped hands tucked beneath his chin. His whole body began vibrating with anger directed inward until he sprung forward with his hands and planted an index finger down on the coffee table between them. Dr. Holmes instinctively flinched backward, but realized the gesture was made to accentuate a point rather than pose a danger.

The patient's watering eyes pleaded with him to understand, "You see, it wasn't me trying to hold him down. That's not why I dismissed Tomal's notion. He was a brilliant man with worthwhile ideas, but ever since the incident with Cleopatra he saw Alpha conspiracies everywhere. This time seemed no different except it was not only Goron, but human nature that worked against me."

"How so?" Jeffrey probed.

"Tomal understood first hand that power corrupts, and absolute power corrupts absolutely," Hastelloy answered. "I created an entity with limitless power. The church knew no borders, and its leaders were obeyed by the poor, the rich, and even the nobility and royalty without question because in their minds the church held the keys to their eternal salvation."

"That absolute power was placed in the hands of one man, the Pope," Dr. Holmes added, "And that power corrupted?"

"Not just Popes. Cardinals, Archbishops, Bishops, Priests and Friars," Hastelloy recited down the church hierarchy. "In hindsight, the fact that any clergy during the Middle Ages managed to do good, let alone most of them, given how much power they held is truly a tribute to the good nature of mankind. Still, enough let the power corrupt them, even without Goron serving as the proverbial devil sitting on their shoulders to whisper evil deeds in their ears. I have little proof, but I must speculate that Goron certainly had a hand in a lot of the misdeeds of that era."

"I'd think meddling with the church elite would make Goron's relic rather easy to locate," Jeffrey pondered. "Wouldn't he just go straight to the top, corrupt the Pope and let it ripple down from there? Couldn't you just raid the Vatican like you did the Temple of Vesta back in Rome?"

Hastelloy managed to piece his composure back together and sat back in his chair again to answer. "Goron was far too clever to do something that predictable. A formless entity does not avoid my crew's tireless searching for fifteen hundred years by hiding in obvious places with the most likely people."

"Occasionally it was the Pope, other times it was a lowly priest or even a peasant girl in France who prompted a revolution," Hastelloy instructed. "Usually he liked to hover somewhere in between. Goron operated wherever he found the optimal mixture of influence, protection, and corruptible personalities."

"Joan of Arc?" Dr. Holmes asked for confirmation of the French peasant girl's identity. Hastelloy obliged with a slight nod which drew a laugh. "Guess I should have seen that one coming. So that's it? The degradation of mankind into the doldrums of medieval times was all because of the Church, which you promoted as a solution to the anarchy you saw coming with the fall of Rome?"

"If bringing down Rome and corrupting church leaders would have been Goron's only disruption, then things would have worked out fine. Unfortunately, his ruthless nature had far more damaging activities in mind that plunged mankind into a dark age it was powerless to resist despite our best efforts."

"I'm all ears," Jeffrey said while turning his notepad back to the current page.

****

Goron felt the unmistakably pompous presence of Archbishop Leonhard von Keutschach approaching. The man was obsessed to the point of madness with expanding his wealth, power and influence. It was an amusing contradiction for Goron to observe a religious figure, supposedly charged with the divine care of others, greedily scooping up everything within reach. All the while his esteemed title provided the freedom to condemn those who got in his way to die in the name of organized religion.

The man's thoroughly selfish nature was revolting, but also extremely useful to Goron. Like a carrot hanging from a string prompting a mule forward, Goron dangled the prospect of riches and power in front of the Archbishop to easily move him to serve Goron's interests.

Archbishop Leonhard shuffled into the hidden chapel Goron ordered built to house his relic. The modest sized chamber was constructed in the heart of a fortress and had only one well disguised point of entry. What the meager chapel lacked in size it made up for in opulence. A hand carved oak door, marble tiled floor and a richly ornamented star vaulted ceiling gave the chamber the proper feel to house Goron's divine presence.

"How kind of you to visit the guiding light behind your prosperity Herr Keutschach," Goron declared in the native German. He felt right at home speaking the local tongue considering he had a heavy hand in crafting the language and its harsh separation of words and phrasing to mimic that of his beloved Alpha language.

The Archbishop visibly cringed upon not hearing the title he so coveted precede his name. One of the few sources of amusement for Goron these days was tormenting the simple man in such ways and this occasion was no exception.

"Tending to your flock in your physical absence my Lord is most time consuming," Leonhard offered while descending to his knees before Goron's stone alter.

Who does this man think he's fooling? Goron thought, but let it slide. "I have determined the fortifications of this castle are still inadequate."

Archbishop Leonhard looked up in confusion. "This fortress is perched on a perilously steep hillside my Lord. What's more, I just finished constructing an outer ring of walls and towers. I respectfully submit the devil himself could not penetrate these walls, let alone mere mortals."

"You will construct another ring of walls and run a rail line down the cliff face to the Nonnberg Abbey below," Goron went on as though the

Archbishop had not spoken at all. "This will provide a means to easily resupply the fortress and an escape route during times of siege."

"More walls?" Leonhard asked in disbelief. "As it is, this proposed rail line will have to pass through four sets of stone walls to reach the abbey. You propose I add a fifth?"

"I propose nothing, I demand it," Goron corrected and allowed his flame to flood the room in a deep crimson hue. "To maintain the power and influence you wield you must, above all else, retain control over the salt mines of Salzburg immediately down the hillside from this fortress."

"But the expense," the Archbishop protested from his knees.

"It is a necessity that is more than covered by the annual income of the salt mines these improvements are meant to safeguard."

In an uncharacteristic display of actually having a backbone, the Archbishop protested further. "Why do we need such protection from your dedicated followers?"

"Because I gave mankind the gift of free will which leaves them susceptible to the devils that I told you about. The ones who cannot die," Goron said as a reminder.

Leonhard offered one last protest, "In my entire lifetime I have never felt their evil draw near."

"When did I instruct Noah to build his ark?" Goron rhetorically asked. "Before the flood, not after; now do as you are told."

Without another word, the Archbishop rose to his feet, bowed at the waist and left the chapel. A deep thud from the heavy oak door shutting let Goron know he had his privacy once more and the oppressive loneliness of his solitude returned. Manipulating the local inhabitants to do his bidding provided some measure of amusement, but the simpletons made it entirely too easy to be even remotely satisfying.

Elohim's relic, despite his many faults, had at least provided a shared consciousness that allowed Goron to practice fortifying his mental defenses, and hone his ability to pierce the barriers of others. Now as the two planets drew closer once more, Goron could only hope his mental defenses and weapons were still sharp enough to dominate the Mars collective.

Goron further lamented the loss of Elohim because his former engineer was a passable sounding board to run plans past for a second opinion. His input was usually worthless, but there were enough occasions of genius for him to be useful. That all ended a thousand years ago when his adversary's masterful strategic vision managed to penetrate Elohim's robust defenses and extinguish his existence.

Shortly thereafter, the pesky little Novi captain nearly got his hands on Goron's relic. A lot of advanced planning and even a little luck were all that saved him. Goron had no intentions of pressing his luck any farther. The fortress overlooking Salzburg would be made impenetrable, no matter the cost.

A flicker of chaos graced the edges of Goron's mind. A hundred thousand minds, each with thoughts and ambitions of their own, shined in like a horseman carrying a lantern approaching at night from a forest. The illumination was there one moment, then shrouded once more by the ever shifting leaf covered branches. The intermittent contact gave Goron ample time to practice his mental discipline. That way when the collective consciousness was fully present without interruption, Goron was in complete command of the situation.

The first moments of sustained contact were always the most taxing. Each life force was busy probing for signs of weakness in the newcomer. An outsider who's leadership only showed up for a few weeks every seven hundred days.

Making the task even more difficult was Kuanti. The frustrating twerp of unremarkable ability or intellect had somehow managed to set himself up as the revered Founding Leader of the Mars colony. Every life force in the collective naturally gravitated toward him for leadership and wresting that control away grew more and more difficult with every passing year.

Goron immediately went on the offensive once continuous contact was established. "Report."

That single word was all Goron needed. Kuanti's naked annoyance at the not so subtle leadership challenge opened the barriers of the simpleton's mind for Goron to get what he needed. Goron instantly knew the situation, the successes, and more importantly the failures on which to scrutinize. The fool was so busy fretting over his leadership vulnerability that his open mind provided the very ammunition Goron needed to undermine that leadership; quite a useful paradox.

"Our last twelve solid fuel rocket launches have all been successful. We have perfected a habitable environment that can be maintained in outer space. What's more, our launch vehicles are powerful enough now to leave orbit to reach the third planet," Kuanti confidently reported.

Goron already knew it was not all roses over there and was not about to let Kuanti only detail the successes. "What about the fusion reactor? All this progress toward solid fuel rocketry is nice for a backup plan, but the flight time of several years between planets is unacceptable. That is too much to ask even the most disciplined of our Alpha warriors to endure."

"Computer models gave us a proof of concept on our design. Construction will commence once enough building materials have been refined."

"Well, that's something I suppose," Goron stated with underwhelming conviction to avoid giving the compliment any undue weight. "That leaves me fending for myself for at least another century. All the while our Novi friends make impressive inroads at repairing the disruptions that I've caused. The unifying force behind humanity's technological and cultural advancement is slowly getting pieced back together."

"It is a race against time," Goron went on. "If they advance these natives enough to construct a transmission device to reach Novus they win. If we get your physical forces from Mars to Earth and destroy the jamming signal that disrupts your communicator, we win. It's that simple."

"The advantage is ours," Kuanti jumped in. "The Novi don't know about our colony, and they are bound by the noninterference mandate of their directive. Our victory is inevitable, no matter how competent the Novi captain may be."

"You have fewer than fifty thousand Alpha in the colony working on technology to reach Earth."

"And the Novi only have five active crewmembers there," Kuanti interrupted. "By weight of numbers we will win the technology race."

Goron's mood brightened with the naiveté of Kuanti's statement. "Do you have any idea how many beings inhabit this planet? Nearly a billion, so if the Novi ever succeed in uniting these creatures in a common goal again, our advantaged position evaporates in the blink of an eye."

"That is on you, Goron. We are all forty million miles away on another planet at the moment; it is on you to disrupt their efforts."

"What do you think I've been doing the last three thousand years? No matter how many humans I can manipulate through their blind obedience to faith or riches, it's not enough. More drastic measures are now required."

"What do you have in mind," Kuanti asked.

"Tell me, did you have the forethought to preserve the biological specimens housed in the weapons hold?" Goron knew the affirmative answer already and felt a strong flicker of recognition from the collective as he continued. "Of even more importance, can you manage the math to deliver one of those solid fuel rockets of yours to Earth?"

"Before being banned, the weapon rendered entire planets lifeless," Kuanti cautioned. "You sure you want to sniff down that path?"

Goron let his sinister side shine through the collective in all its glory. "These humans are stronger than most. Enough will survive to still be useful to us in the future. Yet enough will die to stop the Novi from accomplishing much of anything before you finally get your tails over here."

Chapter 16: Black Mark

POE LOOKED AHEAD and saw his cart was falling behind the rest of the caravan. To correct the matter, he gave his horses a quick crack of the whip which sped the team of nags along. Traveling west and east between the Mediterranean and Far East was dangerous enough. He didn't need to add the peril of making the journey alone rather than among the safety of numbers a caravan provided from bandits.

The pair of horses had served Poe well for the last two years, but nonstop travel to the Mediterranean and back was starting to show in their pace. He resolved at that moment to fetch what price he could for them once he reached Dunhuang and buy a new pair using some of the proceeds from selling his cargo.

He looked ahead of the lead wagon and spotted the familiar square gate house of the Yumen Pass. With the great wall extending hundreds of miles in either direction, this was the place all travelers heading east or west met. Over the years it had become known as the Jade Gate. Not because the doors were made of the highly valued material, but because so much of it passed through the gate for trade. It served as the ideal choke point for the Chinese Emperor to extract taxes from the immensely rich trade route.

The taxes were high, but not quite oppressive. Even with the fees, Poe figured another three or four years spent on the Silk Road and he could retire. He wouldn't quite live like a prince, but at this point anything beat sleeping on the ground, eating mystery stew and feeling the gritty dirt and dung kicked up by horses pulling the wagons between his teeth. Ah yes, retirement would be grand.

Out of nowhere an explosion high overhead shook the very ground and sent an ear piercing shockwave through the air. Poe covered his ears and careened his neck to the side for a look. He nearly wet himself at the sight of a broad streak of fire scorching the sky overhead. The devilish trail traveled from west to east at blinding speed. In a matter of seconds the flaming center passed overhead and nearly out of view over the eastern horizon.

Before any of the travelers could even think, let alone ask 'what in blazes was that,' a blinding white light lit up the western skyline like a second sun. When the light finally dimmed and Poe's vision returned, he saw a towering pillar of smoke rising towards the heavens with a top like a mushroom fanning out on high.

Moments later a terrorizing roar and hot wind laced with green smoke rushed over the landscape and past the travelers. It was as if the gates of hell opened up to release its most fearsome demon upon the earth. Poe felt his wagon teeter up on two wheels as the fierce winds billowed past. He dove onto the tarp covering the back and flung his entire body over the side to provide as much counterweight as possible to keep the wagon from tipping.

After a few harrowing minutes the hot winds died down, and stillness settled over the landscape once more. When the tipping wagon finally settled back onto four wheels, Poe let go and had a look around. Only a handful of carts out of hundreds remained upright. Those that were toppled had their valuable contents spilled across the open grasslands. The lucky ones could simply set their carts upright, reload and continue. Most toppled carts would need repairs to broken wheels and axles. The truly unlucky ones were traders who carried fine powdery spices instead of heavy jade. These now impoverished traders had their cargo spread to the four winds never to be seen or tasted again.

Poe's heart went out to the poor bastards, but he had his own interests to look after. Soon as word got out that a trade caravan was stranded, the bandits would be drawn to the location like flies to dung. He pacified his inner guilt by helping set an undamaged wagon upright, but then was on his way with the two dozen wagons still capable of travel. The city of Dunhuang was only eighty miles away. Poe had no intention of remaining in the open once the flies began buzzing around.

Twenty hours later, just after sunup, Poe and his miniature caravan reached the gates of Dunhuang. The pressed pace of the journey was hard on his aging horses, but also on him; ever since the hot winds Poe had felt a sore throat and stiffness in his joints. To make matters worse, hard black sacs that were painful to the touch had developed under his armpits.

As Poe led his wagon through the torch lit streets he heard all the townspeople talking about the pillar of smoke that occurred earlier. Explanations ranged from a piece of the sky falling to some sort of super weapon of a foreign power to god smiting the Earth with his wrath. As the morning sun rose higher into the sky, Poe began hearing screams of lamentations coming from various houses. As the stories went, people who went to sleep feeling sick the night before simply never woke up.

By the time Poe reached the commerce district he was feeling positively horrible. Amid bouts of cold sweats, he hastily sold his goods for the first price offered and made a straight path to the nearest apothecary to hopefully tend to his illness. Poe's heart sank when he saw dozens of dead bodies with bulging black sacs under their armpits and on their inner thighs lining the streets. At that moment Poe realized his imminent retirement was close at hand rather than several years off.

Chapter 17: Underestimating the Enemy

HASTELLOY SAT ACROSS the table from his opponent under a shaded tree outside his Egyptian home. He watched the youngster's eyes dart across the chess board taking in all the possibilities. He had the boy's rook in jeopardy and the youth was so eager to launch his attack that he failed to protect the valuable piece. Hastelloy captured the rook with his knight, but then his eight year old adversary did something entirely unexpected.

The youngster plowed his queen into a wall of pawns protecting Hastelloy's king. His only recourse was to capture with the king leaving it exposed. The boy moved his bishop into checking position which drew the king further into the open. Next the youngster moved his remaining rook over to deliver yet another check to bring Hastelloy's king even closer to peril. With one final stroke of brilliance, the eight year old moved his knight back to deliver checkmate.

The game was over. For the first time in memory Hastelloy's king was cornered with nowhere to go. He stared in silence with elbows resting on the table and hands clasped under his chin. His opponent had the strategic vision to sacrifice his rook and queen, the two strongest pieces on the board, to launch a brilliant attack which snapped Hastelloy's winning streak of well over a million games.

How could a youth who only learned the game a few years prior have beaten him? Hastelloy sighed softly realizing that his question also delivered an answer. He underestimated his opponent, relaxed his guard ever so slightly and was finally bested by a weaker opponent.

Hastelloy looked out from his introspection to see his young adversary's face radiant with pride. Everyone in the village knew full well Hastelloy did not relax his level of play for anyone. Young or old, wise or dim, the opponent was shown no quarter; how else could they learn to play properly?

To his credit, the boy refrained from boasting with a triumphant shout or victory dance. Instead, the youth extended an open hand across the table. Hastelloy met the offered appendage with a stiff handshake. "Well played, Ashwin. Very, very well played."

"Thank you, Master Hastelloy."

His competitive nature was about to insist upon a grudge match, but the village chieftain's approach altered Hastelloy's intent. "Run along now, it appears a rematch will have to wait for another day."

Ashwin vacated the chair and bounded off to tell all his friends the incredible news leaving the chair open for the chieftain to sit down. "Did I just see what I thought I saw? The ruthless, unbeatable master *finally* lost a chess match. Now be honest, did you throw the game to bolster the confidence of your brightest student?"

Hastelloy glared at the bearded man letting him know the idea of throwing a match was more insulting to him than the defeat itself. He allowed the look to soften before asking, "How does the harvest look this year?"

The chieftain drew a deep breath to puff his chest up with pride. "Plentiful, but that is not why I am here. A messenger just arrived with a letter he insisted was most urgent."

Hastelloy took the folded piece of paper sealed with the wax imprint of Tonwen. "Thank you. Make sure the carts are covered and ready. We leave for market in the morning," Hastelloy ordered and then dismissed the village chieftain with a sideways shrug of his head.

Alone once more, Hastelloy looked down at the chessboard. Had all the years spent in the tiny farming village protecting the Nexus really dulled his abilities to the point he could lose to a child? He quickly pushed the thought aside as he opened the letter.

Entire villages all across the Mediterranean coastline are dying from some sort of plague. It has all the markings of the Alpha Yersinia Pestis bioweapon. I am headed to Florence to join Valnor. Please send word to the others and come as quickly as possible.
-Tonwen

Hastelloy sprang to his feet and ran after the departing chieftain. Sprinting past the bearded man on his way to a horse Hastelloy hollered back, "I'm needed in Italy. I leave the village in your capable hands."

Chapter 18: Resolution

HASTELLOY RODE ALONE on horseback through the streets of Florence, Italy. He would have preferred a quicker gate, but it seemed his mount stumbled every other stride upon the paved street that was in desperate need for repair.

What a difference a few hundred years made, he thought as his horse nearly lost its footing once more. The stones, once perfectly fitted with Roman precision, now jutted and cratered at random intervals making the urban street nearly impassable.

A crumbling infrastructure wasn't the only change. The last time he was in Florence, even with chaos brewing just to the south in the city of Rome, it bustled with life and energy. Now the streets were completely empty, the grand theater and public gardens overgrown and crumbling from neglect. The partially finished skeleton of the Basilica di Santa Maria stood as if a monument to the city's fallen stature.

The ambitious cathedral had been under construction for a hundred years now. Hastelloy was no architectural expert, but by the look of things it would be at least a few hundred years more before completion.

Hastelloy both admired and pitied the multigenerational project. The dedication was commendable, but the designer intended to cap the massive structure with a dome twice the size of any other in existence. The engineering knowledge to accomplish such a feat existed a thousand years ago in Rome as evidenced by the Pantheon and its grand dome, but no longer. Hastelloy feared the cathedral would long stand as a monument to his failure to protect mankind from Goron's meddling.

Rather than risk rendering his horse lame by traveling down the city's decrepit center, Hastelloy chose a side street paved in dirt. Twenty yards ahead he observed a peasant struggling to haul a two-wheeled cart behind him. A rancid aroma wedged somewhere between spoiled meat and sour milk caused Hastelloy to cough and gag. The cargo hold of the wagon was covered with a tarp, but he did not need to see the contents to know what the man carried.

Hastelloy brought his horse to a full stop and watched the peasant set his cart down in front of a house sporting a red stripe across the front door.

He unfurled the cargo hold and then delivered two stiff knocks at the door. It opened, the man went in, and a few moments later he emerged carrying a dead woman with pitch black lesions on her neck, armpits and thighs. He placed the deceased in the wagon, pulled the cover back over the six bodies he carried and moved on to the next marked doorway.

The putrid smell of death only worsened as Hastelloy made his way deeper toward the city center. Hastelloy only saw light from windows or smoke escaping from chimneys in one out of every five houses. By that evidence, he estimated the plague had already claimed a majority of the city's inhabitants. The lucky few blessed with superior immune systems were left to manage a ghost town littered with diseased corpses. The once proud metropolis was unable to function with such losses, and the rest of Europe found itself in a similar way.

Hastelloy finally made his way across the river and came to a crumbling two story structure. The front door was ajar and clung to the doorframe by a single hinge. He did not even bother knocking. He simply nudged the teetering door aside and allowed its thunderous crash to the floor to announce his arrival.

The four men seated around a rectangular table in the center of the room looked up from their bowls of stew long enough to acknowledge the newcomer was indeed their captain.

Valnor opened his arms slightly and gestured around the room. "Welcome to my humble abode," as the broken glass, rotted floor boards and splintered furniture strewn about made quite an impression. So did a curious doll made from a potato sack with sewn buttons for eyes and a painted smile resting on the mantle above the fireplace.

"I love what you've done with the place," Hastelloy commented while kicking debris aside on his way to the table.

"I'd have tidied up a bit for the arrival of such a wise and visionary guest, but I've been too busy caring for the sick and burying the dead. All this was caused by the Alpha relic who, despite lacking a body, continues to allude your brilliant schemes to find him," Valnor responded with nearly tangible anger behind his words.

Hastelloy took the hint and adjusted his tone accordingly. "What happened here?"

"Everything was just fine up until about three months ago," Valnor began. "The cathedral construction was coming along nicely. Commerce was good, the harvests were plentiful. Then one day it all just changed."

Valnor solemnly stared into his stew as he went on. "It started along the docks. A shipment of exotic spices and fabrics arrived from the coast. Some of the flat boat crewmen were already complaining of stiff joints and generally feeling ill. A few days later it seemed anyone who went to the market district developed black lumps all over and dropped dead inside of a week.

"Panic ensued and people fled the city like it was an erupting volcano. The plague followed them though. It hounded everyone no matter where they went to hide. The countryside, other towns, it didn't matter. The pestilence found them and killed them all."

Hastelloy realized Valnor was far too close to the situation to give an unbiased report so he turned to his science officer. "Tonwen, have you had a chance to examine the bodies? Is it really the Alpha Yersinia Pestis bioweapon?"

"Without question it is the Alpha weapon," came Tonwen's sterile response. "It is fortunate these humans have exceptionally strong immune systems to fight off this plague."

At that moment Valnor looked ready to hurl his empty bowl at Tonwen's head. "Nine out of ten people have dropped dead! How is that good fortune?"

"All three instances of the Alpha using the bioweapon before being banned resulted in complete annihilation," Tonwen countered.

"Casualty rates are even lower elsewhere," Tomal added. "I came from the Germanic territories up north and there it is more like one in five has died. It did get worse the closer I came to the Mediterranean Sea, however."

"Regardless," Valnor fired back, "this is a calamity, and it's still going on. All our work over the centuries has been undone in a matter of months. So many have been lost these humans may never recover as a society. This would never have happened if you would have let me put the Roman Empire back together. We could have distributed a vaccine before it ever got this bad."

Hastelloy put his hand up to halt Valnor's diatribe. "Tonwen. We have all been vaccinated against this virus. Can you use our blood to create a vaccine with the tools available?"

"I already have," Tonwen immediately answered. "Creating the vaccine is not the problem. It is producing and distributing the cure on a massive scale that is difficult."

"And expensive," Gallono added.

"A strong central government is the only way to do it," Valnor jumped in, eager to push his secular agenda. "We start with one city state. Let it be known we have a cure for the plague and offer to share it with those who unite under our banner. Once the pandemic has passed the central government will be in position to support the arts and science, and we can get things moving in the right direction again."

The room remained quieter than the abandoned city streets outside for several minutes. Valnor's mind was in an entirely wrong place. The kind of empire building he advocated was not the Novi way. In fact, it had all the ruthless markings of how the Alpha went about doing things.

Hastelloy slowly unclasped his hands and set them flat on the table before speaking. "Even if I didn't find the thought of extorting people's allegiance in exchange for a cure completely repugnant, there is not enough time for it. In just a few short months this city was nearly wiped out, and this is going on all across Europe as we speak."

Valnor erupted to his feet. "What would you know about it? You've been insulated from it all living in Egypt. I've been stuck here living this nightmare day in and day out. This place, this whole continent is a hollow shell now thanks to you insisting we sit on the sidelines while Goron unleashed his poison across the landscape."

"You're out of line, Ensign," Gallono shouted in defense of his captain. "There is no way any of us could have known Goron would resort to this."

"It's called being prepared," Valnor countered directing his ire toward Hastelloy once more. "You used to be prepared for everything no matter how unlikely. If you can't manage that any longer, then it's up to me."

"Valnor," Hastelloy said on the way to his feet. He reached for his subordinate's arm, but was too slow. Valnor scooped the doll off the mantle on his way out the door without another word spoken.

"Well at least I'm not the problem child this time around," Tomal said quietly to lighten the mood, but he only received stern looks from the rest of the table. He dropped the self-righteous grin and asked, "Between the four of us then, what's the plan?"

Hastelloy resisted the urge to chase after Valnor. There was something more to his rage than just seeing the civilization he guided into a golden age regress. The anger was personal, but Hastelloy did not have the time to deal with it at the moment. He reluctantly turned his attention back to the table and shook off the uneasy feeling of self-doubt creeping its way into his mindset. Valnor was right; he should have seen this coming from Goron and been prepared. Had he underestimated his enemy? He set his self-doubt aside to give his orders to the remaining crewmen.

"We will use the infrastructure already in place with the Catholic Church to distribute a cure. By definition public care and outreach is part of their mission, and they already have unparalleled reach and influence throughout Europe," Hastelloy ordered.

"Not to beat a dead horse here, but aren't you concerned Goron has his tendrils into the Catholic Church already?" Tomal asked.

"What proof do you have of that?" Hastelloy insisted.

"History is my proof," Tomal responded. "Pope Gregory the IX establishing the inquisitions to root out and punish heretics. Can you seriously tell me with a straight face that was not Goron using the church to carry out a hit list?"

"Look at the Crusades," Tomal went on. "Popes used religious coercion to send entire generations of Europe's smartest and bravest to die of battle wounds and disease in a worthless desert in a far off land."

Hastelloy felt the discussion spiraling out of hand so he put a stop to it. "Tomal, ever since you broke away from Goron's manipulation you see an Alpha conspiracy behind everything."

"Better to be paranoid than surprised," Tomal countered.

"Priority one is stopping the plague," Hastelloy insisted. "Since millions of people are dying every week we need an immediate solution which means the Catholic Church. Tonwen, you will work to promote the church's social and financial reach to speed along distribution of the cure. Tomal, you will help him."

Before Tomal could voice further protest Hastelloy added, "While you are at it, try and find more solid proof of Goron holding influence over the church. You may very well be right and we are helping to make that Alpha relic even stronger, but it is what's required at the moment."

Hastelloy relaxed his stare affixed on Tomal to address the entire table. "Even when we manage to stop this plague, dark times are coming. We need to lay the foundation for a resurgence in technology and culture when the timing is right. While you two prod the church into helping with that effort, Gallono and I will remain here to keep commerce flowing throughout the region."

Hastelloy looked around the table and saw each of the crewmen lost in their own thoughts contemplating the scope and magnitude of their assignments. "This is why we get paid the big bags of coin, gentlemen, now let's get to it."

Chapter 19: Assistance Is Necessary

KUANTI KNEW IT was coming, but that did nothing to prepare him for the sensation. Feeling the collective consciousness of several hundred thousand relics fade in and out of contact was like trying to watch a display monitor with a short in the power feed. After a few minutes of intermittent contact, they were just gone.

"We are only in contact with Goron now," Kuanti reported to the pilot who dutifully nodded his head in acknowledgement.

Behind the pilot and navigator sat ten Alpha warriors with shoulders overlapping as they squeezed into five rows of seats that ran two across. Amplifying the claustrophobic ambiance was the ceiling resting mere inches above their heads. Completing the cramped accommodations was a narrow shelf along the back bulkhead that housed the flowing liquid metal relics of Kuanti and Cora. There were not many times Kuanti preferred existing as a relic rather than in a physical body, but this was definitely one of them.

Most of the occupants were asleep trying to pass the three day journey from Mars to Earth with their eyes shut. The rest did not budge due to the complete lack of space in the tiny craft.

Everyone would have preferred more room to stretch their legs during the journey, but the required metals were extremely difficult to mine and fabricate into durable alloys. The ship's limited size was out of necessity rather than the designer's masochistic intent to inflict torture upon the occupants. Lesser men would have lost their minds even before leaving Mars orbit; these Alpha were strong. They would perform quite well at their tasks on the third planet.

"We should enter Earth orbit in about two hours," the navigator reported. "I need coordinates of the landing site from Captain Goron."

"Give me a moment," Kuanti replied and then turned all his thoughts and concentration to the now vastly diminished collective: just him, Cora and Goron. "We are on final approach and need to know your exact location."

A curt mental reply came firing back, "I am on the western end of the largest continent in the northern hemisphere, but that is irrelevant for you. I need you to land on the eastern end of this landmass."

"Why? Shouldn't we come together and fight the Novi as one rather than divided? The plan is we land and help you locate the jamming signal while the second transport ship is completed. Then, if needed, it will bring the remaining fifty thousand Alpha warriors from our colony so we can take over this planet and defeat the Novi."

Goron's mind let loose a chuckle that a parent reserves for when their young toddler asks a blatantly obvious question. "These humans are extremely capable beings, Kuanti. Fifty thousand of us, even with advanced weapons, would have a very hard time subjugating a billion of them. I have seen them accomplish remarkable feats when they rally behind a common cause. There is no need to provoke them."

"What do you suggest then?"

"Use them, don't fight them," Goron responded. "Humans in the west are quite pious, and I have significant influence over their religion. They will do as I command when the time comes. People in the east are another matter. They respond to strength."

"If my informants are correct, the mountainous region in the far east is home to the Mongol tribe. A great warrior named Genghis Khan united the tribes and conquered much of the west. Now his grandson has his ambitions pointed east, but he lacks the strength to accomplish the conquest. I think you should get to know this man and fuel his ambitions and capabilities."

"You expect us to find one man," Kuanti responded with disappointment. "You want us to hide in the shadows and help this one primitive conquer a territory rather than seek out the Novi directly and destroy them once and for all?"

"Precisely, and take care not to draw attention to yourselves. A pack of seven foot hound warriors is bound to draw rumors and stories that the Novi will get wind of eventually. We need that time to be as delayed as possible so that when that all too clever Novi captain realizes what is going on it will be too late. We will have him surrounded and outnumbered a million to one with our loyal followers. No one, not even his keen mind, can withstand those odds."

"Excellent plan, sir."

"So glad you approve," Goron sighed to let his subordinate know his approval was the last thing on his mind.

"Who is this person we'll so benevolently assist?"

"Kublai Khan," Goron answered. "From what I hear you will have no difficulty locating him in that mountainous region."

Kuanti liked this plan very much, and he didn't mind allowing his admiration to be detected by Goron. "Navigator, I have our landing coordinates."

The closer the ship came to the planet and the eastern edge of its largest landmass, one specific spot was lighting up their sensors like a landing beacon. Closer examination revealed a perfectly shaped pyramid rising over a hundred meters with all four sides of the base over a quarter mile in length.

The sloped sides absorbed the pulses of energy from the ship's navigation equipment and channeled them to the tip which radiated back to the Alpha ship like a blinding beam originating from a lighthouse guiding vessels lost at sea into port. This was as good a place as any to set down Kuanti concluded. Plus, the potential uses in the future for this structure could not be ignored.

Chapter 20: Catastrophe Avoided

KUBLAI KHAN THREW the entrance flap to his command tent aside and stormed in to deal with his generals. What a catastrophe!

He removed his helmet and chain mail headdress and threw them into the corner. "Three months we have been at this. Three months of frontal assaults, sneak attacks by night and bribing local farmers for a way in has yielded nothing. Nothing!"

"Mighty Khan, it is the terrain that defeats us, not our adversary," a particularly fat general offered. "The mountains to the west and the impassable river to the east make conquest of this valley nearly impossible."

"Get out," Kublai Khan ordered with an angry swat of his arm across the air. "I do not accept impossibilities when it comes to my empire. There is a way, and I shall pray for inspiration. I suggest you all do the same or else incompetent heads will begin to roll."

The six distinguished generals left the tent in complete silence knowing their Khan's words were not idle threats; they were statements of fact. The man had ambitions, and if his current subordinates were unable to fulfill those ambitions then they would be replaced by those who could.

Now alone in the spacious tent that served as his home away from home, Kublai paced toward the bedchamber divider and yanked the curtain aside in frustration. He moved to light the three hanging oil lanterns when his mind suddenly realized the extra illumination was not required. Resting atop the storage trunk at the foot of his bed hovered a robust flame whose inner glow illuminated the entire chamber, and it spoke to him.

"I have plans for you, Kublai Khan," the divine flame calmly stated. "You are better than these feeble attempts to conquer minor territories. Far greater prizes await if you will put your faith in me."

Kublai felt his legs go weak at the realization that his god was speaking directly to him. He instantly collapsed to his knees and bowed forward until his forehead touched the hard ground. "I feel destined for great deeds, yet I do not have the resources for more ambitious campaigns. I cannot even subdue this simple valley kingdom of Dali with the men I have."

"Men are drawn to success like moths to a flame," the radiant flame instructed. "Complete this conquest and the ranks under your banner will know no end."

Kublai raised his head from the ground and sat back on his legs. He shook his head and flailed his arms at his sides in bewilderment. "How?"

At that moment three swords sliced through the exterior of his tent to make a seven foot tall doorway where twelve enormous hounds ducked through to occupy the bedchamber. The sudden sight of these titanic hellhounds nearly caused Kublai to lose control of his bowels. Were they here to kill him or help him?

"My warriors will show you the way and win this war for you," The divine spirit stated with all the certainty of a player declaring checkmate in chess. "Prepare your men for an all out assault. The walls will not be an obstacle for long."

"Thy will be done," Kublai said as he bowed to the ground once more and then rose to his feet to make ready his battle plans.

In the faint morning light, Kublai sat upon his horse in full dress armor at the head of his army. The anxiety among the men was almost a tangible force pressing behind him. His veteran soldiers knew warfare well enough to realize a full frontal assault on the stout barricade walls was suicide. In fact, they had attempted it several weeks before with devastating results and no gain. Would the men follow his lead again if he gave the order to charge? Despite his divine consultation the night before, Kublai Khan quietly harbored doubts.

He looked to the west and shook his head at the towering cliff face. That impenetrable wall of stone ran along the valley's border for hundreds of miles and was the single reason for his inability to conquer the territory. He cursed its existence every day he spent encamped in its shadow. Just then, subtle movements among the shadows of the sheer rock face caught his attention. A closer inspection revealed a cluster of those seven foot hound warriors scaling the cliffs with admirable strength and agility.

Kublai and his commanders had, of course, looked at having a strike team climb the rock face to come over the forty foot high defensive wall and open the gate. The action was dismissed as impossible due to the difficulty of the climb. Even the best and most daring climbers among them said if they had all day and tools they could make it, but attempting the climb at night with no tools was suicide.

Now, these seven foot hounds of his god made the impossible climb look effortless. They clung to handholds barely visible to the naked eye. If no adequate hold was there, the beasts simply used their claws to dig into the solid rock. Even twenty foot wide gaps were easily leapt across with all the effort a man might use to step across a tiny stream.

These warriors were magnificent, but there were only twelve of them. Their meager numbers were hardly enough to mount a competent attack on the wall and gate house protected by several hundred soldiers. Still, Kublai Khan had faith in his god's plan as he watched the warriors descend from the cliff face onto the wall.

Seconds later he saw the body of a soldier launched ten feet into the air come flailing over the wall and crash to the ground with a wet thud. In rapid succession three more bodies plummeted to their death from on top as the hounds made their way towards the first gate house at a frightening pace.

All across the wall Kublai heard warning bells begin to ring along with loud shouts calling men to arms. Now would be the true test. It was one thing to surprise a few guards, it was quite another to overtake an organized defense that was well aware of an intrusion.

From his vantage point Kublai Khan could not see much, but he did observe a cluster of spears forming a phalanx against the hound warriors. When the two forces met, six hounds suddenly used the backs of their fellow warriors to leap fifteen feet into the air and land at the rear of the prickly spear formation. From both directions the warriors savaged the defenders in a chorus of growls and howls mixed in with the death wails of men.

The cruel scene ran a cold shudder up the spine of Kublai as he watched dismembered body parts rain down from on high. Nothing the defenders did seemed to matter: spears, shields, swords, bows. Nothing did much to even slow down, let alone stop, the onslaught from these magnificent warriors of his god.

Shrieks of terror and death rolled all the way across the wall until the gatehouse was reached. A few short minutes later the doors were in the process of opening.

Kublai Khan felt his entire body come alive with aggression. He drew his sword, pointed it toward the now porous defenses of the enemy and yelled, "Charge!" with the utmost confidence his order would be followed by even his most doubtful veteran. The Kingdom of Dali was his this day, and greater prizes would follow, perhaps even the great Song Dynasty of China. Who could stop him now that he had the backing of his god and his hounds of war?

Chapter 21: The Enemy of My Enemy . . .

PROFESSOR RUSSELL AWOKE to find himself lying comfortably on his side atop a firm cot. He opened his eyes for a horizontal view of a cinder block room painted floor to ceiling in brilliant white that amplified the light from a bare bulb fixture hanging down from the middle of the ceiling. The only notable feature of the room was a metal table with four chairs around it dominating the center. He drew a deep breath before sitting up straight and leaning his back against the wall.

Brian looked over to where his head used to face and saw Alex also sitting upright on a separate cot and staring back at him. "Funny, I remember recently getting out of captivity."

Alex nodded with a silent laugh, "The door is locked, I already checked. Like you said back in the tunnel, out of the frying pan and into the fire."

"Any idea who the cooks are tending the flames this time around?" the Professor asked hoping he had slept through some profound revelation that Alex could recount for his benefit. A sideways frown and a shake of her head dashed those hopes.

"All I remember is gunfire and waking up here about a half hour ago with you snoring next to me."

"I don't snore," Brian said feigning great offense.

Alex glanced to the upper right corner near the door with her eyes where a security camera surveyed the room. "I'll bet they have it on tape if you don't believe me."

Professor Russell accepted the mood lightening humor with a gracious smile. "I can't say it will be the first thing I ask our captors, or abductors, or rescuers perhaps? After the week we've had I could see just about anything and not be surprised."

He then looked straight at the camera and waved his arms from side to side over his head to draw the attention of anyone monitoring the video feed. He then repeatedly rolled his arms toward his chest inviting whoever controlled the room to come talk to them. "Come on, you have us here. Let's talk."

A few minutes later the offer was accepted. A frenzy of footsteps and a teeth rattling squeak of wheels needing oil came to a stop immediately outside the room's single locked door. The knob gently turned and the door opened into the room with a gentle nudge, and then the squeaky wheels belonging to a metal cart entered the room.

Pushing the cart along was an oriental man dressed in pure white clothes that someone working in a hotel room service kitchen might wear. The diminutive individual placed two trays full of sandwich meat, cheese and bread along with four bottles of water on the table. With his duties complete, the man wheeled his cart out of the room without a word spoken.

A moment later two Asian men, who also lacked height, but made up for it with muscle mass, stepped into the room. These men both wore dark suits with pristine white shirts and solid black ties; they definitely did not work in the food service industry.

One of them, whose hair was beginning to turn salt and pepper on top, stepped around the table and extended his right hand in greeting. "Professor Brian Russell, it is an absolute pleasure to finally make your acquaintance."

Brian did not know which was more surprising to him, the fact that the man knew his name or how well he spoke English. His speech patterns were overly formal and mechanical, but the words themselves were flawlessly pronounced.

The professor and Alex exchanged a look that seemed to say, 'what do we have to lose?' With that decided between them, Brian accepted the handshake on the way to his feet. "I would like to say the same, but I don't know who you are or the circumstances of our captivity."

The blunt statement did not faze the man in the least. He graciously opened his formal stance backwards and gestured toward the table full of food. "You are our honored guests. Please join me for lunch so that we may get to know one another."

"You expect us to eat food from the people who just drugged and abducted us at gunpoint?" Alex defiantly snapped.

Again, the man's calm composure did not falter. He stepped around the table, took a seat and began assembling his own sandwich from the ingredients provided. "Alex, I believe it is? No guns were ever pointed at the two of you. Besides, if the intent was to keep the two of you sedated, then you would be so right now rather than awake and in these accommodating surroundings. Now please, join me."

Brian accepted the logic and took a seat across from the stranger and Alex soon joined them. The other suited man stayed back and silently stood sentry by the door.

"So...who are you?" Professor Russell finally asked after stacking together a sandwich of his own and taking a few greedy drinks of water.

"You may call me Chin," the man began. "That is of course not my real name, but Chin is the Chinese equivalent to Smith in the United States and therefore works well for me. For the moment I work with the Chinese ambassador to Egypt, at least I have for the last few months since your research project arrived in this country."

"Chinese?" Professor Russell repeated. "Why in the world is China interested in my research into Egyptian landmarks, let alone enough to murder US service men to kidnap us?"

Chin looked ready to respond, but politely held back until he finished chewing his food and wiped his mouth with a napkin. "Rescued is the word you should be using, not abducted or kidnapped or any other synonym. Those service men and operative of the United States government were en route to lock you away for the rest of your lives in some unmarked safe house, were they not?"

Professor Russell was never any good at playing poker. He thoroughly failed to mask his surprise at how well informed Chin was about their circumstance. "I did hear the word 'indefinitely' mentioned when the agent in charge had us loaded into the vehicle. How did you know that, and why was it any of your concern?"

Chin held up a finger as he finished taking a drink from his water bottle. When he spoke again it was with a matter of fact tone. "Where to begin?"

Chin paused for a moment, but seemed to quickly find his place. "The potential application of your sonic density triangulation technology in my country has had my eye for quite some time. While I patiently waited to see how effective your mapping of the monuments in the Giza plateau turned out, I became quite concerned when the two of you turned up missing. You simply vanished without a trace leaving all of your expensive equipment out and about for anyone to take."

Chin, having noticed a furrow cross Brian's brow at the implied theft of his research equipment, addressed the issue up front. "Yes, your ground sensors and helicopter mounted emitter are in my possession. It would have been a shame to lose such valuable equipment to commoners who knew nothing of its uncommon potential."

"Thank you for safeguarding my property, I'd like to have them back now please," Professor Russell jumped in before Chin could move the conversation away from the topic.

"Of course, in due time of course you will have your property back," Chin backpedaled. "In the meantime, my concern for your safety grew even more pronounced when an NSA agent turned up at the location accompanied by a Special Forces team under 'strict' supervision by the Egyptian military. Somehow they managed to reproduce your experiment; probably stole your designs from the patent office. Your country's National Security Agency is quite powerful and would certainly have no difficulty accomplishing that espionage."

"Since they used it to find us I can't say I'm that offended," Alex responded in defense of her beloved government.

"Me either," Brian added, "and I find your accusation quite ironic considering how loosely your government treats intellectual property laws."

"Be that as it may," Chin continued. "Clearly they found something since the strike team immediately got into their vehicles and headed for that warehouse district to raid a tiny building of seemingly no importance. Then a few hours later they come back out with the two of you. A rather curious chain of events don't you think? Would you mind telling me what is inside that little building, and what you found on those sonic density readings to lead you there?"

"In fact I would mind," Professor Russell declared by tossing the remnants of his sandwich down, pushing the plate away and defiantly crossing his arms over his chest. "Now I will ask you again, how did you know where we were being taken, and why did you murder the men transporting us there?"

"I knew because this is not my first run in with my NSA counterparts," Chin quickly responded. "The moment I saw the Egyptian military observer being pushed around at gunpoint, I knew the two of you would be taken to their holding facility out in the suburbs. The place exists outside your government's knowledge or laws so you could be detained there...'indefinitely' I believe was the word you recited earlier."

"Okay, that covers how you knew, now why is it your business?" Brian insisted.

"Other than the satisfaction of helping my fellow man, the self-serving answer is I need your help," Chin admitted. "As an archeologist, I am sure you are already aware that hundreds of man-made earthen pyramids dot my nation's countryside. It is of great importance that you help our team of archeologists use your techniques to see what lies beneath the surface of these magnificent structures. Some, I hear, are significantly larger than even the great pyramids of Giza."

"You could have simply asked me for help," Brian began, but was cut short by Alex springing to her feet.

"No. No, oh hell no," Alex declared while looking at Professor Russell and then focused her menacing glare back on Chin who remained casually seated. "Piss off. You murdered four of my countrymen, you get no help from us. Now hand over our equipment and let us out of here."

"I can do that," Chin said quietly. "I can release you to fend for yourselves against a team of Navy SEALs with a mind to avenge their fallen brothers in arms or the NSA and their vast resources. I must say though, you did not fare very well against them the first time around. I see it ending no better in round two without my assistance."

"What is the alternative, betray my country and work for you?" Alex fired back.

Chin looked toward Brian to be the voice of reason, but the professor simply glowered back with his arms still crossed. "She has a point."

"Telling me what your readings found in the Giza plateau or what happened inside that tiny building might be considered betraying your country," Chin stated. "I am simply asking you to lead an archeological research team to map the inside of these ancient Chinese pyramids. What happened here to cause the NSA to try and detain you indefinitely is really not my concern. I am certainly curious about that whole affair, but it has nothing to do with my request."

For the first time in the conversation, Chin actually became animated. He snapped his arm forward and pushed his index finger into the table right in front of Professor Russell to accentuate his point. "This is your profession and quite possibly the opportunity of a lifetime. It is here, right now, being offered to you with no strings attached. How long did you have to wait to be allowed onto the Giza plateau with your equipment? Five years?"

"Six," Professor Russell corrected while mentally picturing himself and Alex mapping the pyramids across the countryside of China. It was an almost irresistible offer.

"If I let you walk out the front door of this embassy, not only does this opportunity slip away, but you will be taken by the NSA. Then you will likely never have the chance to do research, or even see the light of day again," Chin added. "You saw how easily they were able to operate in this country. Believe me when I tell you, it is like that the world over because most countries are weak, but not China. We have the resources and the will to resist their overtures and repel their attempts at kidnapping and espionage. You will be safe working with us doing archeological research that is your life's pursuit."

Alex took a few deep, calming breaths through her nose and eventually sat down once more. Her conflicted emotions showed through her eyes plain as day. She was also tempted by the offer, but did not for a second trust the man extending it; Brian could certainly identify with the line of thinking.

Chin no doubt got the same read of the situation. "Let me step out of the room for a while and allow the two of you to discuss the merits of my offer in private."

After the two Chinese officials took their leave, Alex was the first to speak her mind. "I don't care if they've fed us and now offer to let us go, I don't trust them. Not for a second."

"Neither do I, but realistically what choice do we have?" Brian asked. "The way I see it, the worst case scenario is our equipment finds something in those Chinese pyramids that makes these people hide us away just like the NSA is trying to do."

"Or they will just shoot us in the head out in the Chinese countryside," Alex objected.

"True, but I put that as an equivalent to a lifetime spent in captivity and as such consider them both the same outcome," Brian countered. A nod from Alex let him know she was of the same opinion. "Now the best case scenario is we find nothing of importance in China and we go home after a few years.

Then we both sign our book deals and do the talk show tours once all the dust has settled."

Alex reluctantly nodded in agreement, but added, "I'm still leery that they're just working us to eventually get information about what went on over the last week."

"Of that I have no doubt," Brian answered, "but for now the enemy of my enemy is my friend."

Chapter 22: Buying Insurance

FROM THE MOMENT Mark closed his phone after talking with Terrance he had an uneasy feeling in the pit of his stomach. The man was a control freak. Almost anything he wanted to know the NSA could get for him, including kidnapping or eliminating anyone he didn't like. His executive powers gave Terrance control; it was practically part of his DNA now.

Dealing with the stalemate this doomsday device created required giving up a certain amount of control. Maintaining the symmetry of tensions was critical, yet every fiber of Terrance's being would demand he try and upset that delicate balance in his favor to regain control. Mark wondered if he made a mistake by informing him of recent events.

When his Humvee rolled to a stop outside the command tent near the Sphinx monument, he immediately stepped out of the vehicle and looked to the partially cloudy sky. He pictured satellites moving into position to better monitor events for Terrance. He could also envision dozens of radar evading aircraft circling overhead while waiting for the order to drop their payload.

Mark redirected his eyes to the sandy plateau where over a hundred Egyptian military personnel still secured the location from the prying eyes of tourists. Soon hundreds of NSA assets loyal exclusively to Terrance and his orders would be on the ground. All so the man might gain control of a situation that was indeed dangerous, but not any more so than it has been for hundreds, if not thousands of years. There really was no need for panic in this situation just yet, but Terrance ran the risk of doing just that.

Mark realized he would very quickly lose his own control over the situation if he didn't do something. This thought caused him to turn around and look into the backseat of the Humvee at the Egyptian Colonel who was meant to be his observer while operating in the country. The man meekly sat between two SEALs and went with the flow so far. It was time to enlist more than just silent cooperation from his government watcher.

Mark opened the back door to the desert camouflaged vehicle and waited for the nearest soldier to exit the Humvee to give him direct line of sight with the Egyptian officer. "Colonel, would you please come with me?" he asked in as cordial a tone as he could summon.

"You have pushed and ordered me around for days and now suddenly you are making requests?" the colonel snapped. "You realize those are my men out there. Once in the open, I can yell for help and I will get it from them and you will be arrested."

"But then you would miss out on having all the answers," Mark interrupted. "Now please, follow me into the command tent."

Mark turned immediately and began walking toward the large tent, which he suddenly realized looked like a miniature pyramid with its tan fabric rising to a point in the middle. He had no doubt the colonel's curiosity would win out and moments later had his confidence confirmed with the sound of footsteps following close behind. They both ducked through the hard plastic door which Mark locked behind them to make sure their conversation would not be overheard or interrupted.

To start things off, Mark extended a hand of greeting. "Colonel Azire, I'm Mark Holmes."

Colonel Azire evaluated the appendage as if touching it might give him the plague. In the end he took the chance and shook Mark's hand. "I am surprised you even know my name given the complete disregard you have shown me so far."

"I make it a point to know all about the men I work with," Mark answered while gesturing for the colonel to have a seat near a computer monitor with a set of screensaver lines dancing across the display. "You, for instance, are just a few years away from retiring and desperately want to reach that next rank of general and the higher pay grade to pad those monthly pension checks. It's curious how you've been passed over for promotion four times and keep being handed mundane assignments by your superior, like babysitting me and my men."

"Bad luck I suppose," Colonel Azire responded so dryly the desert outside the tent felt tropical by comparison.

"More like insubordination," Mark countered. "The way I hear it, you refused an order from your superior to fire into a crowd of protestors while that whole Arab Spring thing was going on in this country a few years back. Considering that uprising led to the downfall of the government your commanding officer was so well positioned within, I don't think that decision helped your promotional prospects."

"What is your point?" Colonel Azire demanded, his eyes now vibrating with anger at the uncomfortable reminder of his actions.

"My point is you're a good man who is willing to do what is right for the bigger picture. I need to call upon that good man now and take him into my confidence. I trust you to be a man of your word. Do I have your word that what I am about to reveal to you will not leave the four walls of this tent?"

Azire clearly valued his word as the man took several seconds to think things through. Finally he looked Mark square in the eye to give his reply. "As long as remaining silent does not endanger my country, you have my word."

Mark cocked his head slightly to the side, "That will have to do I suppose." He then wiggled the mouse resting near the dormant computer terminal to bring the display back to life. Mark watched the three dimensional rendering of the Giza plateau fade in through the darkness along with four glowing red cubes halfway up the Great Pyramid. Next to that rested the Sphinx. The monolith looked like it was suffering from a massive bout of indigestion as a glowing red rectangle took up the entire length of its body along with an underground tunnel leading away from the giant statue.

The colonel, for his part, drew in a deep breath, held it, and held it. Minutes passed and Mark soon began fearing for the man's safety, but finally a mighty exhale came.

"It's not a trick," Mark jumped in before Azire could make the accusation. "The archeologists discovered these chambers with their equipment and were kidnapped because of it. We rescued them from their captors, but are now left to deal with the fallout."

"What...what does this all mean?" Colonel Azire finally managed. "For what purpose are those chambers used?"

"A weapon," Mark coolly responded as he brought another view screen to life. "Are you aware what happened globally a few hours ago?"

"Of course not!" Azire snapped. He took his right hand and wiped it across his sweaty brow and showed Mark his drenched palm. "You and your men have held me at gunpoint inside your vehicle without airflow for hours."

"No guns were ever directed at you," Mark pointed out with a lighthearted grin, "but I suppose you are correct; allow me to get you caught up."

On the view screen Mark pulled up a BBC news feed detailing the devastating effects that numerous earthquakes and instances of tidal surges along the coastlines had caused all across the globe over the last few hours.

Colonel Azire looked on with disgusted wonder. "You are telling me a weapon inside those chambers did all that?"

"Yes, and the weapon is capable of doing much worse," Mark answered. "Cooler heads like me are trying to resolve the situation quietly and with as little collateral damage as possible. Others are on the verge of panic and want to blow the entire Giza plateau off the face of the map."

Colonel Azire was aghast at the mention of his country's national treasures falling under attack. "This is information you expect me to keep from my superiors?"

"For the moment, yes," Mark confirmed. "Right now I am the one in charge, and I don't think blowing up the weapon is a good idea. We have no clue what destroying it would do, and I refuse to take a course of action with a questionable outcome when the stakes are this high. However, elements intent on more aggressive solutions are on their way. When they arrive, my dozen soldiers and I may not be enough to keep them in line. I need to know I can count on you and your men to help me if push comes to shove with the more hostile players in this game."

The colonel looked at Mark with the words 'hell no' blaring from his eyes. The man rose to his feet and pointed toward the exit. "I believe it is time for me to walk out that door and take control of the situation for myself."

Mark quickly sprung to his feet as well and calmly stood between Colonel Azire and the exit. "Don't you mean let that general who stands on your shoulders taking a crap on your head while holding your career back take charge? I have a better solution, one that lets us both get what we want."

"And what is that," Colonel Azire asked while looking ready to physically test Mark's ability to hold him back from leaving the tent.

Mark flicked his head toward the computer desk behind the colonel. "See those two sets of manila folders on the table. I think you will find them both very interesting reading since they concern your boss and the financial prospects of your pending retirement."

Once again curiosity won out as Colonel Azire took his seat next to the computer desk. "These had better impress me."

Mark reached past the seated Egyptian officer and picked up the folders and handed one to the colonel. "I find it ironic that your commanding officer holds you back for not killing protesters during the Arab Spring uprising."

Azire began thumbing his way through the two dozen pages of reports and photos and suddenly looked up in complete amazement as Mark continued speaking. "As it turns out, his son was an active leader in the rebellion movement from behind the scenes during his more playful college years. What you hold in your hands there is the kind of information that ends careers, or lives. Especially for high ranking generals, don't you think?"

Silence with a growing smile was compliance. With that, Mark moved on to his second overture and placed the other folder in Colonel Azire's hands. Again Mark waited for the Egyptian officer to glance through the pages before narrating their implications.

"Dr. Hass of your country's Organization of Antiquities has been a little naughty selling some lesser artifacts on the black market to fund his own eventual retirement. I can freeze or transfer those seven figure Cayman Island accounts of his anytime I feel the need. They should probably go to the proper Egyptian authorities," Mark pondered.

Mark waited a set of heartbeats then snapped his fingers and pointed at Colonel Azire. "Say, you look like an Egyptian and a man with some authority. Perhaps I could turn them over to you."

"What would I do with this dirty money," the colonel demanded in a thoroughly insulted tone.

"Turn it over to your treasury, give it to charity, fund a certain Egyptian authority figure's retirement account," Mark suggested off the top of his head. "You'll be creative and thorough I'm sure."

Colonel Azire looked both offended, yet tempted, by the pages held in his grasp. To force the issue Mark snatched the two folders back from the man and made ready to run the contents through a shredder resting atop a nearby trash can. "I can see these are causing you difficulty so allow me to remove the temptation."

"Stop," Colonel Azire bellowed while lunging after the documents to save them. With the value Azire placed on the leverage Mark held in his hands now known, the Egyptian officer spoke more freely. "Is this how you operate so freely in your country and mine, by using blackmail or bribery?"

"Sometimes I just ask nicely," Mark answered while handing over the folder containing the incriminating evidence against Azire's superior.

"What is it you need from me?" the colonel asked before taking the folder.

"Extra manpower, vehicles, and weapons under your command," Mark answered, "as much as possible around here and back at the warehouse. Oh, I also need a phone number to reach you anytime, anywhere. Do that and we'll talk later about me handing you this other folder," Mark added.

Chapter 23: Expanding Like the Plague

"TRULY TRAGIC, HALF of Europe died within a matter of months," Dr. Holmes commented to his patient.

"Actually the worst of the plague ran its course over a two year period around 1350. Some areas were hit harder than others, but yes, the casualties were upwards of one hundred million people, or roughly half the population of Europe at that time," Hastelloy confirmed.

"The Alpha killed one hundred million people in the hopes of slowing down your progress to bring mankind along technologically," Jeffrey asked in disbelief. "One hundred million?"

Hastelloy slowly shook his head in regret. "That number was just Europe. Asia was hit equally hard if not worse."

Jeffrey felt like he'd just been slapped by the cold, hard hand of reality. This was not Hastelloy's delusion. Two hundred million human beings between Europe and Asia actually died back then. It may not have been the Alpha, since they only existed in Hastelloy's mind, but the plague happened and the magnitude of devastation took his breath away as the patient continued his story.

****

Armed with a fresh batch of vaccine to combat the spread of the black plague, Tomal and Tonwen sailed into the completely vacant ports of Venice in northern Italy.

The docks of this booming port of trade were usually five ships deep waiting for a place to dock, but on this day there was scarcely a ship to be found anywhere in the harbor. As soon as word got out that a city had fallen victim to the plague, sailors steered clear until the epidemic passed. Even then, only the bravest or most desperate traders ventured back.

Their boat stopped just long enough to pay the captain his exorbitant fee and for the two of them to step off the ship. Each carried a crate laden with the vaccine. In all, they transported a thousand doses of the cure, which was nowhere near enough.

"Well, where do we start?" Tomal asked.

"The clergy and physicians," Tonwen answered. "They are the ones exposed to the contagion on a regular basis. If we prove to them that it works they will help distribute the cure more broadly."

"That's a fine plan, Tonwen, but there are over 50,000 residents in this city and we can only inoculate a thousand of them. If word gets out that we have the cure it will be pandemonium."

"That is also where the clergy come in," Tonwen responded. "Their monasteries have the manpower, currency, and a moral obligation to mass produce the vaccine once they buy into its effectiveness. I wrote their rule of conduct. I ought to know."

Tomal looked around at the water filled streets of the sunken city and flagged down two gondolas. "We divide and conquer then. You start on the west side of the city, and I will meet you in the middle coming from the east."

Before the two boarded their respective boats, Tonwen added a word of caution. "Remember, the vaccine only prevents a person from contracting the disease. It does nothing for them once infected so only give it to those treating the patients."

When Tomal stepped off the gondola on the eastern side of the city he was somewhat concerned he would not be able to locate the hospitals very easily. As it turned out, all he needed to do was follow his nose to the source of the most revolting stench he had ever encountered, which included burying the dead on a battlefield a week after the bloodletting happened.

It wasn't just the stench of death. It mixed with sweat, excrement and disease resulting in an aromatic cocktail that made him feel rather lightheaded.

Tomal pushed open a tall wooden door to a church and found the worshipping pews haphazardly shoved aside to make room for hundreds of sickbeds. The potent smell did its best to knock Tomal over as he entered the hot, sweaty caldron of disease and decay.

"Out!" a man wearing a piece of white fabric over his mouth and nose shouted upon seeing Tomal. "All our beds are full. You will need to find somewhere else to take your sick."

Tomal shook his head and placed the wooden crate he carried on the floor and pulled out two thin glass vials, one in each hand. "I do not bring sickness. I bring a cure."

"Yeah sure," the exhausted man laughed loudly. "You and everyone else."

"I am serious," Tomal protested.

The man finished placing a wet cloth across the forehead of the nearest patient and then stopped in front of Tomal long enough to say, "You must be the fifth person to come through those doors today attempting to sell an elixir that will restore all these people back to full health."

The man accentuated his disgust with the abusive practice by spitting at Tomal's feet. "Now get out of here before I get angry."

To the man's back Tomal replied, "Unfortunately, those individuals who are already ill cannot be helped. It is their caretakers I seek to keep healthy."

The man abruptly turned about and looked ready to toss Tomal out by the scruff of his neck if he did not like the answer to his next question. "What's your price?"

"Nothing," Tomal answered. "Except spreading the word to your fellow caretakers and friends once you are satisfied with the results."

"How will I know," the man asked with a little less anger than before. "A few, like myself, seem not to catch the disease. How will I know it is your elixir and not God's favor instead?"

"You know as well as I that nine out of ten people will contract and die from the disease." Tomal bent down and removed a cluster of twenty vials held upright by a wooden frame and handed them over to the man. "Give each of these to a different person you know who is not yet infected with the plague. A week from now if they are all still in good health you will have your proof that it works. Then you can meet me ten days from now in the square outside of St. Mark's Basilica to help deliver this cure to as many people as we possibly can."

The skeptical man accepted the glass vials and Tomal left the building without another word. When he reached the open air he drew a deep breath of relatively fresh air and then moved on to locate the next hospital with his nose.

Ten days later Tomal and Tonwen hosted a gathering of over fifty clergy, physicians and nurses all clamoring for more vials of the vaccine.

"Is this your plan," an angry woman shouted. "Show us the cure and then pretend like you do not have much of it left so you can charge us?"

Tomal raised his arms up to try and quiet the mayhem around him. "Please. Please quiet down so we can talk."

Eventually the chaos died down enough for Tonwen's voice to carry over the din of lingering voices. "We have no intention of charging anyone anything for the medicine. It is our Christian duty to help our fellow man. The difficulty is making enough of it to help this city and eventually those all around Europe. The raw herbs cost money. Trained manpower is needed to properly mix it, and so on."

The bishop wearing a white robe with a bright red half coat draped over his shoulders spoke up for all the clergy in the city. "I can open the unfortunately meager coffers of the church to purchase materials and my monks, priests and parishioners can provide the necessary labor."

"I am afraid it will require significantly more coin than you have available your Grace," Tonwen said with a slight bow of his head.

"We can charge everyone a fixed price for the cure," the first physician Tomal visited on the east side of Venice suggested.

"That would exclude the poor and condemn them to die," the bishop protested.

"What about enticing the wealthy among the city to contribute for the benefit of all," a monk wearing a hooded brown robe suggested.

Tomal shook his head. "No, that will not work. Every person of means is squirreling their money away believing it will somehow help them weather this calamity."

"Then we should convince them that parting with their riches will gain them favor in the afterlife," Tonwen offered.

"You propose we lie to our fellow man. Make hollow promises of riches in heaven in order to extort money from them?" the bishop responded in complete shock.

"It is not entirely a lie," the monk countered. "My studies of scripture reveal numerous instances of favor granted by God for good works here on earth. What could be more holy and noble than contributing to the distribution of a cure that could save hundreds of thousands of lives?"

"Millions of lives," Tomal corrected before the bishop could render his final judgment on the suggestion.

The bishop remained silent for several minutes of silent prayer. Finally he drew a deep breath while nodding his head up and down. "There could be truth to it, and at the very worst it is a deceit at the behest of a noble cause that benefits all of god's creation."

He looked around at all the clergy present. "I will begin work on a series of sermons to deliver the message that financially contributing to the good works of the church will carry favor for the giver in God's eyes."

The order was well received, especially with Tomal and Tonwen who exchanged a subtle look of satisfaction between them as the bishop's plan was put into motion.

Chapter 24: Enlightened Encounter

NICOLAUS SAT ALONE with his notes in the corner of his favorite tavern nestled equidistant between the university and the docks along the Golden Horn. The relative solitude of the establishment was ideal for his work. Bars too close to the docks suffered the distraction of sailors singing songs and getting into brawls. The university taverns on the other hand were laden with intellectuals attempting to outshine one another.

He pored over his observations and calculations for the thousandth time hoping they would tell a different story. He was a man of science, but also faith. What's more, he was not any sort of a rebel. His life's work of studying the heavens was meant to mathematically confirm the church teachings that the Earth was indeed the center of the universe.

This wasn't the case. The data showed plain as day that Sol rest at the center of the system and the Earth and her accompanying planets all revolved around it. The irrefutable conclusion sent shivers down his spine knowing men had died from challenging far less important church doctrine.

"God help me," he said quietly into his beer as he took a long thoughtful drink from the flask.

"Only a man with a lot on his mind utters those words," came a voice from the opposite corner of the establishment. Nicolaus looked up to see a man surrounded by schematics of some sort and a dozen empty beer flasks. "I ought to know, I recite the same prayer many times a day."

The man clearly had his troubles and sought to find resolution at the bottom of a beer flask. At this point Nicolaus had a decision to make: respond to the man and begin a potentially pointless conversation, or play deaf and continue his work. One look at the concentric circles of his own diagram and the inflammatory meaning made the choice for him.

"Knowing the truth behind a great secret is a heavy burden to carry alone, therefore I seek help from the divine," Nicolaus responded.

"Come, join me," the stranger offered. "Perhaps we can share each other's burdens while we wait for divine inspiration to strike us."

Nicolaus had no intention of revealing to the drunken stranger his discovery that would likely see him burned at the stake as a heretic if it ever got out. Still, sharing a drink with another who clearly had a lot on his mind was a welcome diversion from his own troubles. He gathered his papers, stuffed them into his carry bag and joined the man at his table for a drink. "My name is Nicolaus Copernicus. I come from Prussia to teach and study at the university."

"Orban," came a gruff introduction. Rather than offering a handshake he kicked a chair out from under the table and placed a beer in front of it. Nicolaus found the chair occupied by a tattered doll crafted from a stuffed potato sack. He gently picked up the child's toy, placed it on the table and took a seat.

"I arrived from Florence two days ago in order to get away from the plague and those who did nothing to prevent it," Orban said.

"I heard Florence felt the worst of it," Nicolaus said, eager to drive the conversation away from his own issues.

"You have no idea," Orban said into an emptied flask. "Picture four out of five people you know dying a hideous and painful death in the span of a few weeks. Then having to deal with the stench and resulting solitude to ponder what you've lost."

The man's voice croaked and trailed off into yet another mug of beer delivered by the bar maid. "I take it you lost more than just some random neighbors. Parents? Brothers?"

Neither elicited a response, but the mention of wife and children drew a stream of quiet tears running down the side of his tortured face. The man looked to the doll resting on the table and patted it gently with his free hand.

Orban eventually regained his composure enough to continue, "She wasn't my wife and the boy not my son, but we were as much a family as any."

"Tell me about them," Nicolaus prompted. "If they continue in our memories then I believe their existence is immortal."

Orban shook his head and chuckled softly as if the word 'immortal' carried an inside joke for him. "Alice was her name, and Thomas was her eight year old boy."

"I try and picture the two of them in good health and cheer, but the image always degrades to the coroner loading their pale, lifeless bodies onto the burial wagon along with all the other corpses infested with black welts from the plague."

Orban paused to take another drink and gather himself again. Nicolaus decided to focus the conversation on their lives rather than deaths. "How did the three of you meet?"

The sad lines around Orban's eyes noticeably relaxed as he started speaking again. "We had a rather awkward introduction actually, considering she attempted to sell her sexual services to me. She was quite lovely, but paying for companionship is not my way so I declined the offer. For some reason though, I felt compelled to learn why this beautiful young woman was prostituting herself. Over a simple meal I learned she was a recent widow struggling to support her infant son. She had no other family and no one hires a widow, particularly one with an infant child and all the distractions that come along with it."

Nicolaus shook his head with disbelief. "I admire you, sir. Everyone treats widows like the death of their husband was their fault. The fact of the matter is if they have no family to take care of them, then there is little option other than turning to prostitution. Then the snooty socialites look down on them for turning to the only source of income available to them. Life is not fair sometimes."

"Exactly," Orban commented. "That's why I gave Alice a job in my currency exchange office. I even allowed her to bring the boy to work with her. Over the years I grew quite fond of the child. He was happy, playful, and so bright."

"I took every opportunity to teach them both how to read and write. Thomas showed particular promise. At just eight years old the boy could speak three languages. The lad could even read Ulysses and debate philosophy with me."

"Sounds like you were quite the stepfather," Nicolaus commended.

"There was never anything romantic between Alice and me," Orban corrected. "I lost my wife long ago and swore to honor her memory by never being with another. As a result, I never knew the joys of fatherhood until Thomas, and had long forgotten the comfort of companionship until Alice."

"It was a source of great pride and joy helping the two of them through life right up until that fateful day," Orban went on. "Alice was at the market that morning when the flat boats arrived carrying the plague with them. She, along with Thomas, were among the first to fall victim to the disease. Owing to the tireless care I provided, they were among the last to finally succumb to their condition."

The sad lines around the man's eyes returned along with pools of tears gathered in the corners. "I simply cannot forgive myself for failing them. I knew all the sterilization procedures and combination of herbs to support their immune systems, yet it wasn't enough. It required a vaccine."

Sterilization procedures, immune system, vaccine? The man was talking in unintelligible tongues right now.

"I watched them be buried in a mass grave with all the others, and then waited alone in the home we occupied every day. Even when friends arrived I found no comfort. I had to leave. I needed to get away and start anew."

"So you traveled all the way from Florence alone? Was that not a dangerous journey with all the brigands about?" Nicolaus asked as if Orban just said he crossed a lake of molten lava.

"Highway robbers tend to leave the impoverished looking travelers unmolested," Orban instructed. "Plus only the bravest or most foolish brigand is still about. Everyone else is hiding behind locked gates of the nearest city or town to try and keep the plague out."

"Wise considering what the plague brings. I tell myself I am here in Constantinople for the university, but in truth it is protection. The walls of this city are impenetrable and that is truly what keeps me here."

"In my travels I have seen the plague ravage communities with high, thick walls and those with none at all just the same. Being surrounded on three sides by clean water is what preserves this city," Orban continued.

Nicolaus had not considered that. "Regardless, the impenetrable walls do protect the city from conquest. The only possible avenue of attacking the city is a land route to the west that is obstructed by over twenty miles of multilayered fortification walls. The city is impregnable which is why it has drawn the greatest minds of this generation. Above all else, scholars seek safety and consistency to pursue their studies with peace of mind."

"The comfort this city's immense wealth provides cannot be discounted either," Orban added. "With all the taxes raised from ships wanting to traverse the narrow straight between the Black and Mediterranean Seas, it seems no man's purse ever runs empty in this city."

Nicolaus nodded his head in agreement. "True."

For the first time in their increasingly deep conversation, considering how inebriated Orban must have been, the depressed man cracked a smile. "Tell me, how can you claim the greatest minds reside here when so many go uneducated. How many brilliant minds such as Thomas are wasted on the collective illiteracy of the masses? This single city may prosper, but the wider civilization wallows around in ignorance and tears itself apart."

"You speak the truth once more, but what can be done about it?"

"The knowledge and prosperity of this city must be shared with the world for the greater good of mankind," Orban declared and accentuated it by pounding his fist on the table. "We need to bring these artists and thinkers out of hiding and allow the glow of their enlightenment to illuminate the rest of the world once more."

Nicolaus relaxed into his chair a bit realizing he was simply hearing outlandish thoughts of a drunken man. It was an amusing distraction from his own troubles, however. "That is a fine plan, but how do you accomplish it? By force? You cannot thrust civilization onto people who do not want it. We all learned that lesson from the Romans. Besides, every city and town has stout walls and locked gates requiring years of siege to break. The cost is too great and the benefit too small for any prince to try and unite the civilized world under a single banner once more."

"What if a weapon were built that could level those city walls with a single shot," Orban said and thrust a page with a detailed diagram for a cannon of some sort drawn upon it. Not just any cannon but a huge bombardment tool that would probably take fifty oxen and a whole army of men to move if it were ever built.

Nicolaus gave the diagram a closer inspection. He was not an expert, but he knew enough about metallurgy to recognize the design had merit. This was not some drunken boast in a bar, it had real potential.

"Has your recent loss left you preoccupied with death to the point that you would design such a weapon?" Nicolaus asked.

"This is not a tool for death," Orban countered. "It is an enabler for progress and peace in the hands of the right leader. Tomorrow I meet with Emperor Constantine to see if he is such a leader of vision."

Chapter 25: Plan B

AS VALNOR LED his horse away from the last in a string of gate houses defending the city of Constantinople, he felt the ground shudder slightly when the portcullis was locked into position behind him. The heavy wall of iron bars in conjunction with the seemingly endless string of stout walls looked intimidating; impregnable even.

Emperor Constantine certainly thought his city was safe. Valnor shook his head and chuckled at affixing the prefix of Emperor to Constantine's name. It was ridiculous. The word implied the man was master of a massive empire. In reality he was little more than the mayor of a single, albeit wealthy, city.

Constantine scoffed at the idea of using Valnor's heavy bombardment cannon as a means to expand his wealth and influence. The coward was content to hide behind his walls and roll around in his riches while the rest of the world descended into anarchy around him.

The inaction was an unpleasant reminder of Hastelloy and his lack of leadership. If the captain had let Valnor work his plan a thousand years earlier, they would probably already be off this godforsaken rock by now. Instead they were stuck in this quicksand of darkness, death and societal degradation.

His tour through northern Italy and Greece gave a disturbing pictorial of just how far things had regressed. Under the civilized umbrella of his Roman Empire commerce flowed freely, and cities boasted feats of architectural engineering and scholarly study. Now these individual cities featured tall, thick walls with gaudy gatehouses closed tight in an effort to keep the spreading plague at bay. How could Hastelloy have let this happen?

What's more, Alice and Thomas would still be alive. Their condition required a vaccine, a cure that was unavailable due to the disjointed and fractured society Hastelloy stood by and allowed to happen. *Damn that man,* was all Valnor could think as he paced away from the city walls of Constantinople.

Constantine was an infuriating individual. He, more than anyone else on the planet, had the potential to make a difference, but he felt safe behind his walls. So did all the great minds and artists who sought refuge in the place.

Not to worry though, there were other leaders nearby who had far more ambition and vision. Valnor checked one last time that the saddle bags containing his designs were secure and then mounted his horse. He gave one last look back at the towering city walls and then headed north on a mission to topple those very walls.

A week later, Valnor found himself seated before Sultan Mehmed II and a dozen of his military advisors. The twenty-one year old had recently assumed the throne of the Ottoman Empire. He inherited an immense fortune and a strong army. Of more importance to Valnor, he was eager to prove to the world that he had the right to rule.

The city of Constantinople had been a mocking thorn in the side of the Ottoman Empire for generations. The city's command of the straights between the Black and Mediterranean seas robbed the Ottoman's of their ability to tax commerce passing between the two bodies of water. Today Valnor would help them start to remove that thorn.

Valnor decided to open the discussion by laying all his cards on the table. "Honorable Sultan. My name is Orban, and I humbly offer my designs and engineering services to your employ so that you may finally own the Golden Horn and the city which protects that valuable passage."

Valnor observed several men around the rectangular table, including the Sultan himself, straighten their posture a bit. The idea was not universally embraced however.

"It cannot be done," one particularly fat man with a tangled beard barked. "Catapults, trebuchets, sapping tunnels. These have all been tried and failed to breach even one layer of those walls, let alone reach the city itself. This is a fool's proposition and a waste of our time."

Sultan Mehmed said nothing. The young ruler simply opened his arms slightly inviting a counter argument. Valnor was happy to comply. Across the table he unfurled a roll of parchment paper that covered half the table and oriented it to face the Sultan.

When he saw eyes widen with comprehension of his designs Valnor boldly declared, "If the walls no longer stand then there is nothing to impede you from conquering the city."

After a few quiet moments the fat man continued his protest. "Anyone can draw a picture of a big cannon, it does not mean the thing will actually work. Plus, it is too large. How could we possibly move it into position, and once set up it would be too close to the target and draw constant attacks to destroy it."

Valnor was ready for this debate. He took out a stack of smaller sheets of paper detailing the precise metallurgical requirements and shapes for the foundry moldings to render the weapon functional. He set the stack of pages in front of the protesting advisor. "Here are all the facts and figures to prove to your engineers that this is a viable design. It will work."

"I cannot deny the cannon will be heavy," Valnor conceded. "It will take at least sixty oxen and no fewer than five hundred men to move the weapon into position, but all that effort will be well spent in the end."

"The cannon will be able to hurl a six hundred pound boulder over a mile to hit a target," Valnor went on. "Attack from the defenders will not be a concern, and with that amount of force and weight anything it hits will be destroyed. In a matter of days the mighty walls of Constantinople will be little more than a paved entry way for your forces to secure a great conquest."

Murmurs around the table debating the validity of Valnor's claim came to an abrupt end when Sultan Mehmed II rose to his feet. "My engineers will review your designs. If your claims are confirmed, I will make you a wealthy man. If they are not, I will make you a dead man."

With his orders given the Sultan left the command tent without another word. When all eyes fell back on Valnor once more he cracked a confident grin toward the engineers he was meant to impress. "Does anyone have an abacus?"

Chapter 26: Unfair Advantage

KUBLAI KHAN LOOKED out across the open grassland before him and shook his head with wonder. Five hundred yards away a Song army numbering perhaps twenty thousand strong lined up for battle against his men. Surely word of his prior victories had spread, yet the Song generals continued to use the same obsolete tactics ensuring this day would end like all the others.

The Song infantry carried long spears with metal tips and shields. For battle they formed up in square pike formations with the first four rows pointing their spears outward to defend against the now legendary cavalry charges for which his Mongol ancestors were known, but that was then and this was now. Kublai's god had given him a new weapon that rendered pike formations a nostalgic relic of the past.

"Same as before, send the archer cavalry forward to draw their missile fire while the infantry move into position," Kublai Khan ordered.

Like a tidal wave rolling onto the shore, he watched his mounted units accelerate toward the right and left flanks of the enemy's squared up formations. As they drew near, a few riders fell victim to enemy arrows and slingshot pebbles. The riding archers, however, were able to give as good as they got since the Mongols were exceptionally well trained at firing their bows while riding. The casualties were superficial at best, but it did provide a wonderful distraction while the real threat moved in unmolested.

His foot soldiers marched forward with shields locked in protective position to stop any arrows that did happen to come their way. When his soldiers came within a hundred yards of the enemy he ordered the heavy cavalry forward and followed their lead.

Charging a wall of pikes head on with cavalry, even heavily armored horses, was suicide, but those pikes would not be in position for long.

Kublai Khan's infantry came to an abrupt halt thirty feet from the menacing pike wall. The first four rows of his men took their own spears from their shoulders and planted the butt end into the ground and braced it with the instep of their foot. They then leveled the three foot long and one foot diameter tip toward the Song defensive line. To those men it looked like thousands of metal honey combs were pointed at them, but the sting of these weapons was far more potent than any bee.

"Fire," came an order from the Mongol line commanders, and the world erupted with sparks, smoke, and carnage.

From the honeycombed metal cylinders leapt forth hundreds of tiny metal balls propelled by the explosive black powder Kublai Khan's god instructed him to produce.

A wall of angry lead slammed into the Song infantry leveling the first six rows, and sending the remaining ranks to the ground under the destructive force. Thick white smoke billowing up from the Mongol front lines obscured Kublai's vision of the enemy, but from prior experience he already knew their condition and gave his heavy cavalry the order, "Charge!"

A rolling wave of thunder spread across the battlefield as thousands of heavy horses drove their hooves into the ground to produce a mass of armor and lances rushing forward at thirty miles per hour. The Mongol infantry stepped into single file lines allowing the cavalry to pass and do their damage.

Hardly a single spear was still leveled in anger toward the charge as the enemy was busy getting back to their feet and recovering from the shock of seeing handheld explosive weapons flatten their lines. Some bodies flew as far as thirty feet through the air when the charge slammed into them. Others were impaled clear through by a sharp lance, and any man lucky enough to remain raised his hands in surrender and asked for quarter, but none was given.

The only men to survive the battle from the Song army were a handful of officers able to spur their mounts to outrun their attackers.

"Should I order the mounted archers to give chase?" General Kang asked.

Kublai Khan shook his head gently from side to side. "No, let their words carry the terror of this day to the rest of their soldiers and citizens."

His general looked unconvinced. "They will all head for either Xiangyang or Fancheng. Even after laying siege to those fortresses for two years we are still unable to breach their defenses. We can't let them receive even more reinforcements."

Kublai Khan regarded his general with a level stare that slowly morphed into a sly, sideways grin. "Of course we can. This entire campaign has been about corralling all of the Song soldiers and royal family members into one place so that I may deliver a death blow to the entire dynasty all at once rather than allowing pockets of resistance to fester for decades to come."

"Beware what you wish for; you just might get it," General Kang responded with a huff. "I don't see how we will be able to break them. Their defensive walls are too thick for our trebuchets to penetrate and their unlimited access to fresh river water means we cannot starve them out."

Kublai Khan looked past General Kang toward his army's encampment site. He directed his general's attention to the train of fifty horse-drawn carts carrying stout lumber and scrap metal collected from prior conquests lined up along the southern barrier.

"Finish them off and continue moving the army toward Xiangyang to join the siege," Kublai ordered. "My God has a plan for me, and since I started obeying his council we have known nothing but victory and prosperity."

Chapter 27: Follow the Yellow Silk Road

HASTELLOY LOOKED DOWN at the table which had a small pile of finely ground powder with the color and consistency of rust. The prospect was unappealing to him, but he owed it to his guest to try the sample. He calmly licked his index finger, dabbed some of the powder onto the moistened tip and then stuck the finger in his mouth.

The explosion of flavor made his eyelids snap open, and he instinctively opened his mouth to draw in a cooling breath to put out the intense burning sensation on his tongue.

"Intriguing isn't it," Niccolo said from across the table as Hastelloy reached for a glass of water. "It's called cinnamon. I picked it up during my travels in the Far East. Do you think there is a market for it here in Venice?"

Hastelloy took one last gulp of water and set the glass down. "Forget about Venice, I think every baker and chef in all of Europe will want to get their hands on this. How much did you bring back with you?"

"Only a few bags to allow my trading partners to sample the product," Niccolo answered with some regret behind his words. "My brother Maffeo and son Marco depart next week for the Far East again to set up final trade arrangements."

"What else do you plan on importing?"

Niccolo's face lit up like he was already mentally calculating the profits he would make, "Lots of things. Here feel the softness of this silk fabric," he said while handing Hastelloy a patch of the vibrant blue fabric.

"I've also got my hands on some other spices like nutmeg, clove, peppers ..."

"What can we bring to them to earn profits going both directions on the trades," Hastelloy quickly interrupted.

Niccolo reared back his head and let loose a mighty laugh. "You Medici's are always trying to squeeze extra profits into a deal,"

"And you Polos have a habit of always thinking too small," Hastelloy countered and then playfully tossed the silk fabric at his counterpart's chest. "We must have something for them: steel, armor, swords?"

Niccolo looked down at the table and shook his head from side to side. "From what I saw over there, swords and armor might be a thing of the past, even the new steel ones."

"What do you mean?"

"Black powder weapons are being used more and more over there now," Niccolo responded.

Hastelloy was not convinced. "I've seen the local arms dealers try to use those explosive handheld weapons, but they always manage to blow themselves up more often than the enemy targets with them. Besides, the models I have seen don't even have the power to penetrate a decent set of leather armor, let alone chain or plate mail.

"No, I think the loud bang and smoke they billow out might make a good terror weapon against those primitives out east, but here in the civilized world it is just a gimmick, nothing more," Hastelloy concluded.

"It's the wave of the future my friend. Somehow their powder is much more powerful than what they produce in these parts. I heard an invading army from the steppes of Mongolia is using some sort of hand cannon to blast apart shielded pike formations like they are holding a bolt of silk up for protection," Niccolo countered while stretching the delicate silk patch in the air between the two men.

"Really," Hastelloy said with a hint of alarm reaching his voice. It should take hundreds of years to perfect the explosive potential of gunpowder. This smelled of Alpha influence. Things had been relatively quiet around Europe recently. Perhaps Goron had taken his formless existence on the road and was now meddling in the affairs of the eastern empires.

"Oh yes. From what I hear, the weapon is so effective the Mongols are poised to take over the entire region in short order."

Hastelloy took a few moments to ponder his options. "Do you have any extra room in the wagons heading east next week?"

Chapter 28: No Backup

IN THE BACK of an ambulance roaring down the city streets of Cairo with the siren blaring, Frank sat with an NSA network linked data screen on his lap. On the display he watched satellite imagery of the assault carried out earlier on his Humvee. Owing to the triangulation effect of multiple satellites focusing on his distress signal and image enhancement algorithms, he had a video of the events that would make even a Hollywood videographer proud.

Not only could he see a crystal clear image of the action from a top down perspective, the image enhancement programming actually allowed the view to be rotated and render a street side three-dimensional perspective as well. He could zoom in to check license plate numbers and even gauge the approximate height, and weight of the assault team members. The video picked up just as a paneled van sped away from the scene carrying the overly knowledgeable archeologists with it.

Frank watched twelve men dressed all in black with ski masks climb into the back of a delivery truck that had rammed the Humvee from behind. As that vehicle sped away he also saw the sniper come out of a five story building across the street wearing civilian clothes and holding a briefcase carrying his deadly instrument. The man casually walked down the street as if he was going to work for the day.

Frank zoomed the video feed out again and followed the paneled van and delivery truck as they took a direct path to the Chinese embassy where their valuable cargo was unloaded and taken inside.

It certainly explained why most of the strike team members were so short, but the realization that the Chinese were involved in a smash and dash kidnapping of US citizens had him positively baffled. How did they know about the archeologists? How did they know the route to be taken well enough to stage a coordinated attack on a mobile target, and what the devil did they want with the archeologists?

He still had only questions, but he needed to inform Mark of the events. He pulled up a secure phone he borrowed from the NSA field agent driving the ambulance and put it to his ear. "Mark, believe it or not, this entire situation just got a whole lot more complicated."

Frank spent five minutes walking Mark through the chain of events. The man did not value wordy explanations; just the facts, and that is exactly what he got. He absorbed in silence the cold hard fact that the Chinese government was now involved.

"Well that's just perfect," Mark finally said. "Like we don't have enough on our plate right now so the Chinese thought they would add another helping. Alright, it's done."

"It ain't alright," Frank snapped back. "How the hell did they know we were even here, do we have a mole problem in our house?"

Mark's matter of fact answer was immediate. "A Chinook helicopter deposited a SEAL team on the Giza plateau. Three armored Humvees have been driving around the streets of Cairo. That kind of activity tends to reach the desk of intelligence officers pretty quickly. I don't think they used an informant, they didn't need one. The question in my mind is what the Chinese want with the archeologists."

"Seems pretty clear to me," Frank answered. "They wanted to know what was going on and they snatched the two of them to get answers."

"Risking an international incident by attacking US service men and abducting two citizens seems a little brazen to me," Mark countered.

Frank couldn't believe how casually Mark was passing this off. "Considering what those two know, I think it's an exact match for the Chinese's MO."

"They didn't know anything about what went on in that chamber, and depending how tight lipped Alex and Professor Russell wind up being they still may not know," Mark concluded. "It had to be something else."

"Maybe the archeological experiments are what they're after," Frank suggested. "It was certainly useful at finding new chambers inside the pyramid and Sphinx. Maybe they have other areas of Egypt they want to have a peek at?"

"Or back in China," Mark pondered. The long pause that followed let Frank know his partner was clearly conflicted on how to proceed. Finally the orders came. "I wanted you to handle securing the tunnel exit and the Giza plateau while I went back to the states to chat with that Hastelloy character, but that has to change."

"Now I need you watching the archeologists and their new friends," Mark continued. "They will eventually have to transport them somewhere. When they do, be ready to track them, snatch them back, or kill them. Whatever you determine the situation calls for because the sensitive information both of them carry is too dangerous to leave in the hands of the Chinese for very long."

"What resources are available to help me do that?" Frank asked.

"None I'm afraid. I need the remaining SEAL team securing the tunnel entrance. Assets from all over Europe, Africa and the Middle East are en route, but I have a feeling the Chinese will move the archeologists long before they arrive."

"Outstanding," Frank said with a bright, cheery voice that definitely did not match his mood. The Chinese took out a Humvee full of heavily armed Navy SEALs, and now he was supposed to handle them with what, his charm and winning smile? Mark was right though, the tunnel entrance was the immediate priority. He would have to come up with something.

"What about you?" Frank asked. "You need to hightail it stateside to get some answers from that wack job holding your brother."

"Don't remind me. Looks like I will just have to give Terrance another call and let him know he needs to actually earn his paycheck this week," Mark replied just before ending the call.

Frank rested his head against the side wall of the ambulance and closed his eyes to think for a few minutes. Moments later his eyes snapped open and he looked down at the data screen again. He pulled up a search window that would eventually pull down all the registered flight plans for the airports in and around Cairo. He was very keen to find any that were recently filed for private aircraft heading east.

When he found what he was looking for, Frank reached ahead to the front seat and tapped the driver on the shoulder, "Head for the charter gates of Cairo International Airport. I have a plane to catch."

Chapter 29: Catching a Flight

WITH THE AMBULANCE parked just a quarter mile from the charter flight gates of Cairo International Airport, Frank rummaged through the storage cabinets looking for useful supplies. Pillows, a defibrillator, IV bags and syringes were all tossed aside haphazardly until he finally located a portable oxygen tank. He quickly stuffed the two feet long, six inch diameter cylinder along with a breathing mask attached into a carrying bag. To that he added a heavy duty insulated blanket along with an ear piece and fingernail sized listening device he procured from the driver. He then looked back at his data screen once more.

Nobody had left the Chinese embassy just yet, but the presence of four escort cars outside let him know their departure was imminent. Assuming they left the instant Frank stepped out of the ambulance, he figured he had at least fifteen minutes before they reached the airport to board the chartered plane.

The field agent who drove the ambulance had already used a set of high-powered binoculars to locate the correct hangar. The plane with a registered flight plan going to China sat with a flight crew undergoing final checks for departure.

"Do you want me to stick around or cause a distraction for you," the driver asked as Frank made ready to open the passenger door.

"No, I don't want to raise any suspicions that we are onto them yet. Just make sure our asset in the air traffic control tower knows what to do," Frank answered and then slipped quietly out of the ambulance. Before shutting the door the driver added a word of caution.

"Be careful with that oxygen tank. If it were to explode while that plane was in flight it would likely do enough damage to take even an aircraft that large out of the sky."

"Tell me something I don't know," Frank said to himself as he silently closed the door and pressed on it with both hands and his body weight until he heard a soft latch. Then he slung the carrying bag over his shoulder, crossed the street and headed between two concrete buildings with a section of twelve foot tall fencing topped with razor wire tilting outward to prevent unwanted entry.

Frank climbed the fence until he stood just below the razor wire. With two feet and a hand firmly anchored into the chain-link fencing, he pulled the blanket out of his bag and flopped it over the top of the razor wire. He then reached up and felt around until his probing hand located a section of covered wire between the jagged barbs. He reached up with his other hand and located a similar hold.

Even with the thick blanket as protection, Frank could tell this was going to hurt – a lot. With a simultaneous pull from his arms and jump from his legs, Frank hoisted his torso up onto the covered wiring. He leaned his weight onto his chest and then lifted his legs up and over the barrier. As the momentum of his legs caused his chest to pivot on the wire one hundred eighty degrees, Frank felt the agonizing bite of a dozen razor blades penetrate the blanket and his clothing to carve up his chest. It was all he could do not to release his grip, go fetal, and have a good cry in the corner while nursing his wounds.

With his legs now dangling on the airport side of the fence, Frank relocated his hands down to the fence and gratefully pulled his chest off of the covered wiring. He untangled the blanket and draped it over his shoulder as he frantically scurried back down to the ground and crouched low between two metal sided hangars while he packed the blanket back into his bag.

He resisted the urge to look down at his chest to inspect the damage. The nearly unbearable pain let him know it was bad, and looking at it would only make it hurt that much worse. He smeared a hand over his chest and looked at the result. To his surprise only a few light dabs of blood were present, so at least he would not leave a trail of DNA for somebody to find later.

It would have been considerably easier and less painful to use wire cutters on the fence, but he needed his entry to be undetected. Nothing said a bad guy got in like a section of fence between buildings all cut up. The damage would likely go unnoticed for a while, but the Chinese were nothing if not thorough with their security details. It would be spotted eventually and then the already stringent security would tighten up to be nearly impenetrable.

Frank made his way between the hangars until pausing a few steps from the opening. He was positioned right at the elbow of a ninety degree turn of the jet taxiway that led down a path with hangars flanking it on either side.

The target hangar was inconveniently located across the jet taxiway two hangars down on the left. Frank had a perfect view into the large open air hangar featuring a wide body plane parked in the center with four wing mounted engines idling with a fuel truck feeding it.

A cursory review of the hangar's security confirmed what the other agent already told Frank. At least six cameras canvassed the building inside and out along with eight men wearing dark suits patrolling the vicinity. Breaching security that tight would be nearly impossible, but the good Lord blessed Frank with a heavy brain pan and a set of stones to use it.

Frank patiently waited among the shadows between the two hangars until the Chinese caravan finally arrived from the embassy. They hastily loaded Professor Russell and Alex on board without any signs of a fuss. Immediately after everyone boarded the plane the rickety steps were rolled away, the outer door was locked shut and the engines powered up to send the plane taxiing directly toward Frank's position. They certainly were itching to get on the move.

When the Chinese plane began rolling, Frank also spotted a small sized private plane heading toward him from the right. The two planes looked destined to collide right at the bend where Frank had so strategically positioned himself. As the colossal Chinese aircraft completed the turn it came face to face with the relatively tiny incoming plane and skidded to a halt. The two planes stared each other down in a contest that could only be described as David against Goliath. A moment passed and little David began turning around to make way for Goliath.

While that little drama played out right in front of Frank, he dashed out from his cover and jumped onto the stationary set of tires on the plane's back right side. He quickly climbed his way up into the wheel well and pushed open the heavy metal hatch that allowed him entry into the craft's underbelly.

Frank tossed his bag into the plane and then he followed it and shut the wheel well lid behind him. If the Chinese security detail was paying close enough attention they would have had about five seconds to notice Frank's movements among the tires and struts of the landing gear. If he was spotted he would know it in just a few seconds as an onboard security detail would come storming into the plane's cargo hold underneath the seating deck.

The passing of several anxious minutes saw the plane finally rolling again and no guards pointing lethal weapons at Frank's head. Now confident his entry was unnoticed, Frank made his way through the cargo hold searching for an adequate hiding place.

Unfortunately for him, the passengers upstairs appeared to be traveling rather light. Behind walls of cargo netting all he could see were standard sized suit cases and garment bags. He did notice six coffin sized wooden crates, but dismissed them as food containers that would remain onboard the plane when it finally landed in China. A second glance at the crates allowed his eye to catch a black ink stamp on one of them. It stated in bold letters 'Property of Columbia University.'

An angry snarl consumed Frank's face as he shook his head, "Those thieving little bastards."

Frank pried open the lid to one of them and confirmed his suspicion. The Chinese had indeed confiscated the professor's research equipment and were transporting it back to China along with the people who knew how to use it.

At that moment Frank felt the plane rapidly picking up speed. He sat down on the floor and braced his back against the stack of wooden crates as the aircraft took to the sky. Once the jostling of initial takeoff maneuvers were complete, Frank went back to work.

He quickly emptied one of the crates with a ground emitter and Alex's laptop stored inside. He took a moment to pop the casing away from the laptop and attached his listening bug to the inside and hooked the device into the computer's central power supply. He closed it back up and proceeded to cram the computer and extra emitter inside another crate and managed to shut the lid tight again. This left Frank with a completely empty wooden box the size of a grown man to play with.

Frank fought his way through the cold and lightheaded feeling that began overtaking him as the plane rose higher into the atmosphere. Soon the unpressurized cabin would not support life anymore. He hastily lined the wooden crate with his heavy blanket and lay the oxygen tank and mask at one end. He then climbed in and pulled the lid down tightly to leave him in complete darkness.

He secured the oxygen mask over his face and turned the knob on top of the tank to start the flow of air. Instantly, Frank felt his cloudy mind clear. Next, he wrapped the blanket tightly around himself and braced for the long, lonely, and extremely cold flight.

****

Back on the Giza Plateau Mark greeted the arrival of his boss, Terrance. The man did not travel lonely as a cluster of six midnight black town cars came to a stop among the sandy vista.

Mark was not the least bit surprised to see the NSA executive committee member step out of his car still wearing a pressed suit and tie rather than grungy clothes for field work.

"Lucky for you I was attending a conference in Rome when you called," were the first words spoken by Terrance.

"Welcome back to the field," Mark exclaimed and followed it up with a nauseatingly bright smile and an extended hand.

Terrance ignored the offered handshake and simply looked back at the row of black cars and tossed his head forward as if to say 'come on already'. Dutifully, doors popped open and a cadre of hard men began stepping out.

"What do we have?" Terrance demanded of Mark.

"Six SEALs have the tunnel entrance secured while two others and I have been holding down the command area. Unfortunately, the Egyptian military showed up with a few hundred more men here and at the tunnel entrance. That should make things a little more interesting for you, but it is their country after all," Mark responded and then leaned to the side at the waist to look behind Terrance. "Now, what do you have?"

Terrance casually turned his head from side to side evaluating his surroundings. Without addressing Mark directly he answered, "Muscle, and if the President's scientific advisor is worth his salt, I should soon have presidential authority to take whatever action I deem necessary."

"There is no need for that just yet," Mark cautioned. "We have them contained for the time being so give me time with this leader of theirs."

"Speaking of time, you should be going. My plane is set to take you directly there," Terrance said as he walked past Mark like he didn't even exist.

Glancing around at the unloading cars, Mark knew the doubts he harbored about leaving Terrance alone in Egypt were well-founded. He knew the man could be heavy-handed, but soon the President would hand him unlimited authority; which likely included nuclear assets relocating to the region. The situation was definitely trouble.

Chapter 30: The Last Song

WHEN KUBLAI KHAN arrived at the besieged fortress of Xiangyang he instantly understood how the city was able to withstand the siege for so long. The imposing fortress walls stood thirty feet high and utilized the river as a natural moat that was over a hundred yards wide.

All along the shoreline his soldiers manned no fewer than a thousand traction trebuchets. These simple siege engines consisted of a tripod frame with a long arm attached at the top with only a few feet overhanging the front, while the majority of the beam's length extended away from the target. When ready, six men yanked on ropes hanging down from the short end to propel the long arm upward with enough velocity to fling a fifty pound stone high into the air.

Kublai Khan observed the crews launching their projectiles over and over with nearly every shot splashing along the opposite shoreline rather than striking the city walls.

"Come on, put your backs into it," General Kang bellowed. "Do I need the whore from my bed last night to show you how to pull on something to get results?"

That crass little barb did the trick. The six pullers proved their manhood with a mighty yank that sent the missile noticeably higher than before. A few seconds later the stone slammed into the fortress wall about six feet up from ground level and blasted out a chunk the size of a man's head. Between the time it took the trebuchet crew to reset and reload, a repair crew from the fortress was already cementing over the damaged area.

Encouraged by their successful strike, the crew launched the next projectile just as far, but scored a hit at least ten feet to the right of the first impact. A third shot fell short again as the launch crew was now tired.

"We just can't throw them far enough, often enough, and with enough accuracy to do any real damage," General Kang reported in frustration.

Kublai Khan regarded the man with great annoyance. "I have eyes, General. That inability to do damage is why I am here now."

Kang looked away from the city walls toward the new machine being assembled. "This contraption of yours will certainly throw a heavier stone, but I am not sure it will reach the target. You are building it too far back."

130

Mark Henrikson

Kublai Khan regarded the massive weapon with glowing pride. It stood twenty feet high and was built much like the traction trebuchets, only to a much larger scale. Other than sheer size, the key difference was a gigantic wooden bucket attached to the short end of the throwing arm rather than ropes. It was in the process of being filled to the top with rubble to serve as a counterweight for the contraption. Rather than using manpower, the device would rely on gravity to pull down the bucket and fling the projectile much farther than a group of men possibly could.

"Any closer and the fortress might be able to hit it with flaming arrows or caldrons to try and destroy it," Kublai countered. "Come, it looks like they are about ready to fire a test shot. If this is successful, we brought enough lumber in our wagon train to build at least four more."

The two men paced back from the shore line and climbed to the top of a thirty foot tall observation tower erected a short distance from the new counterweight trebuchet. From the top they were able to view over the walls and into the city to see people going about their daily lives as though the besieging army was not even there. That was about to change.

Kublai Khan waited for a team of ten men to load a five hundred pound boulder into the launch channel resting between the frame legs. When the crew stepped away he ordered, "Fire when ready."

Moments later a chorus of creaks and groans from the weapon's wood frame cried out as five thousand pounds of weight was set into motion. There was a thunderous crash when the counterweight bucket rotated to the low point of its drop. Frantic flapping of fabric in the wind soon followed as the sling flung the boulder high into the air.

The projectile cleared the city wall and crashed down onto a wooden bridge built across a sewer canal in the center of town. The boulder reduced the bridge to splinters and imbedded the projectile several feet deep into the ground.

Like a stone lobbed into a lake, terror rippled from the point of impact all the way out to the city walls. Women grabbed their children and dashed indoors, as if the thatched roof would provide any protection when the bombardment began in earnest.

Kublai Khan's self-satisfied glow was immediately extinguished the moment he looked back at his proud new weapon of destruction. The trebuchet still stood, but numerous cracks and hairline fractures riddled the weapon's frame. He and General Kang rushed down from the watch tower to assess the damage.

"What happened?" Kublai Khan asked.

"With that much weight set into motion and suddenly stopping, the damn thing nearly shook itself apart," the lead engineer reported while practically pulling the hair out of his head in frustration as he looked upon the frail machine. "One or two more shots like that and this weapon will be nothing but firewood."

The man paused to look at Kublai and bowed his head slightly in obedience. He did not want his words to in any way be considered a leadership challenge. "Mighty Khan, this magnificent device is your design, how should we proceed?"

Kublai Khan vented a frustrated huff through his nose and headed for his command tent. "I must meditate on it."

He did not say another word, he simply threw open the entrance flap to his tent and let it flop closed on its own behind him. Without stopping he moved into his bed chamber to consult with the divine spirit of his god. Flanking the robust flame on either side of the trunk stood two of his magnificent hound warriors.

Kublai Khan sunk to his knees and addressed his deity with the utmost respect. "Mighty god, the machine is indeed powerful as you promised, but I fear it is too powerful. It nearly tore itself apart on the test fire. My engineers tell me it will not survive launching another volley. I may need the services of your warriors to complete this conquest as I did in the Dali valley."

A shudder rippled through the divine flame upon hearing the request. "My warriors are not at your beck and call. The less they are seen the better. As for the machine, did you mount the trebuchet on four wheels as I instructed."

Kublai Khan sheepishly looked for a hole to crawl into before answering. "Actually no, my engineers assured me the machine would be too large to roll about the battlefield on wheels. A device as powerful as this needed to be anchored to the ground for stability."

"So you chose to defy your god in favor of those uneducated buffoons taking their best guess?" The flame instantly tripled in intensity as it spoke further. "I do not tolerate insubordination in my followers. You either have complete faith in me or you do not."

To emphasize the severity of the situation, the seven foot hound standing to the flame's right drew his blade and stood ready to enforce the divine will.

"I am your humble servant," Kublai begged.

"Then do as I instructed. Mount the trebuchet on four wheels and behold the wonders of my knowledge."

Kublai Khan slowly rose to his feet and bowed at the waist until his chest lay parallel to the ground. "Thy will be done." With that he backed out of the bedchamber and straightened to his full height only after the curtains had closed. Then he paced toward the machine with purpose in every stride.

Two days later the august presence of the counterweight trebuchet rested upon four wooden wheels as tall as a man and just as thick. Knowing that the device being anchored firmly to the ground caused it to nearly shake itself to pieces made Kublai Khan cringe at the thought of what it might do on wheels. However, he trusted his god, or rather feared his wrath, far too much to disobey him.

"Ready when you are," General Kang said standing next to him atop the observation tower once more.

"Then by all means," he said with a hesitant pause. "Fire."

The engineer tugged the release lever and then ran for his life. With the first firing, the counterweight bucket followed a circular arch around the fulcrum point on its way toward the ground. This time the bucket dropped straight down which rolled the entire machine backwards several feet, but then the massive frame suddenly lurched forward, adding speed and momentum to the throw as the weight effortlessly swung under the fulcrum point.

Rather than tearing itself apart with an awkward and jarring motion, the rolling wheels gave the machine a beautifully smooth and efficient transfer of energy into the trebuchet's arm and missile. Not only did the device survive the throw, the added momentum caused it to launch the boulder clear to the backside of the city and obliterated three houses before the stone finally came to rest.

General Kang's face lit up with surprise and immediately transitioned to admiration of the potential. "Brilliant."

"I'd say that is sufficient proof of concept," Kublai Khan calmly stated, while resisting the urge to perform an excited backflip. "Commence construction of the rest."

A week later five massive counterweight trebuchets reduced the city walls to rubble in a matter of hours and the Mongol army consumed the city like a swarm of locusts. For three days the horrifying wails of rape and murder filled the air and carried the three mile distance to the twin fortress around the city of Fancheng.

As Kublai Khan's army approached the new target with their massive bombardment tools, they did not even have to bother setting up. The city gates willingly opened and welcomed them with open arms.

Kublai Khan entered the city surrounded by his honor guard and was greeted by the city administrator holding the last three members of the Song royal family in irons.

"Yes, these gifts will do nicely, and I welcome you into the fold of the Yuan Dynasty," Kublai Khan declared.

Chapter 31: Indulgences

TOMAL LOOKED ON as Tonwen sat at his table atop the steps leading into St. Stephen's Cathedral in Vienna, Austria. The city had an inordinately large population of disgustingly wealthy families due to the high demands for salt found in the nearby mines.

At the bottom of the church steps stood a long line of lavishly adorned citizens wishing to ask questions about their financial contributions to the church. The funds necessary to support the production and distribution of a vaccine for the plague had long since been accomplished, yet Tonwen continued the fund raising with more enthusiasm than ever before.

Half the proceeds were sent to the Vatican to support the latest addition to St. Peters Basilica. Nearly all of the rest went to Archbishop Leonhard von Keutschach to fund yet another ring of defensive walls around his already impenetrable fortress lording over his city of Salzburg like Zeus on Mt. Olympus. Only a small fraction of the proceeds were going to support the well-being of society.

"My sister lost her son to the plague," a middle aged woman wearing jewelry expensive enough to have funded the vaccine distribution program all on its own explained to Tonwen. "The child was only four months old and was never baptized; I fear for his eternal soul. Is there anything I can do on my nephew's behalf to earn him a place in heaven?"

"Why of course there is my child," Tonwen began with his most conciliatory voice. By now he was well practiced in knowing what tone to strike with people to wring the most coin out of them. Tonwen grasped a large wooden box resting beside him on the table with a miniature statue on top of the Virgin Mary holding the baby Jesus in her arms. He moved it in front of the woman.

"As soon as the gold in the casket rings; the rescued soul to heaven springs," Tonwen declared and slapped the wooden box two times with his right hand prompting the woman to open her purse and deposit a hand full of gold coins into the coffer.

"Rest easy my child," Tonwen said while laying a hand of blessing upon her head and then dismissing her to the side so that he might fleece the next gullible fool.

Next, a man wearing fine robes that reached all the way down to his ankles stood across the table from Tonwen, mustering a laughable attempt at a contrite expression. "Bless me father for I am in need of forgiveness."

"What is your sin my child?"

"I have committed adultery with the younger sister of my wife," the man admitted.

Tonwen glanced toward the wooden coffer. "That is a grievous offense against God and his commandments."

"Will thirty pieces of silver absolve me of this sin so that I may still know the blessings of heaven in the afterlife?"

"What?" Tonwen protested and looked to take great offense. "Do you mistake me for Judas? Thirty pieces of silver?"

The man quickly adjusted his offer. "Five gold pieces then?"

Tonwen tapped the coffer with his right hand while making the sign of the cross in the air between them with his left. "May God's many blessings fall upon you."

Five heavy clinks in the coffer later the man went to stand, but was held in place by Tonwen's expectant hand. "And what about the soul of your mistress?" Five more clinks and the man sauntered away feeling renewed.

The whole ridiculous exchange was enough to bring Tomal's blood to a boil when the financial proceeds went to a good cause. Now that it was just money coming in for the sake of a fattened treasury made even Tomal's morally questionable past look quite virtuous.

Yet another individual stood across the table from Tonwen. This man wore a frilly garment of royal blue with a matching hat sporting the plucked feather of a peacock.

"Yes my son, what is your sin?"

The arrogant man did not even pretend to look troubled by his spiritual need. "I have not committed a sin yet, but a man owes me money and I need to make an example out of him. If I kill this man can that sin be forgiven?"

"The gold you contribute will need to provide medicines to save many, many lives if you have taken one," Tonwen said quietly.

"I have not killed anyone yet," the man said and then took a quick glance back at the line. "I am a busy man though. I don't wish to wait in such a long line again to pay my penance. Could I make an adequate contribution now for the sin I will soon commit?"

Twenty clinks of gold in the coffer sent the man on his merry way. That was the proverbial straw that broke the camel's back for Tomal. He stormed forward before the next contributor could approach.

"You fools don't you see what is happening here?" Tomal bellowed from the top of the steps down to the hundreds lined up below. He gestured with both arms toward Tonwen and the church behind him. "They preach only human doctrines that forgiveness and safety from purgatory may be bought. It is certain that when gold clinks in the money chest, greed and avarice can be increased; but when the church intercedes, the result is in the hands of God alone."

"What are you doing?" Tonwen insisted through gritted teeth.

"If men of the cloth are meant to serve the common good, and it is in their power to grant forgiveness and a place in heaven, are they not obliged to perform this service with no demand for compensation?" Tomal went on as though Tonwen did not even open his mouth. "No good comes from this. In fact, it is the height of evil."

Tonwen sprung to his feet and defended his work. "Money raised by indulgences is used for many righteous causes, both religious and civic in nature. A cure for the plague, construction of churches, hospitals, leper colonies, schools, roads and bridges are all results from these contributions. Not to mention the eternal salvation of these fine people's souls."

"It's evil and I want no part of it," Tomal declared and stormed down the steps away from the church and Tonwen.

Chapter 32: Half Way There

FROM THE GROUND, the five hundred foot tall burial mound could easily be mistaken for just another hillside. Its steeply sloped sides made of rammed earth were covered with trees and vegetation just like the surrounding area. However, from the air it lit up the Alpha spacecraft's range finder like a giant landing beacon.

Now two years after landing on the planet Kuanti returned to the mound after helping Kublai Khan conquer the territory with the knowledge that the earthen pyramid served as a mausoleum to Qui Shi Huang, the first Emperor of China. Specifics of the monument were difficult to come by since legend told that the emperor had all seven hundred thousand slaves who worked on the construction trapped inside with the emperor upon his burial so that its many secrets would die with them.

Local legends also stated that vast treasures lay within: piles of gold coins, a scale replica of the empire, a jeweled map of the sky along the ceiling, and rivers of flowing mercury.

Kuanti was not interested in the treasures and models, his engineering mind had other designs for the powerful structure; however the thousands of immaculately crafted clay warriors were also intriguing to him.

Kublai Khan had completed the conquest of this vast land with the Alpha's help and was now in the process of consolidating his power. Kuanti felt comfortable leaving that mundane task to Cora's relic. He planned to use his time more productively, so he made the five hundred mile trek back to Xi'an.

"Kuanti, what are you up to?" Goron asked through the mental connectivity the relics shared. You should be in Dabu with the others making sure Kublai Khan is kept properly under foot. Instead, you pull a half dozen warriors and yourself away for a cross country sightseeing trip?"

"I have an idea to share with you and the others once the planetary orbits come back together," Kuanti cryptically answered.

"That time is now," Goron demanded. "I have felt their intermittent presence for several days now, or is your mental focus so inferior to mine that you could not detect them yet?"

Kuanti allowed the insult to pass without incident. He yearned to respond to Goron's provocations, and if he had a body to engage in physical combat he would. Instead, Kuanti had to endure these mental battles. Over the past two years he found it best to just ignore Goron's incessant little barbs. Failure to acknowledge the mental hits angered him far more than any counter insults could ever achieve.

"I want sustained contact with the Mars relics before revealing my plan."

"Now should suffice," Noren's unmistakable thought pattern communicated from across the forty million mile gap between the planets. He had been Kuanti's brightest student over the years and a natural choice to lead the Mars collective while out of touch with the relics on Earth.

"Report," Goron demanded as he successfully took command of the entire collective once more.

"The second ship is half completed as is the new fusion reactor," Noren proudly declared. "I estimate another two years and we will be in a position to transport all fifty thousand residents of the colony to Earth."

"Your instructions were to quickly construct a ship capable of ferrying five hundred warriors at a time to get the migration underway as soon as possible," Goron chastised.

"Constructing a larger craft is not the limiting factor, it is building the reactor," Noren countered. "If we have the time, we may as well make the ship able to carry as many as possible."

Kuanti felt a surge of pride roll across his consciousness. His former student expertly maneuvered the conversation to maximize the perception of his accomplishment and painted Goron into a corner where he would have to acknowledge the achievement. Victories against Goron were few and far between; Kuanti reveled in it, even if it was truly his student's moment.

"Excellent work, Noren," Goron finally managed.

Kuanti decided the time was right to press his agenda. "What about the relics? Is there room on the transport for them to make the trip with you?"

"No," Noren admitted. "Though the relics individually are rather small, over half a million of them take up considerable volume. In fact, we recently had to open up another network of caves to accommodate them all. Almost every life force now is choosing to remain since they know the ability to return home is finally within our grasp. Transporting them all from here to there will take dozens of trips."

"Each of those round trips could take several months if the planetary orbits are not properly aligned. The whole process could take years," Kuanti added.

"I suppose you have a better way?" Goron snapped back.

It was Kuanti's turn to shine now. "Actually I do. The shape and size of the pyramid I am traveling toward has the ability to harness and focus energy with the addition of the gravity coils from my ship. We spotted its unique properties when our landing sensors were drawn to the structure. I believe the addition of a control chamber within the pyramid will allow me to draw the life force energy of the relics from Mars to Earth without the need for a transport craft."

"You what?" came a resounding cry from the collective thoughts; most prominently Goron.

Goron quieted the masses so he could address the issue. "Caring for and personally transporting our revered elders is natural and righteous. Exerting Mother Nature's resources and energies on the relics in the manner you suggest approaches blasphemy."

"We vilify the Novi for wasting nature's resources to reanimate the dead. This is not the same, but it is taking a few steps in that direction," Goron went on with several others voicing a similar argument.

"It is a slippery ethical slope to be sure, but given our circumstance, I strongly feel it is the best option to get all of the relics safely to this planet," Kuanti responded.

Dead silence echoed throughout the collective and everyone retreated into their own thoughts to consider the implications. In the final analysis, some found the idea repugnant, most thought it distasteful but prudent, and Kuanti was certain a surprisingly sizeable sect would not mind taking a slide down that slope all the way to reanimation.

Goron finally came down with his decision. Kuanti could feel the conflict and hesitation in the back of his leader's mind, but the order came. "You may proceed with your plans for the pyramid."

Oh I intend to, Kuanti thought while struggling to keep his elation private.

Chapter 33: Didn't Walk Here for Nothing

DURING HIS EXTRAORDINARILY long life Hastelloy had the pleasure of visiting royal palaces far too numerous to count. Over time they all, save a special few, ran together with the overwhelming grandeur of one subtly overshadowing another until the memories all ran together. At this point it took a lot to impress Hastelloy, but he was indeed awestruck by the compound Kublai Khan constructed as his royal palace. It was ornate and opulent, but above all it was vast.

As the emperor's honor guard escorted the small group of European merchants, he took careful note of the palace grounds. They included a great park eight miles square enclosed by a wall and ditch with an entrance gate midway along each side. Within this great enclosure of sixty-four square miles was an open space a mile broad, in which nearly a hundred thousand cavalry troops were stationed. These grounds were bound on the interior by a second wall six miles square.

Within the second wall lay the royal arsenals, a deer park, meadows and plush groves. In the interior rose a third wall of great thickness, each side of which was a mile in length and stood twenty-five feet tall. This last enclosure contained the palace proper. The roof was unusually lofty considering the structure itself was only one story in height; it reached from the northern to the southern wall and included a spacious court in the center from which extended a marble terrace seven feet wide, surrounded by a magnificent balustrade.

The travelers were escorted into the inner sanctum of the single story palace where the emperor held court. "Great Kublai Khan, may I present to you members of the esteemed Polo family who have traveled all the way from Europe for the purpose of establishing trade."

Hastelloy was instantly grateful he undertook the difficult task of learning the local language during their year long journey to this kingdom, thus allowing him to understand the verbal exchange. Comprehension of new languages was particularly difficult for Hastelloy, though the task was getting easier the more often he was forced to do it. Quietly he and Gallono watched Niccolo, Maffeo and Marco Polo step forward.

"Mighty Khan, we have traveled far to bring you goods from our lands for trade," Niccolo offered which was promptly translated for the emperor's benefit.

"What valuables do you offer?" the emperor asked while lifting his iron cup for a servant to fill with more wine. He took a drink and winced at the metallic aftertaste the goblet produced.

"To begin with, I can offer a vessel to hold your wine that will not alter the flavor," Niccolo said while gesturing for his son to bring forward the wooden crate he carried. The teenager set it down, and Niccolo reached down and produced a glass wine goblet. "Behold, glass blown from the finest artisans in all of Europe."

Niccolo paced forward, personally filled the glass with red wine and handed the beverage to Kublai Khan. The emperor took the glass and stared at it from all angles. He appeared fascinated at the idea of seeing his drink through the walls of its container. Finally, Kublai Khan took a mouthful, swished it around, and swallowed. Like a sunrise brightened a new day, a broad smile blossomed across the emperor's usually stoic face, "Remarkable."

"I can offer far better wares," Niccolo beamed as he pulled glass plates, bowls, and vases from the box resting on the floor in front of him.

"And what can we offer in return for such wares?" the emperor asked while holding a particularly large wine pitcher up for closer inspection.

"Spices, silks, weapons," Niccolo raffled off.

The great man suddenly lost interest in the glass objects and turned his full attention to the negotiator standing in front of him. "What kind of weapons do you have in mind?" he asked, almost as an accusation.

Hastelloy winced slightly realizing the man's mistake. Niccolo had offhandedly ventured into dangerous territory and the couple steps Niccolo instinctively took toward the exit gave evidence to that fact.

Kublai Khan's sudden rise to prominence revolved entirely around the technological advantages he held over his rivals. The secrets were tightly guarded with lethal force. A stranger trying to pry into those secrets was not welcome at all. In fact, Niccolo's next few words would probably determine if his head would leave the palace attached to his body or not.

Niccolo regained his composure and firmly stood his ground to deliver his reply. "Thousands of miles from here, in the far off lands of my origin there are wars. The combatants in these conflicts would pay almost any price for the advanced tools of war you have perfected. Why not profit from that?"

"Why would I give them my weapons for their money when I can use those weapons to take their money, land and women instead?" Kublai Khan asked, producing a round of laughter throughout the chamber.

"Yes, you could do that, but there are many kingdoms and thousands of miles between here and my intended buyers your majesty. I know. I have seen them on my way to negotiate with you. Do you plan on fighting your way through all of them to reach the gold, lands and women of my buyers who reside half a world away from here?" Niccolo asked.

The edges of Kublai Khan's mustache turned down slightly as the question suddenly muted the room's laughter, "Of course not. Even my grandfather, the divine Genghis Khan, was not able to achieve such conquests."

"Then I respectfully propose you sell the designs for your counterweight trebuchet and hand cannons to my buyers. You or your heirs will never in a thousand years cross swords with these far off kingdoms; and by that time you will have developed even more powerful weapons. I propose that for no effort on your part you can have their gold. You could even use that treasure to buy their women if you so choose, mighty Khan," Niccolo concluded to a second round of hoots and hollers from the emperor's court.

Kublai Khan still gazed intently upon Niccolo which put an end to the laughter and replaced it with a loaded silence. The emperor debated Niccolo's words in his mind for several anxious heartbeats until he finally nodded his head slightly toward the negotiator. "Your suggestion may have merit. You and your travel companions will stay as my honored guests in the palace while I consider your offer."

Never underestimate the greed of men, even one who apparently has everything, Hastelloy thought to himself as he and Gallono followed their royal escort away from the emperor's presence.

Hastelloy noticed a series of family apartments for the emperor and his wives running along the rear of the palace. Behind that, between the palace and the adjoining wall, rose an artificial mound of earth, a hundred feet high and nearly a mile in circumference at its base. The slopes were planted with evergreen trees and crowning the summit sat an ornamental pavilion which served as the emperor's private place of meditation.

"I think we should pay the emperor's private chambers a visit tonight and see what he and his advisors truly think of the Polo's offer," Hastelloy said to Gallono once their escort left them alone in the shared bedchamber along the outer balcony of the palace structure.

"It would certainly be a shame to walk all the way from Italy without gaining a private audience with the man," Gallono said over his shoulder while unpacking a pitch black set of clothes for himself and Hastelloy.

After nightfall the two men climbed over the balcony railing and scaled their way around to the secluded backside of the palace. Hastelloy hoped only a handful of guards would patrol the emperor's private garden considering the nearly impenetrable defenses around the outside, but his hopes were quickly dashed. Every hundred yards or so, a pair of sentries patrolled the hillside and its surroundings on alert for intruders who would be summarily executed on the spot.

When a set of guards moved far enough away, Gallono and Hastelloy slunk out from the shadows and dropped from the balcony into the garden. Gallono absorbed the fifteen foot drop with a graceful summersault to the side that brought him behind a wide evergreen tree without a sound. Try as he may to remain quite, Hastelloy let out a faint grunt when he collapsed to his knees upon landing and barely managed to stagger behind cover before another pair of guards came near. Both men drew their daggers in case the pair got curious, but they passed without incident.

"You sure you're up for this old man?" Gallono teased. "Because I am not walking all the way back here from Egypt if we get caught on account of you sneaking around like a bull set loose in a glass factory."

"Yah, yah," Hastelloy whispered and gestured for the two of them to move across the stone paved walkway to begin climbing the tree covered hillside. The two moved in a leapfrog pattern. One took a forward position, verified the coast was clear and then signaled the other to move up. That man then assumed the forward position and signaled the other to move again when it was safe.

Gallono gave Hastelloy a wave which sent him creeping past his first officer and becoming one with a pine tree twenty feet ahead. Just when

Hastelloy was about to signal Gallono forward, an unusually quiet set of guards rounded the tree Gallono used for cover. The pair paused to look around the general vicinity, but eventually took a noticeable interest in Gallono's hiding place. Something caught their attention.

While the two guards had their backs turned to Hastelloy making their way toward Gallono, he floated out into the open and approached them from behind. The moment one of the guards reached for the soft bristles of the tree, Hastelloy jammed the business end of his dagger into the guard's unprotected neck. He looked over to the other and found Gallono's dagger had delivered a similarly fatal blow to the other guard.

"I can't take you anywhere," Hastelloy sighed while the two quickly dragged the bodies under the tree's low hanging canopy and moved on up the hill toward the ornate temple.

The structure had three layers of curved roof lines stacked upon each other which culminated in a sharp point at the top. Beneath the roof lay an open air gazebo with a stone altar occupying the center. Immediately in front of the altar there was a kneeling pad for prayer.

The temple was unoccupied, but the two did not dare come out of hiding or venture too close. If Goron's relic was indeed the driving force of Kublai Khan's rise to power, Hastelloy knew from prior experience that the Alpha relic had the ability to detect other life forces nearby. Just to be safe, Hastelloy and Gallono took positions on opposite sides of the building and patiently waited.

While silently occupying the shadows they perfected their camouflage coverings by adding pine branches, sap and grass to the point that they were both practically invisible by the time Kublai Khan made his journey to the hilltop temple to consult his deity. It was an odd contradiction to watch an emperor powerful and arrogant enough to reside in such a palace lower himself to his knees and bow before the stone altar.

"I seek your guidance once more," Kublai Khan said from his knees with his arms out wide and chin in his chest. "Foreigners from a far off land offer the opportunity we have been looking for to enhance the treasury to begin the next round of conquests."

"Go on," came a soft, almost feminine voice that sent Hastelloy's adrenal glands pumping. It was Goron's relic, it had to be. The three sets of protective walls, the army of cavalry, and the dense web of interior guards. It was not for the emperor, it was for Goron.

After a thousand years spent searching since the fall of mighty Rome, Hastelloy was finally in position to put an end to the Alpha interference on this planet once and for all. Then his crew could finally focus all their efforts to pull this civilization out of the dark times and on the road to technological progress once more.

"The merchants of course offer to buy our spices and silks, but they also wish to sell our weapon designs to far off kingdoms," the emperor reported.

"And this strikes you as a wise thing to do," the voice asked with a hint of amusement in the tone.

Kublai Khan also sensed sarcasm in the words which caused him to look up in confusion. "We could charge them dear and never run the risk of facing them in battle. I fail to see the downside of making such an arrangement."

"Giving up one's primary advantage is not wise at any price," the voice instructed. "Now tell me about the negotiators. Who are they, how did they learn of our weaponry, and what makes you think you can trust them?"

Before the emperor could deliver his response shouts of alarm rang out from halfway down the hillside. Moments later two towering guards in full armor and headdress dashed from the tree line. Their height was such that the two needed to duck down in order to fit under the swooping roofline as they entered the temple and stood behind the emperor facing the altar.

Hastelloy was prepared to interpret their words spoken in Mandarin, but the series of harsh barks and growls took his mind a moment to process. He was in fact translating the Alpha language.

"Intruders have killed two palace guards just down the hillside," one of them reported as he removed his helmet to reveal the long furry snout and pointed ears of an Alpha.

The sight of two live Alpha warriors still on the planet plunged Hastelloy's stomach into a tailspin. His mind kicked into overdrive trying to play out the scenarios that could lead to a set of Alpha warriors standing in front of him at that very moment.

Had they survived the original crash in Egypt and remained hidden? No, they would have helped Goron back then.

146

Were the Alpha here in force with warships in orbit ready to conquer the planet? No, why would they wait. Why would they be messing around with this human and his little empire? The questions in his mind had no end.

"Quite a coincidence that this intrusion accompanies your new visitors don't you think, Kublai? Do you still think you can trust those men?" the whimsical voice asked rhetorically. "Kasin, escort the emperor back to his palace."

"I will see which members of the merchant party have not been accounted for every second of this evening and put them to the sword," the emperor declared while rising to his feet. He then followed his escort as they both ran down the hillside leaving the relic alone with its foot soldier.

"I just informed Goron and Kuanti of this," the mystic voice reported. "If it is the Novi, they most likely think I am Goron's relic, therefore all their efforts at subterfuge will be focused here rather than his stronghold on the western continent."

"With this fortress, the army, and Alpha warriors protecting you and Kuanti's relic; I like our odds," the Alpha guard stated with excitement hanging from his every word. The giant of a being looked excited enough to jump out of his own sizeable skin. "The thought of a Novi being almost close enough to reach out and strangle with my own paws is almost too much to bear."

"Yes, it's nearly enough to make me want to violate nature and reanimate just for the opportunity to kill one of them myself," the voice added. "How I envy you. Generations spent eking out an existence on that barren red planet has amounted to this, and destiny has chosen you to lead the physical fight, but not yet."

"Yes, one more year," the guard vented. "One more year and the entire colony from the fourth planet will be here so we can end this once and for all and get our transmission out."

"While we wait for that great day why don't you round up the others and search every tree limb, branch, and blade of grass on the grounds," the voice ordered. "I doubt you will find anything, the Novi captain has proven far too clever over the years to commit such an error, but surprises can happen."

Surprises can happen indeed Hastelloy thought while watching the Alpha duck out from under the temple roof and bound down the far hillside letting loose a blood curdling howl as he went to summon his companions.

Hastelloy and Gallono then patiently made their way off of the hillside and out of the palace since their cover was now hopelessly blown.

Gallono was the first to finally break the silence between them while they walked westward along the shores of the Yellow River. "Well that was certainly informative."

Hastelloy just shook his head in bewilderment at the sudden turn of events. He didn't even know where to begin.

"Come on, look on the bright side," Gallono said. For good measure he put his arm around Hastelloy and gave him a playful shake to lighten the mood. "At least we didn't walk all way from Europe for nothing."

Chapter 34: The Right Tool

"ARE YOU PLANNING on walking all the way back to Italy with your tail between your legs?" Gallono finally asked Hastelloy. He had remained silent for most of their two day hike up the Yellow River in order to leave his captain alone with his thoughts and careful planning. Gallono could be a very patient man, but this was getting ridiculous.

Gallono tried to skip a flat rock across the river surface out of frustration, but only succeeded in making a small splash with the first bounce. "Let's review what we know. There are at least three Alpha relics on the planet now instead of just one. We're not sure how many, but there are definitely Alpha warriors alive and well here also. What are they waiting for?"

"Reinforcements," Hastelloy finally spoke. "From that conversation we overheard, it sounds like there is somehow an Alpha colony on the fourth planet. Mars comes closest to Earth in another eleven months. At that time I believe we can expect another shipment of Alpha and relics to arrive. At that time they will locate the jamming signal coming from the Nexus chamber, and it will be check mate."

"How the devil do you think the Alpha established a colony on the fourth planet anyway?" Gallono wondered aloud while attempting unsuccessfully to skip another stone across the river waters. "Escape pods from the battle that landed us here?"

Hastelloy immediately shook his head as though he had already reached a conclusion on this matter a day earlier. "No. We saw no escape pods jettison from their ship after our torpedo hit severed the engineering section from the rest. Besides, the fourth planet is almost uninhabitable and would require far more resources right away than a few escape pods could provide."

"That leaves us with the runaway engineering section then," Gallono concluded. He had to give the Alpha credit for that one. "If that's the case, they survived a massive explosion, and then managed to get half of a crippled ship under control enough to guide it in for a safe landing. That took some stones."

Hastelloy added his praise as well. "They established a colony and made it thrive to the point they can now build sophisticated communications equipment and space craft."

"It's not like they had the benefit of the Nexus to reanimate after death," Gallono went on. "They had to do it the old fashioned way and made it a multigenerational effort."

"It's not the first time," Hastelloy responded. "They spent ten generations building their fleet before launching the war machine against us. They are a very dedicated species when their collective efforts get behind a goal."

Gallono suddenly felt his feet turn to lead weights anchoring him in place. The full severity of the situation suddenly hit him, and it was more than he could bear. "They landed on Mars almost four thousand years ago. By now there must be tens of thousands of them waiting to land and take over."

Gallono picked up another oddly formed rock and hurled it toward the water with all his might and succeeded in generating three awkward skips before the stone plunged below the water's surface. "We can't fight against that even if we had a hundred years to prepare, and all we have is eleven months at best to try and stave off Armageddon. We're completely boned."

Hastelloy came up next to Gallono and spent a few moments staring at the ground. Finally he picked up a flat, rounded rock that was almost a perfect circular disk. He casually reared back and threw it sidearm across the water with relative ease. Gallono marveled as the stone took monstrous skips across the water. It must have bounced thirty times before a soft clink from the far shoreline let him know the stone made it safely across.

"There is more to success or failure than brute strength," Hastelloy said in a calm, level voice while pointing toward the stone now resting two hundred feet away on the far shoreline. "It's about having a good plan and the right tools to accomplish the end objective."

Gallono allowed a sardonic chuckle to escape his lungs. "You just got lucky; this is the dry season and that river is not twice as wide right now."

Hastelloy grabbed both sides of Gallono's head and forced him to look up river until his eyes met a dam made of cut stone, dirt, and rubble that stood over thirty feet tall and three hundred feet across with a dozen flow doors open to allow water from the massive reservoir created behind to gently flow into the river. "Luck had nothing to do with it my friend, that dam did."

The hands holding his head in place were removed and took with them Gallono's state of melancholy. He liked where Hastelloy was heading and he continued following in his footsteps upriver.

"Before this dam was put in place, this river would flood uncontrollably in the rainy season and dry up completely the rest of the year. That dam allows the controlled release of water so the farmers have a steady supply year round. I think it's time we revert back to the old ways, don't you?"

Chapter 35: Operating Above the Law

PROFESSOR RUSSELL AND Alex passed the time on their flight to China pretty much in silence. The first eight hours were spent more or less unconscious as they both caught up on some much needed sleep. The soft cushions of the seats combined with a warm blanket and pillow to lay their heads on was infinitely more accommodating than the cold hard floor in the captivity cage inside the Sphinx.

When Brian and Alex both awoke, they were careful not to say much of anything: important, mundane, or otherwise. The assumption was that every word they spoke was being monitored by their host.

Chin spent his time aboard the flight in the forward compartment immediately behind the cockpit. They did not even see the middle aged man until the engines of the aircraft wound down and the nose tilted forward to begin their descent.

"We will be landing in Xi'an Xianyang International Airport in a few minutes," Chin reported.

"Wait, I thought we were going to Beijing," Alex said, still rubbing the sleep out of her eyes.

Chin pulled his head back slightly in genuine surprise. "What gave you that impression? The pyramids are out in the countryside, and dozens are located near Xi'an. It makes no sense to land in Beijing and then drive six hundred miles to reach any of the pyramid sites."

Brian was as equally unfamiliar as Alex about the size and scope of China's geography, but he was certainly familiar with the name of its most prominent archeological site. "Xi'an? Am I right to assume that we'll begin our research by mapping the inside of Emperor Qin Shi Huang's burial mound?"

Chin bowed his head slightly to acknowledge Professor Russell's familiarity with his nation's history. "Yes."

"Who is Emperor Huang and why is his final resting place so special?" Alex asked.

Brian could not stop himself from shaking his head in disappointment at his assistant's statement. Alex was a wizard with machinery, but her

152

knowledge of history was rather wanting. "Qin Shi Huang was the first Emperor of China. The man was so concerned about the afterlife that he constructed a scale model of his entire empire and built his burial mound over the top of it. He then tried to protect it with an army of clay soldiers."

"Oh, you mean the Terracotta Army?" Alex asked.

"See, you do know your history," Brian applauded.

With the plane making its final descent, Chin took a seat across the aisle from Brian and Alex to continue the conversation. "Our government has strictly forbidden anyone from entering the burial chamber located inside the mound. We are therefore left with investigating the great monument from the outside only. That is where the two of you and your wonderful mapping techniques come in."

"Why not just go inside; why is it forbidden?" Alex asked. "If you know where the burial chamber is located why not open it? If it has truly been untouched for all these years then what's inside would probably make the discovery of King Tut's tomb look like the unearthing of a few broken pots."

"For better or worse, superstition is a prominent factor in Chinese culture," Chin instructed as the plane's tires touched down. "Legend states that if the tomb is opened, then the collapse of China will immediately follow."

Professor Russell jumped in with his more cynical reasoning for not opening the chamber. "Plus the burial mound is a major tourist attraction with the mystery of what lies inside still out there. If you open the doors and nothing is there then the mystique will be gone along with all the tourism dollars."

"That is certainly a concern to some," Chin conceded.

Brian felt the plane lurch to a stop and a melodic tone sounded throughout the cabin to let the passengers know it was safe to stand and exit the plane. Chin was the first to his feet and extended a hand toward the front of the aircraft. "After you."

On his way down the gangplank steps to the tarmac, Professor Russell looked to the rear of the plane and saw his six coffin sized wooden crates being offloaded onto a waiting transport truck. In front of the transport idled three Mengshi off road vehicles, the Chinese equivalent to the American Humvee. These beastly looking jeeps were all black rather than sporting any attempts at camouflage painting that a military vehicle would employ.

Before Professor Russell followed Alex into the back seat in one of them, Brian considered how odd it all felt. There were no customs agents checking the crates or verifying travel papers. Everything he knew about China and its government pointed to a regime that bordered on a state of paranoia; the lack of security was quite disconcerting.

As the convoy of vehicles sped away from the airport and passed through a security checkpoint without even slowing down, Brian could not shake the feeling that Chin was somehow operating outside his government's authority; perhaps even above it in some way.

Chapter 36: An Early End

MARK USED HIS time on the eleven hour flight from Cairo to St. Louis wisely – he slept. He could tell his mental edge was slipping. He couldn't even maintain a constant train of thought to formulate the big picture and his next moves. Considering he was about to come face to face with the leader of an alien presence that had been on earth for over four thousand years, Mark thought it best to be well rested rather than pouring over reports to be well read instead.

It had been an intense thirty-six hours since he last closed his eyes to recharge. He was afraid his mind would have too much going on inside to allow sleep, but the instant he reclined his leather seat back flat and put his head on a pillow it was lights out. Ten hours later he awoke with a clear head and an energized body ready to continue the good fight.

Thanks to the plane flying with the time zones, it was still midday in St. Louis when he arrived. On final approach Mark stole a quick glance out the window to see his favorite feature of the city. Along the Mississippi River front near the downtown skyscrapers stood a reflective, stainless steel arch that rose six hundred and thirty feet toward the heavens. It was a profound monument to the pioneers of the 1800s who conquered their fear of the unknown to boldly expand the nation westward. He drew inspiration from their strength in order to conquer the unknown he now faced.

The small plane did not even come to a full stop before the exit door immediately behind the cockpit was let down allowing Mark to charge down the built-in steps and climb into an awaiting Suburban SUV. The oversized vehicle sped away, left the airport grounds and headed east toward a downtrodden neighborhood that lay directly in the airport's landing pattern.

Mark looked around the vehicle to take a head count. Four local NSA agents were all he had to work with. "We certainly bring the heat when faced with a threat on American soil don't we?"

"Terrance deemed the situation too sensitive to involve the local authorities, and he does not have presidential authority yet to engage the nearby National Guard units," the driver reported. "Besides, we are just going to pick up one man. How hard can that be?"

Mark let the disapproving sneer on his face give the clueless man his answer. At least Terrance did not have presidential authority yet, that was a bit of good news. Mark half expected to wake from his flight to find the entire planet at war with the western power that dropped a nuke on a sovereign Middle Eastern nation.

The SUV rocketed into the parking lot of the Henderson Home Psychiatric Facility which stood a single story high with a dark brick exterior and tall, narrow windows every fifteen feet. The building sat in a valley relative to the neighboring buildings; which happened to be poorly maintained government housing.

Mark could scarcely believe his brother, who was so smart and talented, wound up earning a meager living in a dump like this place. He could be in Hollywood or New York City having the rich and famous pay him obscene amounts of money to whine about their oh so tortured lives. Instead, he earned peanuts tending the incurably insane. He never understood what drove his brother to do this.

With the Suburban parked just outside the front door, Mark and his four helpers stepped out of the vehicle and ran up the narrow sidewalk to reach the entrance shaded overhead with a rickety awning. Mark ripped the door open, but forced himself to actually walk down the long corridor to reach his brother's office in order to not raise too much alarm. He was among the insane right now. They were unpredictable at best so the less disruption the better.

Mark stepped through the open door into the outer office where a strikingly attractive young woman with long dark hair still in her early twenties looked up at him with patient eyes. Ah, Tara, she was exactly how Mark pictured her based on the voice he'd heard over the phone numerous times.

"Dr. Holmes is in a session at the moment, can I help you with something?" Tara helpfully asked. When Mark's four travel companions entered the room a moment later she sprung to her feet in alarm. An index finger pressed against Mark's lips was enough to keep her silent, however.

"I'm his brother, Mark, and he's expecting me," he said quietly and then drew a pistol that had been tucked into a holster near the small of his back under his sport coat. The other four men drew their weapons as well while Tara helplessly looked on in silence.

Mark raised the gun to eye level and reached out with his left hand to turn the knob and nudged the inner office door open. As the six panel white door slowly rotated open, he returned his free hand to the pistol grip and moved into the room leveling his two-handed aim straight at a man seated across from his older brother.

"The session's over," Mark announced to the room while his four companions fanned out around the office.

Chapter 37: We Meet at Last

"OR THE REAL session has only just begun," Jeffrey heard his patient say. For his part, Dr. Holmes was left completely speechless by the sudden armed entry of his little brother into the office. Even though the guns were not leveled at him, Jeffrey was quite sure he needed a change of pants, yet Hastelloy sat cool as a cucumber eyeing Mark as he crossed the room holding a steady aim.

Jeffrey had never seen this side of his brother before; the cold professional. When they got together for holidays and shared vacations it was all jokes and stories of the foolish antics of their youth. Now the little boy he once watched ride his bicycle head long into the back of a parked truck without even looking up stood with a deadly weapon drawn on a man sitting six feet away.

Seeing his brother now brought back the nightmare which interrupted Jeffrey's troubled sleep the night before. In his mind, Dr. Holmes could still see the primal anger in Mark's eyes. Even now he held the same two-handed grip on his weapon as he did in the dream.

Jeffrey felt a cold shiver dance its way up his spine when he recalled the imagery of following his brother, out of loyalty, into his office only to be saved by Hastelloy when his brother turned out to be a monster. In the end, a lifetime of familiarity with Mark won out over a single bizarre dream. That concluded, he still did not like the way Mark was going about things. Hastelloy was a patient under his care after all.

Without even consciously deciding to do so, a wave of professional ethics prompted Dr. Holmes to spring from his chair and stand between his patient and Mark with his arms open wide to provide as much protection as possible. Staring down the barrel of a loaded handgun made Jeffrey's knees buckle a bit, but he defiantly held his ground to ask, "What is the meaning of this?"

"Jeff, get out of the way. Like I told you on the phone, this man is dangerous in a way you've only read about, and he is coming with me."

"To what end?" Hastelloy asked in a very conversational manner. "I am perfectly happy to carry on a discussion with you right here NSA agent Marcus Andrew Holmes."

The last five words passed through Jeffrey like a bolt of lightning to electrify every nerve ending in his body, and make the hairs on the back of his neck stand at full attention. He wasn't sure which realization was more shocking: that the patient knew his brother's full name, or that his brother worked for the most secretive intelligence agency the world over.

Either was enough to prompt Jeffrey to turn around and face Hastelloy with his jaw dropped open wide enough to swallow a battle ship whole. "You two are familiar?"

"Never in person, but when being hunted, it is always wise to know the hunter better than he knows himself," Hastelloy responded while still remaining seated as if the therapy session were still continuing uninterrupted.

Mark stepped around Jeffrey's human shield to stand alongside his brother and put his deadly aim back on the target. "I recently became acquainted with him after spending some time with his partners in Egypt."

"Above ground or below?" Hastelloy questioned.

"Inside your little hiding place if that's what you're trying to get to," Mark snapped back.

"Whoa, wait, what?" Jeffrey stammered.

"Yeah," Mark said with a raised eyebrow and a confirming nod of his head. "It's inside the Sphinx with a three mile tunnel leading to it just like he told you."

Hastelloy shifted his gaze to Jeffrey and looked upon him with grave disappointment. "Shame on you, Doctor, for divulging information told to you in strict confidence. I am very disappointed."

The stern glare then morphed into amusement as he looked back toward Mark who was still pointing a pistol at him. "Then again, this moment might never have happened without your transgression."

"And what a special moment it's been," Mark taunted as he grabbed Hastelloy by the wrist to yank him to his feet. "Now it's over and you're coming with me."

In a blindingly quick motion, Hastelloy yanked Mark towards him with interlocked hands and turned his shoulder under Mark's armpit. The resulting hip toss landed Mark sprawled across the couch clear on the other side of the coffee table with his own gun pointed at him in the hands of Hastelloy.

It all happened so fast Jeffrey's mind barely had time to recognize the complete turn of events before Hastelloy addressed Mark in a commanding tone that only comes from a lifetime spent in military service. "If I truly intended either you or your brother harm, then believe me, harm would be done."

"Drop it or I drop you," one of Mark's armed accomplices shouted.

Hastelloy regarded Mark with the acerbic smirk of a man who owned the moment. "We both know killing this body will not do you any good."

"It will get a gun out of my face, remove my brother from a dangerous situation, and render you trapped back in Egypt," Mark responded calmly as he repositioned himself to sit comfortably upright in the couch with his arm draped over the backrest.

Hastelloy held the kinetic stare between the two men for an extra heartbeat and then turned his aim toward the ceiling and released his grip on the weapon so it hung from his index finger by the trigger guard.

Mark tossed his head to the side slightly which prompted one of his men to take the gun out of Hastelloy's hand. "Cuff him and let's go."

"If I am taken from this room, I will not utter another word and your opportunity to finally have answers will have slipped away from you once more," Hastelloy declared.

"Oh believe me, you'll talk," Jeffrey heard his brother say with a cold hard edge to his words even an arctic freeze could not match. As a humanist, the very idea that his government once used torture on captives during the height of panic following the events of 9-11 brought him deep sorrow and shame. The insinuation that his brother was about to employ those same detestable tactics on the patient standing before him was enough to send Dr. Holmes into action.

"Keep him here, in my office," Jeffrey offered. "Hastelloy has been talking to me for weeks and seems perfectly willing to continue talking right here. What good will relocating him do if the patient is adamant about not talking anyplace but here?"

Mark Henrikson

Mark looked upon his brother as if he were the most naïve person alive. "He is not simply a patient. He used you to get to me. He is an extremely dangerous terrorist who must be taken into custody."

"Funny, you've spent five minutes with him and think you know everything," Jeffrey responded with a very hurt undertone. "I have spent a week and a half getting to know him, and I am telling you your best bet for any kind of answers is talking to him right here. Have these guys stand guard inside and out while the two of you talk. I have other things I need to do outside this office anyway."

"The three of us will talk," Hastelloy objected. "If Dr. Holmes stays as well, I give you my word you will have answers with no escape attempts from me."

A skeptical scowl from Mark prompted the patient to then look directly at Dr. Holmes. "Have I not always been a man of my word?" He then looked back at Mark to ask, "Do we have an accord?"

Mark got to his feet once more and peered intently at Hastelloy taking measure of the man's honor. Next he looked at Jeffrey who did his best to convey to his brother that he did take Hastelloy at his word. Finally he eyed one of his team members. "Two outside the building, two right outside the office. Call for backup and close the door on your way out."

With the room's occupancy down to three, Hastelloy and Dr. Holmes sat down in their chairs once more with Mark sitting across the coffee table on the couch. "Pardon the interruption; please continue," Mark said with legs crossed and hands clasped neatly in his lap.

Chapter 38: Get In Line

"WHY DO WE have to walk so far, Father?" Pang asked for about the hundredth time. It was all Liu could do not to turn around and slap the boy. The Sheng family did not have much, but they did have the tradition of quietly carrying their burdens with pride and honor. There was no honor in the constant whining of his son. The boy was eleven years old now, it was time he understood his lot in life and accepted it.

"We go because master Zhu has called a meeting of the Lords," Liu said between huffs. The journey on foot was indeed long, especially without any food in their stomachs to give them energy. The flood that came from the incompetently maintained dams upriver washed away his crops and food stores. Then the drought caused his planted seeds to wither away in the ground. "Besides, what else is there for us to do now besides sit and die staring at our barren fields?"

The purpose of the gathering was almost certainly to discuss a rebellion against the current emperor. At first Liu did not carry any particular love or hate for Kublai Khan and his leadership. So long as his taxes remained reasonable and the leadership competent, what did he care to whom the proceeds went. Truth be told, even if he were forced to contribute a few extra bushels of wheat per season, it was not worth picking up a sword and risking his life in battle.

Competent leadership was the issue, however. Maintenance on the dams was neglected for years in favor of constructing the emperor's palace; a grotesquely massive and opulent city unto itself. Now the nation starved, and it was time for change, but it would not come easy. Dozens of minor lords constantly fought amongst themselves, but only a unified effort would prevail against the emperor and his legendary armies.

Talk of rebellion could wait, however. Pang's unusually loud whimper let Liu know it was time for a break. He spotted a semicircle of rocks under a large tree by the roadside with a fire pit still smoldering from a traveling party's encampment the night before. "Come; let's rest for a few minutes to regain our strength."

Liu removed his circular straw hat and leaned it against the tree as he sat upon one of the stones. He allowed the sack slung over his right shoulder to fall off to the ground and he reached in to pull out the last fist sized steamed bun for him to share with his exhausted son.

He tore the roll in two and handed half to Pang. "We only have a few more miles. We'd have been there last night if your constant complaining did not force us to stop so often. You are almost a man now. In two more years you will be married and working a farm of your own to support a family of your own. You must accept your responsibilities. To do otherwise is a waste of effort."

"Our family has no food, we should be home hunting so mother and the twins can survive," Pang protested. "That is our responsibility, not marching across the countryside to a worthless meeting."

The selfish arrogance Liu observed in the next generation brought him great sorrow. "Men who are our betters have ordered the gathering. We are under Master Zhu's care and must trust that he knows best."

"And Zhu is under the emperor's care and now orders a gathering to talk about rebellion," Pang countered. "He questions the wisdom of authority over him, and we should do the same rather than just blindly following orders. I only trust our masters to do what is best for them, not us."

Liu vented a huff of frustration through his nostrils and licked the last bread crumbs from his hand. He then snatched his straw hat and fastened it to his head once more and continued walking along the dirt road. Pang did the same and ran to catch up to his father, matching his angry strides. The young man knew better than to press the matter further. The two made the rest of the journey in silence.

A silent hour later, Liu heard the rhythmic beating of horse hooves approaching quickly from up ahead. The dirt road came to a peak in another fifty feet which he recognized as the last hill to climb before master Zhu's fortress came into view. The thunderclaps drew near and Liu put his arm in front of Pang moving them both well off to the side of the road. An instant later a panting black blur whooshed past, and it was not the last. In all, ten horses with riders blew past without a word.

"I wonder what has them in such a hurry," Liu asked as the two continued walking in the weeds alongside the road just in case more would follow. As they crested the hill they were able to see hundreds of tents, large and small, set up across the landscape surrounding Zhu's fortress.

Ten minutes later Liu and his son reached the gatehouse with the portcullis drawn closed with a guard standing firm on the other side. "We are here for the gathering."

"It's over," came a gruff reply.

"What do you mean?" Liu asked with a sense of futility at having made the long journey for nothing. "The banquet was last night and talks were to begin today."

"Everyone at the banquet is dead, poisoned by the emperor."

"E. .everyone? Even Zhu?" Liu managed in a profound state of shock.

The sentry shook his head to the side and allowed a faint smile to grace his lips. "No, Master Zhu fell ill but survived thanks to the care of two visitors from the west. Now he rallies all the banners behind his cause to seek revenge."

Liu let out a heavy sigh of relief at the news. He did not know any of the other lords so he did not mourn their loss. In fact, he drew encouragement from the news as the squabbling factions were suddenly united in a common cause to overthrow that Mongol monster from the north. Kublai Khan was an animal without honor who oversaw an army of animals. When a dog turned rabid it had to be put down, and Liu was honored to join the effort to avenge the wrong perpetrated against his master.

"How can we be of service?" Liu asked, but the question met deaf ears as the guard's attention was turned behind him with the approach of an armed column of pike men marching toward the gate.

"Open the gate," a pale skinned foreigner with an exotic accent ordered in passable Mandarin. The man must have been one of the foreign visitors serving as Zhu's military advisors in return for saving his life.

As the pike men marched past, a second foreigner stopped in front of Liu and Pang. "Who are these two?" he asked of the guard with the same exotic accent as the other man shouting orders to the marching column.

"Late arrivals for the gathering," came a crisp reply from the gate guard.

"Fortune seems to favor you; now grab a pike and get in line," the foreigner ordered in a tone that left nothing for debate. Liu did as ordered without a second thought and Pang followed suit.

Chapter 39: Bombardment

THOUGH HE WAS the architect for it all, Valnor could scarcely believe he was once again standing outside the stout city walls of Constantinople. Three months. Once Sultan Mehmed II was convinced to invest the resources needed to build the monstrous cannon, it only took three months to lay the molds, forge the massive bombard and transport it into position to menace the city.

Accompanying the grand cannon were about eighty thousand of the Sultan's closest friends, including ten thousand Janissaries who served as his elite infantry. This compared to roughly seven thousand defenders who seemed unconcerned by the siege. They knew that many had tried and failed to take the city. They were confident that so long as the walls stood the ratio could be a million to one and the city would still hold out.

As Valnor stood alongside the Sultan under the sizeable shadow cast by the massive cannon, he observed that the walls of Constantinople now looked much less forbidding than before.

"You had better be right about this," Sultan Mehmed said coldly.

"I am," Valnor answered. "However, even with the Theodosian Walls leveled, if all their defenders are focused on our entry point they will inflict heavy losses upon your men."

The Sultan slowly turned his head to look right at Valnor and delivered his cold reply. "In the end, war always turns into a bloody business. Such is the life of a soldier."

"We can make that life much easier on your men by threatening to open a second avenue of attack on the city," Valnor offered. "We should make the naval blockade a credible threat for attack along the Golden Horn. That will force them to man the battlements along the sea wall drawing thousands away from the real point of assault to make victory that much easier and less costly to your ranks."

Sultan Mehmed dropped his arrogant façade for a moment to consider Valnor's suggestion. "That is a worthwhile plan, but they have stretched a series of boom chains across the entrance. There is no way to get through the opening and threaten a landing."

"The peninsula reaching out to create that narrow mouth is only about a mile wide if I am not mistaken," Valnor pondered. "It would not take much to cut the trees and create a road of greased logs to transport galleys over land and into the waters of the Golden Horn."

"Could that really be done?" the Sultan asked one of his many generals clustered around the massive cannon being assembled.

The officer looked at the thirty foot long metal body of the cannon and then at the five dozen oxen used to haul it into position. "Those ships are certainly no heavier than this cannon. I do not see why it would not be possible. It will take a few days to accomplish, but with the three hour reload time this bombard weapon requires between each shot, we should have the time to spare."

Sultan Mehmed pursed his lips in contemplation and then finally gave his orders. "Make it happen. Now, let us see what this grand weapon I spent so much treasure building can do."

All but the crew of twenty men with cotton wadding in their ears stepped a hundred yards back from the cannon. A gunner holding a billowing torch looked up for permission from his Sultan to light the fuse. Mehmed raised his arm and thrust it toward the city walls. An instant later a bone jarring explosion sent a six hundred pound piece of stone on its way.

Five long seconds later, Valnor watched the boulder strike ground three quarters of a mile away. It landed twenty feet in front of the wall and then slammed into it on the second bounce. Even with the severely reduced velocity, the strike managed to topple the upper half of the wall in a section fifty feet wide. The awesome power of the weapon was undeniable.

Valnor lowered the lens of his magnifying viewer and handed it to Sultan Mehmed to inspect the impressive damage inflicted by just one shot that, in reality, was mostly a miss. He looked over at the cannon in time to see the last remnants of smoke clearing away and the crew already at work reloading the weapon with the explosive black powder he concocted for this occasion.

Valnor ran over to the crew to make sure the next shot was even more impressive. "Raise the angle half a degree and load one of the specials now that we have the range set."

To pass time, the Sultan and his entourage of officers adjourned for their midday meal and returned in time to watch the second shot sent on its way.

This time the projectile buried itself into the base of the wall on the fly causing the section of wall to teeter and lean but not crumble.

A few seconds later the fuse on the metal ordinance reached the black powder stored in the center. The resulting explosion blasted the section of wall completely apart with large fragments sent several hundred feet into the air. When the smoke cleared, a gaping hole a hundred feet wide with a crater ten feet deep appeared where the proud defensive wall once stood.

"One down, eight to go," the Sultan proudly declared.

The results were better than Valnor could have ever expected, but he also knew they all would not fall this easily so he needed to temper Mehmed's expectations. "The outer section of city walls was constructed in the eleventh century and is by far the weakest. This will take time, Your Majesty."

"Not nearly as much time as starving them out," the Sultan commended. "Move in the regular troops and take each layer of walls as they fall. Continue the bombardment night and day until we reach the inner city, then send in the Janissaries to finish this business for good."

True to Valnor's prediction, progress after the first ring of walls fell was much slower. The key factor slowing things down was the weapon's propensity to overheat from excessive use. The gunner crews learned early on that loading the cannon too soon after firing left it hot enough to ignite the black powder on its own with disastrous effect. Dozens of crewmen had lost their lives to premature explosions, but the bombardment pressed on.

Eventually, after a month of constant assault from the massive cannon, everything was set for the final push. The navy had drawn thousands of defenders away to the sea walls, and the cannon was bracketed in for one last explosive shell that would unleash the elite Janissary infantry unimpeded into the city.

Before ordering the final shot, Valnor experienced a disheartening moment of introspection. Constantinople was the last echo of prosperity remaining from the Roman Era. The Empire's capital city was relocated to Constantinople not long after the fall of Rome. In his previous existence as Augustus Caesar he almost singlehandedly forced the great empire to be a guiding light for the developing world to follow. Now here he was fifteen hundred years later giving the order that would bring down his creation once and for all. He lamented the loss, but as Captain Hastelloy would boldly declare, it was for the greater good.

"Fire," Valnor ordered and through the darkness of midnight he saw the distant explosion level what was left of the city's last line of defense. A minute later he heard a collective battle cry rise up from the eager Janissaries and bloody tyranny was unleashed upon the last great Roman city.

Valnor followed the flow of Ottoman soldiers into the city as the defending troops retreated towards the harbor. This left Constantine and his loyal guards to their own devices. To his credit, the emperor and his men managed to hold off the Janissaries through the night until morning, but eventually the weight of numbers won out.

In his final moments, Constantine threw aside his purple regalia and led the final charge against the incoming Ottomans, dying in the ensuing battle among the streets along with his soldiers. The man may have lacked the vision to use Valnor's cannon design for his own benefit, but in the end he was indeed quite brave.

After the initial assault, Sultan Mehmed's soldiers fanned out along the main thoroughfare of the city. He had the forethought to send an advance guard to protect key buildings as he did not wish to establish his new capital in a thoroughly devastated city.

The army converged upon the Augusteum, a vast square that fronted the great church of Hagia Sophia. The bronze gates were barred by desperate civilians seeking divine protection inside the building, but none would come. The doors were breached in short order and the troops separated the congregation according to what price they might bring in the slave markets. Such was the scene around the great city as Sultan Mehmed allowed his men to plunder the rich metropolis for three days after the fighting ceased.

Valnor had no interest in the financial treasures found in the posh districts of the city. Instead, he made his way to the university to see if the scholars were more inclined to share their knowledge with the world at large now that their safe haven was no more.

Chapter 40: Rebellion

CORA FELT THE presence of Kublai Khan along with four Alpha warriors approaching her revered location on top of the temple mount inside the palace. These last few months had been the most frustrating of her existence and she was anxious to get an update on the situation.

With the assistance of some advanced weapons, Kublai Khan's army was able to conquer the entire eastern continent and consolidate power in the span of a few years. How could the masterful plan progress so well for so long only to fall apart in the span of a few weeks?

It all started when the levees broke along the Yellow River. The retention basins behind the levees designed to feed crops gradually throughout the dry season emptied in a matter of hours flooding every farm within twenty miles of the river's winding path. The entire harvest was washed away along with millions of farmers who worked the land and most of the grain storage silos. The coup de grace came a few days later when all the water finished draining into the sea leaving nothing with which to replant.

Without agricultural production, the economy ground to a disastrous halt. There was no food or water to maintain the men and cavalry so Kublai Khan's armies melted away until only the most loyal remained, leaving his once firm grip on power tenuous at best.

Rebellious ideas instantly took hold of the peasant population and the soldiers that had deserted joined their ranks. Emboldened by their numbers and the desperation of their situation, the peasant army now converged on the royal palace to oust the man they all felt angered the gods to bring these hardships upon them.

Cora could tell immediately that Kublai Khan was seething, and the fact that he did not even bother kneeling before the altar proved it. "I am besieged and need your help. The peasants have broken through the outer walls, overrun the remnants of my cavalry and now ready siege equipment to topple these walls."

"Report," Cora demanded of her soldiers, completely bypassing the insignificant individual barking complaints her direction.

"The situation has grown desperate. If you intend to leave, we need to go soon or not at all."

"L...leave?" Kublai Khan stammered. "What do you mean leave? You instructed me to build this palace for your protection..."

"No," Cora interrupted, "I instructed you to build a fortress. You were the one who turned it into this eccentric monstrosity that has drawn the hatred and ire of the common man who suffers crippling poverty in the shadow of your opulence."

"What do we do now?" Kublai Khan asked while the four Alpha warriors lifted the cover off the stone altar and removed Cora's shimmering relic. The emperor immediately dropped to his knees and bowed at the reminder that he was addressing his god.

If Cora had eyes she would have rolled them at the pathetic display. To a small degree, she actually respected the man while he tried to stand his ground, but now with his face buried in the dirt he just looked impotent.

"You will take what forces you have left and retreat toward Lake Poyang to the southwest. The freshwater lake there was unaffected by the flooding and you can once again feed your men and horses," Cora instructed. How this whelp managed to lead anyone was beyond her comprehension she thought as her four guards placed her relic inside a wooden carrying case and headed for a hidden tunnel that would take them beyond the palace outer walls.

"If I were you I'd hurry," Cora snapped which sent the little man scampering down the hillside leaving her alone with her men.

"Have the others remain with him to facilitate his escape. He may be an incompetent weakling, but we still need his armies to keep the Novi occupied and distracted from our real objective. Then you four can take me to Xi'an to help Kuanti with his work." Considering the Kublai Khan business handled, Cora mentally opened up to the other relics on the planet.

"Getting a little harsh in your old age?" Goron mocked. "The soft cuddly Cora I knew back on the ship would have bent over backwards to nurture that weakling along."

The intensity of rage Cora took from that insult could have incinerated her carrying case. "When did I ever show that kind of weakness?"

"Your continued devotion to Kuanti back on the ship and in the afterlife is all the evidence I need to know you have a soft spot for weak things. Isn't that right, Kuanti? Kuanti?"

Cora felt Kuanti's existence, but her former mate was completely closed off from her and Goron. Even the intense insult could not bring his attention away from his current project.

****

Hastelloy observed a soft rustling of foliage near the tunnel exit that coincided with a faint vibration from the tiny handheld device he carried. Hastelloy looked at the three inch square display and observed four of the ten tracking barbs he placed on the concealing vines were on the move, presumably clinging to the clothing or fur of the four Alphas.

It took Hastelloy and Gallono weeks of meticulous searching to finally discover the back door exit from the royal palace that they both knew existed. Dealing with Goron and his minions over the millennia taught him that there was always an emergency escape route when a relic was involved.

The covert tunnel was hidden among the vine covered walls of a nearby cemetery crypt. Though well disguised, the raised landscape and direct line to the royal palace gave it away.

"Wow, would you look at them go," Gallono marveled upon seeing the land speed of the tracking device exceed forty miles per hour. "We never could have kept up with that, even on horseback."

"You can outrun me, but not a tracking transmitter's radio signal," Hastelloy said quietly. "Now let's help Zhu and his rebels finish this siege; then we can move on to follow them now that we know where they are headed."

Chapter 41: 95 Theses

TOMAL APPROACHED THE church doors with hammer in hand and a need for revolution in his heart. In the beginning, convincing people they could purchase god's favor served a greater purpose. It had the good intention of financing a project that brought about an end to the plague claiming millions of lives across the continent. Now it seemed the road to hell was paved by those good intentions.

The church now gave its de facto blessing to amoral behavior, particularly in the case of Tonwen selling forgiveness of actions prior to them being carried out. It was evil and had all the markings of a tool the Alpha would use to manipulate parishioners.

Pausing at the base of the cathedral steps, Tomal gave his actions one last thought. Once he openly betrayed Tonwen and his sale of indulgences, there was no turning back. He would once again be working against the interest of his crewmate.

A moment later Tomal steeled his nerve and ascended the steps. He knew in his heart he was right, this evil had Goron's paw prints all over it. He lifted two hand written sheets of paper to eye level against the door and then drove an iron nail through the top of them both. He stepped back and admired the two sheets hanging from the church door for all to read.

The first sheet was entitled *The Ninety-Five Theses on the Power and Efficacy of Indulgences,* and what followed were ninety-five numbered arguments supporting the assertion that since forgiveness was God's alone to grant, those who claimed that indulgences absolved buyers from all punishment and granted them salvation were in error. At the bottom of page two he boldly signed the document with the name of his current identity so all would know this was not the work of a commoner, but an academic study by a Catholic monk named Martin Luther.

The ninety-five points were admittedly overkill to pose the simple inflammatory question: Why does the Pope, whose wealth today is almost without end, build the basilica of Saint Peter with the money of poor believers rather than with his own money? It was necessary, however.

Eventually the position would be heavily scrutinized by biblical scholars. These learned men, some with pure intentions while others carrying loaded political agendas, would cross reference every word and syllable against the Bible. In order to hold up against these examinations the position needed to be air tight and covered from all angles; thus the ninety-five points.

Not at all satisfied with his little act of rebellion which would only garner attention from the local parish, Tomal headed to a local book publisher with a second copy of his theses with a much wider audience in mind.

****

Tonwen sat atop a horse-drawn carriage as it passed through the gates of the local monastery in Weinsburg, Germany. A month earlier he received permission from the local bishop to sell indulgences to his parishioners, and it was now time to settle accounts.

His arrival was greeted by the finely robed bishop himself along with six monks dressed in their typical brown hooded coverture. The moment his cart stopped, the monks silently went to work unloading the two wooden chests resting in the cargo hold.

As Tonwen climbed off the cart he was greeted by the bishop. "Good day to you, Friar Tetzel. I hope my fine flock of dedicated believers greeted you with the same warm hospitality they show me."

"Most did your grace; however, some seem to have their thoughts corrupted by the writings of that Martin Luther fellow," Tonwen reported. "A few reacted most violently to my arrival while others simply refused to listen to my words or contribute to their salvation."

The bishop took Tonwen under his arm and guided him into his office. "I take it those chests are not nearly as full as usual when you finish your work in a particular area."

A dejected expression followed by a subtle nod from Tonwen let the bishop know his assumption was correct.

The bishop sat Tonwen down in front of his desk and then walked over to a bookshelf along the near wall. "When I received my first book produced by that marvelous new invention, the printing press, I praised God. At last the written word could be mass produced and purchased for a modest price."

The bishop raised his hand and slowly circled it around the room to point out the endless array of shelves packed full of leather bound books in his office. He then retrieved a particularly thin book and tossed it onto the desk and took his seat on the other side. "Now I curse its existence for it allows the vile teachings of Martin Luther to spread quicker than the plague. Two weeks is all it took for the whole of Germany to hear his filth thanks to the endless reproduction of his words. Three months later all of Europe speaks of nothing but that man's ninety-five theses."

Tonwen picked up the book and started thumbing through it with an angry stare that threatened to set the pages ablaze. "My sales grow less and less with every passing week as the teachings of that heretic persist."

"How much was the final tally?" the bishop apprehensively asked.

Tonwen took out a piece of parchment from under his robe and laid it across the table facing the bishop. "One hundred and twenty gold pieces, your grace. Half was put into the first wooden chest for your order to keep. The rest I placed in the second chest for you to transport back to Rome so that the Papacy may have its share to further the construction of St. Peters Basilica."

"And the cost for transporting that chest of gold back to Rome will come out of..."

"Your portion," Tonwen jumped in to finish the bishop's sentence.

The bishop shrunk back into his chair and gazed out the window with a troubled stare. "Naturally." He drew a frustrated breath and shook his head. "Much as it pains me to admit it, Martin Luther does raise one good question. What on earth could the Pope possibly need with all that money?"

"Those sixty pieces of gold, less the cost of sending a man to Rome and back of course, will not even fund our outreach to the community," the bishop went on. "Food to the poor, traveling priests, and schools..."

"Books for your library," Tonwen added, which brought the tirade to a quick end. "Much good is done with the proceeds, but let us not pretend it is all noble."

The bishop absorbed Tonwen's rebuke with a simple nod. "Perhaps, but this library still benefits everyone in this monastery. The Pope does build a great basilica from which all Catholics may draw inspiration. Tell me, what greater calling does Archbishop Leonhard von Keutschach of Salzburg serve by adding defensive walls to his castle?"

"Who is he?" Tonwen asked. "I find it odd that I am unfamiliar with a man so elevated in the church."

"He's new," the bishop snapped, obviously annoyed with having to report to the man. "Rumor has it he is still struggling to pay off the debts he incurred while buying his elevated position from his holiness."

The bishop suddenly leaned forward in his chair to fold his arms across the desk. "Not to worry, you will likely get to know him very well. Of all the church voices to lash out against the statements made by Martin Luther, the Archbishop's has been the loudest. He, more than anyone else, needs the proceeds from selling indulgences to continue in order to retire his debts and fund his useless construction project."

Then the bishop's interwoven hands allowed the index fingers to escape and point directly at Tonwen. "You, my good sir, are the most prolific seller of indulgences in the whole of Europe. When the archbishop finally mounts his biblical challenge against this Martin Luther under charges of heresy, you can be certain he will be relying on your insight and testimony."

"And he shall have it," Tonwen exclaimed. "I believe wholeheartedly in my work. I am saving souls and benefitting the church and society at large while tending to the faithful. If this archbishop truly is intent on fighting Martin Luther and the evil he spreads, then I shall make his parish my next destination."

"You do that," the bishop said on the way to his feet. "In the meantime, you can rest assured that the Vatican will receive its share of your services to my parishioners."

"Of that I have no doubt," Tonwen replied on his way to the door. Just before leaving the bishop's office he looked back and added, "After all, I have already sent the accounting results on to the Vatican. They will be expecting it within a fortnight."

That last statement caused the bright smile to run away from the bishop's face carrying with it any notion of short changing the Pope.

Tonwen hated to leave the bishop in such a depressed state. Before turning to exit the chamber, he reached under his brown robes and produced a thick roll of pages and handed them to the bishop. "One man did not have any coin to contribute to absolve his sins, so he turned over these pages. I gave them a quick look; they appear to contain a design for an unusual weapon. I hear the Duke of Helfenstein here in the city is always looking for new and improved weapons for his men. You may be able to sell the designs to him and raise some extra funds for your community outreach. That was not included in my account to the Vatican."

The bishop unfurled the cluster of pages and Tonwen saw a broad smile once again grace the man's lips. He clearly liked the potential.

Chapter 42: Heresy

TONWEN LED A team of two horses pulling his wagon under the city gates of Salzburg and instantly understood the significance of the place. This city was the point where Italian and German cultures met, and that fusion of clashing cultures visually played out across the city skyline.

Against the backdrop of snow-capped mountains, sharp gothic spires rose toward the heavens from churches built right next to distinctly Italian domes capping other churches and government buildings throughout the city. Resting tall and proud on an overlooking cliff face sat the fortress of Hohensalzburg, home to Archbishop Leonhard von Keutschach.

The bright midday sun hit the white stones of the castle's walls and inner keep with dazzling effect. The monstrous fortress seemed to almost glow pure white while casting a darkened shadow over the city below.

While traveling a narrow road that zigzagged its way up the cliffs to reach Archbishop Leonhard's fortress Tonwen took notice of three things. First and foremost was that the castle would never be taken by force from an attacking army. The steep ascent, five layers of walls, and endless array of archer slits rendered the fortress nearly impregnable.

His second observation was the castle's use of a rail system down the steepest portion of the cliff face to bring up supplies. It used a system of pulleys and counterweights rather than some version of a modern locomotive of course, but to his knowledge this was the first such rail line in existence and was a concept way ahead of its time. It allowed the fortress to remain in constant supply without even having to open its gates.

The third, and most comical feature of the fortress Tonwen noticed, was a small outcropping along the tall outer wall of the castle keep. At first he did not know what it was. It just looked like a solid stone wall that had a box measuring two feet wide and deep by five feet tall added to it.

As he drew closer to the odd structure, Tonwen noticed a circular hole on the bottom of it that gave him a clue as to its use. How fitting, Tonwen thought, that the Archbishop could turn his back on the city of commoners below and defecate on them without needing to even leave the comfort of his fortress.

Tonwen passed through a gatehouse that was still under construction and was shocked to see the Archbishop himself just inside the gates. The man pulled his attention away from inspecting the building progress the moment he heard the guard announce the arrival of Johann Tetzel.

"Friar Tetzel, it is an absolute pleasure to welcome your now legendary services into my flock," the Archbishop said with open arms as Tonwen climbed off the cart. He apprehensively moved forward to accept the unexpected embrace when the Archbishop let one arm fall away leaving a hand holding the ring of his office extended. Tonwen resisted the urge to laugh at the transparent power play and instead meekly knelt before the Archbishop and kissed his ring. "The pleasure is all mine your grace."

Archbishop Leonhard basked in his position of power for a moment and then prompted his lesser to rise once again. "Your valuable services could not have come at a better time."

"It seems to me that I come at a time of great peril for the church," Tonwen said with confusion. "Everywhere I go more and more of our faithful seem to turn towards the demonic teachings of Martin Luther. In some towns I, a loyal man of the cloth who faithfully ministers only for the eternal salvation of others, have come under attack."

Tonwen pointed to a stain on his dark brown robe. "In Munich they went so far as to assault me with rotten food; tomatoes to be exact."

Archbishop Leonhard shook his head in disbelief. "The unrest grows more brazen with every passing day. First, the illiterates shout out challenges to the teachings of learned men such as you and I. Next, they pelt the clergy with rotten food. I feel they will soon grow bold enough to rise up in rebellion against those who care for them the most in favor of that man's heresy. That is why I build more walls, so that the faithful may have a place of shelter if the mounting unrest persists."

"Do you really think it could come to that?" Tonwen asked.

The archbishop gestured toward the stain on Tonwen's chest. "They assaulted you didn't they? We must go after the source of the unrest, this Martin Luther."

Tonwen stood aghast at the insinuation. "You do not mean...I mean even if the almighty saw fit for Martin Luther to die of natural causes tomorrow, his teachings are published and in the hands and ears of the public. To right the situation we must prove publically that his teachings are not in keeping with the Bible and therefore in error."

"And thus explains my delight in your arrival," the Archbishop interrupted. "His holiness has ordered these ninety-five theses to be examined for heresy by a panel of experts, and you my good friar are the quintessential expert on the subject of indulgences."

"I am of course privileged and honored to participate, but when and where will this examination take place?" Tonwen asked.

"In Rome, as soon as that slithery serpent can be apprehended," the archbishop declared.

"Rome?" Tonwen repeated with a shake of his head. "Martin Luther will never submit to that, and with the abundance of supporters he now has, the only way you will get that man in front of a heresy examination panel will be voluntarily."

Archbishop Leonhard let out a soft growl realizing there was truth in Tonwen's words. "What do you suggest we do then? We cannot simply allow the man to freely poison the thoughts and actions of the faithful. It will lead to anarchy."

"We all know the results of a heresy examination in Rome are a foregone conclusion, and his words of protest would fall on deaf ears," Tonwen offered. "If the examination were to take place here, up north among his followers at an impartial location, then I believe he would come out of hiding voluntarily to make his case."

The archbishop's face lit up with excitement at the suggestion. "Yes, I like it. And when he is found guilty he will perish in front of his followers as an example."

"No!" Tonwen challenged. "He must be given the chance to recant. It is not enough that he dies, that will only make him a martyr and strengthen his cause. He and his followers must be made to understand that they were wrong."

"But how do we do that?" Archbishop Leonhard interrupted.

"By making our case," Tonwen declared. "There is no need to rig the outcome. We all know that The Bible supports our case and not his. If the examination is conducted thoroughly and properly, then the outcome of a true doctrinal examination is not in doubt. Martin Luther will then be made to see the error of his ways and recant."

"And if he doesn't?" the archbishop asked with a skeptical look.

"Then we will have him in custody and can do it your way, your grace," Tonwen concluded.

"Excellent. I offer you my private library and study to prepare the arguments while I make arrangements for the examination to be conducted at an impartial location in the north."

Tonwen was ecstatic to have the archbishop join his cause against Tomal and his blatant efforts to bring down the church he labored so hard to set up as a guiding light for society to follow in these dark times.

Chapter 43: Animation

CORA WAS NOT easily impressed, but the size and meticulous shaping of the pyramid mound was truly impressive. With modern machinery it would take perhaps a few months to complete an earthen pyramid standing five hundred feet tall and a quarter mile long on each base. The time and manpower to complete the project with rudimentary tools available to these people two thousand years ago was just staggering.

"That is one big pile of dirt," her carrier observed. "Do you know where Kuanti and the others are inside?"

"The entrance sits about a mile east of the mound, and he has guards stationed there at all times who should show us where to go," Cora said.

As her party approached a cluster of four human guards, it did not take Cora long to realize they were also being tracked by a pair of Alpha warriors. They were doing an admirable job of remaining hidden along the far tree line in case they were needed in a fight to repel intruders.

Realizing the newcomers were fellow Alpha warriors caused them to step out of hiding and escort them toward a set of stairs descending into a brightly lit tunnel.

Kuanti must have felt her presence drawing near. For the first time in months, she was able to feel his excitement through his surprisingly stout mental barriers. Something was off though. This was not the mild excitement one might feel before reuniting with a long lost friend. This had the feel of true elation at achieving the grand accomplishment of a lifetime. It put Cora on edge and caused her to look around before being carried down into the tunnel.

Her carrier stopped in his tracks and saw the same phenomenon she did. Harsh sparks and crackles at the tip of the pyramid coalesced into a bright blue light which grew in intensity until suddenly the amassed power pushed downward and out across the four sides of the pyramid. Without a sound, the flash of light washed over the nearby landscape and finally dissipated into the ground like it never was there at all.

The event may have carried no sound or physical impact, but the toll it took on Cora was profound. The animated presence of Kuanti, overwhelming only seconds before, was nowhere to be found. She had shared his mental presence for thousands of years and now it was completely gone.

"What in the name of Mother Creator was that?" Cora insisted.

One of the human guards, who looked almost bored with the whole ordeal, delivered a lazy reply. "Something to do with the new chamber they built inside. It happens at least half a dozen times a day. Don't worry, you will get used to it."

By the laws of nature I will not, Cora thought. "Get me to that chamber immediately. Something has happened to Kuanti's relic. I can feel it, or rather don't feel it."

Her carriers knew better than to ask questions given the urgency in Cora's words. They descended a wooden set of stairs that brought them nearly thirty feet underground. The ten foot wide subterranean corridor would not have felt claustrophobic at all if the ceiling were not so low that the pointed ears of the Alpha scraped along it.

The group moved with purpose for a hundred feet until the tunnel opened up to a forty foot high domed expanse two hundred feet wide and eight hundred feet long. It contained eleven parallel corridors paved with small bricks running east to west. The ceiling was supported by large beams and posts. The wooden ceiling consisted of reed mats and layers of clay for waterproofing. Above ground the structure would have looked just like any other rolling hill.

Facing east and standing at full attention were thousands of life-sized clay soldiers complete with armor, spears and swords coated with chromium oxide to keep them sharp enough to still split hairs.

"What is this place?" Cora asked of their two escorting Alpha warriors.

"About fifteen hundred years ago the fool buried inside that pyramid had a clay army created and set into place to protect his tomb in the afterlife," one responded while leading them between the rows of the inanimate protectors.

Cora admired the craftsmanship as the party made their way through. Each figure had the same basic body shape, but the armor, hair styles, and facial features were all subtly different. "What a waste. That superstitious fool actually thought these clumps of baked clay would come alive to defend him against his enemies or grave robbers?"

She focused her attention on the last soldier standing at attention on the left before they entered another cramped tunnel. Even the figure's mustache showed the fine detail of individual hair follicles. Just when they were about to move past the last clay soldier, a reddish tan arm with a razor sharp blade in its hand crossed their path.

"I find the man to have been a true visionary," the suddenly very animated statue said in the Alpha language.

Without hesitation, one of Cora's protectors grabbed the statue by the throat with both hands and attempted to squeeze the life out of it, but the life-sized figure just laughed.

"Surprisingly durable aren't they?" the statue went on and then delivered a swift punch to the Alpha warrior's stomach that sent him staggering back several paces, "and strong too. Cora you really need to try this."

All six Alpha warriors made ready to gang tackle the statue before Cora finally regained her composure and spoke. "Kuanti, is that you?"

"In the flesh; as it were."

"You...you've reanimated?" Cora managed. "How can this even be possible?"

"The clay that makes up these statues consists of organic materials and minerals," Kuanti instructed. "Given the right transfer of energy, the iron metal can magnetically attract a life force and the organic cells reanimate to allow physical movement once more."

"Energy? You used Mother Nature's precious energy to reanimate your life force once more?" Cora asked in disbelief. "That is the very essence of the Novi's Nexus device that we despise. It's...it's blasphemy."

Kuanti lowered his sword wielding arm to his side and shook his head in frustration. "No, it's not. The pyramid focuses the gravitational forces at work between this planet and its sun. If not used, that energy dissipates without benefiting anyone or anything. I'm not diverting any of Mother Nature's resources away from anything other than the cold, harsh vacuum of space. Come, follow me. You'll see, you will all see."

Without another word, Kuanti moved his newly animated clay body into a corridor that would take them under the pyramid and into the burial chamber. As they all walked the only sound that broke the eerie silence were the heavy, wet footfalls of Kuanti as he lumbered along in his new form.

The shock of it all was too much for Cora. Her mental barriers let down to allow Goron's consciousness inside her inner thoughts.

Even from four thousand miles away Cora felt the full intensity of Goron's rage. "HE DID WHAT?"

"I know," Cora communicated and quickly regained control of her thoughts. "I don't even know where to begin to address this with him."

"There is no beginning," Goron insisted. "There is only an end. You must put an end to this. He intends to bring every relic from Mars to that pyramid and some might choose his path. This could corrupt our entire society, the very essence of what it means to be the Alpha race and not vile abominations of nature like those Novi."

"I know," Cora responded instinctively to the idea of reanimation.

"Do you?" Goron asked with a healthy dose of doubt. "I've been inside your head. Remember?"

Chapter 44: Pawn Sacrifice

"WHAT IS IT with you and large naval engagements?" Gallono asked of his captain on the deck of a modest sized vessel that served as Zhu's flagship for the fleet.

"Oh come on. Once every thousand years isn't that excessive," Hastelloy chuckled while surveying the nearly one thousand vessels in the fleet.

"Next time could you please arrange it so we have the advantage? This being outnumbered three to one stuff, and the enemy having larger ships to boot, is getting old. Are you out to try and prove something?"

Gallono just shook his head as he looked out across the open waters of Lake Poyang. The massive body of fresh water stretched for almost five miles in every direction, but obstructing the view straight ahead was the remnants of the Huang forces assembled to present a formidable armada.

Most intimidating were the highly vaunted tower ships which were basically one hundred foot tall floating fortresses. Each of them featured heavy timbers for armor, hundreds of archers and a half dozen catapults to devastate any vessel unfortunate enough to venture too close. Their only weaknesses were a complete lack of mobility and a requirement to remain in deeper waters during battle.

To combat these shortcomings, the enemy positioned their bulwarks in the lake's center, thus forcing the attackers to come to them. Enhancing the impenetrable center even further were chains running between the ships to hold them together and afloat in case any of the virtually unsinkable boats did start to founder.

Hastelloy put his arm around Gallono. "My friend, have you ever known me to voluntarily give battle when I didn't have the advantage?"

****

When Liu was given command of his own boat he beamed with pride at the great honor bestowed upon him and his son. Zhu and the other great men leading this fleet trusted them to execute instructions without hesitation, and Liu vowed never to let them down in that duty.

Even with the absolute faith Liu carried in the wisdom of his leaders and his vow taken, he found the orders almost impossible to follow. Liu put his arm around his son to steady the young man, and by extension himself. Pang was actually quite brave for his age, but staring straight ahead at a towering blockade of floating fortresses launching arrows and flaming balls from catapults was enough to shake the nerves of a hardened veteran, let alone a wide-eyed farmer and his eleven year old boy.

"Steady. We have our orders to sail directly at them to provide a distraction for the rest. We must trust the wisdom of our betters," Liu said as they both took cover under a makeshift canopy aloft over the steering wheel area to avoid the disturbingly accurate archery fire coming from the enemy ships. Repeated thumps let him know the straw men in clothing positioned around the deck were taking the brunt of the blows.

"Do you trust this is best for them or us?" Pang cynically asked.

To draw strength, Liu and Pang looked behind their boat expecting to see they were not alone in facing the monstrous tower ships, but they were. The trailing fleet was now separating to sail left or right of the floating fortresses leaving Liu's ship and six others on a similar course to fend for themselves. That was the first moment when real doubt entered his mind.

His doubts vanished when he saw dozens of his own ships launch flaming canisters of pitch toward the enemy, but the trajectory looked low. In fact, it looked almost directed at him and the other six vessels sailing directly at the enemy's center. Before his mind could fully comprehend the situation, two flaming canisters landed on the deck of his ship and exploded with flames that quickly engulfed the entire boat.

Dozens of smaller explosions raced across the deck letting Liu know his ship was rigged to blow. He grabbed Pang by the shirt and raced for the railing amid a barrage of enemy arrows and friendly flames alike.

By the searing heat, Liu knew his clothing was on fire, but the plunge below the waves extinguished them immediately. He surfaced with Pang in his arms in time to see the boat he once so proudly commanded plow in between two tower ships. The tiny boat lurched to a stop, but the flames continued moving and spilled over the railing onto the enemy ships. The transferred inferno seemed to double in size with every passing second.

The flames did not take long to find the pitch cauldrons and black powder magazines of the tower ships, igniting deafening explosions that shot tall pillars of fire into the air throughout the fortification towers. Like a suddenly disturbed anthill, men piled out of the towers and jumped overboard to escape the flames, but only a few made it out before the flames and smoke suffocated and charred the soldiers within.

Liu and Pang thrashed and swam with all their might in the water to get away from the blazing heat and flaming debris falling on top of them, but it was no use. As the massive vessels began sinking beneath the waves, suction was created that held them in place and inch by inch drew them in.

Liu drew some comfort from the knowledge that his sacrifice had most likely won the battle. The fact that he and his son would not live to know for sure stole much of the moment's luster, however. In the end, his eleven year old son was far smarter than his blindly obedient father. It seemed great men did indeed do what was only best for them.

Chapter 45: Lake Poyang

"I HATE WHEN we have to do that," Gallono said while holding a blank stare at the blazing inferno that used to be the enemy's impenetrable center formation. "Those poor bastards aboard the fire ships never had a chance."

"Command decisions always come down to the greater good," Hastelloy responded. "Today a few dozen men were sacrificed allowing the rest of our forces to carry the day, thereby making it possible for us to continue safeguarding the twenty million Novi lives in the Nexus."

"Is this all for their greater good or ours?" Gallono countered. "Millions were washed away and drowned when we sabotaged the dams. What makes the Novan lives inside the Nexus more valuable than those lives lost to incite this rebellion?"

Hastelloy hardened the lines around his eyes as they bore down on his wavering soldier. "The fate of these humans and us are conjoined. If the Alpha win and finally get their transmission out, billions of lives will be lost. It is all for the greater good, Commander, now get with the program. This still isn't over."

Gallono visibly straightened his posture and pushed the crisis of conscience aside when Lord Zhu stepped in behind Hastelloy for an update on how the battle progressed. "Looks like the perimeter you advised us to set up is working to perfection," Zhu observed without emotion.

"Their larger ships can't outrun ours and are being corralled back into the flame engulfed center without any difficulty. I'd say the outcome of this battle is almost a certainty at this point," Gallono agreed.

"That is usually when a desperate enemy finds the nerve to attempt the unexpected - when they have nothing else to lose," Hastelloy responded with a matter of fact statement and then silently looked upon the scene of battle to evaluate his enemy's next move.

It was difficult to see much of anything with the towering inferno in the center throwing deep, dark smoke hundreds of feet into the air. He could feel the wind starting to pick up, and saw the tower of smoke begin to lean westward. He then shouted orders to the flag signalers, "Relocate the flag ship grouping directly downwind from their center."

Immediately the three signal men began snapping the flags held in each hand to relay the message to the other ships.

Zhu looked over at Hastelloy as if he had just stuck his head in a tiger's mouth. "We won't be able to see anything coming through the smoke wafting that direction."

"Yes, and neither will they, which is why they would only attempt to flee that direction en masse as a measure of last resort," Hastelloy answered.

A few minutes later the cluster of twenty five ships entered the smoke screen to the chorus of deckhands coughing and tearing strips from their shirts to tie over their mouths and noses. The measure helped with breathing, but still did nothing for the eyes which burned nearly as hot as the flames generating the smoke.

After five long minutes of torture, through the smoke and his tears Hastelloy saw the outline of five ships approaching at suicidal speeds. Unable to change course in time to avoid collision, three of the vessels smashed into Hastelloy's ships. The entanglement held those ships in place long enough for other boats in the fleet to ram them on their sides, sending the doomed vessels to the bottom of the sea in short order.

Another ship broke left out of the smoke screen and was quickly corralled back toward the flaming center by the rest of Hastelloy's fleet.

The fifth ship was another matter. It was smaller and far more maneuverable than the others and managed to navigate the crowded waters admirably. With the wind at its back, escape was a distinct possibility.

Zhu's flagship was running nearly perpendicular to the escaping ship's path. Hastelloy evaluated the waters ahead and spotted several light patches along the fleeing ship's path. Time was short and required Hastelloy to react more out of instinct than clear thought.

"Force them toward the shallows on the starboard side and take us in," Hastelloy ordered.

For the second time in less than a minute, Zhu looked at Hastelloy as though he'd lost his mind. "We'll bottom out."

"Precisely," Hastelloy replied as he grabbed Zhu and braced them both against the upper deck railing before the vessel lurched to a grinding halt against a barely submerged sandbar. Zhu attempted to stand after the initial jolt, but was yanked back down to the deck by Hastelloy. "Not yet."

The enemy ship had been on course to pass immediately behind Zhu's flagship, but the sudden stop of the boat put them on an unavoidable collision course. Twenty feet away, Hastelloy watched the menacing iron ram charge headlong into the broadside of his ship.

The crash was colossal with railings and deck timbers snapping like toothpicks as the enemy vessel plowed halfway through the hull before also grinding to a halt. A shower of a half dozen bodies rained down from the decks of the enemy ship as several sailors did not adequately brace themselves for impact in time.

On the open waves, the fleeing vessel would have plowed right through the side of Hastelloy's ship and kept right on sailing. However, with the boat lodged against a sand bar, the enemy vessel ran headlong into an immovable object. Neither vessel would ever sail again; the fight was now on to claim supremacy over the deck.

There was no need to give an order for the sailors to grab a sword and prepare to repel boarders; the situation was self-evident. He saw a dozen of his men climbing the riggings with a bow and quiver of arrows slung over their shoulders to take the advantage of an elevated firing position. Nearly everyone else already had a sword and shield in hand and braced for a fight.

Hastelloy's eye passed over the decks of the enemy ship to assess their crew compliment. He was quite relieved to find them thoroughly decimated from the battle already. He did see movements among the tall masts and sails letting him know archer fire from above would be an issue for both sides.

Soon the hiss of arrows filled the air above as the archers focused the fire on their counterparts on high rather than the enemy below. Hastelloy released an adrenaline filled breath and attempted to calm the heart threatening to beat its way out of his chest. An instant later a pulse stopping war cry rose up from the enemy decks, and no fewer than fifty men stormed over the railings with their single objective being the death of Lord Zhu. Win or lose this little engagement, the attacking sailors knew they were all dead men when the rest of Zhu's ships arrived. That being the case, they charged forth to decapitate the rebellion's leadership.

The initial wave was not the problem. Those sailors armed with swords and axes were met with similar weaponry and skill. The real trouble came from the second row of ten attackers who leveled spears tipped with long, round cylinders that looked like honeycombs.

Hastelloy and Gallono recognized the dangerous hand cannons immediately and planted Zhu face down on the deck and followed with their own bodies to allow the shrapnel to hopefully pass overhead.

Explosions from the hand cannons leveled the ranks in front of them. Both friend and foe alike fell to their fury leaving the deck completely enveloped with a dense fog.

Hastelloy was the first one back to his feet. He charged headlong into the cloud and took a hack at anything that moved. As the brisk winds cleared the smoke, Hastelloy became a little more choosy where he swung his blade. To his surprise, Gallono did not engage. The commander stood back and dropped his sword in favor of a handful of star shaped disks with razor sharp edges.

In rapid succession he flipped the throwing stars at the attackers who busied themselves with preparing another volley with a second set of hand cannons. Like dominoes, each of the ten men crumpled to the deck while grasping a piece of metal lodged in their throat.

Hastelloy's sword along with archer fire from above was able to finish off the remaining attackers giving him a moment to catch his breath. He was about to draw his first lung full when the crash of a body to the deck from up above caused him to jump back several feet.

He looked up toward the source in time to see six gigantic figures leaping from mast to mast and scaling their way down to the deck with ease. The massive furry figures landed with a collective thud that probably would have sunk the ship on its own had it still been afloat.

A demonic war howl rose from the intruders as the Alpha warriors set about their trade. The overwhelming speed and strength of their race was on full display as they cleaved men in half with a single swing of their sword. They leapt twenty feet in a single bound to maul less brave men who fled from the intimidating sight.

Gallono did not hesitate. He jumped over the balcony railing bringing his sword straight down into the back of an Alpha warrior inducing a death wail from the target as Gallono moved on to the next. He did not try to block their powerful blows with his sword; instead he expertly dodged the strikes and delivered a counter blow that always drew blood and often left a severed limb twitching on the deck. One by one, the Alpha warriors fell to Gallono's skillful hand until only one, who realized the caliber of foe he faced, remained.

"Only a Novi who's lived a thousand unnatural lives could be this skilled with a blade," the Alpha declared in its language while he circled Gallono testing his defenses with halfhearted blows before going at him with blinding speed. Gallono dodged half a dozen swings without finding an opening to deliver a counter strike.

Finally the Alpha managed to line up a slash Gallono was unable to step away from. At the last moment, he raised his sword hand to deflect the blow and had the blade ripped from his grasp by the Alpha's bone crushing blow.

Now defenseless, the Alpha grabbed Gallono by the throat with one hand and squeezed. *"Be sure and tell Captain Hastelloy hello when that mechanical vagina spits you out again."*

Just when the Alpha was about to twist Gallono's head clean off his shoulders, the business end of a sword suddenly burst through the Alpha's chest. The seven foot giant went limp and collapsed to the side revealing Hastelloy standing behind the warrior empty-handed.

"Message received," Hastelloy triumphantly declared while standing over the last fallen Alpha.

Gallono picked himself up off the deck to stand next to Hastelloy. "I suppose taking on all six of them alone was a bit ambitious."

The unexpected levity brought a smile to Hastelloy's lips. "You always did like a challenge."

Just then Hastelloy heard light footsteps approaching him from behind. He whirled around and readied to defend himself when he came face to face with Zhu Yuanzhang standing in the middle of his flag ship's main deck. "What wrath from the gods have I invoked for them to send hell hounds such as these after me?"

Hastelloy would have preferred a heartfelt thank you from Zhu for defeating the terrifying enemy, but instead he had an accusing finger pointed directly at him. "You! This is your fault. You counseled me to poison the other lords to unite the banners."

"Yes I did, Lord Zhu," Hastelloy said in his most contrite tone. He then raised his arms out wide and slowly turned a complete circle. "Look around you, my lord. The rebel factions are united under your leadership, and the Huang armies and ships lay smashed at your feet."

"All I see before me now are these hounds from hell sent to exact a penance for my betrayal," Zhu cut in. He would have continued the tirade, but was cut short by the thunderous crash of a soldier made of solid stone, or perhaps clay, jumping down from the enemy ship's bow onto the deck. If Zhu was intimidated by the sight of six Alpha warriors, his bowels nearly turned to water with the new arrival.

Sailors abandoned ship left and right declaring that the legendary stone army of Emperor Qui Shi Huang was upon them. Zhu stood petrified while the earthen creature stalked forward. He was saved from a mighty swing of the warrior's sword by Hastelloy yanking him backwards by the neck of his shirt. Zhu fell away from the blow and landed on all fours on the deck.

"Captain, look out," Hastelloy heard Gallono yell. The commander managed to deflect the clay warrior's counter strike toward Hastelloy's head at the last possible instant. While Hastelloy scurried away from the blow in desperate search for a sword, the adversary delivered a stiff punch to Gallono's jaw that sent the commander flailing five feet through the air from the powerful blow. Hastelloy picked up a sturdy sword, but swallowed hard at the prospect of facing this new adversary alone.

"*Captain Hastelloy,*" the stone warrior declared in the Alpha language. "*At long last I finally get to face the revered and feared Captain Hastelloy. It has truly been worth stretching the laws of Mother Nature to come alive once more and experience this moment.*"

Before he could find any words, Hastelloy's arm was in motion to parry a sword swing coming from his lower right. He deflected the blade, spun around the soldier's arm and delivered a slice across the creature's back resulting in a nearly imperceptibly shallow gash across the dense, wet clay.

Three more blows were deflected and countered with identical results, inducing a demonic cackle from his adversary. "*It's a pity my ancestors consider reanimating flesh an act of blasphemy. I do so miss the sensation of touch, but bringing life back to hardened clay that feels nothing at all certainly has its advantages.*"

"*Goron, what have you done?*" Hastelloy demanded as he reestablished a firm footing. "*This violates everything you hold dear. Are you so consumed with defeating me that you have forgotten who you are and what you stand for?"*

"That overly conservative traditionalist would never condone my vision, but many others will come around to my way of thinking." The warrior paused long enough to look around at the fallen Alpha bodies. *"I'm quite certain you will see these six warriors again."*

Hastelloy heard a harsh snap followed by a crackling sizzle. He looked to his left and found Gallono holding one of the unused hand cannons with a lit fuse pointed directly at the clay warrior. "Be sure and tell them I look forward to it."

An instant later hundreds of metal shards exploded from the hand cannon. The sheer force and volume of shrapnel unleashed at point blank range shredded the clay figure like a raw egg slamming into a mesh fence. The thick white smoke cleared just in time for Hastelloy to watch the last remnants of an Alpha relic flame hovering where the clay figure once stood fade to nothing.

Hastelloy knelt down and picked up a handful of orange dust that used to be the clay soldier. Apparently without the relic providing life, the figure reverted back to its original fire hardened exterior. Slowly he tipped his hand to the side and allowed the fine red powder to fall back to the deck boards.

Hastelloy was at a total loss. He made a living being prepared for any and all possible outcomes from a situation, but this? This he was completely unprepared to handle. How could he be? "My god, Gallono, somehow they are reanimating. How can we fight them now?"

"We start by assaulting the burial mound of Qui Shi Huang," Gallono said without missing a beat. "Whatever they're doing to make this possible, it's happening there."

"No," a despondent voice shouted from the far corner of the deck. Hastelloy saw the voice belonged to Zhu. "That tomb is cursed, and I will not risk god's wrath any further by desecrating the honored grave of Qui Shi Huang.

"Legend has it that thousands of stone soldiers protect that tomb," Zhu frantically pointed with both hands to the clay shards strewn about the deck. "Clearly that legend is true."

"But the evil must be stopped," Hastelloy began, but was cut short by Zhu.

"No! I must get away from this place. We will head north and drive Kublai Khan and his horde back to the mountain steppes of Mongolia. Perhaps that accomplishment will pacify god's anger with me."

Hastelloy wanted to argue the point further, but he could see it was no use. Zhu was terrified to his core by what he just witnessed and would not be dissuaded from his course of action.

Still, this new and terrifying Alpha threat needed to be stopped, and the job that would determine the fate of the entire planet in the next few weeks rested solely on the shoulders of Hastelloy and Gallono. There was no time to reach the others for help, and his human allies were now hopelessly spooked away.

The concerned look in Gallono's eyes let Hastelloy know he was not the only one who came to that conclusion.

Chapter 46: What a Sight

PROFESSOR RUSSELL SETTLED into his seat as the procession of Mengshi off-road vehicles and trucks drove away from the Xi'an airport. He was about ready to close his eyes to pass what was sure to be several hours of driving through the countryside to reach the burial mound of Qin Shi Huang when Alex jabbed him in the side.

"Look, right there," Alex pointed across Brian's nose and out the side window.

The professor shrunk down in his seat a bit to have a look and was amazed to see a steep sided pyramid partially lit up by the street lighting standing proud and tall alongside the highway.

From the front seat Chin looked back in amusement. "That is just one of many my friends. That relatively small pyramid was unearthed in the early 1990s when the new airport was under construction and the main road to the city was built."

"I was expecting these pyramids to be farther out in the countryside," Professor Russell replied.

Chin let out an uncharacteristically playful laugh at the professor's flawed assumption. "No. They are all over this region in and around the city, so I would not get too comfortable. This will be a short drive."

As the procession of vehicles drove west from the city, Professor Russell and Alex spotted no fewer than twenty pyramids dotting the evening landscape. Some were multi-tiered, others had straight angled sides. Most were covered with trees and other vegetation while a few were only covered with grass to allow their once precise shapes, now worn by weather and time, to be seen.

Chin periodically glanced back at the two archeologists having to wipe the drool from their mouths at the spectacle. "This is only a small sampling. There are many hundreds more out in the unsettled countryside if our satellite imagery is to be trusted. Up until just a few years ago, my government vehemently denied even the existence of these pyramids, but a new era of openness for my country has changed all that."

Forget Egypt or Central America, Brian thought. The future of pyramid excavation was in China. Everyone always thinks of the Great Wall when considering Chinese monuments, but these pyramids were just as impressive. Despite the circumstances of his arrival in the country, he was positively giddy at the prospect of working with these structures.

The vehicle caravan drove westward for about ten minutes. When they came around a sharp curve, Brian saw a view through the front windshield that managed to be both impressive and underwhelming at the same time.

Straight ahead in the dying light of early evening stood a tree covered mound that measured nearly a half mile long on all four sides and stood over a one hundred fifty feet tall. The sheer volume of earth that needed to be moved to build the mound was mind blowing, especially considering it was all done by hand two hundred years before the birth of Christ.

Despite the impressive scope, he found the vista lacking. He could easily tell the pyramid once stood twice its current height making it double the size of any pyramid in Egypt, even the Great Pyramid of Khufu. Unfortunately weather and human activity over the last two thousand years made the mound look like a shrunken cake, or a soufflé that attempted to rise but deflated at the last moment. It would have been truly a grand sight to see in its former glory.

Another lackluster feature of the pyramid was an intrusive trail of steep stone steps that cut a path straight up the middle of the sloped side. With tall evergreen trees covering the rest of the slope except for the middle strip, it almost looked like the pyramid was having a bad hair day where the barber lost control of his clippers and ran the tool down the middle resulting in a reverse Mohawk.

Along the drive toward the pyramid they passed a long, narrow structure with a curved roof that looked almost like the wing of a giant airplane.

"That covers the burial pits where the Terracotta Army is being unearthed," Chin narrated as if he were a tour guide. "If time permits, I think you would enjoy a tour of the facility."

"You think," Alex repeated in disbelief. "Of course we want to see them."

"In due time," Chin responded with his tone now turning serious once more. They drove past the tourist visitor center which was closed for the night. They roared right past a set of barriers and drove across the surrounding gardens until coming to a stop along the far right-hand side of the shriveled earthen pyramid where a large tent with covered sides stood.

When everyone was out of the vehicle, Chin pointed toward the burial mound. "Recorded history through the writings of Sima Qian tells us that automatic crossbows and falling stones guard the burial chamber which is supposed to contain treasures and an ocean of mercury."

"I have my doubts about the former, but the limited testing we have done makes us think the latter may be accurate," Chin went on. "There are high levels of mercury in the surrounding soil, and a magnetic scan of the site revealed that a large number of coins are lying in the unopened tomb."

"If you know all of this already, then why do you need the two of us?" Professor Russell asked as he looked on while the six wooden crates were offloaded from the truck.

Chin once again pointed to the towering mound to their left, "As you can plainly see, the pyramid is quite large. There is plenty of room for other chambers inside, and if the technology exists to accurately map the voluminous interior, why not employ it?"

Accepting the logic, Professor Russell walked back to the wooden crates to oversee their opening. Three already had the lids removed, and the familiar sight of his tripod mounted ground receptors greeted him. Two more crates were pried open to reveal the helicopter mounted emitter disassembled into two halves.

He looked expectantly at the last crate as the workers employed their crowbars. To Brian's surprise, the lid came loose with almost no effort from the workers. He looked over the wooden edge inside to make sure nothing happened to the sensitive equipment during transport. To his great relief, the fourth ground emitter inside looked to be in perfect working order.

Professor Russell looked back at Chin and Alex standing next to each other. "Let's get to work. I need the ground receptors positioned at the cardinal points of the compass around the base of the pyramid and a helicopter to mount the emitter onto. Alex, can you set up the computers inside the tent while that's all happening?"
****

As he hugged the undercarriage of the transport truck with his belt looped around the small of his back and anchored to the truck's frame, Frank counted his blessings. He had the foresight to get out of the crate while on the road to the pyramid. Climbing out the back and underneath the truck while it drove down the road at fifty miles per hour had been tenuous, but in the end, well worth the risk.

Not only did he avoid early detection, but he also was privy to an informative conversation between the archeologists and their handler named Chin – like that was his real name. Nothing of their experience in Egypt was mentioned which was encouraging. The other piece of good news was that Brian and Alex were working under the impression that this was a genuine archeological research project rather than working with the Chinese out of spite to their own nation.

They were being manipulated by Chin, of course, but they could not possibly know that. Short of stealing classified NSA papers, they had no way of knowing the Chinese Ministry of State Security had also detected strong radiation readings during their testing.

When they first read the reports, Mark and Frank gave it a secondary level of importance. The radiation frequency was close, but not an exact match to frequency Alpha so it was deemed a coincidence. Now seeing the lengths the Chinese were willing to go in order to investigate those readings made Frank reassess the level of importance.

Frank patiently waited for everyone to go about their work before he let himself down and slunk his way into the background scenery to keep a covert eye on things, and perhaps extricate Professor Russell and Alex from the extremely dangerous situation they now found themselves in. He would have liked nothing better than to call Mark and report in, but he knew all too well the signal would be a dead giveaway of his presence to the Chinese. Instead, he remained incommunicado until something more profound occurred or was revealed.

Chapter 47: Reading the Man

FROM THE MOMENT Mark sat back down on the couch across from Hastelloy, his line of vision never wavered. He bore down on the man with his scrutinizing stare to evaluate anything and everything the man's body language unknowingly revealed. Tragically, it wasn't much.

Hastelloy had no difficulty maintaining eye contact while reciting his story. As a result, that usually reliable indicator of a subject telling the truth or not was unrevealing. The fact that Hastelloy carried on his story so well while a man aimed a gun and an intense stare his direction was actually quite impressive. It took a level of focus and discipline that Mark rarely encountered.

About the only read Mark got from Hastelloy was when the man paused in his storytelling. Mark watched his eyes very closely to see where they moved during those brief breaks in conversation. Typically, the right side of the brain housed the ability to recall memory while the left side served the more creative functions of the mind to generate fictional tales. Hastelloy's eyes always glanced up and to the right, toward his memory recall. The man was either reciting a story he memorized before, or he was telling the truth. In either case, he was not making the story up on the fly or else his eyes would have moved left.

Mark's instinct was to take control of the room, dictate the conversation and get answers from Hastelloy. Instead, he forced himself to sit there quietly while Hastelloy rambled on about his supposed exploits back in the Middle Ages. There was likely a lot of truth in the story considering Mark's own personal experience with their Nexus device. It was entirely possible Hastelloy and his crew were on earth four thousand years ago to place the gravity manipulation equipment inside the Egyptian pyramid while it was under construction. Was it really so far-fetched that they also tinkered with things only five hundred years ago?

The specific circumstance of the story being told was not particularly important to Mark. He was far more interested in the behaviors shown toward the situations described. Mark found it encouraging that Hastelloy was clearly distraught about the carnage the black plague unleashed upon the world. Then again, Hastelloy bragged about sabotaging levees that drowned potentially millions of Chinese farmers. In the next breath he boasted about poisoning revolutionary leaders to unite their forces under one leader. Next his subordinate engineered a weapon that leveled the walls of Constantinople, unleashing three days of rape, murder, and theft upon that wealthy city. The man had a distinctly ruthless side to him which made the power he held over the entire planet with his gravity weapon absolutely terrifying to Mark.

For the first time in over an hour, Mark looked away from Hastelloy toward his older brother. Jeff just sat in his chair, legs crossed with a note pad in his lap as if this were just another therapy session. Mark knew he had to tread lightly. Jeff did not know the backstory going on here. He knew nothing about the radiation frequencies, or the deep space communications probe tampered with and launched last week, or the gravity weapon. To Jeff, this was just another day at the office with the added shock of his brother barging in holding a gun.

Brotherly love and trust went a long way, but if anything, Mark was sitting on the wrong side of things right now. The visible evidence to this fact was Jeff and Hastelloy seated near each other while Mark sat opposite the coffee table, alone on the couch. Jeff clearly had a strong, trusting rapport with Hastelloy, while the trust he bore his little brother was now shaken by Mark's shockingly aggressive behavior.

Mark may have held the gun, but Hastelloy had masterfully manipulated the circumstance to the extent that he ultimately controlled the situation. A sideways glance from Jeff sent Mark's eyes back to Hastelloy as the man continued on with his story about humanity's past. In the back of his mind, Mark mulled over his options to turn things with his brother back around to his favor.

Chapter 48: Diet of Worms

TONWEN FOUND HIMSELF seated at the center of a long rectangular table. Joining him at this table facing the main gathering hall were six bishops, three sitting on either side. The cavernous hall was filled wall to wall with several hundred onlookers on the main floor and surrounding balcony. The clergy elite sat wearing all the regalia of their position and contrasted against Tonwen's plain brown monastic robe.

The clear mismatch of social and political standing would cause most men to shrink from their responsibility, but this was Tonwen's moment. Once again he had the privilege to be an advocate for the faith his friend Jesus gave his life for all those years ago in Jerusalem.

Despite his lower standing, Tonwen was designated by Archbishop Leonhard von Keutschach to lead the heresy case against Tomal. Tonwen expected the Archbishop himself to lead the proceedings, but the man's paranoia would not allow him to leave the safety of his fortress in Salzburg and travel to the tiny town of Worms resting idly along the shores of the Rhine River. So it fell to Tonwen.

Typically the assembly of estates still considered part of the Holy Roman Empire was not well attended, but this year was another matter. This year the Diet drew great interest as the technically secular meeting now served as a de facto trial of Martin Luther and his Ninety-Five Theses against the church practice of selling indulgences. Both supporters and detractors traveled from all over the land to witness the outcome.

As Tonwen told Archbishop Leonhard would be the case, once granted safe conduct to and from a neutral location, Tomal came out of hiding and agreed to stand under examination of his challenge to papal authority.

Tonwen banged the heavy gavel in his hand three times to render all side conversations in the large chamber silent. "Bring in the accused."

The words were rewarded by the heavy chamber door swinging open allowing Tomal and two armed guards escorting him to enter. The brisk cadence of footfalls echoed around the silent room until Tomal finally took his seat in the middle of the chamber at a small table facing Tonwen and the six bishops.

Mark Henrikson

The two former crewmates of the Lazarus exchanged fiery glares that electrified the air between them. Both men were determined to stand tall and argue the righteousness of their cause to the bitter end. Tonwen was determined to win the staring contest, but was pulled away by his duties as lead inquisitor before either man proved the victor.

"Martin Luther," Tonwen began. "You have been summoned before this assembly to defend your writings entitled *The Ninety-Five Theses on the Power and Efficacy of Indulgences* against examination for heresy."

Tonwen slid back his chair, causing a teeth wiggling screech, and rose to his feet. He deliberately paced around to the front of the judiciary table, picked up a thin leather bound book and dropped it with a clap onto the small table in front of Tomal. "Is this book an accurate portrayal of your writing?"

Tomal took a few minutes to calmly thumb through the pages and eventually placed the book back down on the table and continued looking Tonwen dead in the eyes. "Yes it is."

"Do you stand by the contents?" Tonwen insisted.

"I am the author, but I require time to reexamine the work in order to answer your question," Tomal deflected.

Tonwen snatched the book up in a blur and shook it profusely in Tomal's face. "Nonsense. You admittedly authored the words months ago. In fact, you held confidence enough in their content to publish and distribute them to all of Europe. One does not write such inflammatory nonsense unless you are either possessed by the devil, touched by lunacy, or stand behind your allegations with certainty. Which is the case, Martin Luther?"

Tomal casually reached underneath his plain black robe to produce a copy of the Holy Bible. He placed it on the table and rested his right hand upon it. "Unless I am convinced by the testimony of the Scriptures, or by clear reason, I am bound by the Scriptures I have quoted and my conscience is captive to the word of God. I do not trust either in the Pope or in council's interpretation of these words, since it is well known that they have often erred and contradicted themselves to suit the given situation."

"In these writings you claim the sale of indulgences by the Vatican to its faithful is amoral and unjustified," Tonwen accused with a slightly calmer tone. "Where in the Bible do you pretend to draw this conclusion?"

"The Bible teaches us that salvation or redemption is a gift of God's grace," Tomal said as though he were a guest lecturer at a university. "This

203

one and firm rock, which we call the doctrine of justification, is the chief article of the whole Christian faith."

"Through my studies I have come to understand justification as entirely the work of God. This of course goes against the current teachings of the Catholic Church that the righteous acts of believers are performed in *cooperation* with God. It is my comprehension that Christians receive such righteousness entirely from outside themselves; that righteousness not only comes from Christ, but actually *is* the righteousness of Christ imputed to Christians through faith."

"So you claim that faith alone makes someone just and therefore fulfills the law?" Tonwen interrupted.

"It is not I, but the Bible in Romans 1:17 that states the just person lives by faith," Tomal answered. "Faith is that which brings the Holy Spirit through the merits of Christ. Faith is a gift from God. Since forgiveness is God's alone to grant, those who claimed that indulgences absolve buyers from all punishments and granted them salvation are in error."

"One verse?" Tonwen objected and then snatched the Bible out from under Tomal's hand. "One verse out of this entire text is the basis for your position? Martin Luther, there is not one heresy which has torn at the bosom of the church, which has not derived its origin from the various interpretations of the Scripture. The Bible itself is the arsenal whence each innovator has drawn his deceptive arguments."

"Our theology states that faith alone, whether fiduciary or dogmatic, cannot justify man," Tonwen went on. "Justification rather depends only on such faith as is active in charity and good works. The benefits of good works could be obtained by donating money to the church."

Tomal stared back at Tonwen with vacant wonder and shook his head slowly from side to side. "Errors in my past long ago caused me to seek the introspective healing of monastic life. I devoted myself to long hours of fasting, prayer, pilgrimage and confession. If anyone could have gained heaven through good and holy activities, then I would indeed have been among them. Yet all I came away with from that time of self-reflection was that true repentance does not involve self-inflicted penances and punishments, but rather a change of heart. Now here I sit accused of heresy by the ones I so desperately sought to serve and redeem my soul before. It would seem my good works have not bought me much in the church's eyes."

"Martin Luther, I must warn you. I and the rest of this panel see no biblical support for your assertions. If you recant, then you can work to rebuild your standing with God and possibly still see salvation in the next life. If you do not, then I fear your soul will be lost to the devil forever," Tonwen stated more as a threat than a plea.

"I cannot and will not recant anything, since it is neither safe nor right to go against one's conscience," Tomal answered. "I am a firm believer in Christ and that faith alone is my salvation. So here I sit, I can do no other."

Tonwen paused long enough to look back at the panel of bishops. An affirmative nod from each gave him leave to declare, "It is the determination of this panel that the teachings of Martin Luther are a product of the devil. His literature and teachings are hereby banned and his immediate arrest is ordered."

An explosion of cheers and protests rang out from the audience. The most adamant objections came from a block of spectators seated immediately behind Tomal. The repeated shouts that he was granted safe passage to and from the Diet were impossible to miss or ignore.

Tonwen raised his arms to quiet the chamber. Gradually the shouts and shoving among the audience gave way to silence, allowing Tonwen to be heard. He then turned to face Tomal once more. "You have been granted safe conduct away from this city. That promise will be honored, but know this. The moment you leave these borders you will be alone in the world. You are branded a notorious heretic, and the act of anyone giving you food or shelter will be considered an act of heresy as well."

"Furthermore," Tonwen shouted while raising his head to be heard over the growing anger of those intent on Tomal's immediate arrest. "This council's decree allows anyone to kill this servant of evil without legal or spiritual consequence."

Tonwen looked back toward Tomal to gauge his reaction, but found himself staring at the back of Tomal's robes as he left the chamber with his faithful followers in tow.

Chapter 49: Snatch and Run

TOMAL STORMED AWAY from the main gathering hall of Heylshof Garden castle with such pace that his black robes flowed in the wind behind him like a cape. Feeling his supporters fall in line behind him to join his exit caused Tomal to picture himself as an ocean wave gaining speed and power as it approached the shore.

Like a tidal wave overtaking a coastal village, his rebellious movement spilled out into the immaculately manicured gardens behind the castle. The grounds featured a large circular fountain in the center. From there cobblestone paths radiated out among bright floral arrangements and chest high bushes trimmed with hard edges. The beautiful vista extended all the way to the waters of the Rhine River, which was Tomal's destination.

Exiting the assembly through the main courtyard following the predetermined judgment of Tonwen's show trial was out of the question. Any number of zealots and madmen intent on doing him harm lurked immediately outside the castle walls. To avoid their sinister designs, Tomal arranged to leave via a more private route.

Tomal would have liked nothing more than to stop and smell the roses in the garden grounds, but time was short. He moved with purpose past the central fountain and followed a series of arching bridges and paved paths until he finally reached the river's edge. There, waiting at the dock, rested a long boat with four sets of rowing oars manned on either side.

When Tomal's footfalls transitioned from claps against stone to creaks on the wooden dock, a well-dressed man stepped off the boat to greet him. Tomal met the man with a warm embrace.

"Prince Fredrick, it is wonderful to see you again, but you should not be here," Tomal cautioned. "It was far safer for you to support my teachings from the shadows. Seeing you here now, providing my vessel for escape puts you in as much danger as me."

"An act of conscience rarely leads one down a safe path," the prince replied. "As you feared, all the roads leading away from Worms are blocked with the Pope's henchmen looking to arrest or kill you."

The prince then hastily broke the embrace and ushered Tomal into the boat. As the vessel cast off down the river Prince Fredrick shouted from the docks. "We shall see each other again soon."

Somehow Tomal had his doubts. While the longboat sped away from the dock, he watched his couple hundred supporters get overrun by an angry mob of thousands. Shouts disparaging Tomal and his satanic upbringing carried down the river long after the source passed from view around a bend.

Tomal put his mind at ease by listening to the rhythmic pattern of splash and swoosh the oars made in the water. No one made a sound as the miles passed in silence until they reached a cluster of five horsemen holding a sixth steed in waiting.

A dark brown coat and hood was thrown over Tomal when he stepped off the boat onto dry land. It was not much, but anything to help disguise his identity while out in public following the council ruling was useful.

While Tomal climbed aboard his horse the man holding the reins gave a status report, "It didn't take long for word to reach the roadblocks that you escaped using the river. Search parties are perhaps ten minutes behind us right now."

"Then we have no time to waste," Tomal declared as he spurred his mount north toward Hamburg and the heart of support for his reformation movement against the Catholic Church. He turned in his saddle and yelled back to the boat crew. "Continue down river for another five miles and then make like you sent me toward the south. May God be with you on your voyage."

"Godspeed," he heard multiple men shout back. As if the word speed were his cue, Tomal prompted his horse to a full run up and over the nearest hill. He managed to hold the hastened pace on through to the next rise to make sure plenty of undulating ground lay between him and his pursuers to make sure he remained out of sight.

Eventually Tomal slowed the pace to a brisk trot and allowed the leader of his honor guard to catch up.

"Any word on the prince or our supporters at the dock?" Tomal asked. "They were overrun almost immediately by the Catholics."

"I am afraid not," the man replied.

Tomal shook his head with frustration and regret. "Why did he come with the boat? Why didn't he just meet me in Hamburg like we planned?"

"The prince believed his public show of support for our cause would serve as an example to bring more supporters out of the shadows."

Tomal was mad enough to scream and give his position away to anyone in a five mile radius, but instead, he just turned his head toward the west and watched the sun drop below the horizon. Another hour of travel saw the shadows grow long across the dirt road they traveled and a foreboding darkness settled in.

"Should we pull off to the side and make camp?" the leader asked.

"I am exhausted," Tomal admitted, "but I don't suppose our pursuers will do us any favors and stop as well. I think we need to continue on through the night and then find shelter and rest during the day."

"I was afraid you would say that," the man groaned. "That will limit the distance we are able to travel per day, but I guess it's all we can do."

Not long before darkness completely claimed the wooded path, the group of six horsemen came upon a four wheeled cart overturned across the road with a lone driver struggling to set it right.

The sight instantly put Tomal on edge. The sound of metal swords being drawn by his guards let him know he was not alone in his concern. He kept a close eye out, but as they neared the toppled cart Tomal saw no signs of anyone else nearby.

"I think we can spare a few minutes to perform our Christian duty and help this man," Tomal said. The others must have agreed because four of them dismounted to lend the man a hand getting under way again.

"Oh how kind of you to assist," the man shouted with great delight in a voice that was entirely too loud by Tomal's judgment. While the men worked in cooperation to set the cart back on all four wheels, his sense of impending danger only grew more pronounced as the stranded man looked at Tomal far too often to not be a sign of danger. A moment later his suspicions were confirmed.

Four horsemen carrying torches came charging down the road from beyond the overturned cart. Tomal and his lone mounted escort wheeled about to flee in the other direction, but were horrified to see another group of six riders barreling toward them from the opposite direction.

Left with no other choice, Tomal turned his mount perpendicular to the road and took off down the hillside with ten dark riders in close pursuit. The uneven ground was nearly impossible to navigate in the dark. Tomal realized he was far more likely to get thrown from his horse and break his neck than get away, but he had to try. Capture meant certain death and an end to his rebellious movement against an entity he was certain was controlled by the Alpha.

Tomal led his horse over bushes, under trees, and through overflowing streams in his effort to get away. His guard was able to stay with him for a few minutes, but Tomal soon found himself alone in his flight.

He spotted a tall hedge just in time to prompt the horse to leap over the barrier. On the other side the downward sloping hill took a sharp drop which caused his horse to lose its footing. The animal's hind legs slipped under it, and the animal slid on its backside until finally reaching a flat which allowed it to stand up once more.

Tomal spurred his mount to move on, but the hobbled gate let him know something on the hind legs was either cut or broken. Rather than nurse a lame horse along, Tomal jumped down and attempted to flee on foot.

He managed to scramble a hundred yards further down the hillside, but soon found himself encircled by his pursuers. Every direction he attempted to go found another horseman holding a lit torch searching for him. His ring of freedom grew ever smaller until his only refuge was an attempt to silently climb the nearest tree.

He managed to reach the third branch, about ten feet off the ground, when four horsemen gathered beneath his position and illuminated his hiding spot with their torches.

"Martin Luther, you are many things, but a skilled rider or a squirrel you are not," a familiar voice declared. "Hiding up a tree does not become a man of your repute. Climb down; your destiny waits."

Tomal released the breath he had been holding and then lowered himself down from the branch and let go to drop the remaining two feet to the ground. He rose to his full height and looked up at the speaking rider who pulled back his hood. As the man's face moved into the orange glow of his torch, the smiling face of Prince Fredrick appeared.

"Come," the prince said with an awaiting hand extended to help Tomal up onto the back of his horse. "If I let you keep riding on your own tonight all this effort will be for nothing."

Origins: Reformation

"What happened to the original plan?" Tomal asked as he slid in behind the saddle to sit upon the horse's rump. "Why did you stage an attack rather than just ride up and tell us?"

"Your arguments at the Imperial Diet won over more supporters than even I expected," the Prince announced. "Enough so that I can shelter you in my own castle at Wartburg rather than retreating all the way to Hamburg. I made it look like a clan of highwaymen took you because I have absolute faith in my men and their loyalty, but had questions about those escorting you."

"You nearly scared the life out of me in the process. Wartburg is certainly a shorter ride, but are you sure this will not bring about your downfall?" Tomal asked of his benefactor.

"Of that I have no doubt," Prince Fredrick said and then led the group of riders off into the night.

The morning light greeted Tomal in a very sleep deprived state as the group of riders passed under the protective walls of Prince Fredrick's castle. He cringed a bit at the sound of heavy doors locking behind them. He calmly looked around the castle grounds to get acquainted with his new surroundings. He was virtually certain he would be seeing a lot of these walls over the next few years as travel for him outside would not be possible for some time.

The prince proceeded to escort him up to a private bedchamber with a stone floor and weathered timbers for walls and ceiling. The rather Spartan room featured a simple bed in one corner, a ceramic stove for warmth in another, along with a desk and chair with plenty of paper for further writing. Resting alongside the blank pages was a copy of The Bible.

The prince must have read the gloom in Tomal's face. He reached out to give him a reassuring pat on the back. "I know it is not much, but it beats being burned at the stake."

"With high walls and locked gates, it still feels like a prison. A comfortable and roomy prison to be sure," Tomal immediately added to try and temper any offense given. "What am I to do now locked away from the people who need to hear me?"

The prince picked up the Bible and thumbed through a few pages and then set it back down. "It is tragic that such an important book is only written in a dead language that the clergy alone understand, or so they say. It rather limits both the common and educated man to take the word of priests and their interpretations instead of drawing their own conclusions."

"Yes, it certainly is a convenient tool to focus the power of the Church into the hands of the few," Tomal acknowledged.

"Perhaps a person with a talent for linguistics will one day translate the Latin Bible into a common language for all to read and draw inspiration from," the prince added.

Tomal's mood suddenly brightened to fill the confined space with a radiant glow. "Tell me, Fredrick, do you also have a printing press within these walls?"

****

Hastelloy reached a lull in his storytelling allowing Dr. Holmes to steal a glance toward his brother. It was like looking at a stranger. Where a bright smile and a lighthearted soul usually shined through, Mark now displayed a passive anger and aggression that the victim of a crime might show towards their attacker in a court of law.

Hastelloy was on trial; Mark sat as the judge, and with pistol in hand, apparently the executioner as well. Jeffrey saw his brother's eyes moving his way so he abruptly turned his attention to the notepad in his lap.

"Okay, so Tomal was the one who translated the Bible for the masses," Dr. Holmes exclaimed while thumbing back through some notes he took in a prior session. It didn't take long to find what he was looking for. "Yes, here it is. Back in Egypt you brought up Tomal's remarkable talent for breaking down and quickly learning new languages. You attribute it to languages being very formulaic and logical just like mathematics, physics and other engineering disciplines in which Tomal excels. Of course he would be the first to translate the Bible into a common language."

Hastelloy acknowledged the statement with a sly grin and slight bow of his head. "It was a task not just anyone could do you know. It is a nearly impossible task to force the poetry, rhythm, and meaning of the words from one language into another."

The patient let out a regretful laugh as he went on. "Tomal told me some years later that the ordeal was like forcing the beautiful Latin letters to morph into their barbaric German counterparts against their will."

For the first time since barging into the office, Mark spoke up. "Alright, this Tomal guy translated the Bible into German. Why? How did that help in this magnanimous struggle you so honorably carry on against the evil Christian Church that was dominated by the ghost of this Goron character?"

"It was the key to everything," Hastelloy shot back, apparently flustered that Mark did not see the obvious answer for himself. "The existence of the translation was a public affirmation of the reformation movement. It deprived any elite or priestly class in society of exclusive control over the word of God. It returned the power of free thought to the people allowing them to develop their own informed opinion rather than simply eating what Goron and his puppets were serving."

Before Mark could utter another word, Jeffrey jumped back in to the conversation because Hastelloy's statement provided the perfect avenue to attack the warped logic of his imaginary world. "Okay, I see how it destabilizes Goron and his influence, but isn't the church the tool you intended to use in order to bring mankind back from the Dark Ages? Doesn't destabilizing the church set back the greater good you are striving towards?"

Hastelloy's face lit up like a hunter who just watched a ten point buck step into his crosshairs. "Not at all. In fact, Tomal's creation of an accurate translation of the Bible became a stimulus towards universal education. Everyone wanted to be able to read so they could understand the Bible. Suddenly the relatively unimportant skill of literacy was of paramount importance again. Many thought their eternal salvation depended on it, while others sought the empowerment that came with independent interpretation of the Bible. Either way, from that moment on your people, as a whole, began learning again."

"Tomal sure is quite a guy," Mark jabbed.

"You don't even know the half of it," Dr. Holmes added while turning his notes to a new page to continue the discussion. "He also saved twenty million Novi back in Egypt."

"He certainly had his moments," Hastelloy sighed while reaching for a drink of water before continuing his story.

Chapter 50: Translation Effect

"DAMN THAT MAN!" Archbishop Leonhard hollered at the top of his lungs when he entered Goron's chapel. He slammed the door behind him with enough force to tip the mighty fortress over the lofty cliff face on which it sat. Still wearing his formal robes after saying mass and carrying a Bible, he turned in circles with apparently no adequate way to vent his anger. "Damn him to hell for all eternity."

"Martin Luther?" Goron asked more as a statement than a question. What else could it possibly be? The man was proving to be an absolute menace to Goron's sphere of influence.

The archbishop flung the Bible he carried against the nearest wall with every ounce of his rage as propulsion. The thick book slammed spine first against the stones and tore in two upon impact. The separate halves landed in the middle of the floor with large German lettering from a printing press facing up. Archbishop Leonhard pounded his way across the chapel to stand between the severed halves, and still shaking with anger, pointed to them with extended index fingers. "There is a reason translating the Bible from Latin to any language of the commoners has been forbidden for centuries."

The archbishop bent down and held the severed book in his hands held apart. "This atrocity will be the downfall of your church on earth; mark my words."

Outbursts like this were not uncommon from the easily upset archbishop. Still, Goron felt compelled to at least humor the insignificant man to keep his allegiance strong. "I take it something unpleasant happened at mass this morning?"

"During my sermon, my words to the people inspired by you, a common man of no distinction saw fit to stand and challenge my teachings," Archbishop Leonhard said while pacing in angry circles once more. "Imagine the nerve of that uneducated buffoon to stand up in my church and question me, an Archbishop."

"My church," Goron quickly corrected. "You may be the caretaker here on earth, but my spirit and guidance make it flourish."

Instantly realizing he'd overstepped his bounds, Archbishop Leonhard dropped to the floor with his head pointed straight down. "Of course, my lord; all that I have I owe to you."

After a few quiet moments of reflection, the archbishop looked up with a more settled demeanor. He motioned toward the torn Bible translated into German by Martin Luther once again, "This ... *thing*. Printing presses all across Europe work day and night churning out Luther's New Testament translation. It is not just the aristocracy reading this. It is tailors; it is shoemakers, even women. Anyone with the slightest ability to read is studying it as though it were the fountain of all truth."

"They are committing passages to memory," he went on. "It has only been a few months, yet people already deem themselves so learned that they are not ashamed to dispute about faith and the gospel in the middle of a Sunday sermon."

"My word is the Bible, and it is the truth," Goron insisted. "However, it is full of symbolism and metaphors that the common man is not equipped to comprehend. The gospel was written by multiple hands who do, at times, contradict one another. Common men are not meant to sort through it all without the intermediation of a priest. If unchecked, this translation could bring about the downfall of my church on earth."

The implications of his last sentence struck Goron's consciousness like a bolt of lightning. This was the Novi working against him, he was sure of it. Like so many times before, they sensed his influence over a powerful entity and were moving to subvert it. Once again Goron was thankful for his forethought to strengthen the fortress walls for protection. He drew strength and confidence from the knowledge that he was safe. As an added bonus, he now knew who the Novi were and what they were up to.

When Goron spoke again it was with the methodical tone of an educator. "This Martin Luther has been quite successful equipping every German speaking Christian, to their own peril, with the ability to read and interpret my word for themselves. More and more I am convinced this man is not just a heretic touched by the devil, but truly is the devil himself."

"The one of unnatural birth you often caution me against? The one you have battled throughout the ages?"

214

"One of his demons showed remarkable ability with linguistics in the past," Goron went on. "This translation had to be his doing, and where his demons linger the lord devil is never far away. The stakes are much higher now. If unchecked, this demon and his master may very well break the unity of my church, leaving humanity to twist about in the winds of anarchy without my guidance."

"Then Martin Luther must be stopped at all cost," Archbishop Leonhard declared. "For the last three years he's sat inside that castle in Wittenberg churning out his heretical texts with impunity. It is time to end this once and for all. The man's arrest has been ordered, and it is the obligation of any Christian to carry out that order."

"Breaching the stone walls of a castle is no small undertaking," Goron pointed out. "It requires a massive and sustained military campaign that the church is not equipped to carry out."

The archbishop got off his knees, "Then we put it to the people. In the past, Popes encouraged lords and kings to mount the Crusades. Those men willingly marched thousands of miles to retake the Holy Land for rewards in the next life. Is it really too much to ask that they now cross a few hillsides and lay siege to a local castle to arrest this demon?"

"Yes it is," Goron emphatically answered. "The genius behind the devil's plan is that he owns the unwavering support of the ruling class because Martin Luther's teachings remove my church from over their heads. He enhances their power with every word he writes.

"As for granting my favors in return for conquering that castle," Goron went on. "The whole idea behind his teachings is that faith alone leads to salvation, not deeds performed. Any call to action by the church in return for rewards in heaven only adds strength to Martin Luther's argument."

"What is there to do then?" the archbishop asked.

"Raise the stakes," Goron declared with the fire within his flowing life force doubling in intensity. "Dissect this translation. Show it to be riddled with self-serving embellishments and omissions. Insist the leaders and public servants renounce them. Then seek out, isolate and destroy those who resist. Burn them all down to the ground in the name of your lord."

Goron sensed an uneasy hesitation in the archbishop, so he spelled out the plan in more simple terms. "Make an example of the few to instill fear, and fear will lead to obedience once more. This rebellious movement must be stamped out at all cost. Everything on this earth depends on it."

"Thy will be done," the archbishop said with a bow and then exited the reclusive, private chapel.

****

Tonwen looked through the distortion of the lead glass window and saw Archbishop Leonhard exit his private chambers and cross the stone paved courtyard toward the library. He thought it best to look busy when the archbishop entered, so Tonwen cut his break short and raced back to the room's center table where three separate translations of the Bible in Hebrew, Latin and German lay open.

He inked a quill and made ready to make more notes in the margins of the Germanic Bible when the archbishop burst through the door. "Have you found anything in your review of the translation? Is it accurate? Martin Luther certainly must have altered the text to suit his own ends, and we can use that to discredit the entire work and turn the public against him."

"My review is far from finished, but right now I am forced to admit the translation is remarkably accurate," Tonwen reported with an exhausted sigh. "I will continue my work, and I assure you, we will get our man."

Chapter 51: Peasant Rebellion

"YOU SHOULD NOT be here," Prince Fredrick whispered into Tomal's ear. "You are too important to the reformation movement; outside the walls of Wartburg castle I cannot guarantee your safety."

"For weeks now I have sat in that castle listening to report after report of commoners rising up on account of my teachings only to be put down with murderous force," Tomal shot back while barely managing to keep the volume of his voice under control. "It is time for action, not hiding."

"They rebel against high taxes and low wages while watching their lords build opulent castles and throw lavish parties," the prince countered. "Your teachings are just a convenient message to rally around."

Tomal could only imagine how proud Hastelloy would be of him right now. Attempting to lead an uprising against the excesses of the upper class at the expense of the lower was a complete rehabilitation from his behavior back in Rome. There Tomal was the culprit of upper class abuse of the commoners, and his lust for the finer things left him vulnerable to manipulation by the Alpha relic. Tomal had indeed come a long way.

"Regardless, it is a noble cause, but it desperately needs a central leader," Tomal declared. "All these tiny uprisings are easily put down one at a time."

"Of course they are," Prince Fredrick began, but had his attention interrupted by a man standing a few feet away wildly swinging the wooden handle of a chain mace while holding onto the solid metal striking ball. He released a frustrated huff through his nostrils and then walked over to show the man, whose hands bore the telltale blisters of a farmer, how to properly hold and swing the weapon.

Walking back to Tomal, the prince shook his head and gestured all around the dense forest where twenty other farmers practiced using the unfamiliar weapons they found themselves wielding. "These are farmers attempting to fight against professional soldiers. Every time these peasant groups try and stand toe to toe against knights, trained archers and armored horse they get slaughtered."

Tomal raised a finger which induced a silent pause from the prince. "Correct, so the trick will be avoiding a direct confrontation with their armies and striking where they are not."

Prince Fredrick let an amused smile cross his lips, "Master theologian, linguist, and now general? Did I get all your titles correct?"

"I am a learned man of many talents," Tomal replied and then stepped forward to place a reassuring hand on the prince's shoulder. "Relax, this will be a minor affair. If things go badly, I promise you can kidnap and hide me away in your castle once more."

"And if things go well?" the prince asked with a raised eyebrow.

"Then we change the world for the better," Tomal answered while swiveling his head about to locate the sun. The celestial body was making good time crossing the morning sky. "The executions were set for noon. It's time for us to move."

An hour later Tomal and the prince found themselves herded through the main city gates along with all the other citizens of the town. They all were ushered into the main square at the prodding of armed guards with the lord's inner keep proudly looking over the grounds. At the base of the three story stone structure rested a pile of printed books circling three wooden pillars sporting four sets of shackles each. A quick survey of the literature littered about the ground let Tomal know his writings would provide the fuel for the fire that would see twelve leaders of the local rebellion burned alive.

The townspeople looked on in dejected silence as the twelve men were led one by one to their shackles amid the piles of books. These were husbands, brothers, and friends of those in the crowd, and therefore there was no cheering or taunting done by anyone except the roughly fifty soldiers spaced around and about the silent crowd.

While the parade of prisoners commenced, Tomal made sure to stand near a pair of soldiers issuing cat calls. Prince Fredrick did the same, as did several others from his team who Tomal spotted among the crowd.

The first few prisoners struggled against the guards chaining them to the poles, but the rest saw the futility in the effort and opted to meet their end with some dignity. When all twelve victims were chained in position, the lord stepped out onto a third story balcony protruding from the inner keep. The aristocrat wore all the jewels and fine garments of his elevated station to oversee the proceedings.

In truth, the townspeople were lucky the lord was only executing the leaders rather than every participant in the uprising. No doubt the fat, white haired old bastard's first instinct was to fire the town, but then where would the income to support his life of luxury come from?

Instead, the lord made do with forcing the town to watch their brave loved ones shriek, squeal, and beg for their lives to end sooner as the flames cooked them alive. The town's population was fortunately large enough that a few extra observers were not noticed.

The lord at least had the good sense not to give some pompous victory speech in front of the town's people. He kept it short and to the point. "Get on with it so we can all put this sad affair behind us."

Tomal did not wait for any lit torches to come near the kindling. He calmly drew his dagger and impaled the closest guard in the back through his lungs and heart for a silent kill. Tomal slit the other guard's throat from behind as the incompetent man watched the show rather than perform his guard duties. Tomal then proceeded toward the perimeter of the crowd.

He set his sights on another pair of guards standing near the main gates of the castle when screams and shouts from among the crowd put the men on alert. Tomal sidestepped around one last woman between him and the guards and flung his dagger with deadly effect into the neck of the nearest sentry. The dead man's companion drew his sword while Tomal produced one of his own from underneath his hooded coverture.

Tomal did not possess Gallono's legendary prowess in hand-to-hand combat, but he was certainly no dunce with a blade owing to several lifetimes spent in military service. The guard managed to parry two strikes, but the third drew a gash across the man's stomach which stunned him long enough for Tomal to impale him through the heart.

He paused to look around the dirt paved courtyard to judge the progress of his rescue assault. On ground level, all but a couple of guards lay dead, and those still standing would soon be horizontal as well if the five to one odds had any bearing on their fortunes. The only remaining threat now came from the two archer towers on either corner of the front walls.

Tomal pilfered a triangular shaped shield from one of the fallen guards. He spotted two others from his assault team doing the same and enlisted their help. Holding the shields over their heads, the three men ascended the stone steps to reach the wall walk and made their way across the parapet to the corner tower.

Now at an even level, Tomal pointed his shield toward the archers and sprinted forward to close the gap. The shield was useful, but did not cover everything, and every second gave the shooters another opportunity to hit exposed flesh. One after another, missiles clanked off his shield and the ground around his exposed legs and feet. Only three archers occupied the tower, but they were firing at an impressive rate, which probably attributed to their lack of accuracy.

Just before reaching the shooters, Tomal felt the bite of an arrow graze his right leg, but his adrenalin rush forced the pain to the back of his mind. He rammed shield first into the closest archer, knocking the man clean off his feet, slamming his head against the wall. The archer was probably unconscious from the blow, but Tomal ran his sword through the man's chest just to make sure.

His companions dispatched the other two shooters just as effectively, and they each armed themselves with a bow and a quiver of arrows. Tomal notched and drew an arrow to hit the other tower, but saw his efforts were unnecessary. Prince Fredrick and a few others had already conquered that elevated archer position. He adjusted his aim to the lord's balcony extending over the courtyard from the third story of the inner keep, but found it empty. The lord and his family had retreated inside, trusting the stone walls and reinforced wooden door would hold the rebels at bay long enough for help to arrive. They may have been right were it not for one architectural flaw to the building – the wooden roof.

Down below the townspeople mobbed the prisoners and labored to break the chains of their imprisonment. One by one they were released to the frantic hugs of wives and children. While the joyous reunions were taking place, Tomal and his bow wielding companions stuck a handful of wadded pages onto the ends of their arrows. A touch to the lit torch meant to incinerate the rebel leaders lit the arrows and the six bowmen sent them on their way.

In all, dozens of flaming arrows landed on the rooftop. In a matter of minutes the modest flames took hold of the timbers and grew. Two men from inside the keep attempted to climb onto the roof to extinguish the flames. One did not even make it out of the window before taking an arrow to the chest. The other managed to reach the roof and put out two budding fires before falling victim to an arrow that sent his limp body sliding off the steep pitch of the roofline to the courtyard below.

A brief ten minutes later saw the roof entirely engulfed in flames and it began to crumble and fall into the wood framing below. With no choice other than roast to death in the flames or face the mob, the front door of the keep opened and a dozen guards charged out to do what damage they could, which wasn't much.

Four fell to arrows while the other eight were quickly swarmed and dispatched by the waiting mob. Finally the lord, his wife, two grown sons and their wives and young children stepped out into the open with arms raised in surrender.

A couple of the formerly chained rebellion leaders moved in to execute the lord and his family, but Prince Fredrick interceded on their behalf. "No, wait. They are far more valuable as ransomed prisoners than dead bodies. Take them to Wartburg castle. You have my word the ransoms received will be split among you for the troubles you have endured."

This was the moment of truth. If the rebellion was about God and Tomal's teachings, then the family would be spared. If it was really about raging against the aristocracy, then the entire family would perish.

The earth stood still for a few anxious moments until a man stepped up to Prince Fredrick with a raised sword in hand. "Lord Gringwald saw fit to only punish the leaders; we then shall do the same. No more, no less."

Prince Fredrick turned his gaze to Lord Gringwald who seemed to accept the accord. He quietly took a few moments to hug his family and then willingly stepped away to receive his fate.

Fredrick snapped his fingers and pointed to the family. Twenty of the prince's men immediately went to work binding their hands with rope and leading them out of the castle grounds. When the last of the lord's grandchildren passed under the gatehouse, the prince and the rebel leader looked to Tomal.

"Be quick about it and then meet us on the way to Weinsberg," Tomal said quietly and then left the castle grounds amid the clatter of the inner keep crumbling in on itself and thick black smoke billowing hundreds of feet into the air.

Chapter 52: Identity Crisis

THE RELIC FLOATING before him did not have a body for Kuanti to assess its mood. Four of the warriors who fell aboard Zhu's marooned flagship had already reanimated into clay forms, but these two were being stubborn. He needed a quick answer, but in all fairness, it was a rather vexing decision to make. To suppress his impatience Kuanti turned away from the stone altar to take in the grandeur of the burial chamber once more.

In the center of the room rested a solid bronze coffin interring the remains of the Chinese nation's first emperor, Qui Shi Huang. Surrounding the coffin was a detailed three-dimensional map of the nation complete with flowing streams of mercury representing the Yellow and Yangtze Rivers. The slightly domed ceiling lay twenty feet overhead with imbedded seashells, pearls and gemstones accurately depicting the sun, moon and star constellations of the sky. Hanging from the ceiling, at evenly spaced intervals, were a hundred whale oil lamps which still functioned admirably today.

The only imperfection to the ceiling's portrayal of the heavens was an antenna the size of a man's head, which extended down from the chamber above. His men had spent the last year carving out the chamber to harness and house the relics soon to arrive from Mars. Victory over the Novi, once so certain, was now in doubt. Kuanti needed all the physical soldiers he could summon to fend off an assault by the Novi that he knew was imminent.

A bright flash of golden light emanating from behind Kuanti caused him to turn and face the relic once more. Whatever its answer would be, the relic certainly had strong feelings on the matter.

"I will not comply with that order," the relic insisted. "It blatantly betrays the laws of Mother Nature. I will not dishonor myself by reanimating."

If Kuanti were still a relic flame, his rage would have scorched the entire burial chamber; the selfish arrogance. "You do not have the luxury of saying no, soldier. You are under my command, and I order you to reanimate to take up arms and defend this chamber until our brothers from the Mars colony arrive."

"The Mars relics do not need to transfer here, and those Alpha warriors will arrive on this planet to deliver final victory whether this chamber is defended or not," the relic countered. "This order is all about you. You and your need to be the hero and this blasphemous obsession you have with reanimation."

Kuanti had heard enough. He stalked over to the stone altar, scooped the relic up into his hardened clay hands and carried it over to the flowing river of mercury and held it perilously over the poisonous substance. "You say that like you have a choice in the matter. You will reanimate or your life force will be extinguished for all eternity."

The relic once again flared with intensity to deliver a response. "Then I will enter the afterlife with a clear conscience and Mother Nature as an advocate in my final judgment. Do with me as you deem fit and honorable."

The finality of the statement brought a snarl to Kuanti's face. There was no more debating; he could either make good on his threat, or let it be shown as a hollow bluff. Either way he stood to lose face, but would the example force others to make the right choice? Or would destroying an innocent relic for sticking to its ideals lead to an insurrection?

Cora must have sensed the same dilemma; she stepped toward the stone altar in her new clay form to address the other relic thus far refusing to reanimate. "I suppose you are equally committed to the moral reservations you have about bringing an inanimate clay body to life with your life force?"

"I am," the relic declared without a moment of hesitation.

"These two are as worthless in death as they were in life," Cora stated. "They couldn't even handle one simple Novi armed with a sword. Let them exist in the dark corners of this chamber to contemplate their failures for all eternity until they chose to end their own existence out of shame."

For show, Kuanti continued holding the relic over the flowing mercury to appear conflicted with his decision. In reality there was no decision. Cora gave him a way out without looking weak, and he would take it.

"Very well," Kuanti said and then walked over to Cora and hastily dropped the relic into her hands. "Just be sure to keep these two selfish traitors out of my sight, the very thought of their pathetic existence offends me."

Cora dutifully carried the relic and its rebellious companion off to the far left corner of the burial chamber. As she moved away Kuanti heard a

223

collective exhale from the two Alpha warriors standing watch at the chamber doorway. He turned to inspect their physical reactions further, but had his attention drawn to the two animated statues strutting through the doorway to deliver a report.

"We have finished relocating the landing craft underground to rest inside the fourth soldier pit," they reported.

"And it is adequately surrounded by clay statues?" Kuanti asked.

"Yes, hundreds of them."

Kuanti despised handing out praise, but he simply could not suppress a broad smile from gracing his clay lips. "Excellent. Let it draw the Novi in like moths to a flame."

Chapter 53: The Weinsburg Example

WORD OF TOMAL'S victorious rescue of the rebellion leaders spread about the surrounding townships causing the ranks of his tiny force to swell from twenty to several hundred. As the force moved to the southwest, every minor estate of the social elite was razed to the ground, sending the aristocracy scrambling for the strongest fortification around - Weinsburg castle.

With forty foot high walls that stood five feet thick and a moat ringing the entire complex, it made for an imposing target. Upon seeing the massive structure a few miles in the distance, Prince Fredrick had misgivings about the endeavor.

"This is not just some sneak attack you are attempting here. This will be the siege of a well defended castle requiring thousands of soldiers with heavy bombardment tools," the prince protested. "We only have a few hundred lightly armed farmers. This is beyond us."

While the men rode their horses side by side ahead of the ragtag army, Tomal shook his head in defiance. "No it's not. Five weeks ago Archbishop Leonhard ordered conscriptions from every local lord and duke to form a single large army to overwhelm the separate rebellions around the region to put them down one at a time."

"Yes, it was a shrewd move," the prince admired. "The military maxim to divide and conquer one's enemy is being put on full display. Our scouts report that the large army is still over a hundred miles to the north mopping up a few lingering hotspots."

"I find that a little insulting," Tomal interjected. "Here we are, a sizeable force that managed to conquer a castle and leave a scorching trail of destruction in our wake as we move across the landscape. Yet we still do not merit an immediate recall of that army by the nobles to handle us. Imagine the nerve of them to disregard us like that. Still, it does give us an opportunity."

"I see," Prince Fredrick responded. "You think Weinsburg will be too undermanned to put up a fight against us."

Tomal flashed him a mischievous smile, "The thought did cross my mind."

The prince looked positively baffled by Tomal's plan. He pointed toward the massive walls of Weinsburg with an angry index finger. "It doesn't matter if there are no defenders at all in the castle, we will never make it past those walls. When we show up, I assure you that the Duke and his men will lower their pants and take a piss on us from those walls, and there won't be a damn thing we can do to stop them. Then perhaps a week from now that combined army from the north will arrive and hand our heads to us."

"Who do you think is inside those walls?" Tomal insisted.

"The Duke and his family."

"And?"

"Seventy or more local lords and their families whose homes we burned on our way here," the prince went on. A raised eyebrow from Tomal prompted him to continue the list. "Probably ten or twenty soldiers."

"I'd put it more at fifty soldiers, but that is not even the point. Who else is inside those walls at this very moment?" Tomal asked. He was not at all surprised a man of privileged birth did not see the obvious answer, after all, does anyone ever pay attention to the hired help?

A flicker of comprehension graced the prince's eyes and a broad grin soon followed. "Butchers, bakers, stable hands, servers, cleaners, and the list goes on. With those seventy plus households inside, there must be at least five hundred commoners already within those walls."

"Now the question is, do you think people earning an impoverished wage and enduring a lifetime of being treated like dirt will align themselves with our cause or that of their oppressors?" Tomal asked.

"Our cause is the reformation of the Catholic Church away from corruption, but to most it is about taxes, wages and social standing," the prince answered looking ahead at the castle walls that no longer looked so imposing.

When Tomal's small force set up camp outside the castle walls, the first order of business was to communicate with the commoners inside. Archers shot arrows over the walls with hand written notes attached letting the commoners inside know this was truly their army outside. Their army had arrived to deliver them from the captivity of the antiquated feudal system.

At least one of the notes had an impact; in the early morning hours of the second day, the front gates swung open allowing the castle to fall. It took no time at all to secure the castle since all the hard work was already done by the servants. When Tomal entered the castle, he found the Duke of Helfenstein, along with seventy other noblemen seeking refuge, bound with rope and herded into the central square at sword point.

Tomal could tell immediately that this conquest would not be handled with nearly the same civility as before. Many of the nobles were already badly beaten and wore torn garments. Now the servants hurled rocks, rotten food, and even feces at their one time tormentors. These servants and townspeople had retribution on their minds and would not be denied. A quick look exchanged with Fredrick let Tomal know that the prince saw it too, and moved to be the voice of reason.

"I know, I know," Prince Fredrick shouted as he walked into the open between the nobles and their captors with his arms raised high. The mob quieted to hear his words. "These men have shown you no mercy *ever* so they should be shown none in return. However, we shall hit them where it hurts the most, in their wealth. We will hold them ransom and drain their family treasuries in exchange for their lives so that this rebellion may go on to even greater conquests."

"No," bellowed a burly man covered from head to toe in soot and grime who could only be a blacksmith. He roared forward and grabbed one particular nobleman by the throat and threw him down to the ground next to Prince Fredrick. "This pig forced himself onto my wife and all three daughters whenever he felt the urge. When I tried to resist he would have me thrown in the stocks for a week, sometimes longer."

The man looked away from Fredrick to stare down the man cowering on the ground. "No amount of coin will be enough to right those wrongs. Even death is too good for you, but it is the best I can do."

"No it's not," another commoner called out before the blacksmith could carry out his murder. "Run him through the gauntlet. Run them all through the gauntlet to make sure our message is heard all across the continent."

"No. No!" Prince Fredrick demanded, but the mob's blood was up and there was no reasoning with them. Tomal ran into the fray and pulled the prince away, lest the servants take his nobility as an excuse to kill him as well.

"This is not the Christian thing to do," Fredrick shouted. "Martin Luther, our spiritual guide, is here among us now. I implore you not to shed the blood of these men in his presence."

It was no use. Tomal, Prince Fredrick, and their men were herded to the side as the servants made two lines twenty feet apart and nearly a hundred feet long. They all held long pikes with an axe and spear tip combination at the end. The nobles were tied together in a line at the waist and then sent between the pike wielding columns in groups of ten.

"Any who make it through alive will be free to go," the blacksmith taunted the first group and then swung his sword at the noble who so grievously wronged him and his family. The blow took off the nobles left leg at the knee and sent the entire chain of men running through the gauntlet of pikes for their lives, dragging the one-legged man across the ground as they went.

For over an hour, pikes sliced, stabbed, chopped and bludgeoned the nobles until not a single one drew breath any longer. One particularly speedy nobleman who had the ropes binding his hands cut free actually made it through the gauntlet alive, but collapsed shortly thereafter due to the extreme loss of blood.

While all the commotion was going on outside, Tomal busied himself with the task of locating a specific wagon carrying a particular artifact he needed for the next phase of his plan.

Once Tomal and the rest of his men pilfered anything else useful from the castle, they set fire to the grounds and moved on. A number of servants from the torched castle who felt torturing the nobles took matters a step too far joined them rather than taking part in the despicable spectacle.

After hours of marching, the prince still looked thoroughly disgusted with humanity as he gazed out over the fields with a vacant stare. "That was too far. We should have stopped it. You are a man of God, and having your name associated with that massacre is a travesty."

"There was nothing our meager numbers could do to stop it," Tomal answered quietly to match the somber mood. He intended to continue his thoughts, but was interrupted by the arrival of yet another cluster of peasants asking to join their march. For the tenth time that day he agreed and saw yet another few hundred join their numbers.

"As impalpable as that event may have been to you and I, it certainly has served the greater good. Word of our victory is spreading fast. The peasants have something to believe in now and they join us in droves. Now instead of a few hundred, a capable army of ten thousand approaches the culprit of all things evil and wrong with the Catholic Church in this region: Salzburg and the fortress of Archbishop Leonhard von Keutschach.

Chapter 54: What's In a Number?

UNDER THE COVER of night, Hastelloy and Gallono quietly rolled their invention into position. They both pushed forward a four foot beam attached to an axle with two wagon wheels on either side. Between the wheels sat a five foot by four foot rectangular wooden box that was two feet thick.

Housed inside the box were four hundred cylinders, each two inches in diameter, arranged in a twenty by twenty pattern. Stuffed inside each cylinder was an arrow adorned with a small tube of gunpowder to serve as propellant. Running down from the back of the box was a single fuse to set the entire contraption off at once.

With one final shove, the two men gently dropped the beam to the ground, causing the arrow box to point skyward at a thirty degree angle. Hastelloy stepped up to rest his chin on the box, then held up his range finder which simply consisted of a lens with predetermined distance and elevation markers drawn on it. He found the burial mound and quickly locked in on the well lit entrance to the tunnel leading back to the burial chamber.

"To the right just a bit," Hastelloy whispered. They were almost a quarter mile from the well defended entrance, but voices did carry and had the potential to get picked up by the keen ear of an Alpha warrior.

Gallono crouched down and gently nudged the beam until Hastelloy raised a clinched fist. Hastelloy then pointed skyward with his index finger. Dutifully, Gallono added one inch thick boards under the end of the beam until the angle was where Hastelloy desired.

Gallono relocated some bushes and leaves to conceal the device while Hastelloy pulled out a long wax candle. He took out a ruler that converted time into height on the candle. Hastelloy made a mark, cut it down to size and immediately lit the candle, setting it in place next to the fuse leading to the box. The flame was about an inch higher than the fuse at the moment, but in about fifteen minutes would burn down to light the fuse.

"I sure hope you remembered to carry the one in your math calculations," Gallono said softly as the two men made their way toward the tunnel entrance. "If just one of the twelve batteries we set up is aimed a little off or fires more than a minute or two late, we will be in the line of fire same as our enemy."

"If you have a better way for two men assaulting a well defended position to seem like thousands, Commander, now is the time," Hastelloy hissed. He would have gladly performed any number of lewd acts to procure some radio linked timers to kick off this assault, but it was still a few hundred years too early for that technology and he had to make do with what he had.

Before long they reached their arming point. Nestled beneath a sizeable boulder Gallono quietly moved aside some bushes to reveal a set of swords and sledge hammers. From a nearby tree Hastelloy lowered down four hand cannons mounted on top of short spears. Gallono attached two of the destructive firing weapons crisscross across Hastelloy's back and he reciprocated.

"The barrage should disperse the couple hundred human guards, but we still need to contend with fourteen Alpha who could be either relics, hardened clay or flesh and blood warriors," Hastelloy said softly while attaching the hand cannons to Gallono's back.

Gallono let out a chuckle that dripped of gallows humor. "Just once can we have numbers on our side for a change?"

"What's in a number anyway?" Hastelloy responded while handing Gallono a bow with a full quiver of arrows to attach around his waist. "All hell should break loose in just a couple of minutes."

Without a sound, the two men made their way to the edge of the tree line and waited. A hundred feet in front of them rested the tent city of an army encampment. Beyond the dozen rows of single man tents stood the tunnel entrance with no fewer than fifty human guards standing watch.

To his left and a quarter mile back Hastelloy heard a faint hiss grow from a barely audible whisper to a roaring gust of wind. He glanced behind to see hundreds of fire trails in the sky descending on the encampment and tunnel entrance. Seconds later another barrage landed from the right side raining fire and death upon the small army. Tents caught fire and men, sleeping or awake, took arrows in multiple places on their bodies.

Hastelloy tried his best to keep track of how many barrages had befallen the enemy, but after the first two or three all he saw was an indiscernible firestorm of flaming arrows. A few projectiles fell short of the target and landed in the woods near Gallono and Hastelloy, but they were few and far between. The devastation was all focused on the enemy, and it was time to move.

"Now," Hastelloy ordered once the falling arrows had thinned out to one or two still randomly dropping.

Hastelloy's confidence grew as the two encountered no resistance. Every defender was either dead, dying, or too busy cowering beneath a shield to notice two men sprinting for the tunnel entrance. Then it happened – with still another fifty feet to go, a flurry of hisses approached from above, bringing with it the flaming arrows from a contraption who's ignition candle was cut a skosh too long.

Adding to their peril was a set of Alpha warriors who burst forth from the tree line in a full four-legged sprint in pursuit of Gallono and Hastelloy. The two men had a sizeable lead, but the lightning quick pursuers were closing the gap with every menacing bound.

With thirty feet to go, flaming arrows began landing all around Hastelloy. There was nothing to be done to lessen the danger at this point; it was for fate to decide if an arrow hit them or not.

Hastelloy was the first to reach the protective canopy erected over the descending steps. With arrows and rampaging Alpha on his tail there was no time to take the steps under any sort of control. At the last second, Hastelloy kicked his legs out and twirled to slide backwards on his stomach into the tunnel. Fierce daggers of pain jabbed into his knees, stomach and chest as he bounced his way down half a dozen steps before stopping.

He looked back in time to see Gallono take an arrow to his right shoulder, punching him to the ground just short of the tunnel stairs. Realizing the arrow barrage was reaching its peak, Hastelloy resisted every cell in his body demanding he lay immobile for hours to recover from his injuries to reach up and drag Gallono all the way under the canopy. Behind him, approaching at speeds approaching fifty miles per hour were the two Alpha warriors. One was hit with four arrows at once causing it to crumple to the ground and grind to a stop where three more arrows put it out of its misery.

The remaining Alpha did not seem to notice three flaming arrows sticking out of its back. Just as Hastelloy finished pulling Gallono to safety and reached for his sword, the Alpha leapt for the stairs. Hastelloy's blade sliced clean through the beast as it sailed overhead and landed thirty feet down the stairs with a sickening sound somewhere between a crunch and a squish and moved no more.

By the time Hastelloy redirected his attention to helping Gallono, he found the man on his feet attempting unsuccessfully to grab hold of the wooden shaft protruding from the back of his right shoulder.

"Here, let me take a look," Hastelloy said as he held Gallono steady. Fortunately the arrow hit the triangular shaped trapezius muscle spanning the gap between his neck and shoulder. It had to hurt like hell, but nothing vital was broken or punctured. "The tip won't let me pull it back out, I need to push it through."

Hastelloy grabbed hold of the arrow's shaft, snapped it in half and gave Gallono the free piece to bite down on.

"I have to conclude your arithmetic sucks," Gallono mocked and then chomped down on the piece of wood. "You couldn't have left another millimeter on that candle to give me time enough to get under cover along with you?"

Hastelloy couldn't contain a laugh. "The math was right, you've just lost a step old man." He then pushed the arrow through and out the other side accompanied by a primal grunt from the patient. The gaping wound would need further medical attention, but now was not the time. The two proceeded quickly down the steps toward the well lit chamber housing the ceramic army protecting the tomb of Qui Shi Huang, and now the Alpha.

Chapter 55: Back to Life, Back to Reality

WHEN HASTELLOY AND Gallono reached the bottom of the steps leading to the clay soldier pits, the captain notched an arrow on his bow and followed Gallono who was leading the way with his sword drawn. They reached a ninety degree turn and Gallono stole a quick glance around.

He looked back at Hastelloy and silently pointed to his own eyes then held up two fingers. An openhanded gesture to the left let Hastelloy know his assignment. The moment Gallono turned back around and brought his sword to the ready Hastelloy stepped around the corner, instantly aligned his shot and let loose the fletching while Gallono dashed forward toward his target on the right.

The Alpha standing left of the doorway took an arrow in the throat and dropped to the ground with a muffled gurgle. The remaining guard wasted no time lamenting his fallen comrade. He reflexively swung his sword at the charging Gallono who collapsed onto one leg and slid along the ground to successfully duck the mighty blow. He cleaved the creature's left leg off at the knee causing the beast to topple over.

Before the Alpha's body even touched the dirt, Gallono had already sprung back to his feet and had his sword in motion to deliver the deathblow through the beast's chest. With the immediate threat eliminated, Hastelloy took a moment to survey the gigantic underground chamber they just entered. Forty feet above their heads a dome stretched two hundred feet wide and eight hundred feet deep, supported every twenty feet by stout wooden beams reaching from floor to ceiling.

Thousands of reddish brown clay soldiers, complete with sword and shield in hand, stood in seemingly endless marching columns. Resting tall and proud in the middle of the chamber was the spacecraft that he and Gallono recently observed the Alpha relocate below ground. Knowing that twelve Alpha had to cram into that modest fixed wing craft to make the journey from Mars to Earth made Hastelloy feel a brief sympathetic bout of claustrophobia.

Hastelloy stepped over the Alpha he dropped with his bow and was about to proceed between two rows of clay soldiers leading to the Alpha craft when Gallono yanked him back with an iron grip.

234

When Hastelloy caught his balance again, he followed Gallono's hand pointing to a barely visible tripwire running between the legs of the third row of statues. He then gestured up to the rafters where a set of tightly wound crossbows were trained on the spot.

"It appears the first Chinese emperor didn't plan on hosting any visitors in the afterlife," Gallono whispered. "We'll need to keep an eye out."

"Indeed," Hastelloy acknowledged as he stepped aside for Gallono to take the lead again. Three other tripwires were stepped over before they reached a small clearing in the statues made for the ship.

Hastelloy spotted a human with his back turned standing on one of the wings. He quietly notched an arrow, took aim and fired. His aim was true, but the projectile clanked harmlessly off the man's neck. When the individual turned to face them, Hastelloy realized it was actually a realistically painted clay soldier animated by an Alpha relic.

"Intruders," the soldier yelled in the Alpha language which drew another animated statue to the fight.

As their adversaries stalked toward them, Hastelloy cast his bow aside; his action was quickly followed by Gallono's sword. They both stepped out into the open with their hands clasped behind their backs to do battle with the enemy bearing down on them.

The clay soldiers continued forward uninterrupted. They were supremely confident in their nearly indestructible forms, and that overconfidence would be their undoing.

"I sure hope this works," Gallono grunted and then stepped toward the nearest soldier and swung his arms around at waist level wielding a heavy sledge hammer.

The weapon's blunt end struck the prowling figure just above its left hip. The dense clay material seemed to momentarily reshape around the hammer's head, but eventually gave way to the overwhelming force behind the devastating blow. A six inch wide section of the creature's abdomen was sliced off and flung to the side leaving the torso teetering precariously on top of its separated legs, causing them to dry from malleable clay into fire hardened terracotta in the span of a heartbeat.

Gallono allowed the momentum of his swing to whirl him around to deliver a shoulder check to the clay warrior's chest sending that half of its body backwards to the ground. Without a moment's pause, Gallono swung the sledge hammer over his head with two hands and brought it down with everything he had onto the creature's chest.

His downed opponent appeared to deflate upon impact leaving a vibrant blue haze outlining in its place. A moment later the glow faded away into nothing leaving a shattered remnant of the once menacing clay warrior.

Hastelloy's attack was not quite as successful. His mighty hammer swing connected at the shoulder of the soldier's sword wielding arm spraying clay fragments against the Alpha ship like a shotgun blast. The heavy strike threw Hastelloy hopelessly off balance, leaving him momentarily vulnerable, and the clay soldier did not miss his chance.

The soldier threw a punch with his remaining arm, hitting Hastelloy on the exposed backside of his shoulder. The blow sent Hastelloy twirling to the ground, unable to feel anything on his right side. It was like that half of his body was completely detached from the rest of him. Nothing moved no matter how hard he tried.

The soldier moved in to finish him off with a bone crushing stamp from his heavy foot, but Gallono was having none of that. He struck the clay soldier in the hip with his hammer and sent it crashing to the ground without a right leg.

Gallono wasted no time. He stepped up, drew his arms over his head and whipped the hammer down onto the soldier's chest, yielding an identical result as before. Once he confirmed the life force was no longer in control of that form, Gallono turned to help Hastelloy to his feet.

"You alright?" Gallono asked.

"Nothing's broken, but I've definitely been better. My god those things are strong," Hastelloy marveled as he rotated his arm to get used to the sensation of moving a limb that still had no feeling in it. His attempt to walk on the nerve deadened leg resulted in him stumbling into Gallono's arms.

At that moment Hastelloy's eyes detected a subtle lighting change in the chamber. The reddish glow of the oil lamps was being drowned out by a flash of bright blue coming from a tunnel just beyond the Alpha craft. It was growing in intensity with every passing moment. He shielded his eyes in time to witness a blinding blue flash wash over the chamber and then dissipate to nothing.

An instant later Hastelloy watched a clay statue twenty feet away step forward, look around to gain its bearings and began strutting toward Hastelloy and Gallono.

Gallono quickly slung Hastelloy's arm over his shoulder and began hauling him toward the tunnel from which the light flash originated. "Ever feel like you're bailing water out of a sinking ship with nothing but a tea cup?"

"If the relics from Mars reach this place it will be like an ocean rushing in on us," Hastelloy said as he staggered alongside Gallono.

In rapid succession three more flashes flew harmlessly past them and overtook the chamber. Hastelloy stole a glance behind to see three more statues come to life and join in pursuit of the two Novi.

Twenty feet from the tunnel entrance the clay warriors drew too close for comfort. Gallono gave Hastelloy a hearty shove toward the tunnel and turned to face their pursuers.

"Go shut down whatever is causing them to regenerate," Gallono shouted over his shoulder. "Meanwhile, I'll try to hold back the rising tide as long as I can."

Hastelloy stumbled forward and just barely managed to catch himself before slamming headfirst into the hardened earth wall. Feeling was coming back to his right side and brought with it an excruciating tingling sensation that managed to electrify every nerve ending on that side of his body. Using the wall as a crutch, he ducked into the tunnel leaving Gallono to fend for himself.

"Don't forget to watch out for traps along the way," he heard Gallono say before the voice was drowned out by a thunderous explosion.

Chapter 56: Stone Silence

WITH HASTELLOY SAFELY away, Gallono spun around to the menacing sight of four hardened clay warriors bearing down on him in a spread semicircle formation. He knew one well placed swing of his sledge hammer would destroy one of his assailants, but the remaining three would have him surrounded and he'd be dead soon after.

Rather than facing them out in the open, Gallono opted to back his way into the tunnel and force the clay warriors to come at him single file in a confined space. By the time the tunnel cast its dark shadows over Gallono, his opponents were just a few steps behind.

Realizing how difficult it was to see anything in the tunnel gave Gallono cause for concern about Hastelloy's safety. "Don't forget to watch out for traps along the way," he shouted up the tunnel while working to remove one of the two hand cannons he carried on his back. He jammed the long wooden shaft into the ground and braced it with the instep of his right foot. He sparked the fuse to life and pointed the three foot long canister on top toward the approaching clay warriors.

Gallono closed his eyes and held his breath, but there was nothing to be done about his ears. An instant later the world erupted around him with sound and fury. Hundreds of metal shards propelled by gunpowder exploded out of the hand cannon. In the tunnel's darkness the flash was nearly blinding, even with his eyes shut, and in the narrow corridor the smoke made it impossible to breath. Those disadvantages, however, were far outweighed by the results.

Aligned in a single row, all four clay warriors simply ceased to exist; the largest fragments remaining could fit in the hand of a small child. Gallono stumbled out of the tunnel and into the open again. He exhaled and took a deep breath of the relatively fresh air available to him out there. With his eyesight still washed out from the explosive flash, Gallono did not venture any farther from the tunnel. He needed to defend the entrance and buy Hastelloy as much time as possible in order to destroy the Alpha's reanimation device.

It took a few minutes before Gallono was able to make out shapes with his vision, but he was able to see well enough to notice a bright blue flash rush past him, then another followed by two more. He looked to his left and saw two clay soldiers marching side by side toward him.

"How does it feel facing the same adversary over and over again?" one of them barked in the Alpha language.

To even the odds Gallono gripped his hammer with both hands, raised the handle over his head and flung it at the approaching soldiers. One of them was taken completely off guard by Gallono relinquishing his weapon. The momentary hesitation allowed the sledge hammer to hit it dead center in the chest. The hammer barely paused as it sailed right through the clay warrior, producing an explosion of clay shards with the hammer landing another thirty feet away among the rows of inanimate statues.

"Same opponent, same result," Gallono mocked as he ducked under the remaining soldier's sword swing. He sidestepped another cut and twirled in behind the hardened clay soldier to deliver a leg sweep to the back of its heel.

To his great disappointment, the strike only produced a shooting pain running up and down his right leg while his sturdy opponent didn't even budge. In return the soldier landed a colossal backhanded punch to Gallono's cheek that sent him to the dirt and rolling away just in time to avoid a downward slice of the sword that would have cut him in half.

"Not the result you were expecting I suppose," the soldier said with a soft laugh.

Gallono panicked for an instant when he realized he no longer stood between the soldier and the tunnel entrance. The way was open for the creature to make a clean run after Hastelloy, but it didn't. His opponent was completely fixated on him and that was just fine with Gallono.

On the bright side, Gallono was now free to retrieve his hammer. He dashed three layers deep between two rows of statues and finally found the heavy object on the ground with the handle resting vertically against a statue's leg. Just when he wrapped his hand around the handle, another blue flash overtook the chamber and a moist clay hand grabbed Gallono around his left biceps and flung him backwards through the air like a ragdoll.

He crashed into another clay, soldier toppling the statue to the ground. Gallono rose to his feet again, but noticed the load on his back was significantly lighter. He looked down to see his last remaining hand cannon smashed at his feet.

"Uh oh, you broke your toy," the soldier who launched Gallono through the air chuckled loudly while stalking toward him.

Another flash of blue let Gallono know trouble was near. Suddenly a sword from a nearby statue to his right was in motion. He bent backwards just in time to only suffer a light cut across his chest. Gallono immediately brought his hammer forward again and managed to obliterate the statue before it had time to catch its balance following the overly aggressive attack.

Gallono looked around his position and realized he was among dozens of potential enemies who could come to life at any moment to backstab him. He dashed into the open where three clay soldiers awaited him with a fourth charging at his back.

He headed straight for the tunnel and used the wooden handle of his hammer to deflect a blow and then countered with a two-handed swing. This time the blow was blocked and all he heard was the disheartening snap of wood. The weakened handle broke in half leaving Gallono with a foot long stick to defend against four soldiers armed with swords.

"We're as constant as the northern star," the nearest clay soldier barked in a feminine voice. "Eventually, you will go down."

Out of options, Gallono made a break for the dark tunnel leading to the burial chamber of the earthen pyramid. He did not have the luxury of taking his time; he was in full retreat mode with the clay soldiers now on the run after him. The path was not completely dark. It was lit by an oil lamp about every twenty feet.

High stepping his feet and feeling his way along the hardened dirt walls Gallono frantically searched for anything along the half mile tunnel that would be useful. He wasn't being picky, anything at all would do.

As he approached a lit floor lamp he spotted a hair thin line running between the far wall and the lamp base a few inches off the ground. Gallono looked for any indication as to what the wire might trip, but he saw nothing. No loaded crossbows, no holes in the wall where spears might impale an intruder, there was nothing.

Before he reached the tripwire, one of the pursuing soldiers flung his sword at Gallono which caught him in the leg along his right thigh, tripping him up. Unable to arrest his fall, Gallono dove headfirst over the wire and landed in a crumpled heap ten feet beyond. He attempted to get up again, but the sword protruding from his leg prevented such movement. It was over, and he resigned himself to that fact.

The four clay soldiers slowed their pursuit to a casual stroll when they drew near. "Oh he's down now; down for good."

Gallono's only hope was that the tripwire would trigger something catastrophic. He watched the first soldier step right over the string through sheer luck, but the second pointed out the danger to the others. Out of options, Gallono threw the chopped down wooden handle in his hand at the line and succeeded cutting it clean through.

The soldiers looked concerned for a moment, but let it pass when nothing happened. "They don't make them like they used to I suppose."

A weighty groan shortly followed the clay warrior's words and a stone block three feet thick and twenty feet long crashed down from the tunnel ceiling leveling all four soldiers in its path.

"Down but not out," Gallono sighed while struggling back to his feet. He pulled the sword out of his leg, and removed his shirt to tie a tourniquet around his thigh. He then continued hobbling his way toward the burial chamber that Hastelloy was hopefully demolishing at that very moment. A few minutes later a flash of radiant blue light raced past him to let Gallono know a fight may still lay ahead for him at the end of his hike.

Chapter 57: Not as Things Appear

IF THE FIRST sight of Weinsburg castle and its stout defenses gave Prince Fredrick a moment of pause, then seeing Hohensalzburg Castle occupying an entire hillside towering over the city of Salzburg must have caused his bowels to leave a brown puddle in the saddle. The fortress was absolutely massive, and elevated with only one long, narrow switchback road winding up the impossibly steep incline to the castle.

Archers manning dozens of towers along the walls overlooking the path would inflict devastating casualties before the attackers even reached the gates. Then the attackers would have the insurmountable task of breaking down not one, two or even three, but four separate sets of gate houses in succession as the fortress walls wound their way up the hillside to the castle itself.

As the peasant army entered the city beneath the fortress, Tomal watched as the castle gates were closed and locked tight before the tidal wave of commoners from the city were able to enter and seek refuge from the assault. If locking them out were not enough, Tomal noticed the rail line running down the steepest cliff face continued hauling supplies into the fortress from the town below. The people of Salzburg were simply left to fend for themselves without any provisions while their 'protector' sat on high, safe behind locked doors.

Tomal could not contain a laugh as he crossed the river over a stone bridge to enter the city's business district. He leaned over in his saddle to have a word with Prince Fredrick. "I guess word reached the archbishop already about how we managed to overtake the last castle."

"Clearly," the prince responded without amusement. Suddenly the clatter of broken glass along the right side of the street grabbed Fredrick's attention. He looked mad enough to breathe fire as he spurred his horse to a full gallop toward a store in the process of being robbed by his men.

"Stop this now," the prince ordered drawing his sword to emphasize his point. "We are not petty thieves here to vandalize and steal from fellow peasants. We are here to bring down the arrogant aristocracy that holds you under its boot."

Either the words or sword put an immediate end to the behavior. As a result, most of the townspeople turned away from the archbishop's doors and joined their cause. In short order the fortress was completely surrounded, though the besieging forces kept an adequate distance out of respect for the archers manning the castle walls.

The central square of Salzburg lay two hundred yards away and downhill from the fortress walls. Far enough away so arrows could not reach. Tomal found it to be the ideal spot to set up his command tent. While that was going on, Prince Fredrick received a rider and then walked toward Tomal to relay the message.

"I just received word the archbishop's northern army turned south two days ago and will arrive here by midday tomorrow," the prince reported. "It appears we have until then to break through those walls, conquer the castle, and then rebuild them again to protect ourselves from the pursuing army."

"Shall we get to it then?" Tomal deadpanned back, but received a scowl in return.

"This is serious. When that professional army with twice our numbers arrives we will be slaughtered; every last one of us for what happened at Weinsburg. Either you have a real plan to take that castle without destroying its protective walls in the next twenty-four hours or we need to move on."

Tomal signaled for a wagon to be brought into the central square for unloading. He then put an arm around his friend and turned him to look up at the fortress. "Tell me what you see when you look at the main castle? Not the walls and gates, but the inner castle itself," Tomal asked.

The flustered prince tossed his head from side to side out of futility. "I see an impressive structure that I will never live to see the inside of, what about it?"

"Is there anything unique about the roof?" Tomal prodded.

"It runs the entire length of the structure and has a steep angle to keep the snow off it during winter."

"Exactly," Tomal said with pride. "I have it on good authority that the long roofline is supported by a single ridge beam made of solid oak to give the entire upper level an impressive, yet vulnerable, vaulted ceiling."

"How nice for the archbishop," the prince said dismissively.

"How nice for us," Tomal countered. "Strong as that oak beam is, it cannot handle the additional weight of snow or else it will snap. If that single beam breaks the entire roof will collapse onto the lower levels and possibly allow the walls to follow and bring the entire castle down on top of itself. Then we leave and let the archbishop's army pick up the pieces."

The prince turned his head to look at Tomal with wide-eyed wonder. "Great plan. Let me get my saw." A doubtful tilt of Tomal's head prompted him further. "Seriously, how do you expect to get up there and sever that beam to accomplish your grand plan?"

A shudder of the ground and the groan of wooden wheels struggling to move under heavy weight caused Tomal to turn them both around and face the wagon he beckoned earlier. "We let this new weapon do the job for us."

Before them stood a ten foot long metal cannon mounted on the four wheeled cart. The gunnery team was busy blocking the wheels into position and turning down a hand crank to raise the aim toward the roof line of the castle.

"What on earth is that and where did you get it?" the prince managed to ask with his jaw scraping the dirt at his feet.

"A gun, a big one, that I heard rumors about a while back," Tomal beamed with pride as he inspected the physical incarnation of his designs. "Weinsburg wasn't just about murder and retribution. It was about planning ahead."

The prince's look of awe immediately turned skeptical. "I saw a demonstration once of a hand held black powder gun and was not impressed. Only one in twelve shots even hit the target standing fifty feet away. My archers were able to hit it dead center every time."

Tomal walked over to a second wagon and pulled back the tan tarp to reveal three large kegs of black powder and two sizeable stacks of metal balls, each the size of a man's head. "We have enough powder and ammunition for thirty shots to hit our mark," Tomal declared. "I say we roll the dice and take our chances at scoring a direct hit. What do we have to lose?"

The doubtful frown turned up slightly as the prince looked back at the castle again. "Nothing, I suppose." He turned his focus back to Tomal, but only saw his back walking away toward the city streets. "Where are you going?"

"You have the primary plan well in hand, now I go to see about the backup arrangements," Tomal answered back without turning around.

"Backup plan?" the prince repeated which caused Tomal to stop and turn around for a moment.

"Yes, my mentor once told me he doesn't even go to the bathroom without a backup plan," Tomal responded and continued on into the city streets. "Over the years I have found it to be sound advice," he concluded over his shoulder.

Chapter 58: An Offer He Can't Refuse

AS VALNOR NAVIGATED the desolate streets of Constantinople, he was relieved to hear the roar of Mehmed's rampaging men grow more and more distant. The most advantageous sections of the city to pillage for valuables lay to the south. The opulent apartments and villas adorned with all manner of gold, jewels and artwork were difficult to miss.

Other hotspots for looting and entertainment were the market and brothel districts in the eastern quarter of the city, which left the northwestern quadrant relatively free from devastation so far. The seemingly endless string of run-down apartment buildings that reached six to ten stories skyward would be the last to see looting, vandalism and rape from the occupying army, but it would eventually come.

Thousands of residents attempted to flee the chaos by jumping into the sea and swimming for safety. It was a nearly impossible swim that only a few hundred might survive, but drowning was preferable to being raped endlessly or getting sold into slavery by the occupying army.

Those who knew their aquatic abilities were not up to the task worked feverishly to hide everything they had, including themselves. Walking through the desolate streets Valnor heard a chorus of saws cutting and nails being hammered into place in an effort to blockade doors or make hiding places. Some would succeed, most would not, but it was all they had therefore the helpless civilians worked diligently to finish before the inevitable trouble arrived.

Valnor found his way to the university campus nestled among the six story tall apartment complexes of the Phanar district. His progress was impeded by a blockade made of anything and everything the students and faculty could find. Overturned wagons, crates, desks, and bookshelves were all strewn about making a ten foot high pile of rubble that might keep a few dozen soldiers out, but not the thousands who would eventually come once the wealthier districts were thoroughly sacked.

Valnor took a moment to evaluate the barricade and spotted a book shelf he could use as a ladder leaning against the pile of rubble. When he reached the top, he saw a hundred yard square courtyard defended by a few dozen students wielding swords while looking scared out of their wits.

"Halt," one of them shouted in Latin. He continued in the same language to see if Valnor understood the words. It was a clever test considering most in the invading army would not comprehend the language. "Identify yourself or we will cut you down."

"Relax, I am a friend," Valnor said while scaling his way down from the barricade to the courtyard. "I am looking for one of your visiting professors, Nicolaus Copernicus. Is he still here?"

The armed student hesitated for a moment while his companions drew near to present a united front. "Who is asking for him?"

"Tell Nicolaus his friend Orban is here to present an opportunity to him and his friends."

One of the students ran to the right side of the courtyard and through a door in the center of that wing. Ten minutes later Nicolaus, and no fewer than fifty men all brandishing daggers and swords, stormed out of the building with anger venting from every fiber of their being.

Valnor knew his initial reception would not be friendly, but he hoped to get at least a few words in before the mob's vigilante justice could be enforced. Valnor decided to get his offer out in the open before the group arrived to do god knows what to him. "You have the look of a man with murder in your eyes."

Nicolaus pointed an accusing finger in Valnor's direction. "You ought to know. You brought an entire army of men with that very same look in their eyes to the walls of our great city. Then you gave them a weapon to blast a hole in those walls so they could carry out their murders. Now it's your turn."

Nicolaus quickened his marching cadence which forced Valnor to get right to the point. "You can't kill your only friend on the other side, the man with a plan to get all of you out of this besieged city alive."

"How, as your slaves?" Nicolaus demanded. "Didn't you make enough money selling your weapon of destruction to the highest bidder?"

"Actually, it is I who intends to pay you," Valnor got out just before Nicolaus swung and landed an angry fist to his jaw. The blow sent Valnor to the cobblestone covered ground, and he remained on all fours looking up at his attacker. "That is what this was all about."

247

Nicolaus looked ready to put the sword he carried to use, but those last seven words gave him pause. "Explain yourself."

"I am already rich beyond my capacity to spend in a lifetime," Valnor began as he struggled back to his feet to look Nicolaus dead in the eyes. "I came here to unleash the bottled up knowledge hiding behind these walls to the rest of the world. The collective enlightenment of these great minds must leave this place to bring light back into the darkened world."

"Come with me to Florence. Art, architecture, literature, mathematics, law, linguistics are all poised for resurgence if great men arrive to steer it along to share with the world rather than hide it away in a walled city."

Valnor raised his voice to address everyone in the courtyard. "I offer to sponsor all of you. I will fund any of your artistic and scholastic endeavors if you will join me in Florence."

The look of murder was no longer in the eyes of Nicolaus, but feelings of hurt and betrayal still clearly lingered.

"I know you would sooner run me through and suffer the fate it brings upon you than follow my lead, but this is bigger than you and I," Valnor said looking back at Nicolaus once more. "Look around you. You hold the lives of every man in this university at the tip of that sword you wield. Do with them as you see fit."

Nicolaus held the look of a man torn between two primal instincts: survival and revenge. Gradually the hard lines of anger relaxed around his eyes to deliver a reasoned response.

"Get us all out of this city with our books and notes intact and those who wish to take your offer will follow you to Florence. Those, like me, who find your very existence emphatically vile will go wherever they see fit. Do we have an accord?"

Valnor drew a deep breath through his nostrils and finally extended an open palm to seal the deal. "We do. Now get your things, we don't have much time."

Valnor's misfit gaggle of bookworms following him out of the city drew only a passing interest from the Sultan's rampaging army. When troubled, all he needed to do was show the royal insignia of Sultan Mehmed II. Per their arrangement, Valnor turned over his excessive wages for overseeing the construction of the bombard cannon in exchange for the right to remove as many as a hundred civilians from the city without question.

The Sultan was a man of his word as was Nicolaus. He and a few of his colleagues went back to his native Poland while the vast majority of the rescued scholars and artists accompanied Valnor back to Florence to share their light under his patronage.

Chapter 59: No Big Surprise

PROFESSOR RUSSELL STOOD over the shoulder of Alex as she ran through the last in a series of tests. They wanted to make sure the four ground receptors were well positioned to bounce signals received from the emitter hovering overhead in between each other to map out the interior of the Chinese pyramid.

While waiting, Brian took the time to consider just how much had changed for him and Alex over the last week and also how much was still the same. Just like it was in Egypt, he and Alex sat in a field tent ready to map a pyramid while a government observer looked on.

This time it was a short Chinese man rather than the aging Dr. Andre, who turned out to be an alien intent on their capture to keep the chambers discovered in the Great Pyramid and Sphinx hidden. Brian trusted Chin no farther than he could throw the man, but he did think it quite unlikely that he was also an alien trying to keep a secret. In fact, Chin was the one intent on making new discoveries, but it remained to be seen if Chin would also incarcerate Alex and him if anything important was discovered.

Another prominent difference was the elevated sophistication of the equipment at their disposal. Overhead a state of the art helicopter hovered perfectly steady to give accurate readings rather than an aging aircraft that wobbled about while struggling to stay airborne.

What remained unchanged from before was the laptop computer and C++ program Alex used to display the findings. The tiny monochrome dots were nothing pretty to look at, but it was enough to give a well defined layout of the structure's interior.

"Everything checks out. The emitter is holding steady in position; I think we're ready to give this a shot," Alex reported.

"Let's see what we get then," Professor Russell ordered, which prompted Alex to press the side of her headset with a boom microphone extending from the earpiece to her mouth; another welcome upgrade from before.

"Begin," she said, keeping the message short for the pilot who only knew a few key words of English.

"How long will it take to see the results," Chin asked as he relocated himself to stand over Alex's other shoulder to view her screen.

"With a steady helicopter holding the emitter, not long," Alex responded without turning around.

No sooner had she uttered those words when dots began appearing on the mapping display. First the outer shape of the shrunken pyramid took form. Next, a tunnel leading from the Terracotta Army pits due east was filled in culminating in a large chamber located inside the base of the pyramid.

A twenty foot high ceiling was filled in for the chamber as the dots continued to be laid higher and higher into the body of the burial mound. When it was all done, a one hundred foot tall structure perfectly pyramidal in shape sat directly on top of the Emperor's burial chamber.

Despite the jarring magnitude of this discovery, these readings did not get Professor Russell's juices flowing like they did back in Egypt. Perhaps it was because he had already experienced the wonder and excitement before and now it was old hat. More likely though was the feeling that this was not truly his discovery. The risks and effort the Chinese went to in order to have this test performed made him almost certain something would be found. The result being that there really was no element of surprise this time around.

When Alex spoke up, Brian could tell from her vocal inflections that she was equally unimpressed. "Well would you look at that, another chamber, a big one. Hard to believe no one even had a clue something that large was there."

"Yes," Professor Russell added with a sideways glance toward Chin. "It is very odd that nothing is showing up inside that gigantic chamber. It's as if something is interfering with the emitter readings from inside that chamber."

Chin ignored the conversation between the Americans. Instead, he spent several minutes talking into the headset hooked onto his ear. His words were spoken in Chinese, therefore the specific meaning was lost, but Brian got the distinct feeling that the sanctity of Emperor Qin Shi Huang's burial chamber was very much in jeopardy.

"So what happens now?" Brian asked of Chin once the man took off his headset and placed it on the table next to Alex's keyboard.

"Now we take a little ride back to the Terracotta soldier pits," he answered politely as always, and gestured with his arm for the two archeologists to lead the way out of the tent.

"You plan on disturbing the Emperor's tomb to reach that other chamber don't you?" Professor Russell accused. "Why? For what reason?"

For the first time since meeting Chin, Brian watched the man's accommodating smile that never wavered run flat.

"To further our knowledge of Chinese history of course," the man offered, and grabbed Alex by the arm to forcibly move her along toward the door, but she was having none of it.

Alex rotated her arm backwards and twisted away from Chin's grasp. "Right, and I'm from Mars. If you were interested in preserving history, you would assemble a team of archeologists. They would take months planning out the best way to open the chamber without disturbing the priceless and most likely fragile artifacts inside. Last time I checked you are an intelligence agent. Did you finish your PhD and a lifetime of field work in archeology in the last ten minutes while I wasn't paying attention?"

Her last statement brought the smile back to Chin's lips. "This is China. Things are done differently in my country than in yours."

"Differently or stupidly?" Alex fired back.

Chin allowed the smile to run away from his lips while quickly drawing his pistol and leveling the threatening instrument at Brian and Alex to deliver his response. "Out the door, *now.*"

Alex nodded her head and glanced toward Professor Russell as she began pacing toward the door. "Yeah, that's how it's done in our country too, sometimes."

Brian followed Alex toward the door, but continued pleading his case as he moved. "This is a protected Chinese national landmark. It is illegal, immoral, and not to mention reckless to open that door without proper professionals on hand to preserve the findings. You can't do this."

"Why are you in such a hurry to desecrate this national treasure?" Brian asked with his pleas growing more insistent with every step taken toward the door. Just before stepping out into the evening air he snapped his fingers and turned to face Chin with an index finger pointed right at the short Chinaman.

"Radiation," Brian blurted out like it was the answer to a question worth a million dollars on a game show. "That is about the only thing that could interfere with the emitter readings enough to show us nothing. You knew it was there all along, didn't you?"

Chin raised his eyebrows in surprise at the statement, then shook his head in mild disappointment. "Americans, always thinking for themselves rather than doing as they are told."

"We do things differently in America," Professor Russell deadpanned back.

"Fine," Chin said while turning Brian back toward the door to continue their progress. "We have known about the radiation for a while now, but we were not certain if the readings came from the chamber we knew about already or from another source. Before this discovery I was not certain it was worth the trouble of violating the chamber to reach the radiation source, but now I am."

While walking toward the transport vehicles, Brian could not figure out why Chin was divulging this information to them. He worked for the Chinese intelligence agency. By definition, this made him a secretive individual who horded information rather than dispensing it willingly. This was out of character.

"So what, there's a little radiation in there. You guys already have the bomb. What could you possibly get from this stuff that you don't already have?" Alex asked. "Do you think it's some sort of 'ultra radiation' that could power your whole country for a thousand years or something?"

"The radiation is actually quite benign in strength. It is the frequency that interests me," Chin said while intently watching the body language of his two captives. Both Alex and Brian broke stride at the mention of frequencies. Brian recalled all too well the discussion they were privy to while held captive inside the Sphinx.

"Interesting response," Chin marveled. "You should feel very privileged. Only a dozen people, including your current and living former Presidents, know about frequency Alpha. I cannot say I know what it is, but I do know it is very important to my American counterparts. We shall have to compare notes once we are done here."

When they reached the Mengshi off-road vehicle that Chin guided them toward, Alex was the first to climb into the back seat. Once settled she looked back at Brian as he climbed in with a hateful look that screamed 'I told you so!'

****

Frank heard the words Chin spoke to his men loud and clear through the bug he installed in Alex's laptop. Unlike the two archeologists, he was perfectly fluent in Chinese and understood the order to converge on the burial chamber entrance located near the Terracotta Army pits.

Frank was on the move at a fast jog to try and reach the pits located a mile away ahead of Chin and his men. He had no idea what came up on Alex's screen, but having it described as big and pointing out a source of interference piqued his concern. This was no longer an investigative mission to make sure secrets were not leaked to a hostile nation; this was now a major concern requiring action.

Chapter 60: Defining Evil

AFTER LISTENING TO Hastelloy ramble on about the past for over an hour, Mark decided he had heard enough. Listening to the stories gave him a good feel for what made the man tick; now it was time to put that knowledge to good use.

While Hastelloy paused to take a drink of water, Mark began laughing. Softly to himself at first, but the laughter soon bounced between the office walls drawing awkward stares from Dr. Holmes and his patient. "Let me paraphrase everything that I just heard. The Alpha are pure evil while the Novi are the source of all things noble and good in our world today."

"That is a bit simplistic don't you think?" Hastelloy countered as he placed his drinking glass back on the coffee table.

Mark tossed his hands out wide and shrugged his shoulders. "What can I say, I'm a simple guy. Though I must point out that you killing millions of Chinese farmers to incite your little rebellion, or the poisoning of the nobles to unite that rebellion under one leader does not sound all that noble or good to me."

Hastelloy shifted his weight to lean on the right armrest of the chair and brought his hand up to cup his chin in contemplation. "Well, not such a simple man after all. You of all people must realize that no one is always bad or always good all the time. Everyone lives within the boundaries of black and white in various shades of grey."

"Those actions, along with your man leveling the city walls of Constantinople allowing it to be sacked, look awfully dark to me. In fact, I don't see any white at all in that picture," Mark observed. Hastelloy was trying to sell himself to Mark and his brother as some sort of guardian angel. Mark wasn't buying it and now it was time to make sure Jeff was not tempted to believe it either.

"If you want to judge those individual actions outside the context of the bigger picture, you are free to reach that conclusion. By those rules then, I am free to condemn your acts of water boarding suspects and murdering Valnor's wife in Berlin as acts of evil also," Hastelloy responded with an intense and hateful glare. "Or am I to assume you are a decent man whose despicable actions are performed to safeguard the lives of others for the greater good?"

Mark felt a cold shudder electrify his body with both panic and rage. The last thing he wanted mentioned in front of his brother was the unfortunate necessities of his job. Jeff was an idealist; he would not understand. A glance toward his brother told Mark he needed to cut off this avenue of discussion, but Hastelloy beat him to it.

Hastelloy casually looked over at Jeffrey. "Doctor, you are an impartial observer here. Why don't you be the judge? Was your brother's torturing of Valnor's wife to death in order to gain information about the supposed threat my crew poses to this entire planet of seven billion people good or evil?"

Mark jumped in before his brother could even draw a breath, let alone answer the question. "If there were any truth to that accusation, then the answer would of course be my actions were for the good. Working to safeguard billions is by definition working towards the greater good."

"Now then, can you claim the same noble cause?" Mark continued. "You and your men control a weapon capable of destroying this entire planet inhabited by some seven billion people. All so you can try and safeguard those twenty million Novi lives housed in that Nexus device of yours. The greater good tilts away from you I'd say."

"Good or evil also depends on one's perspective," Hastelloy responded without missing a beat. "Until now the fortunes of humanity and my crew were intertwined. Defeating the Alpha saved humanity from an eternity of slavery and the Nexus from destruction."

"And now?" Mark prodded.

"Now, in addition to the Alpha threat, the safety of the Nexus and my crew are pitted against your leadership's fear of the unknown along with their obsessive need for control," Hastelloy answered in a frigid tone.

Mark paused the debate to assess his brother's situation. One look said it all; he was in complete shock by what he had heard and sat as a mute observer to the exchange.

Mark looked back at Hastelloy and released a skeptical smirk. "You and your men are still around now. Stands to reason you were successful in defeating the Alpha back then."

"Some of us are still around," Hastelloy corrected. "If I ever fail at stopping the Alpha, and you have the misfortune of meeting one of them, you will learn very quickly that they do not go down easily."

"You make it sound like they still might be a threat today," Mark said with genuine concern. "Would you mind telling me how things wound up with the Alpha back then?"

Chapter 61: Extinguish the Flames

HASTELLOY SLOWED HIS brisk jog to an apprehensive walk as he approached the opened doors of the burial chamber. The continued flashing of blue light past him as he ran along the nearly mile long tunnel gave him hope that Gallono was finding a way to hold off the reanimated Alpha relics.

He approached the door with light footsteps, placed the deceivingly heavy hand cannons against the wall, gripped his sledge hammer with two hands and hoisted the heavy end overhead.

"It appears those Novi are putting up an adequate fight," a feminine voice standing just inside the doorway said in the harsh Alpha language. "That makes six reanimations so far."

"Let me know when it gets into the thousands, then I'll start worrying," a domineering male voice responded from deep inside the chamber.

Hastelloy heard the female sigh in frustration and used that brief distraction to the fullest. He burst in through the doorway and demolished the unsuspecting clay figure with a crushing downward swing of his hammer.

The glowing relic inside faded away, but then Hastelloy noticed the vibrant glow reappear above a stone altar along the far wall fifty feet away with copper wires extending to it from a nearby clay vase that stood over seven feet tall. A moment later the relic drew upward into the ceiling and shifted from a glow of deep red and yellow to an electric blue hue. Then the light rushed past him down the tunnel toward the soldier pits.

Hastelloy's preoccupation with the Alpha reanimation process did not serve him well. An Alpha warrior caught him momentarily by surprise and leveled a shoulder led tackle that left them both crumpled on the floor. The Alpha warrior was the first to recover. The beast rose to its full height, towering over Hastelloy with an open hand bearing razor sharp claws ready to strike.

Hastelloy rolled toward the Alpha to bring his hammer up with as much force as possible, devastating the creature with a well placed strike to the groin.

The Alpha stumbled back with a high pitched howl that could have woken the dead emperor still resting in his ornate casket at the center of the room. A second Alpha warrior leapt into action. Hastelloy managed to dodge three punches, but a vicious snap kick connected with the wooden handle of his sledge hammer, breaking it in half and leaving the business end on the floor. The Alpha warrior prowled forward to continue the attack, but was called off.

"No. I've waited three thousand years for this moment, and I will have it," a clay soldier commanded as it strutted forward toward Hastelloy. It stopped momentarily over the Alpha coddling its genitals and then looked at the other. "You two guard the altar. That is your duty. I will secure victory over this enemy Goron was never able to defeat."

Unarmed and nursing a set of cracked ribs from the Alpha's bone crushing tackle, Hastelloy backed away toward the center of the chamber. He looked around for options. His objective was clearly the stone altar and connecting clay vase, but it was now flanked by the two Alpha warriors.

Off in a dusty corner, far from the revered altar, sat five vibrant relics swaying slowly in the air. Their unceremonious position led Hastelloy to conclude these relics chose not to violate their cultural rules and reanimate. Running through the arithmetic in his head gave Hastelloy a moment of relief.

He assumed every relic would be coming after Gallono down in the soldier pits. With two Alpha standing guard, the clay soldier stalking him, and five relics resisting reanimation, Gallono was left to fight against at most six clay soldiers. It was still not an easy task by any stretch of the imagination, but within the commander's abilities.

"Looks like some of your crew still have a shred of self-respect; enough not to violate their most sacred laws at least," Hastelloy said as he walked backwards over a bridge spanning a five foot wide river of mercury. "Having trouble keeping the troops in line there, Kuanti?"

"A frustratingly selfish choice, but inconsequential in the end," Kuanti barked. "Cora and the other five are more than capable of sending your man back to that Nexus device of yours."

Kuanti chuckled softly as he lumbered his heavy body across the bridge to join Hastelloy on an island surrounded by rivers of mercury, housing the solid copper sarcophagus of Emperor Qui Shi Huang. It stood four feet tall with a lifelike rendering of the man inside engraved into the lid. Hastelloy stepped around to the other side to keep the immensely heavy barrier between him and his stalker.

Kuanti strolled up to the sarcophagus and casually scraped a hand over the smooth metallic surface. "It's funny when you think about it: you and the Nexus, us and these earthen bodies. Two sets of immortals locked in endless combat. I suspect the superstitious creatures inhabiting this planet would consider it a battle between gods."

"It's evident you crave power and recognition, Kuanti, but you are not a god. The universe was not so poorly designed," Hastelloy said while circling around the copper barrier which brought the relic altar into clear view for him.

The chamber grew noticeably brighter with the arrival of four glowing relics on the altar. One immediately began rising up toward the ceiling to reanimate again, but then returned to the altar.

"Hmm, immortal no longer it appears," Hastelloy mocked.

Kuanti glanced over his shoulder then back to Hastelloy with a self-satisfied grin. "The process does take quite a bit of power. Give it a few minutes and my men will be back in the fight. If your man goes down, will he be back so soon? No, I suppose not. You probably have that Nexus device tucked away somewhere on the western continent."

"Something like that," Hastelloy acknowledged. "Trick is you have to bring him down first."

"Pretty soon that won't be a problem," Kuanti said slamming his shoulder into the coffin separating him from Hastelloy. The copper fixture groaned and resisted, but eventually gave way. The sarcophagus toppled over sending Hastelloy scrambling to get out of the way. The entire chamber shook with the impact, and a minor tremor followed when the exquisitely sculpted lid fell open upon impact.

Hastelloy took a running jump onto the capsized coffin, then delivered a flying side kick to the head of Kuanti. The painful sensation of kicking a brick wall raced up Hastelloy's leg, but it was worth the price. Kuanti fell backwards onto his back with another reverberating crash.

He half expected the momentary victory to entice the Alpha warriors to rejoin the fight, but they simply looked on with all the morbid enthusiasm of fans watching a gladiator duel.

While Kuanti casually got back to his feet, Hastelloy looked past the red clay figure and noticed a subtle movement among the shadows near the chamber door. He was careful not to look directly at the disturbance to give it any undue attention. Through his peripheral vision, Hastelloy recognized Gallono as the source of movement. He was sneaking along the wall keeping to the shadows, and carried the two hand cannons Hastelloy set near the door before charging into the chamber.

Kuanti was back on his feet again. Hastelloy moved in behind the toppled sarcophagus, but Kuanti leapt on top of the fixture to clear a direct path to Hastelloy.

Kuanti stepped down from the coffin and methodically backed Hastelloy in against the river of mercury. "You are out of places to hide. It's time to face your defeat like a man."

Gallono looked poised to step out of the shadows and blast Kuanti apart with a hand cannon, but a barely perceptible shake of Hastelloy's head waved him off. He flicked his eyes toward the relic altar guarded by the Alpha warriors and Gallono got the message. All Hastelloy needed to do now was keep the show interesting enough for the audience to allow the commander to execute his orders.

Hastelloy briefly considered jumping over the five foot wide river of flowing metal, but opted to keep the spectacle confined to the sarcophagus island. Wandering eyes might spot shadowy movements he did not want noticed. Unarmed and cornered, Hastelloy did the only thing he could; lowered his shoulder and charged.

Kuanti stepped backwards and to the side to absorb the hit. He looped his arms down underneath Hastelloy's armpits and flung him across the island to land against the coffin. Hastelloy scrambled to his feet, jumped up onto the sarcophagus to dodge a punch, then jumped onto the back of Kuanti and held tight with a headlock grip.

Hastelloy stole a sideways glance to check on Gallono's progress while Kuanti swung his waist from side to side attempting to shed the excess baggage. Gallono was twenty feet away and still unnoticed.

A grasping hand finally caught a piece of Hastelloy's shirt, another hand quickly found purchase on his left arm. Kuanti bent forward at the waist and yanked Hastelloy off his back like he was removing a tight fitting shirt. The clay warrior slammed Hastelloy to the ground, then picked him up and threw his limp body down two more times before stopping to put his heavy foot down on Hastelloy's sternum.

"Game over little man."

A sharp snap and sizzle coming from near the altar let Hastelloy know he was free to respond, "It is for you."

Kuanti looked back in time to see Gallono anchoring a lit hand cannon against his foot and pointing it directly at the seven foot clay vase. He took two instinctive steps toward the scene yelling, "Stop him," but it was too late.

Hundreds of metal shards exploded from the hand cannon into the vase filled with the most potent acid known to exist. The aftermath left the nearby Alpha warriors drenched in boiling acid disintegrating their flesh on contact and rendering them wailing pools of pus and blood within a few short seconds.

Hastelloy sprang to his feet, slammed into Kuanti from the side and drove with every ounce of strength he had in his legs until the clay form fell over the river's edge into the mercury, dragging Hastelloy down with him. He managed to draw a quick breath before entering, then found himself completely submerged in a cool, heavy substance that barely allowed him to move.

It was impossible to tell which way was up or down. Hastelloy frantically flailed his arms and legs about in slow motion until he finally felt his left foot hit something solid. He moved his right leg alongside and then pushed off the solid base to bring his head, chest and arms above the surface.

The mercury was about four feet deep and attempting to move around in it was nearly impossible. It took everything he had to shuffle his feet along the bottom just a few inches, making the two foot journey to climb out the side seem like a walk to the moon and back.

Behind Hastelloy, Kuanti rose up out of the silvery liquid like a ferocious sea monster and attempted to give chase, but failed to budge even a single inch. The clay figure swung wildly with its arms to reach Hastelloy, but came up a foot short.

"Frustrating isn't it," Hastelloy chided. "Victory is so close you can almost touch it, yet remains out of reach."

"If I don't get to finish you off, the others will," Kuanti shouted while still attempting to move his heavy frame through the extremely dense liquid.

Hastelloy glanced over at the stone altar and observed no new relics had appeared following the gruesome deaths of the two Alpha disintegrated by acid. "That doesn't look likely to me. There were fourteen of you. Two are now gone, I count eleven relics on the altar or banished in the dark corner. That leaves just you, and not for very much longer."

"Truer words were never spoken," Gallono said from the river's edge as he lit the fuse to the last hand cannon.

"Death is only the beginning," Kuanti defiantly declared before he was blasted to pieces. His relic momentarily hovered over the mercury with a radiant red flame straining to remain above the surface, but then slowly sank down until it lightly touched the mercury. The dull silver liquid drew up into the red flame and snuffed the life force out of it and eventually receded back down into the river once more.

"I've heard that before," Gallono mocked while offering Hastelloy a hand to drag him out of the mercury.

The heavy substance stubbornly clung to its prey, but eventually Hastelloy came free and lay face first on the floor. He took a moment to catch his breath, then rose to his full height. They both walked toward the altar and the six relics resting upon it.

"You take care of these; I will handle the ones over in the corner," Hastelloy ordered.

Gallono regarded the flames with a menacing tilt of his head. "With pleasure."

To their credit, the relics met their end with quiet dignity. No screams, no begging for mercy, simply resignation to the reality of the situation. It still didn't stop Gallono from relishing the moment with one last barb. "Same opponent, same result."

Gallono had the easy task. He disposed of relics who repeatedly came after him with murderous intent and violated their most sacred beliefs to do so. Hastelloy had to face five relics who chose dedication and honor to their beliefs. Hastelloy held the utmost respect for their integrity, but he couldn't very well leave Alpha relics with the potential to reanimate alive on this planet, even if they would be entombed behind sealed doors in this place.

Hastelloy did his duty and dropped the remaining relics into the mercury. He considered resetting the burial casket to make it look like no one was ever there, but knew the weight of the copper was far too heavy for just him and Gallono to move. History would just have to deal with yet another unsolved mystery if the chamber were ever opened again.

On their way out of the chamber, Hastelloy glanced up at the ceiling and instantly recognized it as the night sky he had seen above this planet for four thousand years now.

"Remarkably detailed isn't it," Gallono said.

"All except for that silver ball hanging down. What do you suppose that was intended to be?" Hastelloy pondered.

"Who knows, the emperor was clearly a megalomaniac: building this pyramid, the clay soldiers. It probably represents him ruling his world from among the heavens like a god," Gallono answered.

Chapter 62: Future Prospects

GORON BATTLED THROUGH a complex set of mixed emotions while the profound sense of loneliness he'd endured for millennia on this planet closed in around him once more. One by one, he lost contact with the relics located in the Far East.

The first to vanish from his mind was Kuanti. At first Goron reveled in the blasphemous pup's defeat at the hands of Hastelloy. After giving him grief for thousands of years for not being able to defeat the crafty Novi captain, Kuanti was finally humbled at the hands of that extremely capable foe.

In the end, Kuanti spoke his brave, defiant words, 'death is only the beginning,' but that was just for show. When his clay body shattered and his relic teetered over the poisonous mercury liquid, he showed his true cowardice. Had Kuanti's mind still controlled the urinary track of a live body, Goron was quite certain the pup would have piddled himself. As the mercury slowly snuffed out his life force, Kuanti's mind reached out in an all consuming moment of terror and finally was no more.

Goron privately rejoiced at that moment. Kuanti violated the most sacred law of Mother Nature by reanimating. He got exactly what he deserved. That moment of elation soon morphed to horror as contact with the other relics soon vanished from his mind. The ones who chose to reanimate met their end with the same fear and panic as Kuanti. Those who retained their honor were completely at peace when they met their end, but the end still came for them.

The mental companionship those relics provided was not much, but it was something. Anything, even Kuanti's vile existence, was preferable to being alone again. A weaker man might have given in to the depressing solitude that crushed in around him, but Goron was strong. He did not end his existence in his darkest moment. He would continue to press on with his struggle against the Novi, but knowing he was alone once more in his efforts was demoralizing to say the least.

It took Goron the better part of a week to cast aside his lamentations and refocus his thoughts on formulating a new plan to hinder Captain Hastelloy and his small crew. Before he even had the chance to envision his next instrument of anarchy, his mind was overwhelmed by the sudden arrival of nearly six hundred thousand life forces. The planetary orbits were nowhere near close enough for contact. This fact let Goron conclude that Kuanti's short stay on this planet was time well spent. His modification to the pyramid had succeeded in transporting the relics from Mars to Earth.

Goron was so flabbergasted he could barely communicate a coherent thought. His mind finally regained control over his emotions to say one word, "Report."

"We are all here now," Noren reported for the newly arrived collective consciousness. "What is the status here? We all expected to meet Kuanti, Cora and the others yet do not sense their presence."

Any lingering jovial emotions Goron felt melted away upon hearing Noren's question. Who was he to demand answers from Goron? Still, it was a fair question that needed an answer. "They were arrogant and careless. They disregarded my counsel and as a result, even with a dozen Alpha warriors at his command, Kuanti and Cora were defeated by the Novi."

"Not to worry," Noren declared. "The Mars colony is only months away from transporting fifty thousand Alpha warriors to secure victory on this planet."

"No...they won't," Goron somberly reported. "When the Novi defeated Kuanti's task force, they not only snuffed out their lives, they captured his ship."

The minds of so many in the collective were pathetic and weak. They all thought the words Noren spoke. "So what? The ship cannot space fold, has no communications equipment, and is too slow for its limited life support to keep an occupant alive long enough to even leave the solar system; let alone reach Novus."

"It does have a functioning fusion reactor," Goron pointed out for the others. "I am quite certain that Captain Hastelloy will employ that reactor as a weapon of mass destruction against the Mars colony."

A wave of panic slowly overtook the collective consciousness. The brighter relics understood the dire situation instantly, and their comprehension eventually informed those with slower intellects. "We need to do something; we need to warn them," the collective insisted.

"Why, what an excellent idea," Goron mocked. "We will not be in range to reach the relics still there in time. These humans are many hundreds of years away from building a communications device capable of reaching Mars. Then of course we would have to disable the Novi's jamming signal to get that message out."

The doomed state of affairs hit home for most, but Goron added one last statement to remove any doubt. "The Mars colony will be lost, and there is nothing to be done about it. All we can do now is look toward our future on this planet."

"What future?" Noren demanded. "We are locked away inside this chamber with no way out. Even Kuanti's reanimation process is blocked by copper sealed doors."

"Then my followers will just have to come to the rescue," Goron answered.

Chapter 63: Sacrifice

HASTELLOY SAT IN the pilot's seat of the Alpha craft studying the controls, navigation and communications equipment while Gallono saw to the mechanical components. Everything was in fine working order to make the trip back to Mars.

Gallono leaned in through the side exit hatch. "The fusion reactor is pretty elementary in design, but it clearly got the job done for them."

"The only question I need answered is will it get the job done for me?" Hastelloy asked.

"That's hard to say, Captain. Mars is barely habitable, but the Alpha have been at it for three thousand years. Their base could be pretty large by now. Worse yet, it could be completely buried inside of a mountain and nearly impossible to reach. That said, I can't see anything surviving when this reactor goes critical. Who knows, it might set off a few others they are using to power their base."

Deep down Hastelloy already knew the answer to his next series of questions, but he asked them all the same to give himself a glimmer of hope. "What about the escape capsule you added? Do you think it really has a chance of making it back here?"

Gallono shook his head slowly. "I give it one chance in a hundred. There is enough air to make the three week flight back to Earth, but there are no controls or propulsion. It will be a function of jettisoning at the exact time to take out the Alpha base and hurl the capsule away on a pin point accurate course to hit a moving object some forty million miles away."

For a silent moment he looked Hastelloy square in the eyes and the optimistic bravado between the two gave way to an honest moment. "Captain, we've served together for over five thousand years. I am not going to let our final moments together be filled with false hopes. We both know this is a one way trip, and the Nexus range does not extend much beyond the Earth's atmosphere. This mission is the end of the road for the pilot, and it needs to be me."

Hastelloy closed his eyes and took in the full magnitude of things. They had spent years, sometimes decades, apart while serving on this planet. They all were immune to the emotion of long goodbyes by now, but this truly was the end. After all these thousands of years, this was the last time they would engage in friendly banter or share a disarming smile. They would never again shake hands out of respect or embrace one another in friendship and devotion; there were no adequate words of description in any language. The moment demanded honesty, not false hopes. "You're right. This is the end of the line for me. A little over ten thousand years is a pretty good run though. I reached the big five digits."

Gallono punched his fist against the bulkhead in defiance. "Goron is still wreaking havoc on this planet. Tomal still needs handling. First contact with the humans and final contact with the Novi still needs orchestrating. You are the only one capable of making it all happen. The greater good demands that you stay and I go."

The difficulty was that Gallono made a good argument; Hastelloy was certainly in no hurry to end his existence, but he couldn't give that order. "Both you and Valnor will manage just fine."

"No," Gallono declared and took a step into the ship as though he would attempt to rip Hastelloy right out of the pilot seat.

Hastelloy raised an outstretched hand to arrest Gallono's progress. "I've given the order for others to die because there was no other way: our assault on the Beta sector shipyards, sacrificing the Onager ships so the Lazarus device could escape the battle. I would have gladly made those sacrifices myself, but was in no position to do so. Now that I am, what sort of hypocritical coward would I be if I ordered someone else to go in my stead?"

"Besides, I am the first Novi in ten thousand years to dishonor himself by committing suicide and intentionally reanimating in an altered form," Hastelloy went on. "The four of you are innocent of those charges because I forced you to do it. I made the choice and did the deed of my own free will. We both know that once I get back to Novus I will be found guilty of the crimes and my existence will end anyway. This is just accelerating the inevitable by a few hundred years. My place is on this ship. I will make this sacrifice for the greater good I aspire to promote."

Tears welled up in the corner of Gallono's eyes and ran down his grease smudged cheeks. He, more than anyone else Hastelloy ever knew, was a man of honor. Gallono understood the reasoning and resigned himself to it. Without another word the two friends, brothers in arms for hundreds of lifetimes, embraced for the last time.

Hastelloy absorbed the show of respect and devotion from his friend. "I understand. It's an order you cannot give," Gallono said softly and then rabbit punched Hastelloy at the base of his neck causing a moment of disorientation and paralysis.

He was still conscious, but try as he may Hastelloy could not make his body move. He was a helpless observer of events while Gallono dragged his limp form out of the ship and laid it gently on the ground by a statue.

"You understand that letting my Captain give his life when it could be my own is an order I will not follow," Gallono defiantly declared to his captain. He then climbed into the ship, sealed the hatch and Hastelloy watched helplessly as the craft effortlessly took off and punched a hole in the ceiling of the gigantic chamber to reach the open skies.

As the ship grew so distant that it shrunk to the size of a grape, Hastelloy regained enough of his mobility to reach toward his friend with a wavering right arm.
****

Gallono's hands danced over the controls as he made his final orbital pass around Mars. He ran through the burn-in sequence for the thousandth time and hesitantly locked it in to the ship's central computer and let the countdown begin.

He knew the computer was infinitely more precise than the reaction times of a living person could ever be, but he still hesitated every time he turned his life over to the machines. He glanced back at the countdown and saw he only had two minutes, the moment of truth was at hand.

A rush of stale air greeted Gallono as he squatted down low and sat on the lightly padded floor of the jury-rigged escape capsule. He pulled his legs in, closed the door behind him, and wrapped his arms around his legs in the fetal position to wait.

Time seemed to draw out in front of him for an eternity. His honors, humiliations, joys and sorrows rolled through his mind without end. The first time he played ball as a boy, every single one of his thirty six weddings. The birth of his children came next. He could vividly picture his first child being born, but then the other sixty two ran together.

Then there was his first meeting with Hastelloy. It was at the academy, and Gallono hated the man at first sight. He was so capable, confident, yet

Mark Henrikson

accommodating and unassuming; all the things Gallono was not at the time. He was insecure and ambitious. He viewed Hastelloy as an opponent, a threat to his career path. It took a lifetime for Gallono to finally realize his rightful place as a complement, an instrument to the great man's unparalleled abilities.

A sudden jolt brought him back to the moment. Gallono looked out the tiny viewing window and watched the ship dive toward the red planet below while his miniscule four foot cubed cylinder sailed away with only the faintest hope of finding Earth once more. Making a safe landing was not necessary. He only needed to be within range of the Nexus, and the device would see to his regeneration. Getting within range, however, was the real trick.

Time sped up once more as the ship grew smaller and smaller until it was lost altogether against the red backdrop. Finally, far below he saw an energy ripple cascade out from the center to encompass a thousand miles in all directions. Then another even larger explosion reverberated across the planet's surface and sent a plume of ash soaring high enough to actually achieve escape velocity and eject particles into space.

A second reactor inside the Alpha base must have gone critical from the explosion as well. That was wonderful news for the destruction of the Alpha colony, but terrible for Gallono's prospects of survival.

He felt his tiny capsule begin vibrating and soon lurched and kicked in all directions, tossing a weightless Gallono about like a pinball. When the bucking finally subsided Gallono steadied himself in the middle once more.

What miniscule hope he held onto about reaching Earth was completely gone now. Even if the computer launched the capsule at the precise moment needed, the shockwave from the blast of two fusion reactors nearby most definitely threw him off course. Even a computer couldn't possibly account for all the course alterations that the competing shockwaves would throw off.

Rather than filling his head with false hope, Gallono embraced his end. For the next three weeks he reflected upon the honorable life he lived. It was a life of purpose and distinction. Most important of all, he made a difference in safeguarding the lives of twenty million Novi housed inside the Nexus. How many beings could boast that sort of accomplishment? He carried that feeling of distinguished pride with him all the way to the very end.

Chapter 64: Coming Together

AN HOUR AFTER sunset Tomal sat quietly with his back leaning against the outer walls of Nonnberg Abby near the eastern edge of Salzburg immediately below the archbishop's fortress.

A flash bright enough to rival the rising sun lit up the northern sky and was immediately followed by a thunderous boom that was both felt and heard throughout the city. Tomal's eyes followed the low arch of a flaming ball as it struck the upper fortress wall causing a five foot section to break away and tumble down the steep hillside below.

The damage was impressive, but the aim still managed to miss the ridge beam that lay a few degrees higher on the cannon's trajectory. Five shots had rung out already, but none managed to hit the magical target. Two sailed high, two hit the fortified walls with no effect, but the fifth definitely got much closer. With twenty five shots left, and the target already bracketed in reasonably well, it was only a matter of time before the fortress sustained a catastrophic hit.

The near miss must have gotten the archbishop's attention. Not long after the fifth cannon blast did its damage, the fortress doors opened and released a thousand soldiers along with a few hundred cavalry. Tomal could only imagine their orders were to capture or disable the cannon.

Once all of the Archbishop's forces were through the gates, the heavy wooden doors were locked shut behind them once more. The large body of soldiers snaked their way down the winding road leading into the city at a double time pace. When they reached the central city all hell broke loose as pitched battles filled the narrow streets with the clatter of metal striking metal, and periodic death wails from the combatants filled the air.

Tomal could honestly not predict which force would win out. The soldiers were well armed and organized professionals, but the peasants had ten times their numbers and a burning hatred behind their cause. The losses would be substantial on both sides. Knowing that, Tomal was quite happy to remain safe and hidden among the shadows.

While the battle among the streets raged on, yet another blast from the cannon lit up the night sky. Tomal watched the projectile strike the angled roof of the fortress halfway up the sloped side. It blasted through the timbers and punched a hole out the other side before landing harmlessly on the south side of the city among some fallow farm fields. The shots were getting very close now, which only added to the ferocity of the street battles.

After the blast Tomal allowed his eyes to adjust once more to the darkness. As the bright blotches vanished from his vision, the wooden rail line leading one hundred meters up the sixty degree incline to the fortress came back into focus.

Upon commencement of the siege, the two rail cars attached to one another on the single track made the ascent five times carrying supplies. Even though the siege was to only last a single day, Tomal ordered the Abby seized and the rail line carrying supplies up to the fortress stopped. For hours it had remained inactive, but Tomal had it on good authority that the cars would make at least one more trip up the rails under the cover of darkness.

Five minutes later Tomal's expectations were met. He heard a muffled squeak of wheels grinding against the wooden rail line. Tomal instantly sprung to his feet and ran over to where the rails left the Abby grounds on the elevated track.

He stood between a set of support beams that rose fifteen feet into the air to hold the rail aloft. He put his back against one and his legs against the other and shimmied his way up until he was able to grab hold of the rails above and pull himself up onto the tracks.

Tomal looked down the line and spotted the train of two cars still thirty feet down the track and progressing slowly his direction. He allowed the hemp rope pulling the cars to pass between his legs as he straddled the rails until the lead car came close enough for him to climb in.

There he waited as the cars silently pulled up the steep incline. The fifteen minute journey took him through five openings in the concentric defensive walls of the fortress that were just large enough to allow the cars through before finally arriving at the eastern edge of the central courtyard.

When the cars stopped moving, Tomal apprehensively poked his head over the side. Most of the courtyard was illuminated by ten raised metal baskets holding blazing piles of wood. The only area not lit was the eastern section where the rail line and team of donkeys driving the pull crank remained in the shadows. As expected, the courtyard was nearly empty since all but a handful of the protectors were outside the fortress attempting to silence the cannon.

Out of the darkness a hand flashed in front of Tomal's face. It took a moment of controlled breathing for him to recover from his shock, but he finally grabbed hold of the hand and climbed his way out of the cramped rail car. When he reached the ground and turned around, Tomal came face to face with Tonwen sporting a stern scowl.

"I see the Duke of Helfenstein did not disappoint. He took your designs and forged a cannon that functions quite well," Tonwen admired.

"Yes, thank you for dropping them off for me," Tomal replied. "And I see someone in here convinced the Archbishop that the structural integrity of his entire fortress was at risk if the cannon continued firing. How many soldiers are left inside the castle?"

"Not nearly enough," Tonwen answered with the corners of his mouth turning upward for a rare smile. "I do love when a plan comes together."

"I doubt even Hastelloy could have done any better," Tomal added. "Now where is the archbishop?"

"He retired to his private chapel to seek divine guidance," Tonwen answered.

"How very convenient for us," Tomal beamed. "Lead the way."

Chapter 65: From Alpha to Omega

TOMAL AND TONWEN carefully stuck to the shadows as they made their way around the courtyard until they finally slipped into the main structure unseen by the few guards remaining. Both men wound their way up a tight spiral staircase that let them out into a great room with open, vaulted ceilings that rivaled any throne room the world over.

The entire ceiling was adorned with larger than life paintings of dramatic scenes from the Bible separated into panels by brilliant white plaster with gold inlays. Polished wood floors, tapestries, and two fireplaces with solid marble mantles were just a few of the amenities on display. The view of the huge chamber was only interrupted by two decoratively carved and painted support columns holding up the single wooden ridge beam of the roof.

As Tomal admired the artistry of the columns, another blast from the cannon down below sent a cannonball screaming towards the fortress roof. A moment later, it blasted a hole through the roof and slammed into one of the support columns, delivering a glancing blow only a few feet below the ridge beam. The cannonball came to rest in the center of the chamber along with a similar sized chunk of wood separated from the column, but the support remained standing and continued to perform its duties.

"In retrospect, I may have designed that cannon to be a little too accurate," Tomal admired. "We need to hurry. The next shot, if they manage to get another off, just might do the trick."

Tonwen led them through a door along the far wall which brought them into a dark hallway made of stone except for a thick wooden plank laid into the middle of the floor. Tomal realized the wooden inlay was there so the archbishop could walk around the castle during the cold winter months on warm wood rather than cold stones.

"I am not exactly sure where the chapel is located since I have never been allowed into this part of the castle. These are his private chambers," Tonwen whispered.

"Assuming the chapel is his favorite room to visit, I think we can follow the most worn path in the wood and find it," Tomal offered. "It certainly beats wandering around aimlessly."

Tonwen and Tomal first followed a well-worn groove in the wood runner that brought them to a narrow door along the outer wall of the fortress.

Tomal pulled on the iron loop handle to reveal a tiny closet that had a knee high stone shelf with a single hole the size of a grown man's backside.

"Well that figures," Tomal mused and then quietly shut the bathroom door once more and followed Tonwen further down the hallway. Bed chambers, a library, and a small kitchen came and went without yielding a private chapel that Tonwen knew for certain was there.

The long hallway eventually came to an end with one final doorway which gained them entry to the archbishop's private office. The modest sized room had no windows or other doors leading in new directions. They were at a dead end with no other prospects.

A moment of panic ran through Tomal's mind. Could he be wrong? Could the Archbishop really just be a man whose egomaniacal nature took him down this path all alone? No! The man's actions had Goron's stink all over it; Tomal knew the scent all too well. He refused to give up so easily.

Tomal frantically looked about the office hoping something would catch his eye. The fireplace was apparently real as four large logs were ablaze inside the hearth giving the chamber both light and warmth. The furnishings were nothing substantial: a set of chairs with a small lamp table in between seated in front of a desk. On the desk sat a flickering lamp and a set of loose papers with chicken scratch writing across them next to a stack of books.

The leather bound reading material caused Tomal's scrutinizing eye to look upon the row of bookshelves lining the back wall. He dashed across the room and ran his hand all along the wooden edges of the shelving until he stopped and looked back at Tonwen with a confident glow. "I feel air movement. There is a hidden door behind these bookshelves."

Tomal did not waste any time. He reached for an entire shelf of leather bound books, yanked them all away and tossed them haphazardly into the corner. Tonwen followed suit, and pretty soon the shelves stood bare with a waist high pile of books overflowing in the corner next to them.

With everything removed from the shelves, Tomal stepped back to reassess the situation with the calm mind of an engineer. He let his barely contained anticipation of completing a task over three thousand years in the making to abate.

He knew all too well that only Hastelloy had ever managed to kill an Alpha relic on this planet. He also knew the captain at one time was this close to capturing Goron's relic, but let the opportunity slip through his fingers. Tomal was determined not to make the same mistake, this was his moment.

Tomal would have his revenge on Goron and prove to the rest of the crew that he was truly the better man on this planet. He proved it in Egypt by destroying the Alpha ship; him, not Hastelloy. The one stain on his impeccable legacy was the humiliation of being manipulated into serving the Alpha back in Rome. Now, in the next few moments, that blight would be expunged from his record. Redemption would be his if he could settle his mind enough to open this door.

Tomal closed his eyes and took a deep breath to cleanse his mind of all distractions. He then opened his eyes and looked upon the bookcase in a new light. These were not modern times. This door did not benefit from self-leveling hinges or mechanical release levers. It had to be a simple mechanism at work here.

In the upper left corner of the center shelf Tomal noticed a half inch thick metal rod with the end bent at ninety degrees to give a handhold pointing toward the interior of the bookshelf. He reached up and pulled down on the rod. It moved down three inches and suddenly he felt the entire bookshelf become mobile. He gave it a light push, and the perfectly balanced shelf pivoted around the middle axis as a gimbaled window turned on its side might rotate.

Tomal released the handle and both men pushed on one side of the shelf to turn it completely sideways, leaving two equally narrow entries separated by the askew shelving. Beyond the opening lay a corridor that went ten feet straight back and turned ninety degrees to the right. They heard two distinct sets of voices coming from that direction.

"After you," Tonwen offered, which Tomal immediately accepted and dashed down the discovered corridor with Tonwen pacing close behind.

"Your orders were both foolish and selfish," bellowed a demonic voice from around the corner. "You have left this fortress completely unprotected until that assault force returns, if they return."

"But that cannon my lord," a very weak, human voice responded. "A lucky strike could bring down this entire castle on top of you."

"On top of you!" the winds shouted back along with a bright flash that nearly blinded Tomal as he made ready to step around the turn and enter the archbishop's private chapel. "Such destruction would do nothing to harm my spiritual presence, so you were truly only looking out for yourself. You were so eager to protect your wonderfully opulent quarters that you put me at risk."

"That's what happens when you employ selfish men to carry out your bidding," Tomal declared as he and Tonwen stepped into the chapel to secure the room.

Archbishop Leonhard got off of his knees to face the unexpected intruders. He first looked at Tonwen. "What is the meaning of this intrusion? You have no business violating my private chambers like this."

The archbishop's eyes then moved over to Tomal and simultaneously filled with recognition and hatred. "Martin Luther? This, this can't be." He looked back at Tonwen in desperation. "You two have been working together this whole time?"

"Of course we have, and with your cooperation as well, though your participation had to be without your knowledge. A vile creature like you would never do anything for the greater good that did not first benefit you," Tomal answered on his way to stand between the archbishop and Tonwen. "You played your part beautifully, but now it's time to bring the curtain down on your act."

Tomal did not wait for a retort; he immediately slugged the archbishop square in the jaw with a right hook that sent the man to the stone floor in an unconscious heap.

"That was rather violent for a man of the cloth, don't you think Captain Hastelloy?" a voice admonished from all around the room. "I would commend you for finally managing to corner me after all these thousands of years, but we both know it's not much of an accomplishment. You had a crew of four immortals at your disposal against a formless entity with no arms or legs to even move around or defend myself. You have to admit, this really wasn't your best work now was it?"

"You are remarkably flippant for a being who will soon not exist," Tomal taunted while prowling toward the altar with measured steps. "Considering the captain failed to destroy you for so long, why do you assume he is the one standing before you now?"

"Hmmm, there it is," Goron's voice replied with a mix of surprise and amusement wrapped together. "I'd recognize that self-serving resentment of authority anywhere. Your timing could not be better, Tomal."

"Look at the ground in front of you," Goron ordered. When Tomal's eyes reluctantly complied, the relic went on. "As you can see, there is an opening for a new archbishop to benefit from my guidance. This castle, the wealth derived from the nearby salt mines and all of his subjects could be yours if you would only follow my instructions once more."

"Sounds like quite a plan," Tomal said dismissively as he pulled a small dagger out from under his priestly robes along with a stubby glass bottle containing a dark poison even the light from Goron's relic could not penetrate. "The thing is, even if I knowingly intended to betray my crew, I still wouldn't need you to achieve riches and power. By virtue of my writings and translation of the Bible, I already have a dedicated following throughout the Christian world. I could parlay that into quite a fortune and empire all on my own. Maybe I will do that, maybe I won't."

Tomal abruptly went silent as he slowly drenched the dagger with the dark poison making sure every millimeter of the blade was coated. He then thrust the blade into the flowing life force of Goron and released his grip on the deadly instrument. He looked on with orgasmic pleasure as Goron struggled to repel the tainted metal from his life force, but ultimately failed. The dagger was slowly absorbed into the bright flowing flame which soon after began to dim.

"Either way, you will not be around to see it. Your existence is now at an end. The puppet has at last turned the tables to snip the strings of his puppeteer," Tomal triumphantly declared as the once vibrant flame dimmed further.

Several silent moments passed before a low, haunting laughter rose up from Goron's relic. "At last I am released from my prison of solitude. My crimes at times have been great, but they did not warrant thousands of years spent in solitary confinement. At last the great, all knowing Mother Nature has seen fit to reclaim me. My penance is at an end, but yours has only begun."

As Goron's light dimmed further, the darkness of the chamber drew in around Tomal like a cold, damp blanket. His victory was monumental, yet he could not shake this feeling of guilt eating away in the back of his mind. He had just murdered a defenseless being; albeit a very dangerous one.

Tomal wondered if Hastelloy experienced a similar crisis of conscience when he plunged his dagger into the chest of Julius Caesar. The mere thought of the captain murdering his dear friend, a man Tomal considered a brother, brought anger and resentment flooding back into Tomal's heart.

In silence Goron's life force dimmed further until only a rusty ball teetered above the altar in the dim light cast from the chapel's lone entry point. A moment later the ball dropped and shattered upon the stone altar, releasing a fowl mist carrying with it the stench of death and decay upon the chamber.

For Tonwen, the fumes instantly induced vomiting. Tomal stood his ground and raised his arms out wide in triumph. He breathed deep the vapors, and relished every breath as a victory trophy - his victory.

Chapter 66: The Renaissance

AT VALNOR'S REQUEST, Hastelloy once again found himself walking the city streets of Florence, Italy. It had been over a hundred years since their last encounter when Valnor stormed out of the city intent on singlehandedly resolving the degeneration of society. Judging by what Hastelloy saw of the city, Valnor was well on his way to accomplishing his goal.

The first hint of progress was felt under Hastelloy's feet. The streets were once again paved flat and level allowing easy passage. Another sign was the level of cleanliness around the city.

During his earlier visit to the city he witnessed filled bedpans being emptied in the middle of the street to sit alongside steaming piles of horse dung that sat ankle deep in some parts. Today, he observed regular teams of men walking the streets; their only job was to pick up debris and sweep water and excrement into the central sewer system. The result was a well-kept series of roadways throughout the city.

All these improvements paled in comparison to the city's new skyline. Dwarfing everything else around by at least a hundred feet, stood the Basilica di Santa Maria. A hundred years earlier the structure stood as a monument to failure. Back then the half finished skeleton of the church threatened to never be finished as the ambitious designs called for capping the structure with a dome so large that the engineering knowhow to build it did not exist.

Today, the magnificent church was more commonly known by its nickname – the Duomo. The towering octagonal dome was made of bright orange bricks with contrasting white capped ridges along the eight corners. The structure soared three hundred seventy-five feet into the sky and seemed to defy the pull of gravity by refusing to collapse in or push all the walls out under its own immense weight. Instead it triumphantly stood tall, and was capped with a circular observation level crowned with a gigantic sphere of bronze with a tip directed toward the heavens.

It struck Hastelloy just how different this church was to other great cathedrals still under construction or completed in recent years throughout Europe. All of them were towering structures that relied on flying buttresses to stand alongside the main walls to support the towering height against the stresses of weight and wind. These grand churches to the north also emphasized hundreds, or even thousands, of pointed spires in the Medieval Gothic style. These were regarded as paying homage to the traditional enemies of Italy, so emulating their architecture would not do.

The architects of the Duomo chose instead a style that marked a return to the classical beauty of a freestanding Mediterranean dome. This massive dome measuring one hundred fifty feet across and two hundred feet tall resting atop a set of walls already standing one hundred seventy feet high was an engineering marvel that Hastelloy could not figure out just by examining the exterior.

Hastelloy approached the front doors of the magnificent cathedral and found yet another sight to marvel. A set of tall doors displayed twenty eight bright bronze relief panels depicting scenes from the virtues of hope, faith, charity, humility, fortitude, temperance, justice and prudence. In striking contrast to the golden glow of the panels stood the pitch-black framing of the doors themselves. The artistry on display was simply breathtaking.

He followed a set of devout monks through the doorway and into the church. The floor was flawlessly paved with marble in large, circular patterns that radiated out from the center to the walls. Sunlight shone through the seemingly endless array of stained glass windows to bring the interior alive with color.

Hastelloy continued following the monks down the main aisle until he stood directly beneath the soaring dome itself. He looked up to see the interior of the dome was in the process of being painted with biblical scenes of the last judgment, all forty thousand square feet of the surface area.

A light tap on his shoulder interrupted Hastelloy's marveling gaze. He lowered his line of sight and looked toward the individual vying for his attention to find Valnor's proud face smiling back at him. "Can I offer you a tour?"

Hastelloy returned the smile and offered a stiff handshake. "You may as long as it starts with an inspection of how this dome remains standing."

"Right this way," Valnor instructed and headed toward the left wall supporting the dome. There, nestled around a corner and obscured from view was a set of narrow steps. Valnor looked back at Hastelloy's advancing age of sixty and jokingly asked, "We are about to go up four hundred sixty-three steps; are you sure you are up for it?"

Hastelloy did not know what to expect from his encounter with Valnor. Would he still be angry with him? Was he taking Hastelloy up to the top of the dome simply to push him off? The joke about his age was a welcome sign that things were back to normal. "I'll manage."

He did, but just barely. The initial ascent was no joke and took the wind out of his aging lungs. He envied Valnor for his youthful body that was still in its early thirties. The path eventually flattened out and came to a walkway that hugged the inside of the dome.

"The ceiling is actually two separate domes which we are walking in between right now," Valnor narrated. "To counteract hoop stress forces pushing out, the outer dome relies entirely on its attachment to the inner dome at the base."

"So what keeps the inner dome from collapsing?" Hastelloy asked between labored breaths as they progressed. "I just assumed they followed the example in Rome of the dome over the Pantheon building. There they built a wooden frame inside and poured concrete over the top of it. Once the concrete hardened, they removed the frame to let the dome stand on its own."

Valnor just laughed softly to himself. "This dome presented far more challenges to the builders than that. First off, it is twice that size and stands much taller than the Pantheon. There was not enough wood in the entire Tuscan region to build a frame big enough."

"So how does it still stand?" Hastelloy inquired as the two made their way between the dome trusses.

"The designer is brilliant man named Brunelleschi, who I brought over when Constantinople fell. He came up with an ingenious solution. The spreading problem was solved by a set of four internal horizontal stone and iron chains wrapping around the inner dome to serve as barrel hoops."

Hastelloy gave a closer inspection of the inner dome wall to see that the stones were interlocking rather than mortared together, lending incredible strength and stability to the structure. "Remarkable. Not only have the engineers in this city reached the levels of knowledge achieved a thousand years ago in Rome, they have surpassed it to marvelous effect."

Valnor stopped and looked back at Hastelloy with wide eyes and a flat smile that said it all, but he verbalized the thought anyway. "I know. My plan worked."

All Hastelloy could do was smile and nod; his subordinate was correct, or at least partially so. He let Valnor's arrogant declaration go unchallenged and simply motioned forward for them to proceed.

The four hundred sixty-third step landed them on a circular open air observation deck at the very top of the three hundred seventy foot tall dome, yielding a panoramic view of Florence. It was a clear day, and everything could be seen from the Arno River to the surrounding foothills.

Down below, hundreds of artists lined the river shores working on their canvases. All around the city construction scaffoldings encircled a dozen projects of varying scope and artistry.

"It's a Renaissance," Hastelloy conceded. "A resurgence in the arts and pursuit of knowledge for these people. It's all happening because of you. You were right."

Valnor noticeably straightened his posture at the praise heaped upon him, but then he inclined his head toward Hastelloy. "In Florence, yes, but the movement is radiating throughout Europe thanks to the wealth and unifying influence the church provides. And let's not forget that this all can progress now without Goron interfering since the last Alpha relic on this planet has been extinguished.

Valnor offered a congratulatory handshake. "It was a team effort, Sir."

"Requiring great effort and sacrifice from all of us," Hastelloy added with an introspective frown across his face as he took Valnor's outstretched hand.

Chapter 67: Tomal's Turn

"All is well that ends well I suppose," Dr. Holmes found himself saying at the conclusion of Hastelloy's story.

"How so?" the patient asked while looking rather confused.

Where to begin Jeffrey thought. "For starters, the Renaissance. Valnor got the ball rolling in Florence and then the Catholic Church that you helped propel into prominence took over and turned it into a bona fide movement."

"The question in my mind is how could one city have such an impact?" Mark interrupted. He was the man with the gun in the room, so the conversation followed his lead. "All those thinkers and artists were together in Constantinople. Maybe the revival of mankind's appetite to learn and explore would have happened anyway, with or without you and your crew's meddling."

Hastelloy greeted the loaded question with a disarming grin. "It was not one city. It was one single family that brought about the Renaissance. My cover at that time was as a member of the Medici family. We were able to bring Florence under that family's power, and unlike Constantinople, we opened the city gates to the world rather than locking them tight."

"The biggest accomplishment of the Medici's was the sponsorship of art and architecture," Hastelloy went on. "Owing to the trade routes Gallono and I, along with Marco Polo, set up, the wealth of the Medici family was vast. This was significant because, contrary to popular belief, those artists, teachers and philosophers did not do it out of some noble dedication to a cause. They did it for money."

"During that time artists only made their great works once they received a commission in advance. Name any of the great artisans of that era: Masaccio, Brunelleschi, Donatello, Fra Angelico, Michelangelo Buonarroti, Leonardo da Vinci. All of the greats can be traced back to a member of the Medici family funding their early works."

Hastelloy slid forward in his seat and looked straight at Mark to drive home his point. "The Medici family's notoriety grew beyond the city and into the Catholic Church; some even ascended the ranks to become Pope. The Medici Popes continued the family tradition of patronizing artists in

Rome. Pope Leo X employed Raphael; Pope Clement VII commissioned Michelangelo to paint the altar walls and ceiling of the Sistine Chapel."

"Bravo then," Mark blurted out and accompanied his outburst with a soft, patronizing applause. "You encouraged the Medici family to pay the bills for a bunch of artists who made some silly swirls of paint across a canvas or ceiling. That certainly aided the advancement of science and technology."

"Have you ever heard the term Renaissance Man," Hastelloy countered without pause. "During that era, a man was not considered complete unless he was a master of many disciplines. Those great men were not just painters or sculptors. They were inventors; they were physicians, and they were astronomers."

"He's correct," Dr. Holmes jumped in, sensing the already tense situation growing even more taut. "Michelangelo was a brilliant sculptor and painter, but he also exhumed bodies and dissected them in order to learn how the human body worked."

Mark threw his arms up into the air in resignation. "Fine. You lit the pilot light of mankind's return to learning. Gallono wiped out the Alpha's Mars colony. You killed all of the Alpha/relic/stone reincarnations out in China, and to top it all off, Tomal managed to successfully end Goron's existence. It should be smooth sailing for you right up to this moment."

"Yes, that is how things should have turned out," Hastelloy confirmed.

"Should have," Dr. Holmes repeated. "Why didn't they; what went wrong?"

"An unforeseen human weakness," Hastelloy answered and looked truly pained with the utterance of each word.

"You mean Tomal's arrogance and ambition," Jeffrey suggested.

Hastelloy looked off to the side as he considered his next statement for several silent seconds. Finally he nodded his head slightly. "That was certainly part of the problem. The fact that he delivered the death blow to Goron tore down any mental walls Tomal erected inside his mind to contain his more basic instincts."

"Tell me, how familiar are you with the latter parts of Martin Luther's life?" Hastelloy asked.

"Not at all," Jeffrey answered, and a shake of the head from Mark conveyed his lack of familiarity as well.

Hastelloy drew a heavy breath and let it out slowly. "Where to begin? Martin Luther was the most widely read and published author of his or any generation up until just the last few decades. His notoriety was so pronounced that he was revered as an actual prophet in Germany. Even for the most humble among us, that sort of fame can change a person. For Tomal, it's not that hard to picture fame and fortune taking over his behavior now is it?"

"That was not all though. Another, even more devastating, poison went to his head. A mental sickness that comes with age sometimes," Hastelloy regretfully uttered into his chest.

"Senility?" Dr. Holmes offered.

"Alzheimer's is the modern term for the mental disease that afflicted Tomal, as Martin Luther, in his later years," Hastelloy confirmed. "In the last ten years of his life, Tomal turned decidedly anti-Semitic. In his writings and sermons Martin Luther advocated setting synagogues on fire, destroying Jewish prayer books, and forbidding rabbis from preaching."

A skeptical look from Jeffrey prompted Hastelloy to support his assertion further. "His final written work was titled *On the Jews and Their Lies*; you can look it up if you like. It was filled with his most fiery and venomous ideas. In it he insisted the Jews were the devil's people. He sponsored the seizure of the Jewish property and money. He encouraged people to smash their homes so that the 'poisonous worms' would be forced into labor or expelled for all time."

"That certainly is rancid rhetoric," Jeffrey said. "Why did he single out the Jewish people with his misguided hatred?"

"Because of me," Hastelloy emphatically answered. "In his sick mind he thought they were my people. He went after them to try and hurt me."

"That makes some twisted sense I suppose," Dr. Holmes pondered. "You helped them escape the bondage of slavery back in Egypt and led them to the Promised Land along with Mosa.

"It was just the words of an ailing mind," Mark interrupted.

"No," Hastelloy bellowed in an uncharacteristic display of anger. "In the lead up to World War II, his writing served as the bedrock foundation of anti-Semitism in Nazi Germany. Just about every anti-Jewish book printed in the

287

Third Reich contained references to and quotations from the deranged writings of Luther in his waning years."

"Alzheimer's is an intolerably cruel disease. I see it every day in dozens of my patients. The mind just slowly disconnects from reality and replaces it with anger, paranoia and confusion. It's just...sad."

"Yes it is," Hastelloy agreed. "No such disease affects Novi physiology; this was new ground for all of us."

"The disease of the mind died with that body, right?" Dr. Holmes asked hopefully.

"It did," Hastelloy confirmed, "but in many ways it did not. Those angry, paranoid and confused feelings hung over his mind from that point on like a phantom haunting the place of its murder. Those dark thoughts and impulses were always there, lying just beneath the surface harassing his thoughts and actions. As you said, it is just a sad state of affairs."

Chapter 68: Real Time

WHILE SITTING ON the couch listening to the depressing conclusion of Hastelloy's story, Mark released a breath he did not even realize he was holding. Tomal's fate aside, hearing the Alpha threats on Earth and Mars were neutralized was definitely good news. An added bonus to Mark's mission was that one of Hastelloy's crewmen gave his life to accomplish that final victory; one down and four to go.

Just then Mark felt a vibration on his right hip. He retrieved his phone and brought the display up to eye level between him and Hastelloy. The man politely stopped talking and waited.

Mark saw it was Colonel Azire calling him and immediately snapped up an index finger to pause the discussion permanently and got to his feet. "I need to take this," Mark said on his way to opening the office door and exiting the room.

Outside, he gestured for the two NSA agents standing near the door to step in and watch the target. Mark shut the inner office door behind him and simultaneously felt the phone start vibrating in his hands for the third time. One more and it would go to voice mail so he quickly folded the phone open, "This is Mark."

"For a man who went to such lengths to stay informed about events in my country, you certainly took your time answering," responded a soft voice with an Egyptian accent that sounded like it was coming through a tin can.

Mark looked around the outer office to find the only other occupant was Tara sitting at her desk filing her nails down to almost nothing. He contemplated stepping out into the hallway, but the risk of a random nurse, orderly or even patient hearing something they shouldn't was too great.

"I'm afraid privacy is at a premium, give me a moment," Mark responded and then locked eyes with Tara. He tossed his head toward the exit door with the phone still held to his ear.

The young woman opened her arms out wide and feigned a look of surprise. "Seriously, I'm being kicked out of my own office? I suppose I may as well go since it's time to bring their lunches in anyway."

Tara put down her nail file and stepped around her desk heading for the door, but turned to look toward Mark over her shoulder and playfully added, "I'm going to be back soon though."

"I look forward to it," Mark said softly, which drew a smile as he closed the door behind her.

"I believe you had something important to report, Colonel," Mark said into his phone once he had his privacy.

"This man who replaced you here is out of control. I thought you were bad with your implied threats to my safety to get what you wanted. This man has actually held me at gunpoint ever since you left."

"And what about now?" Mark asked. "Are they letting you call me?"

"No," Colonel Azire snapped. "They are presently focused on bringing high explosives and code breaking equipment I never knew existed into the structure hiding the tunnel entrance. For the moment I am alone in this vehicle with guards standing nearby. You are on speaker to keep the phone out of sight so please do not talk too loudly or they will hear you."

"What about your extra men, are they nearby?" Mark asked while looking at the door leading to the inner office where Hastelloy, his brother, and two agents were. He knew time was running short to let Hastelloy just ramble on.

"Yes. All it would take is my stepping out and shouting an order to fire and our two countries would be at war. I do not want to give that order, but the time is quickly approaching where I will no longer have a choice. I must protect my country."

A loud clatter from behind him caused Mark to whirl around and face the door leading out to the hallway. He saw Tara's well sculpted backside scooting toward him through the door as she pulled along a lunch cart carrying two trays of food featuring what looked like meatloaf and a couple of drinks. Facing Tara, and helping push the cart along, was the orderly named Terry.

Mark evaluated Tara with disappointment which she batted away by shining a bright smile. "Sorry, I only ordered for them since I didn't know you and your companions would be joining the doctor and his patient."

"I don't care about the food; I needed privacy," Mark hissed through gritted teeth while holding his hand over the phone's microphone.

"It's my office," Tara jabbed back with a wink while opening the inner office door and proceeding through. "Besides, more of your friends arrived and I thought you might want to talk with them."

Mark looked back to find six men wearing dark suits standing in front of the hallway exit door; a welcome sight. Briefly Mark turned his attention back to the phone conversation. "Bear with me, Colonel, things are moving right along here. There is no need for rash action just yet."

"Hurry," came a curt reply followed by a dial tone.

Mark pointed to a set of agents standing on the far left. "You two come with me. The rest of you get ready, we'll be moving the target immediately."

The two agents fell in line behind Mark as he turned to reenter his brother's inner office, but he found Tara obstructing his path. The two performed a silent dance from side to side as they both attempted unsuccessfully to get out of the other's way. Finally Mark grasped Tara by both shoulders and moved her to the side in order to finally get by.

"Sorry, I forgot something in the kitchen," Tara said innocently as the three men walked past with pistols drawn.

Mark entered the office to see Hastelloy carrying an amused smile across his lips. He casually took a tray from Terry and placed it on his lap as if five men in the room did not have guns trained on him. The orderly glanced up to the sight and stepped back from the scene with his arms raised high in surrender.

"Are we back to this now?" Hastelloy asked while looking at Dr. Holmes.

Mark watched his brother rise to his feet and stand between him and Hastelloy. "You know his terms for talking."

"Damn it, Jeff, things are moving too quickly for us to continue sitting here listening to campfire stories," Mark explained. "This is the real world with real things happening in real time."

"I can't let you take my patient," Jeff declared, which caused Mark to step in to force his brother out of the way. He pressed the shoulder of his gun wielding hand into Jeff's chest and received a solid right to the jaw from his brother in return.

Before Mark could stop them, two of his men grabbed Jeff by the collar and planted him face first into the floor. Hastelloy couldn't have hoped for a better distraction to unleash his attack.

Time slowed to a crawl as Mark watched Hastelloy fling his lunch tray at one agent while delivering a sideways elbow to the face of another, and wrenching away the agent's gun. Mark's mind sent the signal for his arms to raise his gun and train his aim on Hastelloy. Time once again sped up and seemed to flash forward as Hastelloy simultaneously blocked the progress of Mark's gun arm and inserted the barrel of his pistol into Mark's open mouth.

"I am not going anywhere with you," Hastelloy declared.

Mark calmly stood his ground with the rod of lethal metal protruding from his mouth and watched a dark shadow fall across Hastelloy from behind. An instant later Mark felt his attacker's body go rigid, and the gun barrel fell away from his jaw. Hastelloy's body crumpled unconscious to the side to reveal Terry standing there with the butt of a pistol in his hands.

"Terry, what the hell are you doing?" Jeffrey yelled from under a pile of two agents pinning him to the floor.

"Relax," Mark said dismissively. "He's just earning the salary the NSA pays him each month to protect you in case someone from my life attempts to disrupt yours."

Mark Henrikson

Chapter 69: Violated

FRANK HAD SEEN numerous pictures of the famous Terracotta soldiers. He had even heard several firsthand accounts of how impressive they were. As with most things though, the grand spectacle could only truly be appreciated in person.

The exterior of the museum complex was surprisingly modern. Two castle-like buildings stood among the marble paved walkways and well-kept garden. Rather than garish medieval structures, these buildings were constructed with a fusion of light concrete and stone with large blue tinted windows, giving them a very contemporary appearance.

On the left side of the complex a long, narrow building utilizing the same modern construction theme sported an arched metal roof. The shape instantly made Frank think of an old World War II airplane hangar. Instead of sheltering aircraft though, this rounded roofline covered the entire two hundred foot wide, eight hundred foot long expanse of the first Terracotta soldier pit discovered by peasants attempting to drill a water well in 1974.

Contrasting with the modern exterior, the arched building's interior housed a magnificent window to see into the past. The museum had long since closed to tourists for the evening, making Frank's job of sneaking in a simple matter.

A pair of security guards manned the front entrance, which forced Frank to jimmy a side door and neutralize the security alarm with little effort. He made his way onto the observation deck beyond the security desk without being seen or heard. The cavernous chamber was still dimly lit with every fifth light fixture overhead remaining on at all times. This gave Frank a murky, shadowy view of the entire Terracotta Army standing ready for battle twenty feet below. The army included over six thousand individual figures that were in various stages of being unearthed by archeologists. They stood arranged into eleven latitudinal corridors separated by earthen walls.

The center of the force was dominated by mounted horse and chariot units. Near the very back lay a rectangular slab that sat conspicuously empty. There was a heavily gated doorway leading west back toward the burial mound. This was his objective, but a set of locked gates at the top and bottom of a staircase blocked his path.

293

While Frank mulled over his options to get through the gates, he saw numerous beams of light moving across the vast expanse. He turned around expecting to see a security guard sweeping his flashlight about, but realized the source was actually headlights from three sets of vehicles pulling up to the front entrance. Chin and his men had arrived, which meant Frank needed to move quickly.

Rather than take the conventional route, Frank threw his leg over the hand rail and followed with the other. He climbed his way down to the bottom pipe hand rail to dangle his legs down as far as possible and then let go.

Frank absorbed the force of impact from the twelve foot drop by bending his knees and engaging his quads. He still collapsed all the way down to a squatting position until his rear end bounced off his calf muscles to propel him back to an upright position.

He took a quick glance around to choose his path, but was distracted by the haunting clay faces staring back at him from the darkened corridors before him. Frank forcibly shoved the eerie feeling of being watched aside and made his way down the far left column of soldiers. Initially he slipped around the individual statues with great care, but found very quickly these priceless artifacts were none too fragile. They were solid and extremely heavy and withstood the occasional bump from his hips as he slid past.

When Frank reached a third of the way to the back wall all of the overhead lights came alive. Accompanying the lighting he heard voices from the observation deck. Next, he heard the groan of the metal gates obstructing the steps leading down into the soldier pits being opened. Confident that his movements would not be spotted from up above unless one of Chin's men happened to look directly down his chosen column, Frank continued progressing toward the back wall. It was now a race to reach the back gate first.

"The last time these gates were opened to a foreign visitor to walk among these treasures was for the queen of England," Frank overheard Chin say in English from six corridors over. "Even then the decision to let her walk among this great treasure was highly controversial. You should feel quite privileged to have this opportunity."

"Why are we going down here, where are you taking us?" he heard a feminine voice that could only belong to Alex ask.

"You are correct. The two of you do not need to be down here," Chin answered offhandedly. He then addressed his men in Chinese. *"You two take them back to the observation deck and hold them there until we return."*

"You do not need to be so careful around the statues," Chin said to his men with some annoyance in his voice. *"Despite being made of clay, they are actually quite solid and difficult to break."*

From the direction of the voices Frank could tell that they were making better time than him. Chin's group had already pulled even with Frank's progress, and he was now encountering uneven sections of ground that were still being unearthed by archeologists. He realized he was going to lose the race.

When he finally reached the end of his soldier column, Frank peeked around the tall earthen wall and saw Chin hard at work opening a gate that looked like it had not budged in at least thirty years. Behind him stood six men carrying hand guns in one hand and flood lamps in the other.

All around the rectangular clearing Frank spotted the shattered remnants of several clay soldiers on the ground. Far off to the right of the doorway, a statue was knocked completely on its side. Apparently the heavy statues could be knocked over if one treated the priceless treasures with blatant disregard.

A few minutes later Frank watched a rusted out padlock drop to the ground and endured the mind scrambling screech of rusted metal being forced to move. Two of the armed escorts added their muscle to Chin's effort and managed to pry the door loose and open the barred metal gate completely.

Two of the escorts lit the beams of their flood lamps and fearlessly stepped into the darkness beyond. The rest followed them in with lights of their own leading the way. Frank slipped in behind the group and silently trailed their lead about thirty feet behind.

Less than a hundred feet in they came across an area where a significant section of the ceiling had collapsed. The group was able to slide past the twenty foot long piece of stone single file along the corridor sidewall.

Frank counted his blessings that he was not your typical overweight American and managed to squeeze past with plenty of room to spare. A few times he felt his foot land on something sharp that did not quite crunch beneath his weight. Frank wished he had time and a light of his own to investigate the shards, but the stoic men holding the lights and handguns pressed on.

Ten minutes later the group reached a set of copper doors sealed down the middle with hardened bronze.

"Open it," Chin ordered one of his men carrying a burdensome backpack. The object rang with a heavy clank when the owner set it on the ground. The man bent down and retrieved the nozzle of an acetylene torch, lit the business end with a spark and went to work cutting through the bronze seal.

After five minutes of sparks flying, the torch bearer announced he had finished. Four men, two to a door, grabbed hold of the looped hand holds and pried the doors apart to allow light into the chamber for the first time in centuries.

The flashlight beams reached into the darkness but failed to find anything to illuminate besides the floor. After a more careful look, Frank did manage to spot glistening objects in the slightly domed ceiling twenty feet above. Before he could inspect the reflective objects further, one in particular held his attention. It was a silver sphere the size of a basketball hanging down in the center of the gigantic chamber that had to span at least a thousand feet away from the door.

Frank was not the only one mesmerized by the grand spectacle. Chin and his entire team were enchanted by the sight. Apparently the magnitude of standing in a place no one had laid eyes on for thousands of years was not lost on them. Frank could relate. He remembered a week earlier the thrill of seeing the inside of the Sphinx.

Fortunately for Frank, the sensation was old hat which left him with an opportunity he could not pass up. He drew his pistol, took aim at the acetylene torch's fuel tank and fired. He managed to shield his eyes with his left arm to protect them from the flash, but he certainly felt the concussion wave and heat from the resulting fireball.

A moment later Frank dropped his arm to find four men rolling about on the ground to extinguish the flames licking at their clothing. The other two and Chin were leaning against the copper doors attempting to regain their senses. Frank was not one to let such a distracting opportunity go to waste, so he stepped forward from the darkness and unloaded his weapon.

The first two shots took the men leaning against the door in the side of their heads; dropping them to the ground. Another pair of rounds put two of the burn victims out of their misery.

Chin, out of instinct or exceptional training, did not hesitate amid the surprise attack. He immediately drew his gun and opened fire in Frank's direction. The shots were all over the place, indicating the man still had not regained his vision. Still, even a blind man with enough shots could hit a target, especially in a narrow corridor. Frank dropped onto his stomach and kept count of the number of shots that passed overhead.

He heard eight go off, but then silence followed. Chin was no fool. He was not about to waste all of his shots firing blindly. Frank took the opportunity to take two more shots and dropped the remaining men who recently managed to put out the flames on their clothing. Frank rolled twice to his left until he ran into the side wall and then rose to one knee. His movements were just in time; four more rounds came from Chin's gun and struck Frank's original firing position. The Chinese agent was now alone, but his vision was on the mend.

Chin was now inside the chamber using the doorway as cover. Frank quickly dashed up along the side of the corridor until he stood just outside the chamber with his leading shoulder resting against the opened copper door. He was close enough to Chin now to hear the man's labored breathing and the soft, slippery sound of a wet palm massaging an eye socket to rub out the temporary blindness.

At his feet Frank found a flood lamp still lit. He picked it up and tossed it through the doorway. The sudden flash of motion drew the gun barrel's aim and allowed Frank to step around the corner, grab Chin's gun with his free hand and deliver a blow to the side of his head with the butt of his pistol. The strike had the double impact of smashing Chin's head against the door frame.

Frank slapped Chin's weapon away, grabbed the groggy man by the shirt and threw him into the corridor leading back to the Terracotta army museum.

"My god I'm good," Frank boasted as he shoved Chin farther down the corridor. "In Cairo it took what, thirty of your men to try and take out me and three SEALs. You sure botched that one."

"Now, all by myself I brought down six of your men and managed to capture you alive. Payback is a biiitch," Frank went on, drawing out the last word for added effect.

"Frank Graves, I presume," Chin said while rubbing both sides of his head.

"The man, the legend," Frank responded. "Did you ever consider you just suck at your job? Maybe that's why we always manage to stay three steps ahead of you."

Chin glanced back with a menacing glare nearly as intense as the explosion a few minutes earlier, but then turned back around and paced down the rest of the corridor in silence.

Just before stepping out into the Terracotta Army pit, Frank saw a flash of electric blue light flash past. Then another and another, until a constant stream was rushing past into the open and flooding the soldier pits with a soft haze of blue.

"What in the world is that?" Chin asked of Frank while stepping out into the open and headed toward a row of statues.

"You tell me," Frank countered while holding his aim level at Chin's back as they zigzagged their way between soldier statues. "This is your country and those were your men who opened the burial chamber."

"Yes this is my country, and I am curious how you intend to leave my country? The nearest US embassy is five hundred miles away in Beijing. I have many more men just outside waiting to help me. How about you, super agent Frank Graves?" Chin mocked.

"I figure I'll just wait for the proper authorities to show up," Frank answered casually.

"And you will be shot on sight."

Frank roared with laughter at Chin's statement. "I'm not the one who violated the sanctity of that burial chamber. I expect you will be shot and I will go home with yet another medal pinned to my chest."

"My government does not give awards to foreigners."

"Well then, I'll just have to make one up for myself, won't I?" Frank concluded as they came to the last set of clay soldiers before reaching the steps leading back to the observation deck.

For stability, Frank wrapped his free arm around the waist of the statue and made ready to step by, but in that instant he suddenly felt the statue's arm move.

Frank took a brief moment to question his sanity while he watched the clay statue step down off its pedestal. Reality rushed back to him when he saw the statue's sword wielding hand cut a downward arc aimed at his head. Instinctively Frank dove to the side, rolled back onto his feet, raised his pistol and fired off a trio of rounds to no effect. The statue stalked toward him like he just pelted it with marshmallows.

Out of options, Frank dashed for the steps at a full sprint. On his way Frank glanced around the football field sized dome and saw hundreds, maybe even thousands of statues coming to life. He didn't stick around to perform a head count; he was in full retreat up the steps and onto the observation deck where the Professor, Alex and two of Chin's men awaited him.

"Frank?!?" Alex exclaimed when he reached the top of the steps. "What the hell; you're dead. I saw you dead back in Cairo."

Frank flicked his head toward the now thoroughly active soldier pit down below, "You should know by now sweetheart, death is only the beginning."

Chin and his men took aim with their weapons at Frank which drew a sarcastic sneer, "Really? We have bigger problems don't you think. Now buy me some time; I have a call to make."

Chapter 70: Matter of Trust

"ALRIGHT GET OFF my brother," Mark ordered to the two men pinning his brother on the ground. He pointed to Hastelloy lying still on the ground in front of Terry. "Cuff him and let's get out of here."

Mark watched one man pull a set of cuffs from behind his back as he turned to face his brother. The soft zip of metal gears locking into position let him know Hastelloy was being handled, so he lent Jeff a hand to his feet.

"I guess we will have a lot more to talk about than the good old days when I come visit your family this Christmas," Mark said in a conciliatory tone and an apologetic pat on the shoulder. "We'll catch up later to make this right."

"You're leaving?" Jeff exclaimed. "Now?"

Mark nodded his head, "I wasn't lying when I said time is short. I need to leave with him right now."

Mark heard a commotion behind him and turned to see Hastelloy, with his arms bound behind his back, being carried between two of his men. The captive looked groggy from the head blow, but he was moving his feet as the set of agents moved to the door. Mark joined the other two agents and Terry on their way toward the closed door. His brother just stood dumbfounded in the middle of the room like a man witnessing a mugging, but was too scared to do anything to stop it.

Terry turned the knob, pulled open the office door and led the group through. Mark was the first to notice the four bodies lying crumpled unconscious on the floor in the outer office. Before his brain could process the details, he saw Terry go down gasping for air and holding his throat with both hands.

The two agents not carrying the suspect immediately moved to draw their weapons. With blinding speed a slender leg snapped in from around the door frame and caught one of them in the side of the face slamming the man's head into the door frame.

Following the attacking leg into the inner office was the attractive form of Tara. She brought her left hand down to pin the other agent's gun hand and delivered an openhanded thrust to his windpipe, crushing it.

Mark threw a right hook at the side of Tara's head, but was too slow to connect. She opened her stance to let the blow pass harmlessly in front of her face and then used Mark's momentum to fling him into the outer office. In midflight, he felt the pistol held in a holster at the small of his back get pulled away. An instant later a single shot rang out as Mark crashed into the side of Tara's desk.

He looked back in time to see the agent on Hastelloy's left side fall to the ground with a bullet hole in the center of his forehead. The last agent managed to get a hold on Tara's gun hand to knock the weapon away. The agent went for his own gun, but in the middle of drawing he had the barrel disassembled from the main body of the weapon by Tara's skilled hand.

While Mark lay prone on the floor still recovering from the blinding pain racing up and down his spine from hitting the desk, he observed Tara and the agent square off for hand-to-hand combat. By the look of things, they both knew what they were about in the finer points of martial arts. Still, Mark liked his man's odds considering he had six inches and fifty pounds of muscle on the little lady.

The two exchanged a flurry of blocked punches, with a few snap kicks thrown in, before the agent pressed his size advantage. The man grabbed hold of Tara by the collar and tried to lasso her into a bear hug takedown, but she had other intentions.

On the way back to his feet, Mark watched Tara leap up and summersault over the agent's left shoulder. On her way down she grabbed hold of the man's head with both hands. As the pull of gravity brought her down to the floor with her back against the agent's back, momentum did all the work. The agent's head was pulled backwards, bending him in half. His body had no choice but to follow the head's lead or else suffer a broken spine.

The man's body rotated backwards over Tara's shoulder with his head as the fulcrum and slammed into the floor with the force of a magnitude ten earthquake. Tara wasted no time and delivered a punch to the base of the man's skull rendering him motionless.

Mark charged back into the room to try and tackle Tara before she could reset her position, but he was too late. Still five feet away from her, Mark screeched to a halt and stared down the barrel of a pistol pointed between his eyes.

All he could do was stand there with his arms raised and look about the office and audit the body count. Nine of his men were down. Some were dead, most unconscious, and none would be of any further help in the situation.

His brother still stood frozen in the center of the room as Hastelloy got back to his feet under his own power to stand next to Tara. Unarmed, the ferocious woman faced nine well trained operatives and downed them all in the span of a few minutes. Now she was armed and had Mark and his brother as captives.

"You alright, Captain?" Tara asked.

"I suppose I should have expected the orderly to be working for them," Hastelloy said with a frustrated sigh while holding the back of his head and massaging the base of his neck. He turned his upper body to look toward Jeff. "Dr. Holmes, would you please join your brother on this side of the room. You have my word no harm will come to you."

Mark was busy internally debating how to play the situation as his brother slowly paced over to his side. Jeffrey's perplexed stare never left Tara as he came to a stop to stand next to Mark. To say he was in a state of shock at the betrayal was akin to comparing a category five hurricane to a gentle breeze.

"Your reputation precedes you," Jeffrey finally managed to say. "I see the calculations for your escape pod flight back from Mars were well done, Commander Gallono."

Tara inclined her head slightly to acknowledge the reasoning. "I thought for sure that was the end. I still don't like trusting computers with my life though."

"Am I to discern from that statement, Doctor, that you believe my story to be true?" Hastelloy asked of Jeffrey. "Am I now free to leave this facility?"

"Oh yes, you've made a believer out of me," Jeffrey confirmed. "As I recall though, you checked yourself into Henderson Home. You have been free to leave whenever you wanted. So the question now is, why were you ever here in the first place?"

"For him," Hastelloy said inclining his head toward Mark. "His job is to know everything about me and my crew's activities on this planet. He is the one person on this planet who knows, without question, that the stories I have been telling you are true. Unfortunately, his skeptical nature prevents him from trusting our intentions to be decent or honorable. That's where you come in, Doctor."

"You and I have built a relationship over the last two weeks built on friendship and trust," Hastelloy went on. "I need you to stand by your brother as an advocate of my good, honorable nature."

"Why, to what end?" Mark insisted. "Who cares what I think? You could have remained hidden away for thousands of years to come. Why bother with me and my trust or distrust of your intentions on this planet?"

"The probe," Hastelloy said quietly. "The Novi will be here soon, and I need to be the one they speak to first. Not your president, his security advisors, or even your executive committee overseer. You and I are the only people who can make that happen, but only if you trust me."

Mark was about to respond, but got interrupted by another buzzing and vibration on his hip. Tara stepped forward and pulled the phone from its case.

"Allow me." She quickly glanced at the display screen and then passed the phone over to Hastelloy. "It's his partner Frank."

Hastelloy passed the phone back to Mark. "Put it on speaker. Let's all hear what your feisty Texan has been up to today."

Before releasing his grip on the phone Hastelloy added, "If you feel the need, you may openly divulge your current state of captivity rather than some coded phrasing."

Mark blew a soft chuckle through his nostrils and then pushed talk on the phone. "Frank, where are you?"

"China," came an efficient response. "The archeologists were taken here to run their mapping equipment on the burial mound of the Chinese first emperor."

"Qin Shi Huang's pyramid near Xi'an," Hastelloy added. "We are quite familiar with the mausoleum. What are they looking for?"

"Who the blazes is that?" Frank demanded.

"Frank, meet Captain Hastelloy and his first officer Commander Gallono," Mark said with some annoyance in his voice. "They have subdued my men and now hold me at gunpoint, but they..."

303

"Shut up and listen, all of you," Frank frantically interrupted. "I don't care what is going on over there; this is bigger. Remember a few years back the reports we got about a radiation frequency from inside the pyramid that was close to, but not an exact match to frequency Alpha?"

"Yes, we disregarded it as coincidence and moved it to a secondary threat level," Mark said with concern sneaking into his voice.

"Well the Chinese Ministry of State Security must have put it at the top of their priority list. That's why they kidnapped the archeologists. They discovered a large room above the emperor's burial chamber as the source of the radiation."

Mark glanced at Hastelloy to see if this was new information to him. The creased stress lines running across the man's forehead were a dead giveaway that this was surprising and decidedly unwelcome news to him.

"They opened the emperor's burial chamber before I could stop them, and something happened," Frank reported.

"The Terracotta Army?" Hastelloy offered without emotion.

"Yeah. This blue energy wave overtook the pits and they ... well, as crazy as it sounds, they are all coming to life. We've tried guns and grenades, but the clay just seems to absorb it all with little effect."

"Who is we?" Mark asked for clarification.

"The Chinese and I sorta set aside our differences when this happened."

"Pull everybody back," Mark ordered. "Try and find weapons that work against them, and I'll make sure help is on the way shortly."

Mark ended the call and looked at Hastelloy with his best 'what now' face. "It appears the Alpha are still a threat. Can we follow Frank and the Chinese's example and set aside our differences to deal with it?"

Hastelloy looked at Tara and shook his head fiercely. "I knew that silver sphere was out of place with the rest of the ceiling design. I should have investigated it further."

"At the time, we had the Mars colony to destroy. There were more immediate concerns," Tara offered and handed the pistol over to Hastelloy.

"You know what to do," Hastelloy said to her and then raised the pistol to her temple and pulled the trigger.

"No!" both Mark and Jeff managed to shout in stereo before Tara's lifeless body hit the floor. Mark went on in a rage, "What have you done?

My boss has the tunnel exit under siege. Assuming you bring Gallono back with your Nexus device, he will be trapped inside the Sphinx chamber.

Hastelloy looked over at Jeffrey leaning to the side as he vomited at the sight of his long time secretary's grey matter and blood sprayed against his office wall. "Gallono is fine," he reassured the doctor and then looked to Mark. "You don't seriously think I am foolish enough to only have one way out of the Nexus do you?"

Before Mark could form a response Hastelloy did the unthinkable. For the second time that day he released his grip on the gun controlling the room and handed it over to Mark. "Once again the causes we both fight for are aligned. We are on the same side."

"For how long?" Mark interrupted while helping his brother back to an upright position while shielding his eyes away from the carnage on his office wall and floor.

Hastelloy extended an open palm toward Mark, "If you trust me, get me in front of your president or his science advisor. If not, then send me back to the Nexus and I will deal with the Alpha threat on this planet as I always have - alone."

Mark pursed his lips and shook his head in a moment of contemplation. He hated giving up control, but if his brother truly did trust this man enough to risk his life for him, then that was good enough for him. Mark took the pistol, slid it into the holster behind his back, and shook Hastelloy's hand to seal the arrangement.

Epilogue: Aftershock

LODIE RAISED HIS head and pulled his eyes away from the ground to look toward the sky. Even through the visor of his environmental suit, the deep red tint of the planet's surface overwhelmed his eyes after a while. Dust kicked up by the surface winds made the sky appear pink near the ground, but looking farther up the horizon granted his optic nerves relief with a vista of purple and blue.

He would have loved to rub his eyes, but a layer of clear plastic a quarter inch thick prevented his gloved paw from making contact. He had to settle for blinking and squinting his eyelids to wash out the red blindness. With his eyes no longer screaming for relief, Lodie looked around by turning at the waist to make sure that no one in his team had gotten lost.

After months spent lobbying for the opportunity, Lodie finally had his first command, and he was determined to succeed so that it would not be his last. He looked out across the three mile crater and took count. Thirty men and women were busy testing the soil, while another ten were setting up the core sampling rig. They needed to verify the initial readings that the survey drone flying overhead had detected.

The equipment onboard the fixed wing aircraft had only a fifty percent success rate when trying to detect deposits of titanium. Before investing thousands of valuable man hours to set up a mining and smelting facility, the colony elders insisted the readings be verified, hence the survey crew.

The transport ship was nearing completion, but the current source to mine titanium for the ship's outer hull was just about exhausted. To complete the build, a new source was needed. The one hundred mile distance from the colony mountain was inconvenient, but not insurmountable. A rail line could easily be built to move machinery here and haul ore back. Initial surface readings were promising, but taking a core sample would give conclusive proof if the site was viable.

Lodie was about to walk over and check on the rig when he suddenly felt an odd tremor beneath his feet. The vibrations were subtle enough that he would have ignored it, but several of his team began frantically pointing toward the sky behind him.

Mark Henrikson

He resisted the impulse to immediately turn and look at the spectacle because he did not want to appear as a follower. He was the leader and it would be interpreted as a sign of weakness, and that was the last impression Lodie needed to give during his first command.

An instant later the radio communication channel erupted with panic. "What in the name of Mother Nature is that?" seemed to be the phrase of choice among the frantic team.

Lodie felt the ground tremors intensify, which finally caused him to turn around and join the crowd of gawkers. Once the turn was completed, the sight that greeted him sent a wave of terror through every fiber of his being.

In the distance, near the location of the colony mountain, a towering column of smoke and scorching fire rose dozens of miles into the sky. Lodie watched a shockwave ripple across the red sands toward him. He had just enough time to get down on all fours before the once solid ground bucked him twenty feet into the air.

Lodie managed to control his body enough midflight to come down on his feet. He then crumpled onto his side to absorb the force of impact with his whole body rather than just his legs and knees.

A moment later the air around him began pulsating against his environmental suit, and the sound of a roaring explosion managed to seep through the air tight seals. Lodie looked back toward the horrific scene only to see the calamity grow ten times worse.

A second explosion that originated at ground level propelled a wide column of red soil and ash skyward with so much force that the particles did not dissipate at the top to produce the classic mushroom shaped cloud of a massive explosion. This epic eruption reached for the heavens and met its goal by ejecting billions of metric tons of red rock out into space.

Any hopes Lodie harbored that the colony could have survived the first blast were thoroughly squashed with the realization that the more powerful explosion was the colony's fusion reactor going critical from inside the mountain.

Panic stricken cries and screams of genuine pain reigned supreme over the radio until Lodie put a stop to it all with a primal roar mixed in with his single commanding word, "SILENCE!"

It took less than a second for his order to be followed with only the occasional whiny whimper breaking the dead airwaves.

"If you are unharmed or can still manage to make the trek on your own, fall back to the rovers," Lodie ordered. "If you require assistance, speak up one at a time, otherwise maintain radio silence for those in need."

The final casualty list was not nearly as bad as Lodie initially feared. One team member appeared to land visor first on a rock. The man met a gruesome end as the low pressure of the basically nonexistent atmosphere attempted to turn his body inside out until the pressure was equalized. Three other team members sustained broken arms or legs, but nothing that could not be fixed.

"We are heading back to the colony to look for survivors," Lodie communicated to the team, and then led the way as driver of the lead vehicle. It took the convoy of five square shaped vehicles with six oversized wheels three hours to roll their way back to where the colony mountain once proudly stood. Lodie was not the least bit surprised to find that the colony mountain, the entire mountain range in fact, no longer existed.

After hours of searching, the only evidence that intelligent life once flourished in the location was a mound of twisted titanium half buried under the red soil. It was the remains of the mostly completed space craft. The ship would clearly never fly, but it actually held up quite well given the magnitude of both explosions it sustained.

Lodie crouched low as he stepped through an airlock to the ship that was bent forty-five degrees to the side. He followed his lead engineer through a similarly leaning corridor that opened up to the craft's rather sizeable command capsule.

"It is over here, Leader," the engineer said and beckoned Lodie to his side with a wave of his arm.

Lodie had not believed the reports at first, but seeing the green glow of an indicator light attached to the ship's main computer core gave him hope. Everything the colony had rediscovered over the prior three thousand years was housed in the core: farming techniques, chemical equations, mathematics, engineering diagrams. Most important of all, the still active computer core housed the designs to build another relic altar.

This was not the end of everything; it was yet another new beginning. With only forty-one survivors, it would take hundreds of years, but the colony would eventually return to its former glory.

The engineer had more good news for Lodie. "The ship's fusion reactor is damaged, but I think it can be repaired if we are able to pull up the designs from the computer core."

Lodie nodded his head slowly and allowed a hint of optimism back into his mindset. His first command was going to be a long-term stint after all.

THE END

Help me out:

I sincerely hope you enjoyed the third volume in the story of Hastelloy and his crew. I would greatly appreciate your feedback with an honest review on Amazon.com.

First and foremost, I am always looking to grow and improve as a writer. It is reassuring to hear what works, as well as receive constructive feedback on what should improve. Second, starting out as an unknown author is exceedingly difficult, and Amazon reviews go a long way towards making the journey out of anonymity possible. Please take a few minutes to write an honest review.

Best regards,

Mark Henrikson

SNEAK PEEK:

Most fans of the Origins series are well aware that the back story of Hastelloy and his Novi crew was actually dreamed up by the creative mind of my older brother, Jeff Henrikson, in the form of a brief plot outline. He opted to let me run with it since his writing interests lay in a different project that I am proud to announce will be published on September 1, 2013.

This first installment kicks off a fantasy series about the long war between light and dark elf factions, and a final peace process that will reconcile their differences. The back cover description and first chapter of his book are included here for the interested reader.

Do the Gods Hear Our Prayers?

By

Jeff Henrikson

Book One of the Reconciliation Saga

Back Cover of Volume 1

After fighting for thousands of years, peace between the light and dark elves is within sight. Ordered by the Overlord to settle their differences, the gods from both sides meet to hammer out a treaty, until the unthinkable happens.

Pawns of the gods above, the human kingdom of Kentar and the last elven kingdom of Armena are thrown into war by the conniving genius of the world's most powerful thieves guild. Nations rise and fall as pieces move around the board in this high stakes match for domination of the world, and the heavens themselves.

Two elven brothers and a thief are the mortal foot soldiers in this war between Kentar, Armena, and the Talon Guild. The brothers try to right the most grievous of wrongs, not knowing that their true destiny is to save their race, or die trying. The thief is in it for the power, but is the cost too high, or is he willing to make the sacrifice for his own selfish ends? This is a novel of combat, politics, and religion played out on a three-tier stage where mortals try to win the favor of the divine, wondering all the while if the gods hear their prayers.

Chapter 1: Three Hundred Years of Silence

Evisar double checked the sword in his scabbard and the quiver on his back. Today he was going with Lord Chas to talk with the humans of Kentar for the first time in three centuries. Evisar prayed to Invictus that there wouldn't be any trouble, but it was his job to defend his lord if there was.

In his great grandfather's day the Glenmyr Forest had teemed with elves, but that was three hundred years ago, before the Retreat began. During that fateful time, most of the elves chose to leave the Glenmyr Forest in order to seek a peaceful existence away from the prying eyes of man, orc, and goblin. These races were always encroaching on their territory and cutting down their trees. Those elves who couldn't bear to leave their home stayed behind and formed Armena, the last elven kingdom on the continent of Tellus. Armena was only a fraction the size of the old elf empire, and it was centered on the eastern side of the Glenmyr Forest, away from the humans of Kentar. For three hundred years Armena had been left in relative peace, but time was finally beginning to catch up with it. Humans and other more ghastly creatures were slowly moving into the forest to fill the void left by the elves after the Retreat.

The tiny kingdom of Armena maintained some trade with the human villages to the northeast, near the Ring Sea, but Kentar and Sena to the west and south hadn't seen or heard an elf for fifteen of their generations. Humans were impulsive and their lives were as short as their memories. No doubt a party of elves at the gate of Kentar's farthest frontier town was going to bring quite a shock.

Lord Chas looked at Evisar and his other two escorts and asked, "Are you ready?"

Evisar tried to look absolutely certain as he replied, "Yes my lord," but Lord Chas must have noticed his discomfort.

"Don't worry Evisar, I am sure you will bring honor to your father's name today. Just follow my lead and everything will be fine."

****

A man named Jon walked in contemplation along the stockade wall of the human logging camp that had been dubbed 'Endwood.' The camp was a quarter mile long by a quarter mile wide, and made entirely out of wood. Through the main gate was a large courtyard divided neatly in half by a river that was used by the loggers to transport wood downstream. Across the river and past the courtyard was a town hall, several troop barracks, storage buildings, and a number of houses.

Jon was a simple Lieutenant in the Army of Kentar and he had the day watch. He shook his head as he thought about his dumb luck at being assigned to a logging camp out in the middle of nowhere. To make matters worse, for reasons that surpassed understanding, the king of Kentar had sent an entire battalion of soldiers with the founding settlers three weeks ago, all but ensuring Jon would never see any action. On their trek out to the frontier Jon had heard the settlers talking about the dangers of the woods.

"My friend said there is a huge dragon in the woods."

"When I was a boy my grandfather told me there used to be three villages out on the wooded frontier that were all mysteriously wiped out."

"Did you know the forest is protected by a caregiver?"

"I heard the forest is haunted."

As the column of wagons had pulled up to the site that was to become Endwood, Jon quickly gained respect for the grandfather who talked about past villages that had been wiped out. The foundations of a previous town were clearly visible among the overgrown vegetation.

Mark Henrikson

Since then, everyone had settled into a routine as the lumberjacks set to felling trees and the guards started patrolling. Endwood sprang up quickly and the townsfolk were full of youthful energy. Many of the men had brought their families with them because of the opportunity the abundant forest promised to those who were willing to work hard for their fortune. Jon spent his days lazily walking around the top of the stockade, and today promised more of the same.

Then he caught sight of four figures walking out of the woods boldly up to the gate. They wore brown and green clothes, with ornately carved longbows slung over their backs and swords at their sides. They looked vaguely like humans, but not. The tallest of the four stood only five feet tall and they were all thinner than Jon had been as a boy. In fact, had it not been for their sharp features and pointy ears, they could have been mistaken for children. The four foreigners walked out of Jon's view as they approached the gate, where Corporal Darron had the command.

Jon quickened his pace, and as he climbed down the wooden stairs nearest the gate, he could hear one of the foreigners speaking in a barely understandable form of the common tongue. "… do not understand. … wish to … speak with your leader."

Corporal Darron said, "I can't let you into Endwood. I have my orders. Now, you will have to step back from the gate."

Jon could see the conversation was going in the wrong direction and raised his voice as he approached, "Darron!" Jon quickly closed the distance and said, "What is going on here? Report."

"Ah, yes sir. They claim to be the legendary race of elves. They're askin' to speak with the capt'n."

Jon couldn't believe his eyes. Elves. Here. At Endwood. Like any child of Kentar, he had heard legends about the caregivers of the Glenmyr Forest, but if elves existed at all, they had disappeared hundreds of years ago. If these strangers were here claiming to be elves, then perhaps the legends were at least based on fact. "Thank you, Corporal. I will take it from here. Why don't you go find Captain Sheval and bring him to the gate?"

"Yes sir." With that, Darron saluted sharply before turning around and trotting off.

Jon turned his full attention to the foreigners. "Yes gentlemen. How may I help you?"

The lead elf responded, "I am Lord Chas, and these are my countrymen, Evisar, Laithar, and Falon. Are you the commander of this town?"

"Not exactly. I'm second in command of Endwood." To hear the elf's voice was strange. His voice was musical and rhythmic and his knowledge of the common tongue was rusty and formal. It was as though he had been born a thousand years ago and was a step out of touch with the current world. "Can I help you while my soldier finds the Captain?"

"Yes." Lord Chas began slowly. "Are you familiar with the Treaty of Glenmyr?"

Jon thought back to his school days and answered truthfully. "No, I can't say that I am."

Lord Chas pulled a scroll of parchment out of his brown tunic and handed it to Jon. Jon was one of the few men in town who could read, and the scroll was actually written in the common tongue. The title read, 'Treaty of Glenmyr.' Jon read the first few sentences and was surprised to discover that the scroll outlined a treaty between the elves of the old elf empire and the humans who arrived on Tallus. Jon didn't want to be rude, but he couldn't avoid the facts. "Our history says that the old elf empire doesn't exist anymore, and we are from the Kingdom of Kentar, not Tallus."

Lord Chas shook his head in disagreement. "We are what is left of the old elf empire, and this treaty was meant for any humans living on Tallus, as you are now. This town is breaking the treaty by cutting down the forest. By treaty, the forest belongs to Armena, not Kentar. We have come to ask you to stop cutting the forest."

314

Jon honestly had no idea what the elf was talking about. "I had no idea we might be breaking any kind of treaty. I didn't even know elves were real until I saw you walk out of the woods, but if we are in the wrong then we will make amends."

As Jon finished his statement, Captain Sheval came quickly striding up to the gate. "Lieutenant, what is going on here? Why did you talk to these elves without my leave?"

Jon was surprised by the rudeness of his Captain, and the fact that he knew what an elf was. "Sir, someone reported foreigners at the gate. I simply came out to investigate. Once I saw who they were, I sent for you immediately."

The Captain pulled Jon backwards by the arm and whispered in his ear. "You shouldn't have talked to them at all, but we'll deal with that later." Captain Sheval grabbed the scroll parchment out of Jon's hand and turned his attention to the elves standing under the gate. "What exactly do you want here?"

Lord Chas took note of the Captain's rudeness and continued. "May we come in to discuss our dispute with you?"

The Captain folded his arms across his chest defensively and said, "I don't think so. You can say what you wish right here." Jon stood back and didn't dare say anything, but he saw no reason why the captain should be so cold to the foreigners.

The Captain looked around at the gathering crowd and said, "Get back to work! Get back to your posts!" Everyone except for Jon and the Captain slowly turned around and pretended to go back to their duties, or at least got out of earshot.

Jon eventually found his courage and spoke up to fill the void. "Captain, they claim ownership of these lands and say we are in violation of some treaty between our peoples. They're asking us to stop cutting down the forest."

"Is that so? Well, good elves, I've been expecting you for some time." Jon's mouth dropped open in astonishment. How could the Captain have been expecting these elves? "But it turns out you have no right to ask us to stop logging the forest. The treaty between our peoples was signed by the elves of the old elf empire and the first humans on Tallus, not between Kentar and Armena. Besides, the treaty clearly states that the border shall forever be the forest. As you can see, we are not in the forest. Therefore, the land you are standing on belongs to Kentar."

Lord Chas kept his head about him as he stated, "The treaty also state that Kentar will not cut down any living tree in this forest. If you did not cut down any trees, then there would be no dispute over the border."

The Captain didn't give an inch. "The king of Kentar claims the cleared land. I'm afraid there's nothing else I can do for you gentlemen. Good day." With this statement the Captain stepped back and began to shut the door in the lead elf's face. Lord Chas moved in a blur and slammed the door open. Corporal Darron's hand moved to his sword, but Evisar drew his bow, notched an arrow and fired, in one fluid motion. The sword flew out of the Corporal's hand and an arrow sprouted from his palm. He screamed in agony and fell to his knees.

Lord Chas didn't respond to the violence at all, but simply said in a forceful, strained voice, "You do not respect us. We could destroy you all. We have come in peace, to find a compromise, but you are selfish. Are you saying you will not stop killing the trees?"

Other soldiers drew their swords and moved forward as Captain Sheval responded in kind, "That is exactly what I'm saying. Now be gone!"

With this final statement, the elves backed away and the gate was shut. Jon could hear the elves talking in a foreign, melodic language as they retreated into the forest.

Jon turned angrily to his Captain and asked, "What in the seven hells was that, sir? They came here in peace and you shut the door in their faces?"

"You don't understand, Lieutenant, and there's a reason you were not informed. Return to your duty and remember your place." Jon turned around reluctantly and walked away from his Captain before he said something that would get him thrown in the brig. He resumed walking the stockade and eventually came to the realization that the crown may have sent a full battalion of soldiers to Endwood because they were expecting trouble, or perhaps hoping to start trouble. One thing was for sure, the Captain's treatment of the elves had all but guaranteed a confrontation.